Raves for the Alien novels:

"If you like your futuristic adventure with heapings of over-the-top fun and absurdity, Koch has the series for you. . . . A rip-roaring and outlandish romp!"
—*RT Book Reviews*

"Aliens, danger, and romance make this a fast-paced, wittily-written sf romantic comedy."
—*Library Journal*

"Koch still pulls the neat trick of quietly weaving in plot threads that go unrecognized until they start tying together—or snapping. This is a hyperspeed-paced addition to a series that shows no signs of slowing down."
—*Publishers Weekly*

"This delightful romp has many interesting twists and turns as it glances at racism, politics, and religion en route . . . will have fanciers of cinematic sf parodies referencing *Men in Black*, *Ghost Busters*, and *X-Men*."
—*Booklist* (Starred Review)

"Gini Koch has another winner, plenty of action combined with just the right touch of humor and a kick-ass storyline. What's not to like?"
—*Fresh Fiction*

"Gini Koch mixes up the sometimes staid niche of science fiction romance by adding nonstop humor, blockbuster action, and moments worthy of a soap opera."
—*Dirty Sexy Books*

ALIEN
VS. ALIEN

GINI KOCH

DAW BOOKS, INC.
DONALD A. WOLLHEIM, FOUNDER
375 Hudson Street, New York, NY 10014

ELIZABETH R. WOLLHEIM
SHEILA E. GILBERT
PUBLISHERS
http://www.dawbooks.com

To all the accidental badasses out there who, like Kitty, don't let what's proper stand in the way of doing what's right.

ACKNOWLEDGMENTS

As always, many thanks to my amazing editor, Sheila Gilbert, and all the other good folks at DAW Books. Same again to my awesome agent, Cherry Weiner. And once more with feeling for my great crit partner, Lisa Dovichi, and my super main beta reader, Mary Fiore. You're all fabulous and each one of you makes my writing better every time.

Love and thanks to all my fans around the globe, particularly those on Hook Me Up!, those who are part of Team Gini, every Alien Collective Member in Very Good Standing, my Twitter followers, and Facebook fans and friends. You're the best fans in the world and I love you all.

Special shout outs to: Colette Chmiel for sacrificing hours of her time toward saving my sanity and becoming my distance assistant; Nicole Snyder for fast action and a calming take-charge manner when the pirates were literally at the gate; Sally Janin for going above and beyond to help me out, even during difficult times; Robert Palsma for always liking everything I do; Adrian and Lisa Payne for not only always showing up with books in hand and smiling faces, but also for your eleventh hour fill in during Phoenix Comicon; Chris "Delicious" Swanson and Raul Padron for cheerful support, schlepping, baggage handling, and more, anywhere and everywhere; Kay Moran and Helen King for constant cheerleading, particularly when deadlines loomed; Julie Jones and Marnie Walski for making me grin every day; author Marsheila Rockwell for being there at midnight any time I needed to bounce an idea off another creative night owl; Jan Robinson, Joanne Marie di Biasi, Koren Cota, and Mariann Asanuma for making beautiful and delicious things just for me (sometimes live and on the scene!) and bestowing them upon me at every con; Carien Ubink and Shawn Sumrall for sending fun and yummy surprises that never fail to arrive on just the day I need a smile; and all the wonderful fans who come to my various book signings and make them into such memorable, cherished events, and same again to the wonderful bookstores that host said signings.

My husband, Steve, and I celebrated our 25th wedding anniversary while edits for this book were going on. Honey, thanks for not only your support in my writing career, but for a quarter of a century of a marriage that's easily as good as Kitty and Jeff's—for which the majority of the credit absolutely goes to you. And to our daughter, Veronica, who's as special and super as Jamie Martini, thanks for being both a chip off the old block and your own distinct person. Not sure how you managed it, but well done. And thanks to both of you for being a part of this writing journey—it's always better when the people you love are along with you for the ride.

Stephen Hawking warns that when aliens arrive on Earth, it'll be a bad day for all the inhabitants of the third rock from the sun. I'm not sure if this means the smartest man in the solar system is somehow unaware of reality, doing his part to help with the cover-up, or talking about the aliens that don't already reside here.

I'm going with best two out of three on this one.

Oh, sure, the aliens we have here now are all from Alpha Four of the Alpha Centaurion solar system, or A-Cs for short. And yes, they all look like supermodels, have two hearts, and a whole lot of other nifty things humans don't, like hyperspeed and some interesting talents. But for the most part, they fall on the Superman side of the house—here to protect and serve and maybe score a little human nookie if all goes well.

The other inhabitants of the Alpha Centaurion solar system are pretty all right, too. They don't visit often, but when they do, it's usually to lend a helping hand, paw, or talon. In part because they're cool. In part because they're not sure if Earth is merely talking a good show or really is, as George Thorogood so aptly sings, "Bad to the Bone."

Truth is, we're both.

Which is good. Because there are a lot of solar systems out there in this galaxy we call the Milky Way, and if some of their inhabitants show up here, we're all going to be in agreement that Hawking knows of what he speaks.

But never fear, good citizens! I may be stranded in Washington, D.C., doing the whole Diplomat on Duty thing, but that doesn't mean I'm not paying attention. I am ever vigilant for danger.

Of course, it's not that hard for me, lacking in normal people observational talents though I am. Danger's my best bud forever, as near as I can tell. Plus I have all those nifty A-C skills I backward inherited from my daughter. So, wither danger goest, so goest I, or something like that.

Besides, superpowers or no, the classics—hairspray, a well-stocked iPod, and a Glock .23—never go out of style. It's my own style, sure, but it works for me.

So when the next set of fugly aliens tries to come and ask, "What's the frequency, Kitty?" don't worry. It might look like the end of the world as we know it, but the bad guys won't feel fine.

CHAPTER 1

MY PHONE RANG AT 11 A.M. Sadly, it was a number I knew. Also sadly, it wasn't a number I liked. But even more sadly, it was a number I had to answer.

I heaved a sigh, hit pause on my iPod—right in the middle of the Foo Fighters' "Monkey Wrench"—and put on my Bright and Cheerful Diplomat Voice. "Hello, Senator Armstrong. How are you today?"

Senator Vincent Armstrong was the senior senator from Florida and had come onto my radar during what I called Operation Confusion and most everyone else called "the time the bad guys tried to steal my baby in the first days she was born, while they also tried to kill the rest of us." Our lives were nothing if not exciting.

"I'm wonderful, Ambassador Martini. I was wondering if you might be able to visit my offices today."

I'd become the co-head of the American Centaurion Diplomatic Corps in the aftermath of Operation Confusion. The big test had been six weeks ago, though, when Operation Assassination had gone down at the President's Ball. I represented well, at least, in terms of keeping everyone alive and reasonably unscathed. The less said about the state of my clothing after the event the better, though.

Normally, Armstrong asking for a visit would mean we were both in Washington, D.C. However, currently we were both in Florida. He was in Miami, and I was nearish to the Kennedy Space Center, at what I called Martini Manor and what a stranger to the complex would call Beverly Hills, East.

"Oh, gosh, no. Tied up all day with home stuff." I wasn't. We had no plans at all. But even with no plans, a visit with Armstrong was high on my To Don't list.

"Not able to leave the house at all?" His voice oozed concern, but I knew he was faking it.

"Nope. Jamie's not up to it. Trapped all day, really," I replied cheerfully. This wasn't totally a lie, though Jamie was having a great day today. However, Armstrong had been asking for this meeting for several weeks. And I'd been dodging with different, so far extremely successful, excuses for just as long.

"Well, then, I'm pleased I took the initiative."

That boded. "Excuse me?"

"I had a feeling you wouldn't be able to come to me, again, so, Mohammed will come to the mountain."

I decided not to mention that he was both comparing himself to one religion's revered prophet while managing to insult me religiously three ways at the same time. I was fairly sure he knew exactly what he was saying and that it had been said to get a rise out of me.

"How sweet of you. What day were you planning to visit?" I asked so I could plan to be elsewhere.

"Oh, today, Ambassador. I should reach your location within thirty minutes."

It figured. I ran through all my options very quickly. They seemed quite limited. Armstrong had cornered me well—I'd confirmed I wasn't going anywhere, and there was no way I could officially tell him to drop dead without causing yet another diplomatic incident.

I went for the Cheerful Diplomat voice again. "Wonderful. Guess I'd better go make myself look presentable."

"I've never seen you as anything less than presentable, Ambassador."

This was a flat out lie, but I decided not to call him on it. "Great, see you shortly."

I hung up, cursed quietly, silently told Dave Grohl I'd have to get back to his awesome band later, then ran like hell for where I was fairly sure the rest of the team was.

I ran at human normal, which four and a half months ago would have been my only option. However, I wasn't fully human any more. I'd scored some A-C powers due to giving birth to a hybrid baby whose father had been given Surcenthumain, or what I liked to think of as the Superpowers Drug. So I could have used hyperspeed to zip through the house in a second flat.

Only, I was still having serious issues with control. Slamming into walls wasn't fun, and without an A-C to hold onto and to help control my direction as well as my ability to stop, I had the potential to slam *through* walls as well. I preferred not to, so did my best to keep the hyperspeed turned to "off."

Arrived to find everyone where I'd expected—in the kitchen, hanging out and filching foodstuffs to tide them over between this morning's humongous breakfast and the upcoming huge lunch.

I snagged a brownie that had, by its temperature, just come out of the oven five minutes ago. "We have a big problem."

Of course we—me, my baby daughter, Jamie, Amy, Len, Kyle, and Former Pontifex Richard White—were already in Florida because of a problem. I took said problem out of White's arms and gave her a cuddle.

Jamie was half human, half alien, with me supplying the human side and Jeff supplying the alien or A-C side. Problem was, due to the many internal differences between humans and A-Cs, some things went much faster in child development.

In Jamie's case, while we'd controlled her hyperspeeding well, and Jeff and his cousin, Christopher White, had implanted empathic and imageering blocks into her when she was a newborn, there was nothing anyone could do for her when her teeth came in. All at once.

Jamie had been in agony, and even in isolation, even with every block he had available to him set to eleven on a scale of ten, Jeff, the strongest empath in, most likely, the galaxy, hadn't been able to stand it. His baby daughter was in agony, and he not only couldn't help her, he could feel every bit of her pain. And it hurt him in ways I couldn't even comprehend.

That "fun" had gone on for three days. Then, to save everyone's sanity, preserve our marriage and Jeff's health, and ensure that at least some of us were still able to function in our roles as the current and very novice American Centaurion Diplomatic Corps, I'd packed up my miserable baby and taken her to the one place everyone could feel at least reasonably okay about, which was to Jeff's parents, Alfred and Lucinda.

They'd had to deal with Jeff's empathic talents at birth, so their house was set up for it. They were A-Cs, so they could keep Jamie's hyperspeed in check, and my parents, though awesome grandparents, were both working and human. Plus, as Lucinda had pointed out when I'd called her desperately and somewhat hysterically at 3 a.m. a month ago, my parents saw Jamie all the time, since they'd moved to D.C. to be nearer to us.

"Catsuit time, Missus Martini?" White asked.

"Unfortunately no. But a problem of epic proportions is descending on us."

"Oh, Kitty," Lucinda said with a chuckle. "You're always so dramatic."

"In this case, we really have the drama. Senator Armstrong is going to be here in less than thirty minutes."

"How lovely that he's visiting. I'll set another place for lunch," Lucinda said as she headed for the dining room. My mother-in-law, despite all the evidence to the contrary, seemed to think that most politicians had everyone's best interests at heart.

I heaved a sigh. "Richard, could you please explain to your sister why this isn't quite the social call we'd like?"

"I live to serve. However, I'm sure all of us are more than capable of dealing with the senator. You excel at the diplomatic touch, after all." White trailed after Lucinda.

I managed not to snort. I excelled at certain forms of diplomacy. If it came to dealing with interstellar invaders, I was the go-to girl. When it came to regular politics, however, I was still whiffing a lot more than scoring.

"Great." I appealed to Alfred. "Any way we can pretend to have a big fire or something?"

He laughed. "No, I don't think that's a good idea. But I'm sure you're worried for nothing." Alfred and Jeff really proved the adage "like father, like son" to be true, from their looks and body build right down to their expressions. I was getting the "you're cute, so I don't mind indulging your little whims" look. It was a nice look, but it didn't say "I'm ready to play dangerous word games with the nasty man." And it made me miss Jeff even more than I already did, which did nothing to improve my mood.

Amy snorted. "Right. I stopped thinking Kitty was worried about nothing four and a half months ago."

"Senator Armstrong tried to kill Kitty six weeks ago," Len supplied.

Honesty forced me to correct him. "No, actually, as far as anyone's determined, he was trying to get us into the Cabal of Evil, and was likely deeply in the know about the Paraguayan supersoldier project, but he was not, in fact, one of the people trying to do me in. That was Antony Marling and his bizarre android offspring, and Madeline Cartwright. Now all extremely deceased."

"Armstrong wasn't involved that we know of," Amy countered.

"Per Chuckie and Mom both, they haven't been able to pin anything on him. And believe me, they want to."

Charles Reynolds had been my best guy friend since we were both thirteen, and he was also a self-made multimillionaire, several times over. However, like my parents, he'd been leading a double life I found out about after I discovered aliens lived on Earth.

Chuckie was the head of the C.I.A.'s Extra-Terrestrial Division, so my husband and his very extended family were Chuckie's priority. His other priority was ensuring that those who were trying to destroy all the A-Cs on Earth were taken care of, in all the nasty ways the C.I.A. takes care of people and problems.

"They haven't pinned anything on that Esteban Cantu, either," Amy said. "But per Chuck, he's absolutely guilty."

Cantu was in the C.I.A., though not in the E-T division. He, like Armstrong, was clearly not on our side. He was also, as Chuckie put it, a slippery bastard, and he'd avoided being taken down for Operation Assassination.

"I'm not up on where Cantu's falling on Mom's or Chuckie's Most Wanted lists right now."

"Well, maybe we can find out before Senator Armstrong gets here," Kyle suggested.

"I don't know if we have the time. Armstrong said he'd be here within thirty minutes. If I'm guessing right, that means we have more like ten."

Sure enough, the house intercom buzzed. "Excuse me, Mister Martini, but there's a Senatorial limousine requesting entry," the A-C in charge of the entry gate shared. "They say they have a meeting with the Ambassador."

"Let them in, thank you," Alfred said. "Company will be here shortly, dear," he called to Lucinda.

The Martini complex was huge. It contained both the ginormous house Alfred and Lucinda lived in, an almost-as-big guesthouse, and servants' quarters that would make most millionaires drool with envy. It also took a good five minutes to drive from the entry gate to the main house. Under these circumstances, that wasn't a lot of time.

"We really need to get anything remotely incriminating or telling hidden and out of the way."

Amy shot me a look that plainly said she thought I was crazy. I got that look a lot, from just about anybody and everybody these days. "Kitty, you're acting like we're running a meth lab or something. This senator knows about . . . everyone, right?"

"Right." He did. Armstrong was one of the people who had a very high security clearance, which included getting to know about the Alpha Centaurions who lived on Earth. But he wasn't our friend in any way, shape, or form, and I didn't want him finding some hidden weakness. "But still . . ."

My phone chose this moment to ring. I checked. Not the senator, but indeed another number I'd become familiar with. "Hi, Malcolm, what's up?"

Malcolm Buchanan had been thankfully assigned by my mother to be my permanent watchdog. He'd saved my and Jamie's lives at the end of Operation Assassination. And now, whither I went, so Buchanan went, too. While we were down here he was housed in the servants' quarters.

"You have company coming."

"Yes, we know. Not thrilled about Senator Armstrong's arrival, but there's nothing I can do about it."

"Well, get ready," Buchanan said. "Because there's a lot more than one person in the limo that's just pulling up at your front door."

CHAPTER 2

"WE HAVE MORE THAN ONE COMING IN," I shared as I slammed my phone closed. "How are we going to handle this?"

"I'm getting the door," Kyle said. He nodded to Len. "You're backing me?"

"Of course."

Len and Kyle had been on the USC football team when we'd met in Vegas right before my wedding. Len had been the quarterback and Kyle had been on the line. They'd both given up promising pro careers to work with the C.I.A.'s ET division. Therefore, in addition to being big, athletic guys, they both packed heat. Ostensibly Len was my driver and Kyle was my bodyguard, but neither was a fan of anyone who tried to kill me, in part because those people also tried to kill the boys at the same time.

I contemplated allowing them to open the door with an impressive show of force. Unfortunately, I had a pretty good idea that such a cheerful greeting probably wasn't included in the Diplomat's Handbook.

Jamie gurgled. She hadn't seemed like she was in pain for the past couple of days, I felt outnumbered and unprepared, and I missed my husband more than I would have thought possible. I opened my phone again and dialed.

"Hey, baby, I was just thinking about you. How're my girls doing?" Jeff had to ask because he had to have such strong blocks up in his mind to protect him from our emotions. I really hoped it was time to take those blocks down.

"I think Jamie's fine. I'm stressed out of my mind. Jeff, are you in the middle of anything you can't get away from?"

"We're just doing some Homeland Security paperwork with Reynolds."

"Great. Can you all get down here, right away? We're about to have an impromptu visit from Senator Armstrong, and I don't trust his motives at all."

"Neither do I. We'll be there right away. You want Reynolds along?"

"Please. I have no idea who else is coming, but Malcolm said he saw more than one person when he called to warn me."

Jeff grunted. "He's not in the house is he?"

"Spend needless jealousy on Malcolm when you're here, okay?" I lowered my voice. "I miss you. Use the fast hyperspeed."

"Love you, baby. Be right there."

We hung up, I kissed Jamie's head and handed her to Amy, then headed after the boys. Martini Manor was so huge it was easy to catch up to them before they reached the main entryway. And just in time—I got to them as the front doorbell rang.

"Boys, let's remember that while we don't like the senator, we aren't allowed to act like we're Al Pacino in *Scarface*."

Both boys shot me betrayed looks. Their expressions shared that, yet again, this kind of "fun" was not something they thought they'd signed up for when joining the exciting ranks of C.I.A. operatives.

But they soldiered on. Kyle got the door, Len flanking him, just in case Armstrong actually had a carload of mercenaries along for the ride. Of course, I wouldn't have put it past him, or any of the rest of the Cabal of Evil.

Amazingly enough, Armstrong was in the doorway, no gun or grenade in sight. He was carrying an expensive-looking attaché and, as always, had the Senior Senator from Wherever look going strong. Even though we were now in the Diplomatic Corps, I still didn't pay a lot of attention to politics, but the thought occurred that Armstrong probably had his eye on the White House.

This unsettling notion got pushed aside as Armstrong strode in. Armstrong wasn't the issue—his companions were.

Guy Gadoire followed Armstrong across the threshold, beaming. My mouth fell open. "My darling Missus Martini. You look radiant as always." He raced over to me as I slammed my jaw shut.

Gadoire was a lobbyist for the tobacco industry. He spoke in a fake French accent that made him sound like a less appealing Pepé

Le Pew. He was also bisexual and had, along with his partner, Vance Beaumont, suggested I share a "bed of love" with them only a few weeks prior. Despite all this, somehow, he was not on my list of Potential Adultery Options.

"Guy, what are you doing here?"

"You are surprised to see me, my dove?" He grabbed the hand I hadn't offered and kissed it. Based on his hand kissing alone, I never wanted this man's lips near mine. Gadoire was the only man I'd ever met who could make kissing your hand seem completely charmless and unappealing.

The boys stared at him. They'd heard about him, of course, but this was their first real introduction to Monsieur Love, as I called him in private.

"Ahhh . . ." Gadoire tended to make me speechless, though not for the reasons he assumed.

I heard footsteps behind me, and Gadoire's eyes lit up. I looked over my shoulder to see Amy arriving. She didn't have Jamie with her. I counted that in the win column.

Gadoire let go of me and turned the "charm" on Amy. "And who is this lovely vision with you?"

"I'm Amy Gaultier. Ah, White. Amy Gaultier-White." Amy and Christopher had gotten married right before Jamie's teeth arrived, and she still wasn't used to being married, partially because she'd spent more time away from her husband than with him. But, as she said, that's what you did when your best friends needed you.

Amy made the mistake of offering her hand. Gadoire snatched it to his lips like he had to kiss hands or die.

She gave me the "oh, my God, this is gross" look, but smiled sweetly at him when he straightened up. "Monsieur Gadoire, I've heard so much about you from Kitty."

Gadoire winked at me. "I'm sure you have."

I managed not to gag. "How's Vance?" I hadn't missed anyone from my Washington Wife class while in exile in Florida, but it was polite to ask about someone else's spouse.

"He's well. Looking forward to seeing you again."

"Excuse me?"

No sooner were those words out of my mouth than Vance Beaumont sauntered in. Vance was one of those perfectly put together people the rest of us privately hated. I wasn't so private in my hatred, but that didn't stop Vance from grabbing me and giving me a big hug.

I managed not to go rigid or shove him away, but this wasn't a typical greeting for the two of us. "Hi, Vance."

"Kitty . . . if there's anything I can do, I just want you to know I'm here for you."

"Huh?"

Vance put the Frowny Face of Concern on. I didn't buy it for a New York Minute. "We'll talk about it later."

"Talk about what?"

Armstrong cleared his throat. "Guy and Vance are aware of the . . . situation I need to discuss with you, Ambassador." He looked around. "Is there somewhere private we can go to talk?" He pointedly looked at Amy and the boys, and it was clear he didn't want them along for whatever chat he had planned.

"Whatever we need to talk about can be discussed with Amy, Len, and Kyle. They're all part of our diplomatic mission."

Armstrong shook his head. "I believe you'd prefer to have this conversation in private, Ambassador. Very sure."

CHAPTER 3

SOMETHING ABOUT HIS TONE and expression made me want to pull my Glock. However, my purse was in the room Amy and I were sharing, and besides, if I didn't want the boys to use extreme force, it was worse if I did.

What I really wanted was backup. I'd called for it. So why wasn't it here already? Surely they'd had enough time to get to a gate and over here by now.

The gates were alien technology that resembled airport security metal detectors more than anything else. They allowed you to travel pretty much anywhere in moments. The main gate hub was in the Dome, out in New Mexico, but there were gates all over. The majority of gates were in restroom stalls of every airport in the world, even the tiny ones. For homes, however, if the bathroom wasn't used, the basements were.

So Jeff and whoever else he was bringing along should have zipped down to the Embassy's basement, calibrated, stepped through that gate and out the gate in the basement of Martini Manor. By my count, they should have been here by the time Armstrong got through the door.

But no, I was still backup-less. There was also no way I was having a three on one meeting with this portion of the Cabal of Evil. "I like to live on the edge, Senator. Why don't you share your news?"

Amy cleared her throat. "Why don't we get out of the hallway?"

I really wanted to get Armstrong's info and get him back out the door, but I had to admit I wasn't being gracious or diplomatic. "Good point, Ames."

Amy led us to a nearby study. This was Martini Manor—there was a nearby anything depending on your definition of "nearby." In this case, it was only halfway down the hall.

As with every other room in the house, the study was done in what I called Early American Expensive. The older generation of A-Cs were traditionalists to their cores, and they'd happily adopted Earth traditions the moment they arrived.

It was also decorated in Modern Hunk, since Jeff, Christopher, and Chuckie were sitting in the lovely club chairs this room contained, looking for all the world as though they'd been here for hours.

Jeff was big and broad, with dark, wavy hair, gorgeous light brown eyes, and a mouth that said "kiss me" even when he wasn't speaking. He was built like everyone's male ideal—broad shoulders, perfectly cut, rippling muscles, without being overdone like a bodybuilder. Sure, I couldn't see all that right now, since he was dressed, but I'd spent the last month fantasizing about him, so I was essentially seeing him in my mind's eye sitting there naked.

It was a nice view, but I had to force myself to look away or jump his bones in front of everyone, and I knew without asking this wasn't in the Good Diplomats Handbook.

Christopher was a head shorter than his cousin, smaller all the way around, being lean and wiry, though he had the family rock-hard abs. His hair was straight and lighter brown than Jeff's. Christopher resembled his late mother in almost everything, but he had his father's nose, mouth, and green eyes flecked with blue. They really made them gorgeous on Alpha Four.

Chuckie was handsome for a human, which these days was both a compliment and damning with faint praise when compared to an A-C. He was tall like Jeff but had a similar build to Christopher—sinewy and smooth. He usually moved languidly, but had the reflexes to make you think he could be part A-C. Dirty blond hair, with a bit of a wave in it, but only when it was a little longer than he normally wore it. Blue eyes that radiated intelligence—no matter where he went, Chuckie was always the smartest guy in the room.

Speaking of his eyes, Chuckie's caught mine, and he gave me a look I was familiar with—the "play it cool" look. Know a guy more than half of your life, you know when he wants you to act nonchalant.

Amy was obviously in on the news, because she didn't look at all surprised. Armstrong, Gadoire, and Vance, however, clearly hadn't been expecting this kind of company. I chose not to wonder which one of the three men Guy and Vance would proposition first to share their "bed of love"—it would be a tough call either way. And for all I knew, Amy was going to get the next proposition. Vance was giving her an approving look, so I figured she was his type. I was Gadoire's, apparently. I was lucky that way.

Armstrong, unsurprisingly, rallied the quickest. "Ambassador Martini, how good to see you."

"Senator," Jeff said with a nod. "I didn't realize you were bringing along additional visitors."

Armstrong managed a weak Campaign Smile. "Well, you've got additional people too. Nice to see you, Mister White, Mister Reynolds."

Christopher gave Armstrong a cold nod. Chuckie smiled without any warmth. "I'm sure you weren't expecting us, Senator. But it's more social this way, isn't it?"

Armstrong shook his head. "I'm not here on a social call, in that sense. Ambassador," he said to Jeff, "what I have to discuss affects you and Missus Martini. Are you sure you don't want to ask your associates to wait outside? I have to stress that it's a very private issue I need to discuss with you."

I always turned right back into Mrs. Martini any time Jeff was around. Supposedly I was the co-Head Diplomat, but no one seemed to buy that story, other than Jeff, who steadfastly insisted I was his equal.

"If it's so private, I have to ask why Guy and Vance are here," I said, before Jeff could respond.

"We're here to help," Gadoire said. Vance nodded. They looked serious and concerned, and a part of me wasn't so sure it was an act.

Amy and I looked at each other. "Help with what?" she asked.

"Again, it's a private matter for the Ambassadors," Armstrong said. He gave Chuckie a long look. "Though Mister Reynolds might want to remain, as well."

"All of us," Jeff said. "There's no one here we need to hide anything from."

Armstrong sighed. "When you change your mind, I want you to remember that I requested privacy." He put the attaché on a nearby table, opened it, and pulled out a large manila envelope. The rest of us crowded around the table. Jeff was behind me and he took and squeezed my hand.

Armstrong pulled some pictures out of the envelope and spread them out on the table.

We all stared.

"Whoa," Kyle said finally.

"Wow," was Len's contribution.

Jeff, Chuckie, and Christopher didn't make a sound. Neither did I. I was still trying to process what I was seeing.

"Kitty," Amy whispered, "what did you do?"

CHAPTER 4

I CONTINUED TO STARE AT THE PICTURES. They showed me and Chuckie having a really good time. An amazingly good time, in fact. A very good, very naked, time.

These pictures weren't from our one week fling in Vegas years ago. Both of us looked about our ages now.

"Now do you see why I wanted this meeting, and for it to be in private?" Armstrong asked.

Jeff let go of my hand and picked up the pictures. "Huh." He handed them to Chuckie.

"Interesting." Chuckie handed them to Christopher.

I managed not to mention everyone was looking at my audition for Hustler Girl of the Month. I was still too shocked to think about much at all, other than wondering when Chuckie and I had blacked out and consummated this torrid affair, because it certainly wasn't an event I remembered.

Christopher grunted and put the pictures back in the envelope, which he held onto.

"Thanks for stopping by," Jeff said to Armstrong. "Let me show you out."

"I understood you were still in Washington," Armstrong said, not budging.

"This is my parents' house. My wife and child are here. What's surprising about that?" Jeff smiled widely. It wasn't a very nice smile, not like his normal one. I got the impression he was controlling himself from hitting someone. "Of course, I can see how my being here puts a real monkey wrench into your plans to blackmail my wife."

"Sorry about that," Christopher added, in a tone of voice that said quite the opposite.

"See the senator and the other gentlemen out, will you?" Chuckie said to Len and Kyle.

The boys nodded and moved closer. Gadoire and Vance took the hint. "Call if you want to talk or need a shoulder, my dove," Gadoire said to me as Kyle none-too-gently nudged him and Vance toward the door.

"After you, Senator," Len said. He also looked like he was controlling himself from hitting someone.

Armstrong shook his head. "We need to talk about this," he said to me. "These pictures were sent to me, and they're going to be used against you."

"Unless what?" I asked.

"I don't know," Armstrong said. "Look, I know we're not the closest of friends, but I didn't come here to blackmail you. I came to warn you."

"We're warned," Jeff said. "We'll be in touch." He nodded to Len, who took the senator's arm and led him out of the study. Chuckie locked the door behind them.

"Kitty's been here the whole time," Amy said. "We're sleeping in the same room, too."

Jeff rolled his eyes. "We know. Christopher, what do we have?"

Christopher took the pictures out again and spread them on the table.

"Crap, Armstrong left his attaché here." I reached for it, but Chuckie grabbed my wrist. I looked up at him, and he shook his head strongly.

"We'll send it to him," Jeff said.

"These pictures are real," Christopher said. "I'm sure we don't want them being leaked."

I opened my mouth, and Chuckie put his hand over it, giving me a "you're really being dense" look.

"We'll figure out what we need to do once we're back home, then," Jeff said. "I'll deal with the two of you later," he added.

Only, he wasn't looking at me, or Chuckie, or even Christopher. Jeff and Christopher were looking at and talking to the attaché case.

Amy's mouth opened, and Chuckie rolled his eyes and shot her a "shut up, shut up" look. We'd all gone to high school together, so she recognized the look and slammed her mouth shut.

"Let's get out of here," Christopher said. He gathered the pictures and put them back into the envelope.

We all filed out of the study and went into the kitchen. This was not where I wanted to have the powwow. However, the three men still looked as though they didn't want me or Amy to talk.

To my surprise, no one I was expecting was around. Instead, there were two field teams, each comprised of an empath and ima-geer, patiently waiting. Like the rest of the men, they were wearing black Armani suits with white shirts and black ties. A-Cs loved their Armani and formality, usually in that order.

"Search the house, quietly, quickly, and carefully," Jeff said in a low voice. "I'm assuming the only bugs are in the study we just left, but let's be positive."

The agents nodded and zipped off at hyperspeed. In the olden days I wouldn't have been able to see them. Now I could. Sort of. So far, if I wasn't concentrating at all or was concentrating really hard, I could see A-Cs using hyperspeed. But if I was in that middle phase of normal focus, they still sort of disappeared.

"Does anyone want to tell me and Amy what's going on?"

Christopher went to the counter and spread the pictures out yet again. This time, though, I could tell he was actually examining them using his imageering talent. "It's really Kitty and it's really Reynolds," he said finally. "But . . ."

"But?"

Christopher shook his head. "Something's wrong."

"Aside from the fact that Chuckie and I haven't been having an affair, you mean?"

Christopher nodded. "I can't explain what, though."

"Do the Go Team move."

Jeff chuckled, which was kind of a relief. He put his hand on top of Christopher's. Empaths, if they were good enough, could read an image through an imageer, if the imageer was good enough. Jeff and Christopher sort of defined "more than good enough."

Jeff looked thoughtful. "Huh. Well, you're both really enjoying yourselves. But if you were cheating, baby, it's nice to know what you were thinking about was me."

Christopher nodded. "Yeah, the only thing I can get from this specific moment is a focus on you, Jeff."

"Same with Reynolds. He's not thinking about Kitty . . ." Jeff's eyes narrowed, and he shot a glare at Chuckie. "Interesting."

Chuckie shrugged. "I'm allowed to have a personal life. You, of all people, should be happy about that."

"I am. I suppose." Jeff took his hand away. "Anyway, these pho-tos are doctored."

"You guys are all really calm. Amazingly calm. Calmer than me and Amy, and I guarantee Len and Kyle. Jeff, I'm not unhappy you're not trying to kill me and Chuckie, but I'm sort of surprised. I mean, I want to ask questions, and I'm in the pictures. Of course, my first question is, how the hell am I in these pictures?"

"I got a tip," Chuckie said. "Filtered through our favorite paparazzo."

"How is Mister Joel Oliver?"

"Worried about your reputation. He called me and said he was sure there were incriminating photos of the two of us." Chuckie chuckled. "I think he thought they were real and was warning me so Martini wouldn't kill me."

"They look real."

"They are real," Christopher said patiently. "This is really you and really Reynolds. Only from what Jeff and I can pick up, you're not having sex with each other."

"Reynolds and I talked about this over two weeks ago," Jeff said. "But until something surfaced, Oliver didn't have more to go on other than the juicy rumors, to use his phrase, we had other, more important things to focus on, and we figured it would be better not to worry you in case it ended up being nothing."

"How did they get naked pictures of Kitty and Chuck doing the deed, with each other or anyone else, in the first place?" Amy sounded repulsed and horrified. Great.

The light dawned. After all, Operation Confusion hadn't been all that long ago. "The secret lab. The bad guys had a bank of screens, and cameras all looking at our bedrooms. But I thought that was so they could make accurate clones of everyone."

"We destroyed the lab and those clones," Chuckie said. "But that doesn't mean we destroyed any videotapes or pictures kept elsewhere. I know we haven't found everything related to the lab and the people involved with it."

"I'd ask why they saved them, beyond being too cheap to buy their own porn, but I can clearly see the advantages for the Bad Guys Club."

"I think we should have questioned Armstrong and his cronies more," Chuckie said to Jeff. "It would be helpful to have a clearer idea of who's behind this."

Jeff shook his head. "It was all I could do not to pound them into the ground. Too much longer and I would have created a diplomatic incident."

"Yeah, I understand. But the P.T.C.U. wants this investigated before it has to be turned over to Homeland Security, and I don't want to have nothing to tell Angela when she calls me, let alone have to explain this to Cliff if I can help it."

"Why is my mom involved at all?"

Chuckie shot me a look that said my being in Florida for a month had obviously killed brain cells. "Buchanan called your mother to advise her of Armstrong's visit, and she called me to find out what's going on," he said as Len and Kyle rejoined us. "Oh, and duh."

Two and a half years ago, this wouldn't have been a really stupid question on my part. Admittedly, by now, yeah, it was, because, as I'd discovered when I met Jeff and the rest of the gang from Alpha Four, what I'd believed my parents did was only sort of right. My father's cover was history professor at Arizona State University. What he did for fun and much more profit was cryptology for NASA, in their Extra-Terrestrial Division.

My mother, as it turned out, was a consultant, just as I'd always been told. Only she consulted on antiterrorism, since she was actually the head of the very clandestine and very kick-butt Presidential Terrorism Control Unit. She was also the only non-Israeli, non-Jew to be in the Mossad. A long story I'd never fully gotten out of her, but basically my mom wrote the book on kicking butt and taking names.

"Why would this go to Homeland Security?"

"It would go to Homeland Security because Senator Armstrong has the highest-level security clearances, and you're part of American Centaurion, and these pictures indicate a severe security risk if you and I are having an affair, particularly if it's perceived that Armstrong is trying to cover it up," Chuckie said patiently.

"So, who's Cliff?"

"Clifford Goodman, the recently appointed Head of Special Immigration Services. He reports directly to the Secretary of Homeland Security."

"Special meaning extraterrestrial?"

"Yes."

"You like him?"

"Yes."

"Really?" I tried not to sound shocked and failed, if Chuckie giving me a rather snide look was any indication.

He shrugged. "He's no worse than your average younger politician and better than most. He's been quite helpful to me, and to Centaurion Division, since he moved into the position. And he's a decent guy. You've met him."

"I have?"

"At the President's Ball. After all the excitement was over. The President introduced you to him personally."

We'd met so many people that night, after almost dying so many times, most of them were a blur. But Chuckie didn't hate this guy, and he wasn't in the Cabal of Evil, so fine, I could file this information in my To Be Worried About Later folder. I had a much more pressing concern. "So what does Mom know about this?" I sort of hoped absolutely nothing.

"She knows what I did before coming here today, and she also knows that if there are pictures, they're either from years ago or doctored. They're doctored; she won't be upset with you." Chuckie grinned. "So you can stop worrying."

"For about five minutes," Christopher added. "Because I don't think that threat Armstrong made was an idle one."

"No, it wasn't," Jeff agreed. "However, I didn't pick up what I was expecting to."

"What were you expecting?"

"Devious intent, triumph, those kinds of emotions, baby. What I got, however, was a lot of concern and, of course, lust from Pepé Le Pew." Jeff shook his head. "Armstrong might have been telling the truth."

"Great." Chuckie rubbed the back of his neck. "So, who's out to get all of us this time? And why?"

CHAPTER 5

"N O IDEA," JEFF SAID. "But lunch is ready, so let's eat."

Christopher put the pictures once again into their plain brown wrapper and handed them to me. "Thanks. I want to put these into my purse or something," I said to Jeff as the others headed for the dining room. "I do *not* want your parents to take a gander."

Jeff smiled and took my hand. "I'll go with you."

He zipped us off at hyperspeed, so we were in the bedroom in about a second flat. "So, miss me?" he asked as I shoved the pictures into my purse.

I turned around, flung myself at him, and kissed him. His kiss was, as always, amazing—deep, sensuous, his lips and tongue owning mine.

He ended the kiss slowly. "So, when were you going to tell me?"

"Tell you what? I didn't know about these pictures, and I absolutely wasn't having an affair with Chuckie, or anyone else for that matter."

"I know, baby. There's no way you could hide that from me. No, I mean about Jamie being ready to come home."

"She isn't." I looked at his expression. He was upset, much more about this than the naked pictures. "Tito, Melanie, and Emily are supposed to come down tomorrow and check her out. Then, if they all think she's done teething, we can head home."

"She hasn't been in pain for three days."

"And just how do you know that? You're not supposed to be monitoring, her or me, remember? That's the whole reason we've been here for a month."

He looked just a little guilty. "Yeah, I know . . ."

"But you have been, haven't you?"

"Yeah. When Reynolds told me about Oliver's warning, I figured I'd better check. So I've done random checks over the past couple of weeks."

"To make sure I wasn't doing the horizontal mambo with Len, Kyle, or Malcolm?" I asked, a tad more sarcastically than I'd intended.

"No." Of course, his eyes now weren't meeting mine. Most A-Cs couldn't lie to save their or anyone else's lives, and Jeff was pretty much the prime example of this lack of skill.

I snorted. "Right, because my husband, Monsieur Jealousy, would *never* worry about something like that."

Jeff sighed. "I trust you, baby, I do. I just . . . I needed to be sure. I haven't really seen you for so long . . ."

I leaned my head against his chest and let the sound of his heartbeats calm me. It felt so nice to be together again, I didn't want to bicker or fight. "I know. I've missed you so much."

"I know." He kissed the top of my head. "I could feel it. I could also feel that Jamie wasn't in pain."

"Your parents didn't want to take the chance that we were wrong and that she might still have issues, and I didn't want to get your hopes up, or mine, and then have to say, 'Oh, sorry, false alarm.' It's been fine being here, but it sucks without you."

"I understand. And I can't really blame you, either. We brought Tito, Emily, and Melanie with us. They're with Jamie right now."

I looked up. "Really? So, if Jamie checks out, we can all go home?"

Jeff grinned. "Yep. There's no way I'm leaving my wife and child here any longer unless I absolutely have to. You're not the only one who's felt lonely in a room full of other people."

It was nice to know he'd missed me as much as I'd missed him. The desire to rip his clothes off and see if we could figure out when the naked pics of me had been taken by reviewing our entire sexual repertoire was pretty much overwhelming.

Jeff's eyes smoldered, and he got the sexy "jungle cat about to eat me" look on his face. I loved that look. I'd missed that look for four straight weeks.

We'd have undoubtedly gone for it, people waiting for us in the dining room or not, but there was a knock on the door.

Jeff heaved a sigh and let me out of his arms. I managed to refrain from snarling when I opened the door. "Oh, hi, Tito."

Tito Hernandez had joined us in Vegas, when some of the many invading bad guys had tried to kill another one of my best friends. Tito had been working three jobs while going to medical school, while cage fighting on the side for fun. Now he was a full-time doctor who still practiced mixed martial arts because he used it regularly—not in the octagon so much as a part of our daily lives.

"Sorry to interrupt," he said in a tone that indicated he really wasn't. "But I figured you'd want to know Jamie's test results right away."

I tried not to tense and failed if Jeff massaging the back of my neck was any indication. "Is she okay?"

Tito grinned. "She's fine. It looks like she's past all the teething she's going to do for a good long while."

I contemplated jumping up and down but figured I'd save my energy for sex. "So we get to go home?"

"Whenever you want."

"Now's good."

Jeff chuckled. "Right after lunch."

I sighed. "And here you said you missed me."

CHAPTER 6

THE THREE OF US JOINED EVERYONE ELSE in the dining room. Jamie was there sitting on Lucinda's lap, and she made her "Daddy's here!" sounds at the top of her lungs.

Jeff zipped over, and took her out of his mother's arms, then he and Jamie had some serious Daddy and Daughter Love Time.

Lucinda took the opportunity. "So, Christopher, we've been discussing a wedding party."

Amy put on a fake smile while I cringed inside. When I'd first met her, Lucinda hadn't liked me at all, and the feeling had been mutual. But we'd gotten past that before my wedding, and these days I got along with my mother-in-law pretty well.

However, Amy and Christopher had made the decision to get married without any fanfare, based on Amy's quite accurate belief that any time all of us were dressed up some big fugly attacked or politician went nuts.

This decision had sat just fine with White, Christopher's father, but not with his aunt and uncle. Because Christopher was also part of the Royal Family of Alpha Four, they'd expected to host a huge wedding for him and Amy. They'd apparently been looking forward to it, especially Lucinda, since she would get to do the mother of the groom job again, because Christopher's mother, Terry, had been dead since he and Jeff were ten years old.

So they'd been less than thrilled to discover Christopher and Amy wanted to tie the knot with absolutely no fanfare. Alfred and Lucinda had been in attendance, but the rest of Jeff's family hadn't been invited. All the A-Cs on Earth were related somewhere back there, but Jeff was the youngest of six, and his sisters were all married with children. Even though they were cousins, Christopher and Jeff were closer than brothers, and Christopher was treated like another member of the family.

This treatment hadn't always been the best, for a variety of reasons, most pertaining to the talents Jeff and Christopher had combined with Alfred and Lucinda's desire to, as they'd put it to me, "keep the boys from thinking they were better than everyone else, even though they were better than everyone else." I'd given up arguing about or questioning this logic three and a half weeks ago.

However, Christopher not having the immediate Martini family in attendance was apparently a thorn in almost everyone's sides. Lucinda had, therefore, spent much of this past month subtly indicating to Amy that she wasn't really an official member of the family yet, because she hadn't done some big ceremony. Lucinda had also none-too-gently been pushing the idea of a big "we're married" reception type thing to make up for Amy's evil idea of not doing it up right in the first place.

"Why have we been discussing anything about any weddings?" Christopher asked. He looked and sounded confused, probably because he was—Amy hadn't mentioned this situation to him when she'd called during our time in Florida.

"Well, you and Amy just ran off and eloped," Lucinda replied. "We need to have an official reception for everyone."

"Why?" Christopher sounded completely uninterested. "We didn't elope—you and Uncle Alfred were there. We're married, we're both happy about it, and everyone knows, so why would we need to have a reception?"

"No one's been able to send you a wedding gift," Lucinda shared.

"So what?" Christopher shrugged. "We live at the Embassy, so we don't need anything. I don't see why we need to bother with anything about this." He looked as though he thought this conversation was over.

"It's proper protocol," Lucinda countered.

"We're drowning in protocol right now, and I'm really sure some party like this isn't necessary to our success as diplomats."

Jeff looked up from his baby snuggling and shot Christopher the "shut up, shut up" look. But it was too late.

Lucinda had the Stern Mother voice going. "You have an obligation to our people. You've married someone no one knows, and you did it in such a way that almost no one knows you're married. Are you ashamed of her?"

"Of course not!" Christopher sounded shocked and looked confused. "What is this about?"

Jeff winced. Either he'd taken his blocks down or the emotions in the room were so strong he couldn't help but feel them. I had no clear idea which option was the winner.

"I'm not good enough for you," Amy snapped. "That's what it's about, and what it's been about for a month."

"That is absolutely not true," Lucinda said. "We have traditions, however, and you completely ignored them."

"I didn't know what they were, and no one else had a problem with it," Amy retorted.

"You never bothered to find out," was Lucinda's comeback. I'd heard this argument, which always ended in a stalemate, for a month now. It never got any better.

I looked around. Those who'd been with us all this time had "I'm not really here" looks on their faces. Even White hadn't been able to make any headway with this issue—Lucinda merely turned her righteous wrath onto him, since, as Pontifex, former or otherwise, he knew what all the rules were, and she felt he should have forced Christopher and Amy into the huge wedding.

Melanie and Emily looked as though they'd expected this somewhere along the line. Tito was taking the cue from Len and Kyle and pretending he wasn't here. Jeff was clearly struggling with the strong emotions.

That left me one person to appeal to for help. I shot Chuckie the "get us out of this" look. He heaved a sigh and cleared his throat, loudly.

Lucinda and Amy both stopped snarling at each other and looked at him. "Thank you, ladies. Under the circumstances we are, have been, and likely will be in over the next few weeks at least, I have to insist that no one in Centaurion Division is allowed to throw what I'd consider an overly excessive party."

"And why is that?" Lucinda asked haughtily.

"Because a huge formal affair leaves all of Centaurion exposed and in danger in ways we can't afford to risk at this time." The way Chuckie said this indicated the No Parties Rule was in full effect and would be enforced by the U.S. military.

"My son might have something to say about that." Lucinda sounded even haughtier, if such were possible. She also glared at Alfred, clearly expecting his support on this one.

"He might, but it won't matter," Chuckie replied calmly. "I outrank all of you."

"You have no rank within Centaurion Division," Alfred said, wisely supporting his wife.

Chuckie laughed. "I don't need a rank. My position within the C.I.A. ensures that I control all of Centaurion Division. I don't like to constantly remind all of you of such," his eyes and voice went icy, "but with one word I can make your lives miserable in the extreme. Now, this discussion is over, because if one more person tries to suggest Centaurion needs to throw a big party, I'm putting Centaurion officially under C.I.A. control."

Lucinda opened her mouth. White spoke first, however. "Agreed, Mister Reynolds." He looked at his sister. "You're done. Complain to Alfred, in private, but we cannot afford for the C.I.A. to feel forced to exercise their authority."

Lucinda looked over at Jeff. "You're not going to argue with him?"

Jeff shrugged. "I'm no longer the Head of Field, remember? You can argue about this with James and Paul, but I can guarantee they're going to back Reynolds."

I wasn't sure what the next words were going to be or who would say them. But I decided it was time to toss out some diplomacy. "Hey, I'm starving. What say we eat whatever delicious meal Lucinda's prepared?" It was sure to be delicious—she was a great cook.

The others quickly took up the "I'm hungry" chant. Lucinda smiled graciously at me. "Well, since our guests are ready to eat, I suppose we can table any further ideas about the reception for a time when we're not in a state of emergency." She got up and headed for the kitchen.

Everyone else looked at each other. It was clear no one really knew what to say. I didn't want us discussing the only state of emergency I knew about, which involved naked pictures of me and Chuckie. I could tell Amy and Christopher didn't want to talk about weddings or receptions or anything remotely similar. Chuckie had his "you owe me" expression going and I knew it would be a bad idea to try to make him come up with a legitimate state of emergency excuse. I'd used up my only idea already.

"I smell meatloaf," Tito announced as if nothing untoward had happened, thankfully breaking the uncomfortable silence in the room.

Jeff groaned. "It figures."

CHAPTER 7

CHUCKIE GLANCED AT ME. "I think you should help your mother-in-law in the kitchen."

I was about to ask when, in all the years he'd known me, my helping in a kitchen had ever been a good idea, when Jeff nodded. "Yeah, please do, baby."

The idea of arguing appealed to me, but I decided to do as asked. Surely they both had a reason for this request.

Sure enough, they did—I trotted into the kitchen to hear the sounds of someone crying quietly.

Lucinda had her face buried in a dish towel. Okay, this wasn't good. I went to her and put my arm around her shoulders. "I'm sorry we can't have the party." It was a lie, but sometimes you had to tell a whopper to make someone else feel better.

She shook her head, face still buried, shoulders still shaking.

"Um, sorry you and Amy had a fight. She just really wants you to like her." This was true, though Amy probably wasn't going to be pleased I'd told Lucinda so.

Lucinda took her face out of the towel. "I do like her." She took a deep breath and let it out slowly in that way you do when you're trying really hard not to lose it again. "I don't understand why Richard isn't insisting on this party. Just because he's retired as Pontifex doesn't mean he should be ignoring things."

Things. Not traditions. "Um, what things, exactly, is Richard ignoring?"

Lucinda heaved a sigh. "The fact that without a big wedding, or at least a reception where I can show Amy off, no one believes we want her in the family."

This was a twist I hadn't seen coming. "Why not? I can't believe that in all A-C history no one's chosen to skip the big wedding parade and just get married quietly."

"Oh, of course, many don't do a large wedding. However, Christopher's position within the community and our family . . ." Her voice faltered. "It's so hard to deal with talented children when you have no talents yourselves."

I chose not to ask what this had to do with anything we were discussing. "Oh?"

"You can't hide the things from them that you can from other children. So when you're cross or they've been bad and you have to punish them, they think you hate them. They can't understand why you might be jealous of someone even though you love them. They just see the negative and assume that's all there is to your feelings for them."

She was talking in generalities, but it was easy for me to put in the specifics. Christopher's mother, Terry, had been an empath, which was rare for A-C females. Because his powers had been off the charts at birth, she'd had to take Jeff when he was a baby, so she'd been like his mother, too. When Terry had died, the boys had come to Alfred and Lucinda, and I knew they considered Christopher their "other" son.

But as far as I knew, Christopher didn't think of Lucinda as his mother, and his father was alive. And as the most powerful imageer in the galaxy, I had to guess the odds of him touching pictures of his parents and Jeff's parents would be high. Alfred and Lucinda were big on pictures—they had photos of their family all over their humongous house, and I knew Alfred had photo albums at work.

That Lucinda had been jealous of Terry was something I'd known early on. Jeff and Christopher knew this, too. Of course, I didn't know all the reasons why. I could pussyfoot, but it seemed extremely relevant, so I decided to go for it. "Why were you jealous of Terry?"

"She married my brother, she had to take my only son, my son and hers still love her more than me even though she's been dead for over twenty years—you tell me why I wouldn't have some jealousy issues."

Nice to know where Jeff's jealous streak came from. "Ah. But weren't you happy that Richard was happy?"

"Of course! I loved Terry. She and I were friends, that's how she met Richard and I met Alfred." She sniffled. "I lost someone precious to me, too, when she died. But the boys only see the loss as their own, and all I ever hear is how much happier they were when Terry was alive."

"I can see how that would hurt your feelings." I could. Lucinda wasn't a monster, she was just a regular person with failings, like anyone else.

"And Christopher didn't even take the time to bring Amy down to meet us before they started living together, let alone before they got married."

"Well, things happened pretty fast. And Amy wasn't in a great position to meet parents at the time." Since she'd found out her father had murdered her mother at the same time she discovered he was a charter member of the Evil Lunatic Scientists Club.

"I know. I'd hoped that maybe Amy would see us as her new parents. But we barely got to know her name before they were married. I can't tell anyone anything about her, because much is classified, and I don't know anything else." Tears ran down her face. "And all our family, all my friends, they think we're ashamed of her and Christopher. I'd hoped that by focusing Amy on traditions and protocol, I could convince her to let me throw a reception. And now Mister Reynolds says we can't, and by the time he lifts that ban, everyone's opinions will be set."

"Why didn't you just say this, straight out, to Amy?"

"And have her realize that she wasn't fully accepted into the community?" Lucinda looked and sounded aghast. "Better she should only hate me, rather than feel as if she's an outsider all the time."

Wow. Lucinda was taking one for the team, and no one had known about it. I felt particularly crappy that I hadn't picked this up in the slightest way. I'd been here a month, watching the interactions and hearing what she was saying, but none of it had registered.

Of course, I could do something about this now that I knew. But *what* was the big question. Marching into the dining room and sharing that this had all been a big misunderstanding didn't seem like the smoothest way of handling the situation, but I didn't have any other ideas.

A throat cleared, and I looked over my shoulder to see Chuckie standing in the short hallway between the kitchen and dining room. He wasn't alone. He had his hand over Amy's mouth, and Jeff had a hold of Christopher.

I glanced back at Lucinda. She looked trapped.

"Hey, guys. What's up?" I sort of felt trapped, too.

Chuckie rolled his eyes and let Amy go. She shot him a dirty look, then walked over to me and Lucinda. "I don't care if anyone else likes me," she said to Lucinda. "I only care that the people who matter to Christopher like me. And you matter to him, no matter what you might think."

Jeff now let Christopher go. Christopher shot Patented Glare #1 at him, then came over to us. He took Lucinda's hand. "You are my other mother. I just don't always know how to let you know that."

Lucinda started crying again. I backed away while the three of them did the group hug thing A-Cs all seemed to do naturally.

Jeff took my hand, and he and Chuckie walked me to the other side of the kitchen and out into the Great Room, where I was fairly sure the Martini grandkids performed Shakespeare when things were quiet, simply because it was certainly big enough to handle both the performers and a decent-sized audience.

"You handled that well," Chuckie said.

"How long were you watching?"

"Most of the time," Jeff said. He looked at Chuckie. "If you knew, why tell my mother we couldn't have the party?"

"Because I didn't think she'd want to discuss this in front of everyone. Oh, and duh."

"How is it the two of you figured out what was really going on when I've been here a month and had no clue?"

Jeff sighed. "I'm an empath. Passing Reynolds' 'duh' along to you, baby."

"I'm observant," Chuckie mentioned. "As you know. So, doubling that duh."

"True enough. Okay, fine, don't hand out another duh, I'm at capacity. So, while this is all working out, Lucinda brought up a really big issue—if Amy's not being accepted by the A-C community at large, you know that means whoever's still holding a torch for the whole purity of the race idea is going to use this to their advantage."

Chuckie sighed. "Very true. But since there are other things going on that you know nothing about, we need to get back to D.C. and determine what ranks where on our list of priorities."

"And we need to involve Alpha Team," Jeff added. "Reynolds didn't create a fake excuse for my mother not to throw a big party."

"I hate being out of the loop."

"Well, don't worry," Chuckie said. "We'll be catching you up quickly. As soon as you've taken and passed the HSAC we can bring you up to speed."

This was a new one. "Excuse me? I'm not heading to law school. Am I?"

Chuckie heaved a sigh. "No. The HSAC stands for High Security Administrative Clearance."

"I have a really high security clearance."

"Yes. You do. You don't, however, have HSAC clearance."

"How do you know?"

Chuckie gave me a look that clearly said I was dancing on his last nerve. "Because I have the complete records of which Centaurion Division personnel have what clearances. You don't have this one. At least none of you who've been in Florida have it. The others have been cleared."

"You have?" I asked Jeff.

Who shrugged. "It's just a test, baby. It's something we have to take as part of the Diplomatic Corps. Doreen said it's been around for as long as she can remember. She took it again, even though she'd taken it before."

"Great. I haven't studied."

Chuckie rolled his eyes. "There is nothing you can study for. This is a standard test, but it's testing your reactions more than your knowledge."

"Clear as mud."

He ignored me. "However, it's a U.S. Government test designed for anyone who works with or for Centaurion Division in a non-military capacity."

"So I didn't have to take this before because I was the Head of Airborne, as opposed to now, when I'm in the Diplomatic Corps."

"Nice of your brain to join the party."

"Careful, Secret Agent Man. I know where your bodies are buried."

"Which is precisely why you and the others have to pass this test. I need to get the rest of you passed and approved. It's a small thing, but a large check in the column that matters to my superiors. And to your mother."

Jeff cocked his head. "I realize you'd prefer to do this back at Langley, but I know NASA Base is set up for this kind of testing."

Chuckie nodded. "That would work. And it would also be a logical cover story for why you, White, and I are down here."

"Hey, and we can visit Alliflash and Gigantagator while we're at it."

Jeff shook his head. "Only my girl."

CHAPTER 8

EVERYONE CALMED DOWN and lunch was eaten. Lucinda showed yet more personal growth by whipping up something special for Jeff while the rest of us snorked down as much of her meatloaf as possible.

Jeff seemed both genuinely shocked and touched that his mother had a strip steak for him and that she hadn't complained at all that he didn't want meatloaf, which he loathed. Amy and Christopher moved so they were sitting right next to Lucinda, so the meal ended up a lot more cheerfully than it had started.

The need for the HSAC test was explained to everyone, and reassurances were given by Tito, Melanie and Emily that the test was a no big deal kind of thing. Alfred confirmed that the proper personnel were on site or on call even though it was the weekend, and Chuckie made a couple of calls to set things up. The best part, however, was that the A-C Operations Team was told to start packing our team up in preparation for going home.

The Operations Team handled things like cleanup, maid service, providing supplies, cooking if you wanted it, and more. What I—and apparently whoever had set this team up in the first place—considered the dirty, boring jobs.

Every official A-C facility was supported by the Operations Team. They were impressive to the extreme, and I'd tested their abilities all over the world and at thirty thousand feet in the air. But I'd never seen them.

Christopher liked to explain how the Operations Team worked, but his explanations always sounded just this side of crazy. I thought of them as the A-C Elves, using magic to do their jobs quickly and invisibly. This was honestly a less crazy explanation than any Christopher had tried to pass to me.

Lucinda was a wonderful cook, and it was something she loved to do, so she never had the Elves help out with food prep. I tried not to contemplate how much weight I'd probably put on while down here—on a daily basis we had three big meals, two snacks, and munchies available at all times. All homemade, all delicious. While getting home sounded great, I was definitely going to miss the food.

But even though the Elves didn't have to cook at Martini Manor, they certainly did everything else, as packed suitcases sitting in our room easily proved.

"Does Jamie stay here or does she need to take this test, too?" I asked Jeff as I pulled the salacious pictures out of my purse and shoved them into my suitcase.

"She's still a tiny baby, she stays here."

"Hey, just checking. Are you sure this is an easy test to pass?"

Jeff sighed. "It was easy for me, baby. I'm sure you'll do just fine."

"Can I take my iPod?"

"If I tell you no, will you actually leave it here?"

"Only if you tell me whoever's running the test will confiscate it."

"They'll only confiscate it if they can find it. Since you'll have it in that black hole you call a purse, I doubt anyone will find any of your stuff, even if they use x-rays."

I contemplated my options. "If they confiscate it, will they give it back?"

"I'm sure they will. I can't imagine why anyone would want to steal your things while you're taking this test."

"What if they don't let me take my purse in at all?"

Jeff sighed. "I'll be there. I'll take care of your purse, baby."

"Works for me."

We took Jamie back to Lucinda and Alfred, who were, understandably, less excited about our going back to D.C. than everyone else. "Be good, Jamie-Kat," I said as I gave her a big kiss. "Mommy and Daddy will be back soon."

Jamie didn't seem happy about us leaving, if her clinging to Jeff and starting to cry was any indication. "Should I stay here?" he asked.

"I think she's just being like this because she missed you so much." I'd certainly missed Jeff a ton, and if he were leaving right now, I'd probably also be clinging to him and making a fuss about it, so I couldn't blame our daughter for feeling the same way. "Maybe you *should* stay." I didn't want him to, but I was willing to take one for my daughter and let her have some alone time with her daddy.

Melanie shook her head and took Jamie from Jeff. "No. Emily, Tito, and I are staying here. She's just doing what we more experienced parents call Baby Blackmail."

Jeff didn't look convinced.

"You can stay if you want to," Chuckie said. "White and I can escort everyone to NASA Base without you."

Jeff heaved a sigh and kissed Jamie on her forehead. "No. Jamie will be safe here. Kitty, on the other hand, can find trouble without looking for it."

"I resent that."

"But you can't deny it," Christopher said.

"True enough." We said our good-byes to those staying at Martini Manor, then those of about to test gathered at the front steps. Len went to get the limo, and I sent a text.

"Who are you talking to?" Jeff asked.

"I'm letting Malcolm know where we're going and why."

"Nice to see you keep in constant contact with him," Jeff said far too snidely.

Chuckie sighed. "Buchanan's down here doing a job the head of the P.T.C.U. wants done. You feel free to call your mother-in-law and complain to her that you're jealous of the man assigned to protect her daughter and granddaughter. But, please, put it on speakerphone so we can all enjoy Angela ripping you a new one."

Since Chuckie had basically said what I would have, I let Jeff's whining pass without comment while he grumbled under his breath.

Len brought the limo around. Like every A-C limo, it was gray and had an impressive number of extra A-C bells and whistles on it. I was particularly fond of the surround-sound speakers and the laser shield features.

We piled in. I took the rear seat, Jeff and Chuckie joining me. Christopher, Amy, and White faced us. Kyle shut the passenger door, took shotgun, and we took off. I looked behind us—sure enough, a black Escalade was pulling out from in front of the servants' quarters. Buchanan had insisted that I always make sure he was the one driving, so I looked carefully. Yep, there was a big, good-looking, brown-haired guy behind the wheel.

"Done checking out the competition?" Jeff asked.

"Jeff, for God's sake."

"No, let him go on," Chuckie said. "It's so nice to hear him complain about someone other than me."

While Jeff grumbled and the rest of us laughed, "My Humps" by the Black Eyed Peas came on the sound system. I had a feeling Kyle had chosen that song on purpose.

I decided it was time to get us off of Jeff's jealousy issues. We'd been apart for a month, after all, so I had to figure the loneliness and horniness was causing most of his jealousy right now. Sadly, couldn't do anything about the horniness, for either one of us, but I could get us talking about something else. "So, why are we driving instead of taking a gate? The last time we went to NASA Base for anything we went as 'just folks' and all almost died in about a hundred different ways."

"It's the weekend," Jeff replied. "It'll raise fewer questions if we show up and go in through the front door."

"I'd also like to have our own car this time," Christopher added. "Just in case. It'll be a lot better to escape from alligators in a limo than in a VW Superbug."

"That was the fun part of Operation Drug Addict."

On cue, everyone I could see winced. No one else really seemed to appreciate my names for things; apparently the boring, official names were the popular ones. "I hate your name for that," Jeff muttered.

"Besides, you didn't think it was fun while it was happening," Christopher reminded me.

"True." Of course, Jeff and I had had some amazing sex during that time.

Jeff nuzzled my ear. "Love where your mind's at."

"Don't start," Chuckie said flatly. "I know the four of you have been separated for weeks, but the rest of us really don't want to watch the reunions."

"Spoilsport."

"That's me. I'm sure I don't need to say this, but just in case, don't mention the pictures to anyone until you've all passed the HSAC test and we're all alone."

"I was thinking I'd just grab the receptionist and tell her all about it," Amy said, sarcasm knob headed to eleven.

"What if they ask us about it during the test?" Len asked.

"That's a good question," Chuckie said slowly. "They shouldn't . . ."

"Who else knows about those pictures? Or should I ask who doesn't know?" I prayed my father was firmly on the side of "doesn't know."

"From our side, only those of us in the car and Mister Joel Oliver," Jeff said.

White coughed. "I have no idea what you're all talking about." True enough, he hadn't been in the room when Armstrong had shared.

Everyone looked uncomfortable. Kyle was already blushing, Christopher was looking at his hands, Amy was staring at the ceiling, and I didn't have to look to see the expressions on Jeff's and Chuckie's faces—they were right next to me and I could feel their embarrassment.

I opened my mouth, but Len beat me to it. "Senator Armstrong has faked dirty pictures of Kitty and Mister Reynolds. Mister Joel Oliver gave Mister Reynolds the head's up and he advised Ambassador Martini, which is why everyone's calm. Ambassador Martini isn't sure if the senator is trying to blackmail us or help out."

"Succinctly put. Thanks, Len. So, Richard, it's a spin on our usual fun and frolic."

"Ah. I'll have to examine the pictures at another time." White looked as though he was really trying very hard not to laugh. "I think I might have to insist, safety of the mission and the Embassy and all that."

"Great," Jeff said with a half growl. "You love to torture me, don't you, Uncle Richard?"

White did laugh now. "As much as I can, Jeffrey. As much as I can."

CHAPTER 9

NASA BASE WAS SEVERAL MILES from the Martini estate, but it didn't take us too long to get there. We had enough time to fill White in fully and confirm that Chuckie didn't know who else might have copies of the dirty pictures while listening to Steel Panther's "Death to All But Metal" and, to apparently ensure all the musical bases were covered, Culture Club's "Church of the Poison Mind," and then we were there.

Unlike the last time we visited, we went to a normal reserved parking lot, checked in at reception, and walked through the halls to get to our desired location. There were plenty of security folks around, as well as a variety of NASA personnel bustling about, and none of them tried to kill any of us, nor was a mad bomber tossing explosives from out of nowhere.

Sure, our former mad bomber was now the Head of Imageering, but Serene had been the bad guys' first Surcenthumain test subject, so it wasn't really her fault. And Mom, Chuckie, Alfred, and others had removed the remaining bad ones out of NASA's Barrel of Security Bad Apples, so there was no reason for me to be jumpy.

Only I was.

"What's wrong?" Jeff asked me quietly as we waited at an elevator bank we'd reached by wandering the rat maze that were the hallways of NASA Base. This wasn't my favorite place on Earth to visit. I wasn't hungry, thankfully, but I still felt like I would, ultimately, find either a big piece of cheese or a steel trap whenever we reached our destination.

"I think I'm having flashbacks."

"Ah." He rubbed the back of my neck. "Don't worry, baby. We'll all be fine and heading home shortly."

The elevator arrived and Chuckie insisted we all pile in together. Nine people in an elevator is a lot, especially when most of them are big guys, but I was okay being smooshed up between Jeff, White, Len and Kyle. Jeff had made sure Buchanan and Chuckie were on the other side of the car, which was sort of on the sweet side of his jealousy meter.

Once we were all in the elevator, instead of pushing a button for one of the floors, Chuckie used a special keycard. A panel I hadn't realized was there opened and a keypad slid out. He entered a passcode he ensured none of us could see. The reason for us all being chummy in the elevator was explained.

"Are we having a *Get Smart* moment?"

Chuckie heaved a sigh and ignored me. Well, he shot me his "seriously?" look and then ignored me.

We headed right down into the bowels of the earth. This, more than anything else, confirmed we were heading into the A-C controlled part of the facility—A-C bases tended to go down, not up.

The doors opened onto a part of NASA Base I hadn't seen before. It looked like we were entering the floor of a typical office building. A sterile, very white, very quiet office building.

We trooped down a long hallway. "You know, this is sort of like *2001: A Space Odyssey*. Or *Men in Black*. Or both."

"It's the secured floor," Chuckie said.

"Secured for what? There's no one here but us."

"Almost no one." Christopher pointed to the end of the hall. There was a reception desk, manned by a young Hispanic woman with large glasses and long black hair. Matching the rest of this floor, she was dressed in white. She didn't smile when we finally reached her.

She wasn't ugly, but she wasn't Dazzler level in any way, so it was a safe bet she was human. Most A-Cs at least shot you a smile the first time they met you, too.

Chuckie handed her his badge. "I have personnel for the HSAC exam," he said without preamble. "You should be expecting us."

The woman didn't look impressed by the badge, which was a first in my experience. She examined it and sniffed, then examined all of us and sniffed again. Not the "what's that smell" kind of sniff, but the "you're beneath me" sniff. I wondered if she'd ever met Mrs. Darcy Lockwood, my Washington Wife class instructor, or if she'd picked up how to be supercilious all on her own.

Her clothing didn't scream "impressive." The suit was okay but a little baggy on her, and her blouse was sort of wrinkled.

Before I could ask if she'd recently lost weight, she deigned to speak to us. "My name is Sandra. I'll be monitoring your activity during the HSAC."

"Does that mean you're administering the test?" Chuckie asked.

"No. We have someone for that. I'll be there to ensure there is no cheating."

"Why would we cheat? It's not like we won't get into a good college or something if we flunk."

This earned me another dismissive look. "You'd be surprised." Sandra turned back to Chuckie. "I had five individuals listed."

"There should have been six." Chuckie indicated Buchanan. "He should be on the list, too. May I see it?"

Sandra handed a small clipboard over, a tad unwillingly if I was any judge. I was sure she'd recently lost weight, because the clothes just didn't fit her right. Maybe she was still dieting and so hungry. I didn't like to miss a meal, so I could cut her some slack over being a little testy due to limited caloric intake.

"Huh." Chuckie showed the list to Jeff, who grunted.

"What?"

Chuckie looked at me. "Your name isn't on the list."

"Cool! I'll just wait out here with all of you, then!"

"You have to take this test, Kitty," Christopher said, shooting me Patented Glare #1.

"Apparently I don't."

"Kitty Katt?" Sandra asked.

"That's me, yes. Well, my maiden name."

"Ah." She pulled out a slip of paper from her jacket pocket. "Yes, I have you here. Kitty Katt-Martini. You're supposed to take the test alone."

"I beg your pardon?" Chuckie and I said that one in unison.

Sandra shrugged and handed her slip of paper to Chuckie. His eyes narrowed. "This is highly unusual. I'll have to clear it. With much higher level personnel," he added meaningfully.

This didn't seem to bother Sandra, who shrugged again. "Suit yourself. We'll take the others in now."

"No," Chuckie said firmly. "They all test together or they don't test at all."

Sandra heaved a sigh while Chuckie tried to make a call. "No reception," he said finally.

"That's because this floor is insulated in all ways," Sandra said. She didn't add "duh," but it was obvious she was thinking it. "So you can leave to make your phone call, or we can follow the orders given."

Chuckie seemed torn. I couldn't blame him. I didn't want to let Sandra win this one on general principles, all oddities aside. Plus, I wasn't wild about being tested all by myself in the first place, and I was certain Mom wouldn't be pleased that Buchanan wasn't in the room with me.

Then again, getting this test over with had advantages, and we were already here. "I'll be okay," I said quietly to Chuckie.

Jeff took my arm and Chuckie's and moved us away from Sandra's desk. "I'm not getting anything but annoyance from her," he said in a low voice. "She wants us to stop wasting her time so she can get her job done and go home, but that's all I've gotten. No malicious intent, other than the fact she's not happy to be here on the weekend."

"I don't like it," Chuckie said. "There's no reason for Kitty to be tested separately, other than to have an easy way to attack her when she has no backup."

"You want to go back and do this at Langley?" Jeff didn't seem excited by the idea. "We have a lot going on that we have to handle the moment we're back in D.C."

Chuckie heaved a sigh. "No, you're right. I'm probably seeing things that aren't there."

"First time for everything. Chuckie, seriously, if you don't think this is safe, let's go and we'll deal with this back at the Embassy."

"I can't read any of you in on what's going on until you've taken, and passed, this test," Chuckie said. "And I need to be able to read you in, quickly. And your husband hasn't picked up anything dangerous."

"Then let's just go for it. If someone tries anything, I have hairspray with me."

Chuckie shrugged. "I'd prefer it if you had your Glock."

"Left it at home, under the correct assumption the many security checkpoints here would have taken it away from me."

"Okay, against my better judgment, let's go for it. What's the worst that could happen?"

"Superbeing formation and attack," Jeff said without missing a beat.

"Superinsulated floor," I reminded him. "I'd expect an assassination attempt, if I were you."

Chuckie rubbed his forehead. I had a feeling he had a migraine on the way. "Then you're the one who needs to be on the alert, Kitty, because you're the one who'll be alone."

CHAPTER 10

AS EXPECTED, Buchanan was no happier with this turn of events than Chuckie, Jeff, or I were, but after some more quiet arguing the others dutifully trotted into their room to the left of Sandra's desk and I was taken by her into a room on the right.

The room was big enough to handle a full-sized classroom, but there were only two desks and three chairs in it. One desk was all by its lonesome in the middle of the room, and it looked like a deluxe high school desk. Clearly, this was where I was supposed to hang out. The other desk looked like a teacher's desk, was close to the far wall, and had a normal office chair with it. There was no one in said chair.

"Put your purse in the basket under the chair," Sandra instructed as she went to the third chair that had no desk partner. It was a high swivel-stool with a back and arms. She looked liked the Good Humor Lifeguard sitting in it.

I did as instructed. It was difficult to shove my purse in, in part because my purse was big and stuffed full of things I felt imperative to have with me at all times—like my iPod, speakers, Jeff's adrenaline harpoon, teething biscuits, baby wipes, hairspray, and more—and also because the basket seemed set up to not let you get your stuff out once you'd foolishly shoved it in.

"Can I have my iPod out?"

"No. Nothing."

"Why not? If this place is as insulated as you say, there's no way I'd get some cheater transmission or anything."

"Those are the rules."

"Screw the rules," I muttered under my breath. But despite my desire to flip Sandra the bird, I left everything in my purse and sat in the chair.

Sandra seemed about to say more when the door at the other end of the room, near the teacher's desk, opened. An older man with wire-rimmed glasses, sandy hair, and a well-kept moustache poked his head in.

"I'm looking for Susan," he said. "She's supposed to be helping me administer the HSAC."

"She went home sick," Sandra said. "I'm covering."

"Then why are you in here?" He seemed to notice me for the first time as he stepped fully into the room. He wasn't too much taller than me, and though he was dressed all in white, just like Sandra, his slacks and mock turtleneck fit him properly. He smiled warmly at me. "Ah, there's my missing student. I'm John. I'd say welcome to your HSAC test, but you're in the wrong room."

"Sandra said I was supposed to be tested alone, but I'd much rather be with the rest of my diplomatic mission."

John gave Sandra a confused look. "I didn't get any instructions like that. I have six students listed on my roster. I can't start the test without Missus Martini." He looked at me. "You *are* Katherine Katt-Martini, right?"

"Indeed!" I wasn't going to let this opportunity pass. I got up and got my purse. It was close to impossible to get it out of the basket, but by using some of my hyperstrength I was able to do it. Then I trotted over to John. "Let's join the others."

"Suit yourselves," Sandra said quietly.

We left my Solitary Confinement Classroom and went to another room. It was set up similarly to how the room we'd just left was, only this had plenty of desks and also had the others to be tested in it. Buchanan looked relieved to see me, but he wiped that expression off quickly.

"You need to have at least one desk between you and anyone else," John told me. I picked a spot in the middle between Amy and Len, which was in front of White. Kyle and Buchanan were both nearer to the back of the room.

There was a stool for Sandra in this room, too, and she perched on it. "I was sent additional questions," she told John.

He stared at her. "Why? And why were they sent to you? I'm the administrator of this test in this facility."

She shrugged. "Maybe they couldn't reach you."

"You can ask your questions at the end," he said firmly. "These folks have been delayed long enough."

Sandra sighed and pulled out a packet from her jacket. I had no idea how she'd hidden it in there. "Official orders."

John took the packet and examined it. "Sealed." He shrugged. "Looks right, so fine. Now then," he turned to us, "please put all your personal items, including any electronics, in the basket under your seats and we'll get started."

Amy's purse was already in her basket. I reluctantly put mine away again. Happily, this desk's basket seemed normal and not like it was trying to take my purse captive and never let it go again.

John handed out a folder and mechanical pencils to each of us. The folders had our names on them. "This is not a timed test," he shared as he went back to the teacher's desk. "So there's no pressure. Just choose what you believe is the best answer for each question, and when you're done, turn your test over and raise your hand. Obviously, no talking amongst yourselves."

He sat and watched us while we got going. My mother had trained me to always read the test through fully before answering, especially if there was no time limit given, so I followed Mom's teaching and did so.

At least, I read the first few pages. Then I surreptitiously checked out what Amy and Len were working on. Their pages seemed normally thick. Not my set. It was like I was holding the Fall Fashion issue of *GQ* in my hands—my special test had a *lot* of pages. Sadly, most of them were not ads featuring handsome men in great clothes. All of them were filled with questions I was expected to answer.

There were a lot of convoluted questions, some multiple choice, some yes/no, some requiring an essay answer. I refrained from asking if we were actually taking the SATs again, because the questions weren't about algebra or literature. I did recognize the types of questions they were, however.

This was a psych evaluation, and a really complex one. My father had given tests like this to me, Chuckie, Amy, and Sheila, my other best friend from high school, and, as I thought about it, to all my sorority sisters somewhere along the line. Always under the guise of either having fun or using us to see if a test was too hard or too easy. That none of us had questioned why a history professor needed to give psych evaluations was probably not something I needed to ponder at this precise moment. However, I did know this kind of test when I saw it.

There were a variety of questions, all asking the same things in different ways, all trying their hardest to ensure that the testee wouldn't have any idea what the "right" answer was, nor be able to fake replies for too long.

While I contemplated which response was the most accurate for me in the question of who I would save during a bank robbery—when the offered replies were Other Bank Robbers, Bank Manager, Your Accomplices, or Best Hostage Option—the balance of my mind was trying to figure out what this test proved and why everyone working with Centaurion Division in a nonmilitary role had to take it.

Every question seemed to be determining what level of bad guy the responder was. I scanned the test again. Sure enough, every question I saw seemed more suited to The Club of Evil Megalomaniacs Entrance Exam than the HSAC test, at least insofar as it had been described to me. I couldn't imagine Jeff and Christopher thinking this test was no big deal.

"Yes, Mister White?" John said.

I looked up and around. White had his hand up.

"I'm done." White smiled at me. "I saw no reason to prolong the experience."

Ah. He'd used hyperspeed. Lucky duck. I wasn't able to control it well enough to read and write like an A-C could. I wanted to ask White what he'd thought of the questions, but John had him bring his test forward, then had White sit at the front, near to him.

One by one, everyone else finished. I was still struggling with how to answer any of these questions and not sound like my next act after the test was going to be blowing up the Base. Maybe they'd put this into effect after Operation Drug Addict, because of Serene and the Security team infiltration. But even so, this test wasn't going to tell anyone anything realistic about our crew.

The others were all sitting in a row in front of me by now, and they were clearly antsy. I couldn't blame them. I normally didn't take forever to do a test.

I flipped to the back, to see if there were any normal questions before I gave up and asked for a room so I could eat and sleep while finishing the test version of *War and Peace*. As I did so, Sandra spoke again.

"Why don't we let the others go? Clearly Missus Martini isn't close to being done yet."

"It's not in the rules," John said.

They argued quietly about this, but I stopped paying too much attention, because a set of questions had caught my eye.

Who is Esteban Cantu and what is his position within the United States Government?

Well, I knew the answer to this one. Cantu was part of the C.I.A., the head of their Antiterrorism Unit, to be exact, and he'd been involved in some ways in both Operation Confusion and Operation Assassination. He was also, absolutely, not a friend to Centaurion Division or anyone who protected the A-Cs in any way.

What is Esteban Cantu's affiliation, to the best of your knowledge?

Evil, bad, pick a negative adjective, probably affiliated with whoever wrote this test. He'd been in league with John Cooper, when Cooper had run Operation Confusion. And he'd been in league with Madeline Cartwright and Antony Marling, the head of Titan Security, when they'd been putting Operation Assassination into action. He was also chummy with Senator Armstrong and what was left of the politicians and lobbyists I called the Cabal of Evil.

But I didn't write any of this down. I read on.

What are your thoughts on Paraguay? Do you feel the situation there is under control?

No, I did not think Paraguay was under control. Marling had confirmed there were more supersoldiers than the ones we'd captured at the end of Operation Assassination, and I was sure some were in Paraguay, just as I was sure some were in Paris or the general surrounding area. But like so many other Weapons of Mass and Scary Destruction, whenever our teams descended on the confirmed locations, the WMDs had been moved to a new secret lair.

Why does Charles Reynolds oppose integration of Alpha Centaurion personnel and the U.S. Military?

Huh? We had Chuckie questions now? Cantu was always trying for the Wedge of Separation between me and Chuckie, because Chuckie was the person who did the most to block Centaurion from becoming the War Division. And he opposed this integration because the A-Cs were actually pacifistic at their cores, and they were also here for reasons other than running the military-industrial complex.

Is Charles Reynolds' biggest weakness: a) his intelligence, b) his willingness to be insubordinate, c) his affection for aliens, d) his inability to see the big picture?

There was no "none of the above" choice, unfortunately. In reality, and Jeff would be the first to confirm this, Chuckie's biggest weakness was probably me. He'd been in love with me for half of our lives, though I was pretty sure he was over that. But I was also his best friend, and we loved each other as best friends do. I knew he'd die to protect me, or Jamie. And probably Jeff, too, because I loved Jeff and he was my husband, and my safety and happiness mattered to Chuckie, just as his mattered to me.

I looked at the last question.

Are you prepared to answer these questions or are you prepared to die?

Uh-oh.

CHAPTER 11

"EVERYBODY DOWN!"
I followed my own order and flipped myself out of the desk and onto the floor while grabbing for my purse and wishing I'd brought my Glock and just dealt with a few extra minutes at the security checkpoints. I flung the strap over my neck—no reason to lose my purse, I was sure I was going to need its contents soon enough.

The rest of the team were all experienced by now, and all of them, even Amy, were on the floor. Kyle was using his body to shield her.

I looked to the front of the room. John was still sitting at his desk, gaping at me in shock and confusion.

Sandra, however, was already moving. Straight for me.

My brain worked at its own version of hyperspeed. Jeff hadn't picked up anything dangerous from her, and he'd definitely monitored. But she'd done every low-key thing she could to get me in a room with her alone. Her clothes didn't fit her right, and Susan, whom John had been expecting, wasn't around. I had a feeling she hadn't gone home sick but that she'd gone home dead.

And I knew androids—really good, really believable-as-human androids—existed. Androids so good they'd fooled Jeff based on their emotional output.

I didn't have a lot of options, but there was a really good way to tell a human from an A-C and an A-C from an android. I jumped to my feet, grabbed the desk, and swung it at Sandra with all my strength.

The desk shattered. Sandra jerked a little and kept on coming. It so figured.

"Android attacking! Len, Kyle, get Amy and John out of here!" That was all the time I had before Sandra was on me.

She grabbed me with one hand and held me at arm's length. I tried to break free, but her grip was far too strong. The other hand she held out, fingers slightly splayed and pointed at Buchanan, who was running toward us, while Len grabbed John and Kyle picked Amy up as they ran for the door near the teacher's desk.

"Malcolm, down!"

He ducked just as bullets sprayed out of Sandra's fingers. Antony Marling had told us, right before he'd killed himself, that the super-soldiers we'd found in D.C. were our friends compared to what else was out there. If we had weaponized androids running around freely, he'd undersold what was coming.

The bullets missed everyone, but not for Sandra's lack of trying. She spun us around, still firing out of her fingers.

Sandra wasn't that big, as people or androids went. I hit her with a strong front ball kick to her side. She seemed to feel it, but only a little. Bummer. I grabbed another desk and hit her with it. She staggered a bit while the desk fell apart, but that was all.

She was still shooting bullets, and we were still spinning. Getting dizzy and sick was going to be in my near future if I didn't do something. These rooms were insulated, so no help was coming from Jeff, Christopher or Chuckie until Amy and the boys found them, and by then one or more of us could be hurt or dead.

Buchanan, using desks as shields, was getting closer. Sandra stopped spinning and focused her firepower at him. The desks didn't last long, but as near as I could tell, Buchanan wasn't hit yet. I couldn't spot White anywhere. I was sure he hadn't run out the door with the others, but I hadn't seen him while we were spinning like a really badly made dreidel.

Of course, as someone tackled Sandra from behind and both of us went down, maybe I hadn't seen him because he'd been using hyperspeed to stay behind us.

Because Sandra was distracted by White, I was able to get out of her grasp. As I scrambled away, she flipped around and slammed White into the ground, while she landed on top of him. He was strong, because he was an A-C and a big man, but he wasn't enhanced. Buchanan had made it over and was trying to help White. And while he was a big, strong guy, he was a human. Even if Len and Kyle came back to help, I didn't think the four of them were going to be able to stop Sandra.

After all, the only person who'd been able to stop the androids who'd been passing as Leslie Manning and Bryce Taylor had been Jeff. And he'd been high on adrenaline in order to do it.

I was still experiencing control issues with my powers, and I hadn't been able to work with Christopher at all while in exile in Florida. However, the one thing I knew for sure by now was that if I wanted to kick butt in a really serious way, rage was my friend.

It didn't take much to get really angry. I just had to focus on the fact that I hadn't had sex with my husband for a month and that if this heinous robot won I might never have sex with him again. Presto, pissed.

I grabbed a broken desk and pulled a solid piece of metal off, as Sandra landed a good hit to Buchanan's sternum. He went flying and slammed against a wall. She kicked White right in the gut with both feet and he flew into a different wall. Both men were down and they looked out.

Not a problem. Just made me angrier that she'd hurt my friends.

Sandra looked a little mussed up, but she got to her feet easily. "You will complete your test," she said. Her voice sounded a little slurry, which meant the men had managed to do some small damage at least. We circled each other, like fighters in the ring. I wished Tito were here—he was a really good coach for me when it came to Mixed Martial Arts fighting outside of the octagon.

"I don't think so. I'm planning to flunk this exam."

She feinted and I swung my metal bar at her. I hit her head. The bar bent. Her hair and the skin on her face were kind of messed up, but other than that, not a lot of damage done. I tossed the bar away as I jumped back to avoid her reaching for me.

"You can't win. I'm so much better than you." I waited for her to shoot projectiles of some kind at me, but she didn't. So either she was out of ammo or I was supposed to be taken alive. Either option was better for me.

"Blah, blah, blah. I've heard that one before. So, you killed Susan?"

She shrugged as she moved her neck in a weird, totally nonhuman way. "It was expedient." Her voice wasn't slurring any more, and what I'd done to her head didn't look nearly as impressive now, either. Too bad, the damage wasn't much. Yet.

"John in on this plan?"

"Hardly. He, like the others, will be dead soon."

"How's that? I'm not letting you out of here alive. I mean, alive for you, which, I guess, means I'm yanking your battery."

She shrugged. "I am only one part of the operation." She smiled nastily. "I won't have to listen to you much longer, though. And you'll never see your husband and friends alive again."

This was probably supposed to scare me and maybe make me offer to come quietly as long as they left the others alone. But I knew how "they" worked. I had no clear idea who was behind this, though Esteban Cantu was up there on my Perennial Top Three Suspects List. But the League of Evil Masterminds all rolled the same way—lie to get you to do what they wanted, then kill you and anyone else they felt like. Well, not this time.

All Sandra's threat did was move me from really pissed off up to enraged. Excellent.

"So, who's pulling the puppet strings on this one, Pinocchia?"

She gave me a nasty look. She had to be one of Marling's creations—the man had been a loon of the highest order, but he'd done amazingly good work, and he was particularly good at creating androids so unlikable you'd never suspect them of being more than human. "The last person you'd ever manage to suspect."

Sandra hadn't attacked yet. We were still circling each other and she was likely stronger, even if I was at my most enraged state. So what was she waiting for? Me to attack? Reinforcements? The signal that my husband and friends were dead or captured?

"So, who's that? If you're going to take me dead or alive, might as well tell me who's giving the directions for you to do so."

She smirked. "Why not? My instructions were given to me by Charles Reynolds."

True, this was the last person I'd ever suspect of these machinations. And also true, the fact that the smartest guy around had been stymied at every turn lent a certain credence to the idea that he was in charge and therefore ensuring nothing concrete was found. And maybe if I'd only known Chuckie for the past few years I'd have believed it.

But I'd known him for more than half of my life, and I still knew him better than anyone alive. And among the many things he wasn't was the kind of person who would do these evil, underhanded things. I also knew how much our enemies hated him. It didn't take a lot of mental effort to figure that Sandra had been told to tell me Chuckie was in charge in the hopes of slamming the Wedge of Separation between us so strongly that it would never come out.

That was the goal, I was sure. Only that wasn't the outcome. The outcome was that I was now seeing red I was so furious.

I lunged at her. Either she really hadn't expected it or I was moving so fast she couldn't tell, but she wasn't able to block me. I slammed into her, and we slammed into the wall behind her.

And broke through.

CHAPTER 12

I WAS TOO MAD TO STOP, and besides, we hit another wall almost immediately because we were going so fast. We broke through that one, too.

Clearly my mutation wasn't over, because I hadn't been able to do this before. I knew A-Cs were strong enough to break through walls—Jeff, Christopher, and Michael Gower had had to do just that the last time we'd been here, after all. But I was breaking through the super walls on this level, and they had more than drywall and the fluffy pink insulating materials in them.

The positive was that I was breaking through using Sandra as my ramming mechanism. Not only was this ensuring that I wasn't getting hurt, but it was obviously affecting her.

I sped up.

We slammed through, by my count, over a dozen walls before we hit something I couldn't get through. Right, we were underground. I stopped running, and Sandra managed to fight back. Not as much as she'd done before, but still, I didn't enjoy getting punched anywhere.

"Who's really in charge?" I growled at her as I slammed her against the wall again.

"Charles . . . Reynolds . . ." The words were slurred and coming out slowly. "He . . . is . . . your enemy."

Goody, my rage spiked again. I slammed us into the wall that didn't want to give a few more times. This was fun, but I wasn't sure if it was going to short her out or not.

I heard voices. I wasn't sure where we were or who might be coming, but if it wasn't our team, what the NASA folks would see was me beating up someone they'd assume worked here. No time for that. I was fully revved and running on waves of fury. Time to go up.

I ensured I had a really good grip on not only her clothes but her body, and then I ran us around the room twice to build up speed, then up the wall. Happily, my plan worked and we slammed through the ceiling and kept on going.

My memory shared that we'd gone down about five floors, so after we slammed through four more ceilings, I turned so we were once again playing nicely with gravity, gave it a shot, and headed us toward a wall. Breached it as if it were tissue paper, and lo and behold, we were outside.

I didn't know this area very well, but the landmark I knew best was the lighthouse. I could see it, and I headed us for it. We were moving so fast I was certain no human could see us. I wasn't sure if any A-C who wasn't enhanced could see us, either.

We reached the lighthouse and I actually managed to stop us by the water's edge. I didn't want to go into the lighthouse, not yet anyway.

"We're right by the alligator preserve. I guarantee that you can't beat a full contingent of 'gators, even if you were at full power, which I know you're not. Now, you tell me the truth or I toss you in and watch to see if my friends Gigantagator and Alliflash show up to reminisce."

"I don't have to tell you anything." Her voice sounded funny—metallic and recorded, not real like it had before. Her eyes looked funny, too—they were glazed and looked like glass marbles with irises painted on them.

My brain none-too-gently reminded me that every recent super-being cluster that had formed in either Paris or Paraguay had self-destructed before any of the good guys could manage to capture or disarm them. That Sandra had a self-destruct protocol installed seemed likely.

I spun her around and checked her back. Circuitry was definitely exposed. High school science shared that the body of water was big enough and the voltage probably small enough that no 'gators would be harmed. Worked for me.

I picked her up, chose a good spot in the swamp to aim for, and threw her in, hard.

Water splashed up and I saw a little smoke escape as Sandra went under. I waited. No explosion.

She didn't bob to the surface, which made some sense. She had metal and wires and such and so probably not the same amount of air humans did, ergo, she was going to sink versus float.

I saw what looked like a lot of floating logs converging on the area where I'd tossed her, which was still reasonably close to the shore. Time to get to higher ground.

I zipped to the lighthouse and up the stairs, doing my best to slow down along the way. Either my technique worked or I was out of hyperjuice, because by the time I reached the top, I was both going at a human walk and utterly exhausted.

Dug my phone out of my purse while watching the 'gators. They were still in the area and not following something moving, so I could hope Sandra was really shorted out and at the bottom of the preserve's swamp as opposed to walking away underwater while laughing at me.

Jeff answered on the first ring. "Where are you? Are you okay? What the hell happened?"

"At the top of the lighthouse, enjoying the view and having Operation Drug Addict flashbacks. I'm really tired, but otherwise I'm fine. Sandra was an android and I tossed her in the swamp. I'm hoping that means she can't self-destruct, and I'm also hoping someone can come and fish her out before the 'gators eat her and get sick."

"Only my girl. We'll be right there, baby."

"She seemed to believe the rest of you were going to be dead or captured."

"Might have been if Reynolds hadn't been antsy. He insisted on the three of us snooping around, so we weren't where the attack squad thought we'd be."

"Interesting. Is everyone else okay, Richard and Malcolm in particular?"

"Yeah, they're bruised up but insisting they're okay. Per Christopher, we can wait to get back to my parents' before we have them go to medical."

"So, did you or Christopher pick up anything untoward going on?"

"No. Whatever that floor's insulated with, we couldn't get any reading from it."

I chose to refrain from cursing, but only because it would have required more exertion than I felt up to. "Figures." I spotted what I was pretty sure was a floater gate and shared as much with Jeff.

"Alpha Team is on the way." As he said this, I saw Tim Crawford, the Head of Airborne, aka the guy who had my old job, step

through. To human eyes, he would have appeared out of nowhere.
I had no idea what it looked like to alligator eyes, but I could see
some of them start to take an interest.

"Oh, good. Maybe one of them can carry me down from the
lighthouse. After we've set up an electric fence to keep the 'gators
at bay, that is." I wanted to check on Gigantagator and Alliflash, if
I could spot them in an alligator lineup, but I wanted to do this from
a distance and with the really heavy animal-enclosure glass between us.

Jeff cursed quietly and in a moment I wasn't alone on the top of
the tower. I hung up and dropped my phone back into my purse as
he picked me up. "You really overdid it, baby."

"I could have let the evil android kill us all and take me captive,
true. I officially never want to come here again. Just sayin'."

He chuckled as he hypersped us downstairs, which coincided
nicely with the rest of Alpha and Airborne teams exiting the gate.
Well, the male portions of those teams were in attendance, meaning
Paul Gower, James Reader, and the five flyboys were in here along
with Tim. Serene was too pregnant to make any situation calls, and
Lorraine and Claudia were still the mothers of newborns and therefore enjoying the last part of their maternity leaves.

The rest of the team with us arrived now, accompanied by
Michael Gower, who was both Gower's younger brother and an
astronaut. Michael worked at NASA Base, so him being here
wasn't a shock.

"Who or what the hell broke through over fifteen walls and
floors of the Base?" Michael asked before anyone else could speak.

I raised my hand. "Guilty. It messed the android up a lot, though,
so it was all worth it. I think."

Reader shook his head. "We can't leave you alone for a minute,
girlfriend."

"This wasn't my fault!"

"It's never your fault," Gower said. He heaved a sigh. "This is
going to take some Pontifex-level charm to smooth over, isn't it?"

"Yeah, I think it is. Good thing you're so good with the smooth-
talking, isn't it?"

"Why are we waiting for the alligators to eat us?" Jerry Tucker,
my favorite flyboy, asked.

"Kitty probably wants to catch up with old friends," Reader said
as he winked at me.

"I really want to take a long nap and figure out what the hell's going on. But if we can toss a couple cases of chicken carcasses to the 'gators, I'm not against it."

"I am," Chuckie said firmly. "This is an unmitigated disaster. Thankfully, we can get some A-Cs here to do fast repairs to the building that you almost single-handedly destroyed."

"Hey, it's still standing. Besides, Sandra the Nasty Android really pissed me off."

"Why so?" he asked.

"She said you were the one in charge of all the supersoldier stuff and my enemy."

Chuckie gaped at me. So did most of the others. Reader and Gower, however, exchanged a very meaningful glance, and it wasn't romantic.

"What?" Chuckie asked finally.

"We've gotten some anonymous messages insinuating the same thing," Reader said.

Chuckie was still basically speechless. I could tell he was furious, hurt, suspicious, and the conspiracy wheels were turning.

I was about to reassure him that I, at least, didn't buy it. But Amy spoke before I could. "As if."

Everyone stared at her in shock, Chuckie in particular.

Amy rolled her eyes. "Look, Chuck and I have basically never gotten along, but there are a few things I know about him—and the number one thing is that he would never do anything to hurt Kitty.

"And maybe you all don't remember Paris, but I sure do. There is no way he's in charge of anything going on against Centaurion Division. All the bad guys wanted to kill him in even more horrible ways than they wanted to kill everyone else, and they weren't exactly shy about beating the crap out of him. He was closer to dying than any of the other guys when we were captive. I don't buy that even anyone as smart as Chuck is would want to be about three seconds from dying, no matter how much he might have expected Kitty and Richard to come save the day.

"The people who were friends and allies of my father's aren't taking direction from Chuck. They'd rather die. And no matter how sneaky all of you think he is, there's no way he's that good a liar. At least, no lie Chuck's ever tried to pass has fooled me." She looked at him. "Starting with the 'Kitty and I are just best friends' line you tried passing to me in ninth grade."

Jeff grunted and Amy rolled her eyes again. "Jeff, seriously, Kitty's missed you a lot this past month, but I have to be honest when I say I haven't missed your jealousy crap one little bit. Chuck's over her romantically, catch the obvious clues, will you?"

"You're in a mood," Christopher finally got out.

"People trying to kill me and everyone else while pinning it on a really easy, obvious, and yet so clearly innocent target pisses me off. Kitty and I aren't *all* that different, you know."

Everyone else was still basically stunned into silence. "What Ames said. So, um, let's fish Sandra the Android out of the swamp, assign some teams to fix the buildings, and get Malcolm and Richard to medical while we regroup and try to figure out what the hell is going on."

"Let's do what Kitty the Android Killer says," Reader said. "I want our flock out of Dodge as soon as possible." He patted Chuckie on his shoulder. "For what it's worth, Paul and I agree with Amy and Kitty—it's not you, but someone sure wants us to think it is."

"Who?" Chuckie asked.

I snorted. "Pick a target, we're spoilt for choice."

Reader sighed. "Just like always."

CHAPTER 13

"SO, DO WE DRIVE OR TAKE A GATE?" I asked.

All of Alpha and Airborne snorted. Jeff and Chuckie looked resigned. Christopher came through, though, and hit me with Patented Glare #3. I truly felt it was his favorite. "Alpha and Airborne didn't arrive via floater gate to get to you more quickly. They used a floater because they had to—you destroyed the main hub apparatus for all of the gates at NASA Base while you were breaking down walls, floors and ceilings."

"Bummer."

Christopher switched to Glare #4 as Jeff rubbed the back of his neck, Chuckie rubbed his forehead, the flyboys grinned, and Tim, Reader, and Gower gave me a variation of the "why me?" look.

"Hey, sometimes the buildings in Metropolis get trashed while Superman's protecting the world from Darkseid and Lex Luthor. It happens. I didn't do it intentionally." Well, not with malice afore-thought. "So it's a good thing we drove, right?"

"Nice spin," Chuckie said. "Do you want me to stay?" he asked Reader.

"No. Get out of here along with the rest of our demolition crew," Reader said. "We'll call you if we need you to flash the badge, but right now, anyone who was down on that floor isn't popular with NASA."

"No time to stop and feed the 'gators?"

Jeff picked me up. "You seem tired, baby," he said as he strode off quickly, the rest of our team following.

I waved to the guys who were staying behind. The flyboys waved with enthusiasm, the others not so much. Oh well. Surely they wouldn't be mad at me for too long. Not forever, hopefully.

Jeff sighed. "No one's mad at you. Not very much, anyway. It's just an expensive, awkward situation to be in."

"I thought we in Centaurion Division didn't care about money."

"We don't mind spending it. But wasting it's another story."

Now I felt bad. It wasn't like I'd given the destruction of the base a lot of thought. My destructive thoughts had been focused solely on Sandra. The destruction or at least stoppage of a dangerous android had to count for something, right? I really related to how the Justice League and X-Men must feel when they'd saved the world—again—and yet all said world wanted was to discuss the bill for damages.

Jeff sighed again. "It happens. Stop worrying about it."

"I'll do my best."

The less said about the ride back to Martini Manor the better. White and Buchanan weren't feeling great, and while White had faster healing and regeneration because he was an A-C, getting mule kicked by an android wasn't something even the toughest person just shook off.

Everyone else was in some kind of stress-related mood, to the point where I wished I'd mastered the A-C talent of napping wherever and whenever the opportunity presented itself.

Once back, happily, Tito didn't demand that I go immediately into isolation, preferring to get everyone back to the Embassy before Treatments of Doom were handed out.

We said fast but heartfelt good-byes to Alfred and Lucinda, reclaimed our small child, ensured our belongings were already back at the Embassy, and took a nauseating gate trip back home.

I'd expected to be happy to be back in D.C., and I was at first, what with getting a lovely greeting from everyone who'd been able to avoid going on Exile to Florida. None of them seemed upset that I'd sort of trashed a building. I was even happier when Tito decided I could merely go to bed really early, as opposed to going into isolation.

Christopher and Amy dashed for their rooms. White and Buchanan went with Tito, Emily, and Melanie to the medical bay. Len and Kyle went across the street to say hi to everyone at the Romanian Embassy, Olga and her granddaughter Adriana especially. And I got another set of hugs from everyone whom I hadn't seen for a month.

The Embassy was a full city block wide and long, seven floors going up, one real floor going down, with one underground parking floor, and then a bigger drop down to the Secret Lab Section that the former Diplomatic Corps had secretly had installed when Jeff and Christopher were little boys. The Embassy, like Martini Manor, was one of the A-C showcases, so it was quite opulent and had pretty much anything you could want in terms of business and home layout and amenities.

Happy Embassy Hellos done, I really wanted to go up and lie down. Only I could tell Chuckie was still upset and I wasn't an empath. "You want to hang out here a little while?" I asked him.

Chuckie shrugged. "Not sure it's a good idea."

Jeff sighed. "You need it. Come on." He led us to one of the small studies on the third floor. "Hang out here while we get our things squared away."

Chuckie looked uncertain. "If you're sure."

"I'm sure we have a lot we need to go over," Jeff said.

"Like how in the world Sandra the Android knew to attack us at NASA Base."

"And what we're going to do when those pictures hit the news-stands," Chuckie added morosely.

Jeff pulled out his phone and dialed. "Hey, Naomi. Back in D.C. Nope, all here. Yeah, finally. Look, are you and Abigail available? Great. Yes." Jeff rolled his eyes. "Thanks ever." He hung up and shook his head.

"What's going on?"

"Naomi and Abigail are going to come babysit Reynolds. Apparently they were waiting for my call and feel I should have asked them to help out in Florida."

"I don't need a sitter," Chuckie said with a laugh that didn't sound remotely real.

"Yeah, to quote Amy, you really can't lie to me, because there isn't an emotion you have I can't read. You need company while we're upstairs, and we need to go over things sooner as opposed to later."

As Jeff finished talking, the Gower girls arrived. They were younger than Michael, but, like their brothers, they were dark-skinned and beautiful to behold. They were also hybrids, which, because human genetics were strongest for external and A-C genet-ics strongest for internal, was why they resembled their mother, Erika, who was a beautiful dark-skinned African-American human, much more than their father, Stanley, who was also part of the Alpha Four Royal Family, though a few inheritance places farther away than the Martinis were. The Gower girls were also incredibly talented.

Abigail was the youngest, and she was like a reverse empath—she picked up thoughts but they filtered to her like emotions, so if someone was thinking angry thoughts, Abigail felt angry. There were also gases common to Earth that could cause mass hallucinations for the majority of humans that the A-C field teams were able to manipulate. The Field teams needed implants in their brains to do the manipulations. Abigail didn't.

Naomi's talents were more like her eldest brother's, dream and memory reading, but greatly expanded. Naomi could also alter dreams and memories. The girls tended to work together as a team, and they were the C.I.A.'s main test subjects for what hybrids could do now and might do in the future, so they spent a lot of time with Chuckie.

That the Gower girls hadn't conspired to take over the world, or destroy it, had much to do with ACE. ACE was a collective super-consciousness I'd managed to move into Paul Gower during Operation Drug Addict. But even before that incident, ACE had helped the Gower girls to control their powers when they were young, and now he was doing it with all the new babies, Jamie in particular.

The Gower girls took one look at Chuckie and sighed. "You were right to call us over," Naomi said as she went and sat next to Chuckie. "You need to relax, mister," she said with a grin.

He managed a smile. "Right. Let me tell you about our day so far, and then you can tell me to take it easy."

Abigail chuckled. "Let's get him calmed down, Sis. Our boy's all riled up." Of course, it took A-Cs with special talents or people who'd known Chuckie a long, long time to tell that he was upset, but for everyone in this room, it was obvious. Abigail smiled at Jeff and me. "We'll say 'great to see you' when you two get back."

Jeff and I knew when to take a hint, so we headed to our apartments, which took up half of the seventh floor and were larger than the house I'd grown up in. But I was getting used to living in them and had missed the privacy while in Florida.

Before we were through the door, I was greeted by a tide of canines. My parents had moved to D.C. right before Operation Assassination had rolled, and they were in a no-pets building. This meant that we now claimed ownership of four dogs and three cats. The pets seemed to be okay with their permanent vacation.

The dogs having proved they'd missed me and Jamie and loved us best, I trooped into our bedroom to the welcoming sounds of loud, demanding mewing mixed with equally loud purring. The cats were lounging on the deluxe cat trees I called Poof Condos, surrounded by a whole pride of Poofs. I gave up on the idea that Jeff and I could get some quality naked time in the next few minutes and focused on the fur balls.

The Poofs had been our parting gifts from the Alpha Centaurion Royal Family during our wedding, aka Operation Invasion. They were small bundles of fluffy fur, with cat ears, bright, button eyes, and tiny paws. Poofs were basically the cutest things in existence. They also had the ability to go Jeff-sized and very toothy, so they were great personal protection providers.

They were also androgynous and could mate with any other Poof. They mated when Royal Weddings were afoot. We had a lot more Poofs than our wedding or Christopher and Amy's would have warranted, but I didn't mind. Poofs for everyone and more Poofs for me was one of the mottos I lived by.

In the Poof's world, if you named it, you owned it. We had the unnamed Poofs living with us, so while I was gone, Jeff had gotten to enjoy all the Poofy wonder by himself. I was envious—I'd missed all the pets, the Poofs in particular.

For whatever reason, the Poofs hadn't come down to Florida with us. They had a lot of powers no one understood, among them the ability to go wherever and whenever they wanted. But none had wanted to visit Florida, not even the Poof that was obviously Jamie's. I'd tried to bring them along, but they'd done a runner and come back to D.C. before we'd been at Martini Manor an hour.

However, Jamie's Poof was in her arms now, snuggling and purring up a storm, while she giggled and cooed. Two Poofs alighted on my shoulders. "Harlie, Poofikins! Kitty's missed you so much!"

I got a lot of Poof purrs and rubs. The cats deigned to take an active interest beyond yowling at me for my desertion and jumped onto the bed, mewing and purring.

"I was hoping to be the first one you cuddled with in bed," Jeff said, "but clearly the animals missed you two as much as I did.

"Sorry."

"It's okay. I'll bide my time. So cuddle with the cats, baby. I know you want to, and so does Jamie."

Thusly encouraged, Jamie and I got on the bed and were soon buried under cats and Poofs. It was a lovely thing to come back to.

In the midst of our little love fest, Jeff wandered out. I heard a strange voice. "I love Jeff!"

CHAPTER 14

I SAT UP. "WHO'S THERE?"

Jeff walked in, a large parrot on his shoulder. The parrot was gray. It was also kissing him. Literally.

"Meet Bellie," Jeff said. "Jeff loves Bellie, and Bellie loves Jeff, doesn't she?" he cooed at the bird, who did the parrot version of a coo right back before she leaned her beak back for another kiss.

I watched my husband snuggle this bird for a good few seconds before I could manage to come up with a question that wasn't going to start a fight. "Um, is that . . . ours?"

"Yeah." Jeff beamed as he brought the bird over to the bed. "You'd just left and we got a shipment. It was addressed to you, but since it had no return address, we figured we'd better open it at Home Base, just in case."

"So you went to Area 51, and this popped out of the box?"

"Yeah." He fished something out of his pocket. "This came with her."

He handed me a note.

Miss Katt,
Have taken your advice. All traces removed. However, the bird is innocent and will likely be destroyed. Sending her to you, therefore, since you appear to be an animal lover. With my best regards for your continued good health,
Your Uncle

I stared at it, then stared at Jeff and the bird again. "So, my 'uncle,' the notorious assassin, Peter the Dingo Dog, removed all traces of his being hired by Titan Security, that I understand. But, in an act of animal kindness, the scariest hit man in the business sent Antony Marling's African Gray Parrot to us? And you're okay with that?"

Jeff was clearly okay with it. To the point where I was worried he was going to kiss the bird with tongue.

He nodded. "Your mother and Reynolds didn't object. They examined the note and got everything they could from it. Bellie's been checked, and she's healthy, and there are no hidden things on her anywhere."

"Oh, good. So, why did you keep her?"

Jeff looked aghast. "She was going to be sent to Animal Control if we didn't keep her!"

"There are plenty of exotic bird rescue groups out there."

"I couldn't send Bellie to one of those. She's a very sensitive creature. And she's very affectionate." He had the same expression that I was used to seeing toward Jamie—possessive and protective.

He and the bird had another little nuzzle-fest while I controlled my nausea and my annoyance. It was time to be diplomatic again.

"I can see that." Fine. We had a bird. And not just any bird. We had our last Major Megalomaniac's Beloved Birdie. And my husband had attached to her just as her former owner had. No problem.

I shoved a smile onto my face. "Okay, no worries." I put my hand out. "Can I pet Bellie's pretty feathers?"

The bird looked at me, and I recognized the expression. It said clearly that Jeff was *hers*, and I wasn't included in their Special Love.

Because I had fast reflexes, I was able to pull my hand back right before her beak closed on my fingers. Instead, she bit air, and she bit it viciously. I didn't need to consult an ornithologist—this bird didn't like me.

"Wow, guess I'm not allowed to pet the bird."

Jeff looked shocked. "You must have frightened her. She's not like that with anyone normally."

I let the many sarcastic comments I wanted to say pass as I thought about it. "Who does she like?"

The bird looked at me again. "Bellie loves Jeff," she shared.

"Yeah, Bellie, I got that one. Jeff, who else does Bellie love or at least like?"

"Well," he said, while petting the bird, "she likes Christopher, Pierre, Tito, even Reynolds, Irving, Kevin, pretty much everyone."

"Uh-huh. Does she like Doreen?" Doreen and Irving Weisman were part of our Diplomatic Mission. Doreen's parents had been the head Diplomats for American Centaurion before I'd had the Poofs eat them. Fortunately, Doreen was both nothing like her parents and not holding any kind of grudge for their deaths.

"Doreen hasn't really tried to do much with her. She has a new baby, after all."

True enough. She'd given birth right at the end of Operation Assassination, a couple days after Lorraine and Claudia had. "What about Nurse Carter?" She was our Staff Nurse because after going through all we had with her during said Operation, it seemed logical for her to stick around.

"Magdalena says she doesn't like birds much."

"Uh-huh. Did she say that before or after Bellie tried to take her hand off?"

Jeff had the grace to look a little guilty. "After."

"Right. So this bird loves men, and she clearly adores you, but she doesn't like women, and she hates me already, because I'm your wife."

"I'm sure it's just because she doesn't know you yet."

"Right. Well, if she so much as puts a beak or claw in Jamie's general direction, she's dinner. Otherwise, don't let me intrude upon your love that knows no bounds." I had an awful thought. "Where is this bird sleeping?"

"Bellie sleeps with me."

"Not any more she doesn't." Wow. I'd been gone a month, and if someone had asked who I'd guess my husband might have a torrid love affair with in my absence, a lunatic's African Gray Parrot wouldn't have even made my top thousand guesses. "And she sleeps in a cage, because I don't want to be murdered in my sleep."

"If you insist."

"I emphatically insist." I looked around the room. The dog beds weren't against the wall. "Where have the dogs been sleeping?"

Jeff mumbled something.

"What? Didn't catch that."

"They don't like Bellie. So I put them in the nursery. Along with the Poofs and cats. I move the Poof Condos out during the day," he added quickly, as if that were going to make it alright.

I was honestly speechless. No advice, no comic, no movie, no TV show, had prepared me for this kind of rival for my husband's affections.

Fortunately, the many things I wanted to say were forestalled by a voice on the intercom. "Chiefs, it's Walter. You're needed."

CHAPTER 15

"NEEDED WHERE, WALT?"

"Naomi asked me to let you know that you're fine to rejoin them any time you want, Chief Katt-Martini."

"Great, be there in a bit," Jeff said.

"Ah, I think they'd like you there sooner than later, Chief."

Animal greetings or no, I'd still hoped to at least fit in a quickie while the girls calmed Chuckie down. Of course, Jamie was wide awake, and the people waiting for us seemed impatient. On the other hand, it'd been a month and I'd been horny for Jeff from the first hour we were apart.

"Does Bellie want to go for a visit?" Jeff asked. The bird, not me. In a voice normally reserved for our daughter, only.

I looked at the bird. Bellie looked right back at me. Before this experience in surreal horror, I'd have said the only animals capable of looking smug were felines. I reversed that judgment. The bird looked smugger than I'd have thought possible.

"Bellie missed Jeff," the bird shared as she rubbed her head up against his cheek.

"And Jeff missed Bellie," he shared right back.

Well, that did it for me. There was no way I was going to be in an amorous mood while that bird was around. "Great, Walt. We'll be right there."

"I'll let Naomi know, Chief Katt-Martini."

"The bird stays here," I said after the com went off.

"Why?" Jeff seemed completely unaware of my emotional state.

"Because Jamie's coming with us, and I don't want that bird around Jamie."

"Her name is Bellie."

"Her name is going to be Carcass if you don't put her away in a really sturdy cage."

Jeff looked hurt and disappointed, but didn't argue. While I settled the Poofs, dogs, and cats down, and moved the dog beds back into our room, Jeff took care of Bellie. Apparently she didn't go into her cage without a romantic interlude with my husband and several bird treats. It was official—I hated the bird.

Bird hatred gave me energy—I wasn't nearly as tired as I had been, so that was one for the win column. I slung my purse back over my shoulder and looked inside. Happily, Harlie, Poofikins, and several other unnamed Poofs were snuggled up inside, snoozing.

Jamie needed neither feeding nor changing, the benefits of her having been with Lucinda while I was out being She-Hulk. I slung the diaper bag over my other shoulder, Jamie clutched her purring Poof, I picked her up and the two of us, at least, were ready to go. Jeff was still saying good-bye to Bellie. I wondered if I could ask Chuckie to have some shadowy C.I.A. killer off the bird for me, but figured he was too upset to broach the subject at this precise time.

No problem. There was always tomorrow.

I stalked out of the bedroom to find Jeff waiting for us. He took Jamie from me and cuddled her. "I'm sorry you're jealous of Bellie."

"Wives tend to be jealous of mistresses."

He sighed. "I don't love her more than you, or Jamie."

"But you do love her as much." And she was not only some bird who was stealing my husband's affections, but she'd been the bird of a man who'd tried to kill me in many different and nasty ways not very long ago.

I tried to continue my stalk to the front door, but Jeff grabbed me and pulled me to him. "That's not true. But I do feel about her like you do about the Poofs and the other pets. I know she belonged to one of our enemies. But she's an innocent animal."

"Animal maybe." I wasn't buying innocent. That bird had been around the block more than once.

"We can debate it later. But I didn't mean to hurt your feelings, baby. You and Jamie were just having your love time with the cats and the Poofs, and I wanted . . . I wanted you two to meet Bellie, so she could be a part of that, too."

"Which might have worked better if Bellie wasn't clearly a one-man bird, emphasis on 'man.' "

"I'm sure she'll adapt to you and Jamie being home."

"I'm not." I still wanted to be angry, and really, I was, but it felt nice having Jeff's arm around me, while he held both of us. "But I'll try to give the bird a chance."

"Great!"

"I'm making no promises, Jeff. I'm not much of a girl for birds."

"Maybe Bellie can change your mind about that."

If that was her goal, Bellie was a total failure in creating a bird lover out of me. But I chose not to say that. Instead I contemplated my options. "Can Chuckie and the girls wait for us for a few more minutes?"

Jeff got a faraway look. "Yeah. They're waiting but not impatient."

"Okay. I'm sure Jamie would like more undivided Daddy time before we go pay more attention to things other than her." She was clinging to Jeff, so this wasn't so much my being a great, intuitive mother as me stating the obvious. In part to show willing and in more part to give Jeff and Jamie some private time, I pulled away. "I'll go see if Bellie and I get along better without you in the room."

Jeff looked pleased. "Her cage is in the living room."

Wonderful. I went to have a look-see. Cage was the wrong word. Her bird habitat was in my living room. In fact, there was far more bird habitat than living room now. Bellie had a better setup than if she'd been housed in the Washington Zoo. Better than any zoo I'd seen.

I walked over to the nearest part of her enclosure. She flew up to me and latched onto a nearby swing. She stared at me, I stared at her.

"He's mine, you know," I said finally.

"Jeff loves Bellie."

"Too true. But he loves Kitty and Jamie more. And you'd better get that through your bird brain, before I brain you."

She seemed unperturbed. Shocker. "Bellie loves Jeff."

"Yes, I know." I decided to try another tack, since intimidation was clearly not working. "What else does Bellie love?"

The bird seemed to contemplate this question. "Bellie loves treats."

"No argument. Does Bellie love anything else?"

"Bellie wants treats."

"You just got some. What does Bellie want besides treats?"

"Bellie misses Daddy."

I assumed this was Antony Marling. "Daddy is not coming back."

"Bellie knows the secret."

"What secret?"

"Daddy's secret."

Interesting. "Will Bellie tell Kitty what Daddy's secret is?"

The bird gave me a look that clearly said "talk to the tailfeathers." This bird had derisive down to an art form. "No. Bellie loves Jeff."

"Will Bellie tell Jeff Daddy's secret?"

"No."

"But if Bellie really loves Jeff, Bellie should tell Jeff what Bellie knows."

The bird actually seemed to be considering this. I was wondering how it was that I was doing an avian interrogation. But that's what was going on. African Grays were the smartest birds out there, and they had the best language skills. And Marling had adored this bird as much as my husband did now. Clearly, she was the Marilyn Monroe of the parrot world.

So it was conceivable that Marling had kept the bird with him when he was working, while attending meetings of the Association of Crazed Evil Geniuses, and perhaps more. I didn't doubt that Bellie knew something. But whether it was information we already knew—his "children" had actually been amazingly good androids—or information we didn't was the question of the moment.

Jeff joined us. "See? You two are getting along great."

"Yeah, right. Um, Jeff, is it time to join Chuckie and the Gower girls?"

"Yeah, that's why I came to get you. They're starting to wonder where we are."

"Great. You give me Jamie. I want you to bring Bellie with us."

"Really? She'll enjoy that."

I shook my head. "I don't care if she loves it or hates the experience down to her giant talons. Bellie has intel, and I think you and maybe Chuckie are going to be the only ones who can get it out of her."

CHAPTER 16

BELLIE WAS REMOVED FROM her luxury accommodations. She happily perched on Jeff's shoulder and seemed quite content to stay there. I got the impression she'd been riding around the Embassy like this a lot while I was gone.

"How is it that if a Poof is on your shoulder you feel unmanly, but you're all over this bird sitting there?"

"Bellie's different."

"Whatever you say, Cap'n Jeff."

"Huh?"

I decided not to elaborate. We headed for the elevators. The doors opened, but the elevator wasn't empty—Buchanan was in it.

He smiled at me and Jamie. "Hey there, Missus Chief and Baby Chief." Then he took a look at Jeff and gaped. "And Captain Chief."

"What's with all the captain stuff?" Jeff asked as we got into the elevator and he stood between me and Buchanan. "And call her Missus Martini."

"Malcolm can call me whatever he wants." He'd started calling me Mrs. Chief the moment we hit Florida. I liked it, in part because it always made me want to giggle. "And, seriously, Jeff, you have a parrot on your shoulder. All you need is an eye patch or a fake peg leg and you're all set for Halloween, which is far away, or Purim, which you're more than a little late for."

"It's a great look, really," Buchanan added. He and I looked at each other and burst out laughing.

Jeff glowered. "It's not funny."

"Actually, it's hilarious. But whatever. Malcolm, were you coming to see us?"

"Yeah. I wanted to talk to you about the incident at NASA Base."

"Great, come on down. We're meeting up with Chuckie to discuss that and other fun facts."

Jeff wasn't happy about this, but I no longer cared. He was carting Bellie around; I'd take Buchanan along. At least my plus one was human.

Buchanan looked closely at the bird. "Isn't that Antony Marling's parrot?"

We got out of the elevator. "Yeah, it is. How'd you know?"

"I researched everything related to you. I thought the bird would have gone to an animal rescue of some kind."

I brought Buchanan up on the specialness that was the "gift" of Bellie to me by Peter the Dingo as we joined Chuckie and the Gower girls.

Bellie cawed happily when she saw Chuckie. "Reynolds! Reynolds! Reynolds!"

"I see she likes you."

Chuckie shrugged. "The bird's seen all of us a lot." He winked at me. "Captain Martini likes to have her around."

"Seriously, stop it with all the captain stuff," Jeff snapped. "It's not funny."

"It's pretty funny," Naomi said as she and Abigail both giggled.

"Captains of industry," Bellie said. "Captains of science."

"What other captains are there, Bellie?" I asked.

She looked at me. "Captains of military."

"Any other captains, Bellie?" The bird seemed to be considering. "Mimi, Abby, can either one of you see what the bird's thinking?"

"No," Naomi said. "We don't do animal minds."

"They don't think like humans," Abby added. "They don't have emotions like humans, either."

Pity. It was never nice to find limitations to our side's powers. "Well, it was worth a shot. Jeff, you ask her."

"Ask her what?"

"Ask Bellie about captains. And secrets."

Jeff gave me the "you so crazy" look. "Why?"

"Just do it." I managed not to snap. I didn't want Bellie upset with me.

He sighed. "What other captains does Bellie know about?" he asked the bird in a goo-goo voice. Naomi and Abigail both put their hands over their mouths. I was certain they were trying not to laugh out loud.

"Captains in place."

Chuckie sat up straight. "Captains in place where, Bellie?"

Bellie looked at him. "Paraguay and Paris! Paraguay and Paris!"

We all looked at each other. "Jeff, ask her about Daddy's secrets. Keep on talking to her in that lovey-dovey way you seem to have acquired while I was out of town."

He gave me a dirty look but did as requested. "Can Bellie tell Jeff about Daddy's secrets?"

The bird did a jerking thing with her head. I couldn't tell if she was trying to nod yes, no, or just had a twitch. "Secrets for keeping. Bellie misses Daddy. Jeff misses Kitty. Jeff has Bellie. Bellie has Jeff."

Interesting. Presumably Jeff had shared his loneliness with the bird and vice versa. I made a mental note to ensure this bird was never around when we were having sex. I didn't need her imitating my yowling.

"Yes, Bellie has Jeff," he confirmed, as if there were any doubt. "Bellie, tell Jeff Daddy's secrets."

Bellie did the head shake thing again. "Bellie knows Daddy's secrets."

"Jeff needs to know Daddy's secrets." The bird didn't answer. He looked at me. "Any ideas?"

Jamie gurgled, and I kissed her head. Which led to inspiration. Always nice when that happened. "Bellie, Jeff is your Daddy now. So he should know Daddy's secrets."

Jeff nodded and looked back at the bird. "Jeff is Bellie's Daddy now. Tell Jeff Daddy's secrets, Bellie."

The bird seemed to be considering her options. "Jeff is Daddy?" she asked. She sounded uncertain, not that I was any real judge of bird tonal inflections.

"Yes," he said firmly. "Jeff is Bellie's Daddy now."

She did that head thing again. "Daddy's secrets are ready to go. Captains in Paris and Paraguay. Bellie wants a treat."

Jeff reached into his pocket and gave her a treat. I managed not to be either horrified or shocked. Of course he was now carrying around bird treats in his suit. Naturally. I wondered how many meetings outside of the Embassy he'd gone to with the bird along. Had a horrible feeling I'd find out at the most embarrassing times possible.

"Now tell Jeff Daddy's secrets, Bellie." Jeff stroked her head. "Be a good Bellie."

"Good man. Good man. Captain is good man." I doubted that, because it was unlikely anyone Marling had in place was good. "Can do. Can do. Captain can do." This one I could buy—whoever was in place was likely able to do whatever evil actions he was assigned.

Bellie preened. "Bellie wants a treat!"

Jeff sighed and gave her another. "I don't think she's got any more, baby."

"Or else she's not ready or willing to tell us."

"It's a bird," Buchanan pointed out. "How much do you really think it can tell us in the first place?"

The bird looked right at him. "Time to tell the dog to kill the cat."

CHAPTER 17

I COULDN'T SPEAK FOR ANYONE ELSE, but my mind was going at top speed. "You know, I think my 'uncle' sent this to me for more reasons than him having a soft spot for abandoned animals."

Chuckie nodded. "That sounds like the order Marling would have given to have you assassinated."

"Only it was Madeline Cartwright who'd set up the assassins. She told me so." And I didn't doubt it, either, not based on all I'd seen and gone through.

"Doesn't change things," Chuckie said. "The bird must have heard the order given."

"Wouldn't you think she'd need to hear it more than once?" Buchanan asked. "To be able to repeat it, I mean."

"Maybe." What I knew about parrot learning skills could fit into one of Bellie's treat pellets and have room to spare. "I guess we'll find out."

"True." Buchanan looked at Chuckie. "Let's deal with something more pertinent. How did they know to set up the attack at NASA Base?"

"I've been asking myself that since it happened," Chuckie said. "I honestly have no idea."

"We're so screwed." This remark earned me a glare from Jeff, a sorta-smile from Chuckie, and a laugh from Buchanan. "I also had a Very Special Test asking me some really interesting questions." I filled everyone in on the weirdness that was in my special packet.

Buchanan shook his head when I was done. "My test was perfectly normal. I'd assume everyone else's was, too. Why didn't you say something?"

"At first I figured I was just being singled out because of everything that always happens around me. By the time I read ahead, I was too busy going 'what the hell' and being attacked by an android to do much else."

"Why give her that kind of test?" Jeff asked. "Even if it was legitimate, the results would be thrown out because the test was so clearly biased."

"I'm more interested in how the attack was put in place so quickly," Buchanan said. He was looking at Chuckie again and he didn't look all that friendly.

"I sweep for bugs regularly, so my phone wasn't tapped. Martini's and White's weren't either."

"How do you know that?" Jeff asked.

"I have a mobile sweeper I carry with me."

A thought occurred and I decided to share it before the men could start arguing or fighting. "Our phones aren't bugged. But we have enemies all over. I'll bet NASA Base's phones are tapped, big time. Langley's, too."

"All these areas are routinely checked," Chuckie said patiently.

"Yes, but let me remind everyone that the last time we went to NASA Base half of the Security team was part of Club Fifty-One and working for Howard Taft and Leventhal Reid and pointedly out to kill us all. Just because they're long dead doesn't mean someone else hasn't picked up those pieces and started rebuilding."

"Why would they be tapped for this?" Buchanan asked. "It seems almost . . . random."

"It wasn't." I thought best running my mouth, so I kept on talking. "Look, it's no secret I was down in Florida for a month. Whoever's behind it—and we can be sure they were best buds with Antony Marling and probably Madeline Cartwright—they're a long-term thinker, right? Because most of our enemies are."

"Right." Jeff looked thoughtful. "You think they were just waiting to see where you'd go to take this test?"

"Potentially, yeah. I mean, why the hysterical rush to get this test taken care of?"

"It's protocol," Chuckie said. "It's not a hysterical rush. We're late in doing in."

"Even better. It's something you have to have us do, so no one questions, right? And you're late, so you're in a hurry to get this taken care of so that less people in the C.I.A. lean on you, right?"

"Go on." I could see Chuckie's conspiracy wheels starting to turn again. Good. He was far too upset about everything. We needed him calm and thinking.

Which meant more yapping from me. Never an issue. "So, they were monitoring for wherever you'd ask to have the last of your A-C flock tested. Maybe the phones aren't bugged. Maybe it's just a couple folks at each location where we could take the test who get an extra fifty bucks or something if they share that we're finally taking this test. They might not even know they were doing wrong. Someone high up saying 'let me know when this finally gets taken care of' wouldn't raise alarms, and a grunt worker would be sure to advise the bigwig, because, well, that's part of their job."

Chuckie nodded slowly. "I can buy all of that. The tests are required to be taken in the type of rooms we were in—extremely secured and impregnable. It's a perfect place for an ambush."

"I buy all that," Buchanan said. "But why give Kitty a special test? If I'd been handed something like that, I'd have brought it up immediately."

"Whoever's in charge knows Kitty," Jeff said without missing a beat. "She's not thrown by weird."

"And she's inquisitive," Naomi added. "She'll hunt leads down to see where they go."

"Willing to take risks and a little foolhardy," Abigail added.

"Geez, guys, I'm in the room. But, yeah, I can buy that whoever set Sandra's lasers well beyond stun must have had some idea that I wouldn't question."

"Wouldn't have mattered if the instructor hadn't hunted you down," Buchanan added.

White put his head in the room. "Ah, Mister Reynolds, glad you're still here. I had a question for you. What happened to our instructor, John? Was he injured?"

Chuckie opened his mouth, but Walter's voice came out. "Excuse me Chiefs, but there's a video upload for Mister Reynolds that's just come over from NASA Base."

"Send it to my office," Jeff said. "We'll watch it there."

Walter signed off, and we all went to the first floor. As we passed the kitchen, I trotted in. Hey, I'd gotten used to snacking a lot while with my in-laws.

Pierre was there and he beamed. "So good to have you and our little princess back, Kitty darling." Jamie giggled and held out her arms to Pierre, who scooped her out of mine. "I see my Jamie missed her Uncle Pierre," he cooed at her. "I also see you're all bustling off about more exciting diplomatic business. Shall I just hold onto our little one and leave Mommy's arms free?"

There was no way Jeff was going to have time to give Jamie attention right now, and I wasn't going to let him hold her while Bellie was on his shoulder anyway. "Sure, Pierre, that'd be great. Ah, is there anything to eat?"

He grinned. "Yes indeed. Your lovely mother-in-law called and told me to ensure all of you kept on eating well once you were back here. I believe she's worried about your Jeff's eating habits, too."

I snorted. "Jeff's a healthy eater. I'm not. So, um, any brownies around?"

"Indeed there are." He went to the pantry. "A plate of Lucinda Martini's brownies, if you please." Opened the pantry door, there they were. The Elves had come through once again. Pierre handed them to me. "I must say I love working and living here."

I grabbed a brownie. Considered, and took the plate. "Me too. I'm going to bring these in for the others." I was willing to take one for the team, especially since that meant I could snag another brownie while being kind and generous.

Gave Pierre a one-armed hug, gave Jamie a big kiss, and headed off down the hall to Jeff's office.

Fortunately his office, like everything else in the Embassy, was spacious, because we had more people in here than I'd left in the hall.

Our in-person additions were Christopher and Amy, both of whom looked slightly mussed and only somewhat happy to be here, along with Kevin Lewis, who was my mom's right hand man in the P.T.C.U. and assigned to a permanent berth at the Embassy, Tito, Melanie, and Emily. There was a video conference going, and I could see Alpha and Airborne on screen.

Everyone in the room and on the screen looked at me as I came in. "About time," Christopher snapped.

"Sorry. I'm not the one who dragged you out of bed for the latest War Room discussion. Brownie? They're Lucinda's."

Christopher, Amy, White, and Buchanan all grabbed a brownie before anyone else. Yeah, we'd gotten used to the good eating, even Buchanan. Sure he'd housed in the servants' luxury pad, but Lucinda had insisted he eat dinner with us every night and had ensured he had plenty of snackage during the day.

I took the plate around to everyone, in part to be polite and in part so that the brownies stayed near to me. Jeff sighed as he took one. "Where's Jamie?"

"I traded her for a plate of brownies and some magic beans. She's with Pierre, getting cuddles and tons of one-on-one attention." I managed to stop myself from mentioning that the person I'd expected to be doing that was Jeff. We were occupied. And, of course, he had his bird.

Who, it turned out, had her own Special Perch in his office. I wondered if there was some sort of Parrots Anonymous group I could drag Jeff to. Soon.

"So, now that you're all snacking, can we get back to business?" Reader sounded annoyed. Probably bummed there were no brownies wherever Alpha Team was.

"How did the cleanup go?" I asked.

"And I'd very much like to know how our instructor, John, fared," White added.

"Thankfully we were able to call in field teams as well as the Operations team, and because they evacuated the humans, they were able to use hyperspeed," Reader said. "Everything but the gate hub is fixed and like new. The hub's a little trickier, but it should be completed by tomorrow if not sooner."

"And the instructor's fine," Gower added. "Shaken, but in a safe location, being debriefed."

"Was he in on the attack?"

"No," Tim said. "NASA had surveillance tapes running. Watch."

There were several screens running. Actually, there were a lot of screens, with a lot of images running, but our particular focus was only on a set of them. With this and Serene in the room I realized Alpha and Airborne were at Imageering Control, or what I called the Bat Cave Level of the Dulce Science Center. I felt a pang. I still missed living there. The Embassy was great, but it wasn't the Lair.

I pulled my focus back to the screens. One showed us arriving in our limo, with Buchanan right behind us. The other cars arriving raised no suspicions.

The employees parking lot showed John arriving in an older Toyota Corolla. He drove and parked carefully, but rushed out of his car and to the employees' entrance. I checked the timestamp—he'd arrived about when we had, which would make sense if he was called in to manage the test.

There were plenty of other feeds, including some that showed walls, floors and ceilings exploding. Each explosion left a rather human-sized hole. I was kind of impressed. You couldn't see that the cause of the explosions was me and Sandra slamming through.

"It's like watching a Bugs Bunny cartoon," Tim said, as the feeds started over again. "Nice job, Kitty."

"Yeah, well, you try fighting off an android without weapons of any kind and then complain to me about some building damage. Speaking of which, what's the status on my least favorite robot?"

"You tossing her in with the 'gators shorted out her self-destruct mechanism," Reader said. "So, damages aside, this could really be an actual win for our side. She's being examined now. Lorraine and Claudia are overseeing it. They'll let us know what they find."

"I want to see the results as soon as possible," Chuckie said.

"Oh, yes, sir," Reader snapped. Clearly there was something about being the Head of the Field—it meant you weren't nice at all to the guy who you reported to in the C.I.A.

"You know what I don't see in all the video feeds running on constant replay?" I said before any more alpha male sniping could continue. "I don't see the people who attacked Jeff, Christopher, and Chuckie arriving. Nor do I see Sandra arriving."

"Maybe they were already there, lying dormant," Serene suggested.

"That would be a remarkably poor use of resources," Chuckie said. "The android, fine I suppose you could leave her in some kind of stasis until activated. But the people who attacked the three of us were humans."

"You're sure?" I asked.

Christopher nodded. "They were a lot easier to beat than the androids we've faced. They could have been a problem if they'd surprised us, but they didn't. Jeff and I handled them pretty easily."

I thought about this. "They weren't prepared for an A-C to be there. Maybe Richard, but he was in the examination room with everyone else." And every bad guy who knew that the former Pontifex now kicked butt was dead. "I wonder . . . Chuckie, did you mention that Jeff and Christopher would be along?"

"No. It wasn't relevant to the test."

"You think they were only after Reynolds, girlfriend?"

"Yeah, James, I do. I think they wanted to get rid of me and Chuckie."

"What about the rest of us?" Amy asked. "We were all in the room, and that horrid android shot at us."

"No," Buchanan said slowly. "She really only shot at me and Mister White because we were trying to help Kitty. She ignored the rest of you. I think she would have killed you if you'd gotten in the way, but you weren't her target."

Jeff looked thoughtful. "The only reason we moved from the waiting area was because you were antsy," he said to Chuckie. "If we hadn't had the incident with the senator earlier in the day, would you have been as jumpy?"

"Probably not," Chuckie admitted. "And that means I'd have been right where they expected me."

"So Senator Armstrong, Monsieur Love, and dear Vance weren't actually involved with or connected to the NASA attack."

CHAPTER 18

EVERYONE IN THE ROOM AND ON-SCREEN looked at me. "Mind explaining that, Kitty?" Tim finally asked. "What does Senator Armstrong have to do with any of this?"

I looked at Jeff. "Don't they know?"

He looked uncomfortable. "Not really." Chuckie and Christopher looked equally embarrassed. So they'd kept this Embassy-Only. This news wasn't going to make Alpha Team happy.

"Jeff, what's going on?" Reader asked. Interesting. He had a Commander Voice now. And it was on full.

All the men in the room with me seemed remarkably embarrassed. Chuckie I could understand, in that sense. Maybe Jeff, too. But not the others.

"Oh, for God's sake. How old are all of you, twelve?" Amy turned to the screen. "Someone doctored up dirty pictures of Kitty and Chuck doing the deed. That reporter who's always hanging around warned Chuck they were out there. Senator Armstrong showed up with that weirdo, Guy Gadoire, and his husband, to share the pictures with us today. The senator said he wasn't trying to blackmail Kitty and that the pictures had been sent to him anonymously. Not sure any of us buy that, but what Kitty's saying is that if the senator was involved, then whoever set that android on us would have sent a hit squad capable of taking out Christopher and Jeff, too, not just Chuck."

"Succinctly put, Ames." She was really coming along. I felt all proud.

Alpha Team seemed shocked into silence. Airborne, however, were also in attendance, and my flyboys never missed a beat. "So, can we see the pictures?" Jerry asked, miraculously with a straight face. "Purely in the interests of law and science."

"Yeah," Matt Hughes agreed. "We should know what the fake pictures look like, so we're able to denounce them."

"And so we can be sure we're looking for the right negatives," Chip Walker added.

"We're married men," Randy Muir said, as Joe Billings nodded his head. "So we can look at the pictures safely, since there's no way we'd be looking for any reason other than investigative interest."

"How many shots were there?" Joe asked. "I mean, enough for a full calendar, or just a poster-type one with a single photo?"

"Oh, I'll bet there were plenty," Jerry said. "I mean, you can't blackmail someone with just one shot."

"True enough," Hughes agreed. "There are probably extra sets hidden in various hideouts, too."

"I say we get right on it," Walker said. "We don't want dirty pictures of Kitty in anyone's hands but ours."

"Awww, you guys just warm my heart. And while I think it's great of you to offer to sacrifice yourselves for the cause, I actually had another unit in mind for this job."

Once again, all heads swiveled toward me. "Just who were you planning on bringing in on this?" Jeff asked. He sounded lost, frustrated, and a little freaked out. Why? He'd known about this weeks longer than I had. Surely he'd had time to adjust to the idea that this "news" was going to get out one day.

"Really? Well, first off, the person who let Chuckie know what was going on in the first place. And, to assist him, I'm going to do what any normal person in this situation would do."

"Pay the blackmail?" Naomi asked.

"Make a sex tape with Jeff to show your range?" Abigail suggested.

"Go on Leno to confess and say you're really, really sorry?" was Amy's contribution.

"Request your own reality show?" Melanie chimed in.

"Go back to your roots to 'find yourself' and reconnect with the simple girl you used to be?" Emily offered as her option.

Clearly the gals were on the same wavelength as the flyboys. The others seemed clueless. Alone on my own wavelength. Always the way.

"No. What normal people do when they're being blackmailed is to go to professionals for help. We have a special K-9 unit that owes us, big time. I'm going to get Mister Joel Oliver and Senator Armstrong together, and we're all going to go to the police."

"I don't want you going to the police," Jeff said in the growly man voice he seemed to still somehow believe I obeyed anywhere other than in bed. "We can handle this ourselves."

"Blackmail tends to fall to the F.B.I.," Kevin said quickly. "Though I'm not recommending that we contact that agency for help. I'm just pointing out that the police rarely focus on those kinds of cases."

"The K-9 guys are a special unit. They may have been somewhat unimpressive in terms of their taxi services, but they were spot on when it came to surveillance. So we set a team of spies to catch a team of spies."

Chuckie sighed. "I can't argue with the idea. In part because you haven't actually taken or passed the HSAC test."

"Seriously? You're actually going to insist we go through all that again?"

"The instructor actually had everyone's tests in his hands," Gower said. "He'd clutched them in panic, and they made it out of the building with him. I asked, as Pontifex, for them to be processed immediately. So, ah, everyone other than you, Kitty, is approved."

I let this one sit on the air for a moment. "So, what you're saying, Paul and Chuckie, is that everyone other than me can discuss whatever the hell is going on that Jeff, Christopher, and Chuckie spent time stressing was a bigger deal than my faked photos. But I can't. Is that right?"

"Right." Gower didn't say this with a lot of enthusiasm I was fairly sure I saw Tim and Reader wincing. Checked the expressions of the men in the room with me. Check, they all looked ready for me to get seriously mad.

"Correct," Chuckie said. He looked at Jeff. "Let her go to the police and handle this with Mister Joel Oliver, who also hasn't taken the HSAC test. It'll keep him out of our hair, keep Kitty occupied, and possibly get that problem fixed before we have to worry about the bigger issue."

"She shouldn't be doing that," Jeff argued. "It's not a good idea for an Ambassador to head to police headquarters to show off naked pictures of herself. And I don't want those getting out."

"Guys, I'm in the room. Still. I clearly have to mention. And, the pictures are already out, Jeff. Since I can't do anything else until I'm all alone in another special room with another android trying to kill me while I take a ridiculous test that makes no sense, let me handle this. Chuckie's right. It'll distract me."

Jeff gave me a look that said he knew I was up to something and, even though he had no idea what it was, he didn't approve. "I don't like it."

"I don't like your new avian mistress, but I'm dealing." I looked to Chuckie. "That plan sit okay with you, Secret Agent Man?"

"Yeah. Take Len and Kyle." He looked at Buchanan. "You'll go back to being her shadow?"

"Yeah. I don't care about the other issue, whatever it is."

I got the distinct impression Buchanan was lying like a wet rug, but I was also fairly sure the others weren't picking this up. Jeff might have been, but if so, he didn't say anything.

"I'll accompany Missus Martini as well," White said. "I'm sure I'll be more helpful there than here."

White was lying, too. Well, it was always nice to have backup.

"So I won't be alone." I went over to Jeff and gave him a quick kiss. Bellie cawed and squawked indignantly. "I love you. Do something about that bird before I get back, because she's dancing on my last nerve. I'm going to take Jamie to Denise, so Pierre's free. I'll check in as needed."

Jeff stood up and hugged me. "Be good, baby, and be careful. Call if you need anything or think you're being followed by anyone other than Buchanan."

I hugged him back and went to the door. I contemplated suggesting that, barring Bellie having taken and passed the HSAC, they refrain from talking about whatever was going on in front of her.

Then I reconsidered. Bellie was a bigmouth. I'd find out what was really up one way or another, even if it meant giving my feathered nemesis bird treats.

CHAPTER 19

WE WERE NEAR THE FRONT DOOR when the doorbell rang. I could have waited for Pierre to race over to get it, but I was right there, so I opened the door.

A tall, blond-haired man who looked to be somewhere in his mid-to-late thirties stood there. He was dressed like every other go-getter in D.C. seemed to be—expensive, tailored navy suit, nice wingtips, official political haircut that was just this side of a Marine high and tight. He also radiated a look I'd gotten used to from spending over half my life around Chuckie—intelligence.

He looked vaguely familiar, but I couldn't place him at all. "Can I help you?"

He nodded. "I'm looking for Charles Reynolds."

"And you're looking for him at the American Centaurion Embassy why?"

He smiled. "I'm sorry. I'm Cliff Goodman, the Head of Special Immigration Services for Homeland Security. Chuck told me he was here."

"Oh! Sorry, come on in, Mister Goodman." Per Chuckie, I'd met him already. I was thankful he didn't bring it up, since he still wasn't looking anything more than vaguely familiar.

"Thanks. And please, call me Cliff. You must be Kitty. Chuck's told me a lot about you." He was going for the polite pretend, I assumed because it was clear I'd had no idea who he was.

"Has he?"

"Yeah. He's very proud of you. I can't blame him. You've really moved fast in your career."

"Thanks again." I had no idea which career or careers Cliff was referring to, and figured Chuckie would appreciate my not sharing in case Cliff wasn't in the know about everything.

Buchanan, who'd been nearby and witnessed all this, went down the hall, presumably to get Chuckie. White extended his hand. "Richard White. Nice to meet you, sir."

Cliff smiled again as he shook White's hand. "It's an honor to meet you, Former Pontifex White." Well he knew enough to know who White was. Whether this was good, bad, or indifferent, I had no guess. "I'd hoped to meet you at the President's Ball, but that did get a little out of hand."

"You win the Understatement of the Year Award." I decided we should stop faking it. "I'm sorry, I know we met at the Ball, but most of it's a blur. I appreciate you pretending I wasn't just incredibly rude."

Cliff laughed. "I know how many people Ambassadors tend to meet in any given month. Considering what had gone on, and what you helped avert, I'm amazed you can remember that the President was there, let alone anyone else. This is a much better introduction, for both of us."

So, Cliff was in a high level of "know." Not a surprise, based on his position. But I'd been trained to not give away everything, even though I might think the person I was talking to knew everything already. Mom and Chuckie both had been big on that mindset, and Dad had supported it, too.

Buchanan returned with Chuckie in tow. "Cliff, thanks for coming." They shook hands without the usual male posturing coming from Cliff that I normally saw around Chuckie, which was refreshing. At least there was one guy in power out there who viewed Chuckie as a person to be valued as opposed to killed or discredited.

Buchanan stayed back and didn't seem eager to be introduced. I was going to do the introductions anyway, but Cliff spoke before I could. "So, Chuck, can I get a debrief on what really happened at NASA Base?"

Chuckie looked a little uncomfortable. I took the logic leap. "Can you do that in front of me?"

Cliff chuckled. "You were a part of it, so yes. I understand there was a problem with your HSAC test, though."

"Yeah." I looked at Chuckie and shot him the "what do I say" look.

He nodded. "You can give Cliff the full details, Kitty. Including all the details about your attacker."

"Oh, what fun. Shall we get out of the hallway to do this? I mean, we're not exactly lacking in available rooms."

"Oh?" Cliff asked. "I'd heard your Embassy was pretty much filled to capacity."

"Not really. We try to avoid having the fire marshals called in."

Cliff laughed. "Good point. I don't want to take up a lot of your time—I was just nearby and figured this was a good way to get the unofficial answers before I'm asked for the official ones."

"True enough," Chuckie said. "Kitchen?"

"Sure, I never say no to the comfortable room." Cliff looked around. "Though I'd bet every room here would be comfortable."

"It is." I didn't add that it was plush and a showcase—Cliff looked smart enough to figure that out on his own. Chuckie led him into the kitchen, with White trailing them. Buchanan stayed in the hall. He looked like he was pondering something. "Coming?"

Buchanan shook his head. "No. But remember, we have things we want to do. Things that aren't necessarily going to make some people happy."

I figured he didn't want me to share with Cliff that we were planning to head out to grab an influential senator and the top paparazzo to see if they could help us solve the mystery of dirty pictures featuring me and Chuckie. I was certain Chuckie wouldn't want me to mention said pictures, either. I nodded. "Gotcha."

Buchanan gave me a half-smile. "Don't be long."

I joined the others in the kitchen. Pierre, with Jamie on his hip, already had everyone settled at the small table for four with a beverage each and a plate of fresh veggies and dip, and Chuckie was giving Cliff the high-level debrief, with White adding in as needed.

Jamie gave her "Mommy's Here!" squeal, and I took her from Pierre, got a Coke, and sat in the open chair, opposite Cliff. A part of me wondered why Jeff, Christopher, or any of the others weren't joining us, but I figured Chuckie had wanted to keep this meeting as small, and as fast, as possible.

Chuckie summed things up, and I had nothing to add—he'd actually given my statement about Sandra the Android and what had happened pretty much verbatim but without my, as Christopher called them, Kittyisms added in.

Cliff sighed. "Another mystery mess. I'd like to find the Evil Geniuses Headquarters and catch them all at their next monthly meeting."

I burst into laughter. "I thought I was the only one who called them that."

Cliff grinned. "Nope. I wouldn't say that to too many people, of course, but Chuck's special, just like the rest of you here."

"Thanks, we try."

"And you succeed. But that reminds me—why has Senator Armstrong been so desperate to have a meeting with you?"

I didn't remember Chuckie mentioning Armstrong at all in his debrief. I controlled myself from looking at Chuckie, or White. I had the feeling this was a test question. My mind worked fast—I had a variety of ways to answer this, but Cliff wasn't my mother, ergo, Cliff wasn't likely able to tell when I was lying, especially if I told the truth that was still, in that sense, a lie.

"Oh, he wants us to use our influence for some of his projects. It's the usual political cr—ah, stuff."

Cliff grinned again. "You can say crap in front of me. It's a nicer word than I'm used to hearing, believe me." He looked at Jamie. "Whoops."

I laughed. "It's okay, and thanks. Anyway, I think the senator feels I'm the weak link, so he's trying to get me on his side so I'll influence my husband."

"And probably Chuck, too. Everyone knows you two are tight."

"I suppose. It's hard to say with politicians."

Cliff nodded. "True enough." He smiled at Jamie. "Beautiful baby."

She gurgled, then turned her face into my chest. "Aww, she's gotten shy. But thank you, we think we'll keep her."

He grinned. "Well, I'll bet there'd be a lot of takers if you wanted to give her up."

"Uncle Pierre is first in line," he said as he scooped Jamie out of my arms. She cooed and snuggled next to him as he did the Uncle Pierre version of the Baby Dance.

I figured we should get the conversation off of Jamie, in part because I knew Jeff and the others were probably waiting for Chuckie to rejoin them. "What did you do before you became the Head of Special Immigration Services? You seem really young for the job, so I figure it was impressive."

"It was," Chuckie said. "He was the second in command of Andrews Air Force Base."

Cliff shrugged. "I joined the Air Force right out of high school, worked hard and worked my way up. It's not that impressive, really."

"Yeah, I hear that line from Chuckie all the time, too, and I've never bought it from him, either. Are you still in the Air Force?"

"Nope. I retired to take the Special Immigration Services position. Neither the President nor the Head of Homeland Security asked me to, by the way, but I didn't want to appear biased toward any one branch of the military, and I didn't want the temptation to go back hanging over me."

"Why would that be a temptation?"

Cliff and Chuckie both snorted. "The pressure of our kinds of jobs make going back to the comfortable familiarity of the military appealing, believe me," Cliff said.

"Dude, you're not just whistling Dixie. So they passed over the head man at Andrews and gave the position to you?" Cliff nodded. "Does that mean said head man is thrilled for you or wants your job?"

"I'm honestly not sure."

"The head man doesn't like you," Chuckie said. "Or me, for that matter."

"I think he doesn't like you because you're friends with me," Cliff replied. "He's angling for a different promotion, anyway. He's career military, so Secretary of Defense is his goal."

"What's his name?"

"Colonel Marvin Hamlin," Cliff said. "He may not like us, but he's still a good man."

Chuckie shook his head. "You say that about everyone."

Cliff shrugged. "I'm the trusting one, you're the suspicious one. We make a good team." He looked at his watch and stood up. "I'd better get going."

"Tell whatever committees that I take full responsibility for what happened at NASA Base," Chuckie said, as he stood, too.

"Why? None of it was *your* fault."

Cliff nodded. "Kitty's right. Don't be too hard on yourself, Chuck. Things happen, and we can't foresee or stop everything. I wish we could, but we can't. You're doing not only the best you can, but you're doing a better job than anyone else in the position has or would."

Chuckie managed a grin. "Always nice to have a cheering section."

"Well, I know you have one in Kitty. And you should know you have one in me." Cliff smiled at me. "Take care of our man here, and don't let him beat himself up."

"Will do."

We all shook hands and walked Cliff to the door. We said our good-byes and he walked off down the block into Sheridan Circle.

"He doesn't have a driver?" White asked, as we saw Cliff hail a taxi and get in.

"No, he's big on public transportation." Chuckie shook his head. "I'd prefer it if he had a driver. He leaves himself too open."

"You know, he mentioned that Colonel Hamlin is a good man. Think that the Colonel could be the good man Bellie was referring to?"

Chuckie shrugged. "Could be. Cliff's last name is Goodman, so it could be him, too, I suppose."

"Only you don't think he's a bad guy."

"No. I don't. Of course, I could be wrong."

"Like when does that happen? Exactly never?"

"Hey, I was wrong about where Hoffa was buried," Chuckie said ruefully, as Buchanan rejoined us.

"That's right. Where is —"

"Ambassador Martini's getting really impatient," Buchanan said. "I think you need to get back in there. They can't do anything without you."

Chuckie nodded. "You're right." He hugged me. "Thanks, and be careful. And don't tell me what you're doing so I don't have to lie to Cliff about it." He sauntered down the hall, again looking relaxed and like the guy I was used to, not Mr. Tension Overload. He'd needed Naomi and Abigail, but Cliff's visit had helped him just as much.

"You look pleased," Buchanan said quietly.

"It's nice to see him have an actual friend here, other than me or the Gower girls, I mean."

Buchanan nodded but didn't say anything.

"You don't agree?" White asked.

Buchanan shrugged. "Like I told Missus Chief not that long ago, you want to be sure the people who appear to be your friends like you for yourself."

"And Cliff sure seems to like Chuckie for who he is."

"His last name is Goodman," Buchanan said flatly.

"And he said his former commanding officer was a good man. We discussed this before you rejoined us. Chuckie trusts this guy, and that's always been and always will be good enough for me.

"Goodman is a common last name," White said. "And there are plenty of good men out there. I don't believe we have enough yet to point a finger at anyone, especially based on the word of a parrot."

Buchanan nodded. "Too true, Mister White. Now, Missus Chief, I think we have another task at hand that you wanted to get moving on. We either get going or we table it for tomorrow, your choice."

"Let's roll."

Buchanan chuckled. "You sound so 'street' when you say that."

CHAPTER 20

WHILE WHITE AND BUCHANAN went to get whatever it was
they'd need for our latest adventure, I retrieved Jamie from
Pierre again and headed to the fourth floor.

Pierre had insisted we put in a school and daycare center within
the first days he was with us. Because they were living at the
Embassy now, too, and she wanted something to do while her husband was fighting the various fuglies we were always up against,
Denise Lewis was the teacher and daycare worker. Right now, we
didn't have a lot of students, just their kids, Raymond and Rachel,
and Jamie. However, we had a number of infants whose mothers
were about to go back to work full time and another set of babies
on the way—Denise wouldn't have it easy for too long.

Denise was a gorgeous blonde with a fabulous figure and perfect
teeth. She wasn't a Dazzler, which was what I called all the female
A-Cs to myself, but she gave them a good run for their money.

She gave me a huge smile. "I didn't want to suggest it, but I was
hoping you'd bring Jamie in for a while. I've missed her."

"She's missed you, too, I'm sure." I gave Jamie a big hug and
kiss, then handed her and her diaper bag, which I'd been carting
around all this time, to Denise. "Not sure when I'll be back. I have
breast milk stored up, but since her teeth have come in, she's started
solids."

Denise laughed. "Pierre talked with your mother-in-law. We're
fully stocked for everything our little girl here needs. Besides,
you'll be back soon."

"Huh?"

"It's almost dinner time."

I gave Jamie another kiss, then rejoined White and Buchanan at the front door. "Shall we go retrieve the boys from Romanian soil? I don't think we can do much else today—Denise pointed out that time has flown."

"That happens when we're fighting off dangerous forces and taking impromptu politically charged meetings, Missus Martini," White pointed out.

"Sure, let's get the kids," Buchanan said. "I want to discuss something with you before I do my fast fade anyway."

We closed the door behind us and went down the steps. "You mean you want to share that whatever's going on that I'm not allowed to know about ultimately has to do with me in some way, or else Jeff wouldn't be worried about my being followed."

Buchanan grinned. "Never let it be said you're not intuitive, Missus Chief."

"Never let it be said I'm not used to this kind of crap happening all the time, either. I'd just like to be on record that protocol which prevents the target from actually knowing what's going on is protocol designed to ensure the target gets killed."

"I'm not going to allow that," Buchanan said calmly.

"I'm sure you're not," White replied. "I'm not either. However, Missus Martini has a point. Are you sure you shouldn't stay and find out what's actually going on?"

"Let's go get your official C.I.A. bodyguards."

White and I looked at each other. "So," I said, "what you're not saying, Malcolm, is that you already know what's going on."

"I might be saying that, yeah. I might, on the other hand, want you to get your official guards around before I disappear."

"Or you want the boys to hear what's going on, too. Great. Let's include Adriana and her grandmother in this vague intel debrief. If, as is so much more likely, Olga doesn't already know more than anyone else about what's going on."

We trotted across the street. Either they'd been expecting us or someone was right by the front door, because it opened before we could even knock.

"Come in, Ambassador," Adriana said from behind the door. "And Mister White. Nice to see you up close, Mister Buchanan."

"Never mind," I said to Buchanan and White as we all crossed the threshold. "I presume Olga knows exactly what's going on."

Adriana laughed as she closed the door. "Grandmother is aware of many things and has been eagerly awaiting your return to town. Don't worry—it's only Grandmother and me here right now."

The last time the entire Romanian diplomatic mission had been gone, they'd been touring their country's visiting president around D.C. I chose not to ask if that was the case again or not. We had other issues.

As we followed Adriana upstairs to the second floor, which was much warmer and inviting than the entry area, I asked myself why Olga never used a telephone. Then reminded myself that it was because, as former KGB, she knew how easily they were tapped.

We found her at the end of the long hallway, in her study that had two floor-length windows, one facing our Embassy, one looking out onto Sheridan Circle. It was a nice room, and the handicapped handles around the windows were done, like everything else here, tastefully.

Olga was in her wheelchair, flanked by the boys, who were busy stuffing their faces with a variety of Romanian treats. Yeah, we'd *all* gotten used to eating well, and a lot, while we were in Florida. I would have mentioned that snacking here would ruin our appetites for dinner later, but I already knew that none of us had shown the least issue with scarfing everything in sight for weeks. Maybe it was good that the game was so very clearly afoot—we were all going to need the exercise.

We officially introduced Buchanan for the sake of politeness, even though she already knew about him. White gave her a little bow and kissed her hand. He always did this better than Gadoire, a classic example of damning with faint praise.

I went over and gave Olga a big hug. "It's so nice to see you."

"And it is always nice to see you. How is your beautiful baby? All through with her traumatic teething experience?"

"I won't even ask how you knew, but yes, all her baby choppers are in, and she seems back to her usual happy self."

"That is good, and not a moment too soon. And I knew because your husband visited me to show off his lovely bird and have some company that did not require him to be the Ambassador, merely a husband and father missing his family."

Nice to know Jeff had missed us. I really wished he'd attached to one of our existing pets, though. We certainly had enough dogs, cats, and Poofs around. But no. He'd gone for the bird. My luck was always consistent.

"Great, so you've met Bellie, the new love of Jeff's life. I'm sure you realized whose bird she was before anyone told you."

"Oh, yes. But the bird is innocent of her former owner's wrongdoing. However, she is quite bright." Olga looked at me expectantly.

Adriana brought each of us a glass of lemonade; the boys already had some. There were more chairs in here than the last time I'd visited—clearly they'd been expecting us. White, Buchanan, and I settled down as Adriana brought in more goodies. I snagged a cookie to keep up my strength.

"For once, we're not miles behind you. It's pretty clear Bellie heard everything Marling was plotting. She's sort of told us. She knows 'Daddy's secrets' but so far we haven't gotten really clear answers."

"Ah. Well, do remember—it *is* a bird. It will not speak, or reason, as humans do."

"Point taken. So, are we going to pussyfoot, speak in vague homilies, or actually cut to the chase?"

"I understand you did not pass a required test."

This conversational shift was classic Olga. I didn't even blink or miss a beat. "Wow. Just how many contacts do you have, and where? I'm truly shocked you know this soon. Not that you know, mind you, just that you know only a couple hours after the fact." Okay, maybe I blinked a little.

Olga shrugged as if to indicate still waters continued to run deep. Not that there was any doubt. "I also understand there is a scandal brewing."

"Oh, yeah. The dirty pictures. They're fakes."

"I'm sure they are. Your loyalties have never been questioned by me."

Loyalties, plural. Did she mean my being in a committed marriage, new Beloved Birdie aside, my friendship with Chuckie . . . or something else? It was Olga. Asking straight out so rarely worked. I figured it was because, being mostly confined to a wheelchair, she wanted to prolong her fun as much as possible. No problem. Extra time spent with Olga, Adriana, and their foodstuffs was not an issue.

Though Adriana, as per usual for these types of meetings, didn't stay in the room. I was quite clear that Olga briefed her later. The possibility that Adriana watched us from a secret room was also quite high. But she made sure we had plenty of food and drink and then trotted out.

"Do you have any recommendations for how to deal with the scandal?" White asked. "You do have more experience here than we do, Madame." He was always courtly, but he turned it up to eleven for Olga. And it was also clear that Olga ate it up.

It was slowly dawning on me that White was, quite frankly, a ladies' man. It had only taken, what, close to two and a half years with almost constant contact for this to dawn on me, but at least the realization was finally arriving, wearing a Belated Clue sign.

Olga laughed softly. "I suppose this is true. In some cases it's best to meet things head on. In others, it is not."

I sighed to myself. Vague innuendos it was going to be. "Which tactic do you think we should use for this scandal?"

"Whichever tactic will work at whichever time."

I really liked Olga, and not only because she'd sent Adriana along during Operation Assassination to ensure I didn't die, but there were times she drove me crazy. Any time she had information we needed, especially.

"Someone sent the pictures to Senator Armstrong and insinuated they were going to be released. He also told Guy Gadoire, at the least, about it."

"Interesting choices." She said this leadingly.

It was always Remedial Class whenever we chatted with Olga. She was a lot like my mother—usually about ten steps ahead of everyone else but determined to make you work for it so that you'd remember how to do it by yourself next time.

"The senator and Gadoire both insist they aren't trying to black-mail me and want to help."

"They could be telling the truth." She didn't say this definitively enough for me to feel truth was a given.

I went for the frontal attack. "Okay, my plan was to get Mister Joel Oliver and Senator Armstrong, both of whom have seen the pictures, and go see if the nice guys from the K-9 squad could help out."

Olga nodded. "Your strategy has potential." She didn't sound like this was an awful plan, but it also clearly wasn't first on the list of Olga's Recommended Ideas. And I also wasn't sure if by "potential" she meant potential to succeed or potential to be disastrous. Or both.

"What would you recommend, Madame?" White asked again. He was always the one most willing to put up with Olga's playing around. Maybe this was a form of flirtation in the older set. I still wasn't a fan.

"Oh, I imagine anything you try will be fine."

There was something about how she said this that made me want to really think about the next words that were going to come out of my mouth. "You don't see these pictures and whatever scandal they might cause as a big deal, do you?"

"Oh, they can and likely will be made to be a very 'big deal,' " Olga said gravely. "But they are hardly the biggest deal, so to speak."

Buchanan finally spoke up. "You think the pictures are just a distraction, don't you?"

"A distraction from what?" I asked this one, because I knew Buchanan had a good idea of what was really going on.

"A distraction from more important things," Olga replied, speaking to Buchanan, not me. "You are prepared?"

He shrugged. "Not really. The mess at NASA Base ensured the Ambassador can't actually know everything that's going on." He smiled at Olga. "At least, she can't hear about it from anyone who officially knows."

Olga beamed. Clearly Buchanan was moving straight to the head of the class. "Ah?"

Buchanan grinned. "However, it seems fortunate that no one in this room has been briefed on anything yet. So there's no one here who could compromise their security clearance, since they don't know what is or isn't classified."

Olga nodded and looked to me. "Definitely keep Mister Buchanan close at hand, Ambassador. He will be most useful to you and your Mister Reynolds."

CHAPTER 21

BEFORE I COULD QUESTION WHY Olga had mentioned Chuckie and not Jeff in terms of Buchanan's usefulness, Adriana popped her head into the room. "I'm sorry, Ambassadress, but the Ambassador just called. He'll be home shortly."

"Ah, then I must ask our guests to take their leave. My Andrei will be wanting his dinner right away."

We all took the hint. We were on Romanian soil while in their Embassy, and Andrei wasn't quite as aware of things as his wife and granddaughter were. I was quite willing to continue to keep him in the dark.

We said our good-byes, and I noted the boys both hugged Adriana. I knew without asking that it was hard for her to be trapped in the Embassy as much as she was, even though it appeared she spent the downtime training in how to be the best New KGB operative ever. But I didn't begrudge her some handsome male attention, and the boys were happy to provide it—she was a cute girl.

Buchanan walked us across the street. "I'll find you tomorrow."

"You're not coming for dinner?" I'd gotten used to eating with him. He shook his head. "Your husband won't like it."

"I'll bet you twenty bucks that bird will be joining us."

He laughed. "Probably. But we're back home now, and we need to have things appear to be normal."

"Whatever you say."

"See? That's only one reason you don't want me at dinner." He grinned as I blushed. "See you later, Missus Chief. Try to give the bird a chance. And if you really can't stand her, I promise she'll meet an untimely death due to a sniper's bullet."

"You'd shoot Bellie if I asked you to?"

He nodded as he turned and walked away. "Yeah. My job has nothing to do with making your husband happy."

I waited to go in until Buchanan turned the corner. "Does anyone else want to know where the hell he goes?" To date, I'd never been able to spot or find Buchanan unless he wanted me to find or spot him. And I'd tried. It was as if he had Dr. Strange's Sorcerer Supreme powers. Jeff hadn't liked it when I'd mentioned that comparison.

"No," Len said shortly.

"Ditto," Kyle added.

Come to think of it, the boys hadn't liked the Dr. Strange comparison, either. There were times, like now, when I felt the boys saw Buchanan's existence as my mother saying the boys weren't good at their jobs. I knew this wasn't true, but now probably wasn't the time to get into that particular discussion.

"I'm just curious. He sort of comes and goes like the wind."

"I don't care where he goes as long as he shows up when you need him," Len said. "I want to know what's really going on."

"Me too," Kyle agreed. "From what he said, it sounds like we should avoid finding out, though."

"I agree," White said. "I think our little team would be better off remaining out of the loop, at least for now."

"What do we say if someone tries to tell us something?" Len asked.

"Tell them part of the truth—you don't want to know because you don't want to have to censor yourselves around me. I'm sure Jeff and Chuckie will agree."

White nodded. "It's quite reasonable. And true. Now, let's do as Mister Buchanan suggested and get ourselves as back to normal as we're able to."

Every apartment in the Embassy had its own dining area, and the kitchen had two nooks, an island, a table for four that could extend to a table for eight, and a bar where you could eat. However, the Embassy also possessed a huge formal dining room, and that's where we found the others.

I was pleased and surprised to see Bellie nowhere in sight and Jamie in Jeff's arms. Good thing Buchanan hadn't joined us—I'd have owed him twenty bucks.

I got the "Mommy's Here!" squeal. It was always nice to know my baby missed me, even if I was only gone from her for about an hour.

"See, Jamie-Kat?" Jeff said. "I told you Mommy would be home soon."

Jamie was bouncing with excitement. For her, this had to be the best night in a long time, because she had both of us. I sat next to Jeff and took Jamie while he put his arm around me. Everyone else was here, chattering away, catching each other up on what had gone on while we were gone. Even Nurse Carter, who was sitting next to White, seemed relaxed and part of the group. It was pleasant and comfy. I leaned against Jeff. "It's nice to be home."

"It's nicer to have you home." He hugged me and kissed the top of my head, then nuzzled my ear. "I missed you, baby. More than you can imagine."

Humongous dining table filled with people and our baby in my lap or not, I started to drool just a little. It had really been far too long since I'd been naked with my husband.

Jeff chuckled. "Nice to see your mind's gone straight back to the priorities."

I chose not to share that my mind hadn't left the priorities for the past month, but I was too busy trying not to let the drool get onto Jamie.

The conversation was pointedly kept on either what interesting things our Embassy personnel had done while we were gone or mundane Washington stuff. Of course, mundane meant scandals, snubs, and the like. Pierre was, unsurprisingly, a fount of all that was Insider: Washington.

Doreen and Irving were also loaded with stories about all the interesting things we'd missed, including their baby's first smile. Doreen insisted Ezra had given her the first, Irving felt he'd gotten it. Pierre's expression indicated that, as far as he was concerned, Ezra's Uncle Pierre had scored the first smile in reality.

I would have liked to exchange stories with Doreen about what cute things Ezra and Jamie had done while we were gone, but Jamie had spent most of her time being miserable, and now wasn't really the time anyway. I wasn't all that interested in who was sleeping inappropriately with whom, mostly because I couldn't keep it straight and tended to either forget or mix it up at the wrong time, which meant when I was with one or more of the people being indiscreet.

Amy, however, was fascinated. Chuckie looked like he was taking mental notes, which, as I thought of it, he probably was. I checked everyone else out. Yep, they were all hanging on Pierre's every juicy word, even Tito and Christopher, who I wouldn't have thought would care at all about who was zooming whom. The thought occurred that I should maybe pay attention.

"And the lovely people from the Czech diplomatic mission were our neighbors, but only for a fortnight." Pierre shook his head. "We barely had time to visit before they had to move right back to their old haunts, which are inadequate for their needs but are at least livable."

"What happened?" Amy asked.

"All the pipes in their building's basement burst. All of them. Flooding up through half of the first floor. Cleanup and repair will take months."

"Not if A-Cs did it," I said. "Speaking of which, are NASA Base's gates all back together?"

Christopher nodded. "Good as new. James told us they'd finished up just a couple of minutes before dinner. Though I don't think NASA wants you to visit again any time soon."

Before I could say, yet again, that it really wasn't my fault, Amy spoke up. "What's going to happen to the building the Czechs had?" I wasn't sure if this question was asked purely out of interest or because NASA Base was now on my Don't Ask Don't Tell list and Amy was getting the conversation back onto a safe track. Had a sinking feeling it was the latter, which was confirmed by catching Chuckie giving Amy a little nod.

Chuckie and Amy were working together and I was out of the loop? Could this homecoming get any worse or more bizarre?

Pierre threw up his hands. "No idea. The building's owner was practically sobbing. He had to refund all deposits to the lovely Czechs, understandably of course, but he now has no capital with which to do the repairs. A broken man, if you ask me, financially and emotionally, poor thing."

There was general murmured consensus that plumbing issues sucked, and everyone felt bad for the building's owner and glad it wasn't us going through this homeowner's nightmare.

I'd figured we'd finished with all the gossip, but I was wrong. "Pierre, what happened with the Bahraini Embassy?" Amy asked. I would have sworn she'd spent all her time since we got back to D.C. in bed with Christopher or in the debrief she couldn't talk about in front of me, but clearly they'd spent the time reading the last four weeks' worth of gossip columns instead of doing the deed.

"A break-in, darling. But nothing was taken. At least nothing the Bahraini Ambassador will admit to."

"Did they catch whoever did it?" Hey, I could still ask questions.

Pierre shook his head. "Not yet. Of course, the Israelis are being blamed. But they insist they had nothing to do with it."

"Did anyone ask my mom?" All heads turned to me and everyone gave me the "what the hell" look. Why? It seemed like an obvious question to me. "Um, she's former Mossad. If anyone would be able to confirm Israeli guilt or innocence on this break-in matter, I'd think Mom would be the one to do it."

"There are other suspects," Pierre said. "Including some of the other Middle Eastern diplomatic missions. As well as the idea of a common thief."

"I've seen the Embassies in that area," Kyle said. "They're all protected like Fort Knox."

This was pretty much true. We were housed in the area nicknamed Embassy Row. Embassies were everywhere, interspersed among homes, businesses, hotels, and more. Half of the Embassy doorways were practically at the street. Most were architecturally pretty, some saying "look at me," some just going for the understated look so popular with Old Money. Our general Embassy neighborhood was a friendly-feeling area.

However, the Israeli and Bahraini Embassies weren't really in our part of town, so to speak. I thought of the section where these particular Embassies resided as The Bunker.

In The Bunker's section of D.C., every Embassy was gated and secured, the buildings set well back from the street and no doorway was close to the gates, and the buildings weren't nearly as pretty as the ones in our area—because they looked as though they'd been built for stolid usefulness and defensibility as opposed to architectural beauty.

"That might be why they're thinking it's the Israelis," Len said. "It takes real skill to break into an Embassy set up to keep you out."

"Mossad aren't the only ones with those skills," Chuckie said. "There are plenty of options. There's also always Middle East intrigue going on. But it's a police matter, not something the head of the P.T.C.U. needs to worry about."

I was going to ask if this was standard intrigue or intrigue related to what I now no longer got to know about when Jamie yawned. Widely.

"Time for someone to go to bed." I handed her back to Jeff, who put her gently onto his shoulder. Jamie snuggled her little face right into his neck and sighed happily.

"Time for you, too, Kitty," Tito said sternly. "You overdid it today and didn't take the nap you were supposed to."

Under most circumstances I would have protested, but frankly Tito was both right and ensuring that I at least had a hope of getting to see my husband outside of his clothes. "Okay, Tito, whatever you say, you're the doctor."

"I expected more of an argument about it," Tito said with a grin. "But I can understand why you're more tractable than normal."

Jeff stood up holding Jamie with one hand while he took my hand in the other and gave it a squeeze. "I'm going to turn in, too, then. Have to take care of my girls."

Everyone at the table gave us looks that said they knew exactly what we were going to be doing the moment the baby was in bed. I saw no reason to deny the obvious.

"So, don't knock or call unless it's a dire emergency."

"And even then," Jeff added as we headed off, "really think twice about it."

"Long and hard about it. So to speak."

Jeff chuckled as we left the dining room and headed for the elevator. "Long and hard's coming, baby."

"Promises, promises."

Jeff waited until we were in the elevator. "Baby, you know I keep my promises. And then I improve on them."

Then he kissed me, and my mouth was far too busy to talk.

CHAPTER 22

I WAS IN A HAPPY GLOW and ready to go for it by the time we reached our door.

"Bellie missed Jeff!"

Well, that put a damper on the mood. "Go take care of your girlfriend. I'll get Jamie started."

"You sure?"

I refrained from heaving a sigh, but it took effort. "Yes, I'm sure. Put a lid on her. She stays out of our bedrooms. Unless all you want to do is sleep while I stay awake with a Poof trained on her."

"No. I fed Jamie before you came to dinner. Denise said she'd just changed Jamie before I picked her up, too." We went into the nursery and Jeff put Jamie gently into her crib, stroked her head, and gave her a soft kiss.

While he got the Poof Condos and moved them back into the nursery, I covered Jamie with her blanket. She still had her special Poof with her, and it snuggled next to her side. Several of the other Poofs joined them in the crib, as did the cats, with Sugarfoot at her head and Candy and Kane at her feet. Much purring ensued. Put her half of the baby monitor into her crib, and as Jeff closed the door softly, I put our half onto the nightstand.

Jeff had left one Poof Condo in our room, and Harlie, Poofikins, and several other Poofs were in it, snoozing away. The dogs were in their beds, looking happy. "Who's taken care of the dogs and cats while I was gone?"

"Walter assigned some of the Operations Team to do it. They've had no issues."

I didn't like this answer, but Bellie was squawking. "Seriously, get that bird shut up so I can sleep." There was no need to mention that if I could hear the bird, we weren't having sex. I wasn't going to let him touch me if I could hear the bird. Why he'd left the door open so I could hear the bird at all was beyond me.

Jeff nodded and hypersped to his beloved, thankfully closing the door behind him so I didn't have to hear him make out with Bellie before he came back to me. I had to figure the dogs and cats hated the bird easily as much as I did, since they loved Jeff and wanted his attention. It occurred to me that the Poofs might have stayed in D.C. because of the bird, too.

Whatever Jeff did worked and he was back fairly quickly. "She's all set. I have her cage covered."

"With what? Her 'cage' fills our entire living room."

He mumbled something.

"Sorry, missed that."

"I had a special covering made."

This surprised me not at all. Chose not to fight about it. "Whatever, as long as she goes to sleep and shuts the hell up, not necessarily in that order."

"She will." He fiddled around with the iPod dock.

"What're you doing?"

"I made a special play list for whenever you finally came home."

"You make it sound like I'd run off to the far reaches of the earth."

Jeff pulled me into his arms as "Sea of Sin" by Depeche Mode came on. "It felt like it."

"Love the song choice. Looking forward to the whole mix. However, will the music wake your bird up?"

"No. I'd have to have the volume turned up to full for Jamie to hear it through the walls, let alone Bellie. She'll stay asleep. You, however, will not be sleeping any time soon."

"So you claim."

His eyelids drooped just a bit and he got the sexy "jungle cat about to eat me" look on his face. I loved that look. I was also made pretty tractable by that look, to sort of quote Tito. "So I know."

We started kissing, slowly at first. Well, slowly for about a second. In the next second we were ripping the clothes off each other. Five seconds after that we were in bed.

Jeff buried his face in my breasts. "I can't tell you how much I've missed these."

"They've missed you, too," I gasped out, as his tongue swirled around one nipple and then the other. He took each one between his teeth in turn and toyed with them until I was howling. The first orgasm he'd ever given me had been at second base, and even with no practice for a month, he'd lost no skills whatsoever.

The soundproofing in the Embassy was excellent, which was good because I didn't want to wake Jamie, Bellie, the pets, the Poofs, or anyone else. The animals in the room with us had gotten over the novelty and chose to remain asleep. No one else seemed to notice my yowling. This was, so far, the only place where my sounding like a cat in heat was only shared with Jeff. It made for a nice change.

Jeff made for a nice change, too, and headed his mouth southward. As he licked and nipped, my hips started bucking. I grabbed his head as his hands slid up and fondled my breasts. The music switched to "Just Can't Get Enough." Clearly Jeff had been on a Depeche Mode kick. Not that I could argue with his musical choices—I could never get enough of this.

It didn't take much more to cause another orgasm to crash. In between howling I managed to convey that foreplay was still great, but the real thing was, I sincerely hoped, still better.

Jeff slid up onto his knees, picked me up by my waist, and slid me onto him, so that I was kneeling, too. He wrapped his arms around my back as mine went around my neck, then kissed me deeply while pressing me down so that he went deeper into me, too.

I ran my hands through his hair while we thrust together. My movements were frantic, at first. But Jeff slowed me down, as he stroked my skin with his fingertips.

He moved his mouth to my neck and the real screaming started. My neck was one of my main erogenous zones and Jeff knew exactly where to kiss, lick, nip, or bite to get a full orchestral experience out of me.

"I missed you so much, baby," he whispered in my ear. "I'm going to show you how much, all night long."

I moaned. I wasn't really able to talk much when he had me this far over the edge. Happily, being with the galaxy's strongest empath meant he knew exactly how I felt, even if I couldn't tell him.

Going more slowly like this was sexy and romantic. Jeff was the world's best kisser as well as the world's best everything else. Rubbing against his body, feeling the hair on his chest against my breasts while we moved together and his tongue twined around mine, was erotic and loving, and I never wanted it to end.

However, when Jeff shifted me just a little and I felt another climax start to build, I wasn't going to argue. I mean, romance was great, but orgasms were better.

We started moving faster, with me rocking my hips forward and him pressing me back and down. My skin tingled anywhere it touched his and, as he went deeper still, I screamed my orgasm against his neck as he roared as he erupted inside me.

As our bodies shuddered, I kissed my way up his neck to his ear. I nibbled his earlobe and felt him start to harden inside me. "I missed you, too," I whispered as I ran my tongue along his ear and he growled softly. "I missed everything you do and how you do it. And no one does it better than you."

I took his head in my hands and kissed him strongly. He purred and flipped us so I was on my back, but we were still in the same position, with my knees bent and up by his waist and his knees bent and under my butt.

Jeff grinned as "Master and Servant" came on. "Baby, you haven't seen anything yet."

CHAPTER 23

AFTER SEVERAL MORE HOURS of truly amazing, orgasm-filled, sexual athletics—including the Alpha Centaurion Love Knot and an array of versions of the said Position Supreme—I was finally satiated enough that sleep was knocking on the door and I was willing to let it in.

Jeff knew, of course. He wrapped himself around me, I snuggled closer, took a deep breath, relaxed, and was out like a light.

I woke up a few hours later. Jeff was asleep, and we were still wrapped around each other. Jeff had turned the music off before we went to sleep, so it wasn't hearing a song or hearing silence after music had stopped that had disturbed me.

I listened to the baby monitor. I could hear Jamie, the Poofs, and the cats all snoozing peacefully. I checked the dogs and the Poofs in our room. All were fast asleep, making either soft baby purrs or having happy but rather quiet doggy dreams.

So, why was I awake when no one else was? Wondered if I was still asleep, but it didn't seem like a dream. I listened harder. Nothing.

Looked around the room. My night vision had improved due to the mutation. I was adjusting every day, but all in all, I liked my new abilities. Getting back to pre-pregnancy shape within two days and without any effort still seemed worth almost any price, let alone one that had made me more able to kick butt. And I felt like I needed to kick butt right now.

Jeff was still asleep, and I really wondered if I was dreaming. He normally woke up if I was moving around too much. And we'd been apart for a month—I would have thought my moving would have woken him up faster right now. A part of me wanted to let him sleep, but all the hairs on the back of my neck were standing up. I nudged him and put my hand over his mouth.

I could feel him wake up and nod against my hand. Felt him move to look around the room, then he sat us up slowly. "What is it?" he whispered in my ear.

"No idea," I answered in the same way. "But I feel like we're about to be attacked."

He nodded, slipped out of the bed, and hypersped into the nursery. He was back with Jamie in his arms. I took her, she seemed fine. Several of the Poofs came along for the ride. Still nothing.

I was about to apologize for clearly being overly dramatic when Harlie and Poofikins both growled and went large. They were facing the bedroom door and were in major protection mode. Jeff grabbed me and hypersped me and Jamie to the closet. We dressed quickly in the blue pajama bottoms and white t-shirts that were standard A-C nightclothes. We both put on slippers, too, just in case. Then Jeff put me and Jamie behind him.

The other Poofs were awake now, and to a one they were growling. We had a lot of Poofs, and that meant the growls were loud. The dogs, sensing that the game was afoot, all stood up. They were growling low, too, but not barking, which, for our dogs, was extremely unusual.

Jamie's Poof hadn't gone large, but it was quivering and I got the feeling it was waiting for some signal from Harlie, who was the head Poof. The rest of the Poofs were also still small, but I got the impression they were also waiting for Harlie to give them some kind of Poof Enlargement Go-Ahead.

The intercom crackled to life. "Chiefs, are you awake?"

"Yes, Walt. All the Poofs are on major alert."

"Mine, too." I'd insisted on Walter getting a Poof. He'd been so thrilled it had almost been embarrassing. Walter was determined to be the best Embassy Head of Security ever. I really liked Walter. Walter didn't have a problem with his Poof being on his shoulder, either.

"Can you spot anything?" Jeff asked, his Commander voice on. He'd been the Head of Field Operations for all A-Cs worldwide for over a dozen years, and a man didn't lose his authority just because he'd changed jobs. At least, mine didn't. Commander, Chief, really same thing, right?

"Sensors show nothing, sir. All cameras are on, and they show no activity in the general areas or outside the building. I've checked with the other residents. All Poofs are awake and growling. All personnel are awake and prepared for attack."

I considered. It was late enough that it was safe to assume that everyone had been in bed. It was a safer assumption that anyone who'd been naked wasn't any more. So that meant we were all in our nightclothes. I didn't call that prepared. "Jeff, do you think it's someone coming in through the secret tunnel?"

"Reynolds insists he's got that secured. So unless he's completely incompetent—and before you snarl at me, I know he isn't—I don't think we're being infiltrated from that source."

"Mister Reynolds is in the Embassy, as are Abigail and Naomi Gower," Walter shared. "They were here late, and Doctor Hernandez and Former Pontifex White insisted they all sleep here."

"Same issues with their Poofs?" I asked.

"Yes, ma'am, Chief."

"This is bizarre."

"Chief, Doctor Hernandez is asking if you think this is Jamie's doing."

Tito had good cause to ask. Jamie had certainly made things interesting the night before she'd been born, or what I liked to call the start of Operation Confusion.

Jeff put his hand onto her head. "I don't get anything from her that's wrong. She's uneasy because we and the pets are uneasy, but that's it."

"Could she have had a nightmare that triggered all this?"

"She was fast asleep and looked happy when I got her, baby. Walter, tell Tito I really don't think it's Jamie." He closed his eyes. "It's not Ezra, either." We weren't sure yet if Doreen and Irving's son had special A-C talents, or extraspecial ones for that matter.

"Chiefs, I've alerted Gladys to our situation." Gladys was the overall Head of Security. She housed out of the Dulce Science Center and was technically Walter's boss. "Building is being scanned. I also checked the sensors and scanners Mister Reynolds installed in the tunnels. No sign of any infiltration there. No alarms have been triggered." Walter sounded tense. "Chief Martini, what would you like me to do?" This was Walter's way of saying he had no clue. Which was fine. I'd accepted long ago that most men didn't like to admit when they were scared and clueless.

Jeff sighed. "No idea, Walter. Sit tight for the moment."

The Poofs hadn't stopped growling. I sniffed. Nothing. "Walter, flood, fire, electrical issues?"

"No, ma'am, Chief. Again, I've checked. Have Dulce Security on com with us now."

"Gladys, how goes it?"

"Fine, Chief Katt-Martini. Dulce Security lives to serve, at any hour of the day or night. Chief Martini, have scanned the building, nothing shows as wrong."

"Gladys, everyone, and by that I mean every man, woman, Poof and other animal, is up and freaked out. We'd all like to get back to bed. Any chance of that?"

"No idea, Chief Katt-Martini. Scans show nothing."

"I woke up with a feeling we were going to be attacked. Then the Poofs woke up. And the dogs. And so forth. Something's going on."

"I agree with Kitty." Christopher was on the group com now. "I woke up, too, before Amy, Toby, or Mignon." Toby was Christopher's Poof and Mignon was Amy's. Amy had given her Poof a French name—mignon meant cute in French. I had no argument with the name, but Jeff felt it was only slightly less silly than Poofikins. "But they woke up soon after, and both Poofs went large and are at full alert."

"Chiefs, have inquired," Walter said. "Only Consul White and Chief Katt-Martini were awakened before the Poofs or other personnel."

"What would wake up me and Christopher but not anyone else?"

"Good question, baby. I have no answer."

No sooner were these words out of Jeff's mouth than a bright glow showed under our door. Bellie started shrieking her head off—loudly enough that we could hear her through the soundproofing. And every Poof, including the one with Jamie, went large and toothy.

CHAPTER 24

THERE WAS A THUD OUTSIDE the door and the glowing stopped. "Everyone else just get a package shipped via Creep Out Express?"

"Yes. Confirmed, Chief. Unidentified objects outside all inhabited bedroom doorways. Including guest rooms." Walter sounded tenser than I felt.

"Only the inhabited ones?"

"Yes, confirmed." Gladys also sounded tense. "Impenetrable to our scanning equipment."

"They're from outer space."

"Why?" Jeff wasn't arguing, just asking.

"We can scan everything else."

"What if it's from my stepmother or Al Dejahl?" Amy sounded freaked out but also very angry. Couldn't blame her. LaRue Demorte Gaultier and Ronaldo Al Dejahl were not our favorite people.

"Why would whatever it is wake me and Christopher up, first?" I really wanted this answered. Unfortunately, I had a feeling one of us was going to have to do something besides cower behind a door.

"Have put all personnel onto the com, Chiefs."

"Thanks, Walter." Jeff took a firm hold of my hand. "I don't want anyone trying to be heroic right now. That's an order, and it applies to everyone, including anyone who thinks they report into the C.I.A. before Centaurion Division." Clearly he was worried about Chuckie, Len, or Kyle being overly brave in this situation.

"Fine, but I'd like to know how you expect us to get out of our rooms," Tito said. He didn't sound as scared as everybody else.

Then again, one of his many hobbies was being a professional cage fighter. Tito didn't scare easily, ever.

I started to get angry. There was something in here, threatening everyone, threatening my baby. Jeff's hand tightened on mine. "Baby, keep it together. You feel as angry as the Poofs."

Something kicked in my brain. If the Poofs were angry, not afraid, why would that be? "Mister White, do Poofs have natural enemies?"

"Not that I know of, Missus Martini. However . . ."

"However, what, Richard?" Jeff was just this side of snapping, and that meant he was as scared as everyone else, because he rarely snapped at the man who was both his closest uncle and his former religious leader unless he was at the end of his rope.

"Have you advised the Royal Family of Jamie's birth?"

"Of course. Months ago. Once Operation Confusion was over, we did the whole official announcement thing." They were our friends and family, after all. I'd essentially put Alexander on the throne. After the Poofs and I had gotten rid of the old king. "You think they've finally decided to get upset about good ol' Adolphus and sent out Poof Extermination or something?"

White coughed. "No. I think it's possible that these are, ah, gifts."

"Gifts that scare the crap out of an entire Embassy? Wow, Jeff, your relatives just rock the giving."

"There are traditional gifts for a child of royal birth," Gladys chimed in. She sounded underwhelmed. "Those same gifts also apply to the formation of a new principality."

"We're a principality?"

"King Alexander might consider it that way," Chuckie said. "Councilor Leonidas might, also."

"Why send us gifts right now?" Jeff asked. "Jamie was born almost five months ago. Ezra was born over six weeks ago."

"I have a better question. Are these safe gifts?"

"Relatively speaking," Gladys said. "In the same way the Poofs are safe." She still didn't sound enthused.

"Gladys, the Poofs protect us."

"Yes, and God help the person they don't like, right? These, if Richard is right, are similar."

"They aren't snakes, are they?" Royal gift or not, no snakes were coming into my house. Okay, they would already be in my house, but they were going to be Poof Chow if they were hoping to stay.

"No. Just a moment." White didn't sound worried.

"Richard, stay in your room!" Jeff wasn't bellowing, but he was close.

No answer. I could feel everyone holding their breath, waiting for screams or explosions or something.

Instead, White came back on the com. "It's what I thought. Safe to open your doors and open the boxes."

"Can't wait," Jeff muttered. "You stay here," he said to me, in the growly-man voice. Jeff was really attached to the idea that it worked outside of bed.

In this case, because I had Jamie in my arms, I chose to let him think I was obeying. He went to the door, and I readied myself to grab or tackle him out of the way of danger. But nothing much happened. Door opened, big box was there. Jeff turned on the lights. Still looked like a big box. Poofs were still growling. Dogs looked ready to lunge. Cats had come out and were on the bed, also looking ready. Bellie was quiet.

He looked at me. "Ready, baby?"

"I guess. Let's open it and see what kind of scary jack-in-the-box pops out."

Jeff flipped the lid and jumped to the side.

I had to admit, it wasn't anything I'd have guessed in about a thousand years.

CHAPTER 25

A BIRD THAT LOOKED A LOT LIKE a peacock flew out, screaming its head off. Then another one, this one pure white. There was a card tied to their legs, keeping the birds together.

This was a good thing, because they both attacked Jeff as if he were the person who'd put them into the interstellar shipping box. Wings flapping, claws flailing, beaks snapping, screams of displeasure echoing. Shockingly, Jamie started to cry.

The Poofs didn't move, though their snarling and growling was at the Heavy Duty Kill level. The cats flattened, hissed, then bolted into the nursery. The dogs all were great jumpers, and they confirmed this by leaping over our bed and following the cats' lead. Whatever these things were, Earth animals were afraid of them.

"Get these things off me!" Jeff was bellowing now, and Jamie was screaming at the top of her lungs. "Get away, stop it, go home!"

I didn't fear or hate birds the way I did snakes, but they'd never done much for me pets-wise, and Bellie was confirming my dislike and disinterest. I was a feline, canine, and Poof girl. Horses and their compatriots were fine. Otherwise, the animal kingdom was on its own, unless I was eating it. I had no idea of what to do, but in times of great stress, I did my best to channel my mother.

"Birds, SIT!" Amazing. The bird butts hit the floor. "Jeff, are you okay?" I raced over to him.

"Fine, I think." He was bleeding in a couple of places, but A-Cs healed fast. "Keep the baby away from these things."

I pointed to the card. He grabbed it, tore open the envelope, and read, "Many congratulations on the birth of your first heir to the

Earth Throne." Jeff looked at me and groaned. "They still don't get it, do they?"

"No, finish the card."

He sighed and continued. "May these Royal Peregrines provide protection and beauty for your palace and your child. Many happy returns, Alexander, King, Alpha Four."

I still heard lots of unpleasant noises coming from the com. "Did everyone get a set of Royal Peregrines?" I yelled.

"Hell, yes!" Christopher shouted. "And God alone knows why!" I heard Amy screaming in the background.

Pierre wasn't speaking. He was shrieking. "Back, you horrible creatures! Get back!"

He wasn't the only one. It was a cacophony of terror coming through the com. This had to stop. "Walter, make sure my voice goes into all the rooms."

"Yes, Chief! Ahhhh! Down, down, dammit! Go ahead, Chief!"

Handed Jamie to Jeff, raced to the com, took a deep breath, channeled Mom. "ALL BIRDS, SIT!"

"I love you, Kitty," Christopher said.

"I worship at your altar," Chuckie said, sounding shaken. "Because I already tried telling them to sit, and it didn't work."

"Us too," Abigail and Naomi chimed in.

"The strong authoritative voice didn't work until you used it, Kitty," Kevin confirmed. Raymond and Rachel were crying in the background with Denise trying to soothe them.

"Boys, you okay?"

"You're my personal Jesus, Kitty," Len said. Everyone was on a Depeche Mode kick right now, apparently.

"Mine, too," Kyle added, voice only shaking a little. "You want to hear some Depeche Mode?"

"Not sure music's going to calm these savage beasts, but if it'll help the rest of the Embassy, go for it."

I hadn't realized we had an Embassy Surround Sound System, nor that it was tuned to my iPod, but the sounds of "Personal Jesus" came softly through the air. Couldn't speak for anyone else, but music always helped me.

"I was ready to break some bird necks," Tito said. "Glad you got them quieted before I had to. I'm going to take care of my wounds first and then do room service, if that's okay."

"Sure, Tito. Richard, you okay?"

"Yes, Missus Martini. I knew how to calm them."

"Just how is that?" Jeff asked while he cuddled Jamie, who was still crying.

"You grab their feet."

"Wow, Richard, that would have been a great plan for the rest of us, but ours all had claws and such."

"I'll teach you how to control them in the morning, Missus Martini."

"Cannot wait. Walter, you okay?"

"Somewhat."

"Pierre?"

"Now that these beautiful gifts of vicious mass destruction aren't attacking me and destroying my living area, yes, darling, I'm fine. I have no pride attached to standing and fighting, and I've proved I'm just a trifle faster when running away screaming than these things. Either that or they weren't trying hard."

"No idea yet on that, Pierre. Magdalena, how are you?"

"Ah, I'm fine," she said. "I'll go assist Doctor Hernandez."

"Works for me. Doreen, Irving?"

"We're okay, Kitty." Doreen sounded shaken. I could hear Ezra crying. "I think Irving needs stitches, though."

"Good lord. They sent these as presents? For an infant? What's wrong with the people on Alpha Four? Are they all crazy, is that it?"

"Don't know, baby. We left, remember?"

"Geez, you sure it wasn't actually intelligent choice, versus exile?"

White laughed. "They're not that bad once you get used to them."

"Cannot, literally, wait." Our two birds were still sitting, looking around for what they could destroy, at least if I was any judge of avian behavior. "You know, around Earth, the only peregrines we have are falcons. These don't look like falcons."

"They're guardians, bred for both beauty and protection." White still sounded unperturbed. "They're quite a lovely gift."

"Oh, yes, lovely. We have at least half of our staff nursing wounds, but they're great." I went into the bathroom and got some things to take care of Jeff's variety of cuts. The Poofs were still growling. "By the way, Richard, why do the Poofs hate the Peregrines?"

"Job rivalry."

"Oh, you have got to be kidding me!"

Jeff winced as I put some salve on the biggest cut. "I hate that stuff you humans use."

"Oh, my big baby." I kissed his arm. "There, does that make it better?"

He gave me the jungle cat smile, bent and kissed me full on the mouth. "That makes it better," he purred as he pulled away from me.

I tended to the rest of his thankfully minor wounds, then we sat back down on the bed, staring at the Peregrines. "Richard, are the colored ones the males and the white ones the females?"

"Yes, well done, Missus Martini."

"I did amazingly well in my animal life sciences courses in college. So we have, what, thirteen mated pairs?"

"I believe we have twelve pairs. Enough to start a new flock, yes." White didn't sound perturbed. I decided not to ask who'd lucked out into not getting the special avian present right now.

"Guys, I'm thinking two words here—Washington Zoo. We make a lovely donation of, erm, native birds, and maybe the dirty pictures and whatever else is coming won't matter."

"You'll hurt Alexander's feelings to no end," White said.

"Richard, where in God's name are we going to keep them? They're big-ass birds! We don't have an aviary, let alone a yard. Bellie taking up my entire living room is already more bird than I want in here. And, lest anyone other than me not realize it, birds are dirty. Unlike Poofs and cats, who understand the concept of the litter box, or dogs who can learn to hold it for their walkies, birds crap wherever, whenever."

"Bellie doesn't," Jeff said. "But I agree—she's different."

Now wasn't the time to mention how different Bellie appeared to be. She was also still silent, which I was sure was because she was still afraid. I couldn't ignore that. "Jeff, get her and a perch and get her into the nursery with the other terrified animals."

He gave me a quick kiss and hypersped off. He came back and edged around the Peregrines. Bellie was on the perch, huddled. The Peregrines turned and stared at her. Bellie stared back. The Peregrines stared harder, clearly sharing that they could stare like this for days. Bellie looked away.

I closed my dropped jaw as Jeff came out of the nursery, shutting the door behind him. "I'll move the dog beds in there later. The animals are terrified."

"Who can blame them?"

There was a knock at our door. Jeff went to answer it while I did a very slow version of the Mommy Dance. Jamie was calming down now that the horrid screeching birds weren't attacking her father, but she was still crying, albeit quietly. Jeff came back with Tito and everyone else in tow. They'd brought all the birds with them.

"Wow, great. So I get to have two dozen of these things in here with my baby? You're all thinking, good, good."

"We just don't want to let them out of our sight," Christopher said, snark on full, Patented Glare #5 going strong. I couldn't really blame him. "Where's your Glock? I'm open to just shooting them. Maybe they cook up nicely."

Tito sighed. "We can't get rid of them." He handed a card to Jeff. "This came on my set."

Jeff read it aloud. "Doctor, please be aware that these birds provide more than protection and beauty. They are considered essential in helping the particularly talented deal with their gifts."

We were all quiet. "Richard, did you know that?" I asked finally.

"It's considered what you'd call an old wives' tale," White said. "However, my father did have a pair of Peregrines. They were killed by the King's order when he was exiled to Earth."

Interesting. I moved a little closer to the birds. The white one that had come in our special Box o' Fun craned her neck up. I squatted down and let her look at Jamie. I was enhanced—I could get us away from the birds if they tried anything.

But the birds tried nothing. The white one looked at Jamie and cooed. Jamie stopped crying. The bird cooed again, and Jamie giggled. The bird extended her neck slowly and put her head down so her beak was pointing at the floor and the top of her head was right by Jamie.

Jamie reached out and patted the bird, then squealed with what certainly sounded like joy. The bird put her head up and gave me a look that clearly said I could take the clue and relax now.

"Huh. Um, good Peregrines." Got happy bird looks. At least I chose to think they were happy. Who could really tell with birds? "Richard, truly, where in God's name are we going to put these things?"

He studied them. White resembled Timothy Dalton, only a little younger and hotter. He made the Thinking Frowny-Face, which reminded me of when James Bond was deciding on whether or not the minor evil henchman needed to be taught a lesson or killed for expediency's sake. "We need to convert part of the Embassy into an aviary," he said finally.

"You're kidding. Who has an aviary in an Embassy? And where would we put them, anyway?" White looked at me and shrugged.

"Richard, you're not serious. I realize this place is humongous, but what if the future Ambassadors don't want to keep these things?"

"The future Ambassadors will be A-Cs, either by birth or marriage. Therefore, they will want to keep the new Royal Flock in good stead." He was serious.

"They aren't going in our living quarters." Jeff had his Commander voice back on full.

White shrugged. "They do need sunlight."

"Buy up the building next door and gut it."

"You're kidding," Jeff said.

I pondered. "Actually, no, I'm not."

Christopher nodded. "For this area, it's dirt cheap, too."

"I don't want to know." I didn't. The A-Cs treated money the way probably everyone should—as a tool. They were extremely casual when they dropped huge sums that made me physically ill to even think about.

"It would ensure we didn't have neighbors we don't like," Doreen said. "But it might make us stand out too much. The last thing we want is to be showy in the wrong ways. That draws the wrong kind of attention."

I looked at the birds. They looked back. "Not if we turn it into a gift."

CHAPTER 26

"PARDON?" DOREEN SOUNDED CONFUSED. I looked around. Okay, unsurprisingly, everyone was looking confused. Well, everyone other than Chuckie. He looked rather proud. I didn't let it go to my head.

"If we buy the building, we say we're doing it to help the economy. We earn the current owner's gratitude and sound like we really care about moving the ol' dollars around. Then, we turn it into an aviary that's also a park or museum or something. Where people can, for a small fee, come in to view the lovely birdies and such. We make income, which we can in turn donate to the zoo or something, meaning that we come under nonprofit status, which is advantageous. We house the Peregrines safely, don't piss off Alpha Four, come across as total caring folks from wherever the hell everyone thinks we're from, and extend our real estate holdings. Good from both a financial and public relations viewpoint. In fact, if we do it right, the tax benefits alone could pay for itself, potentially with profit."

Everyone stared at me, some with open mouths. Other than Chuckie, who was in the back of the group. He applauded silently. I managed not to laugh.

"Peregrines got your tongues?" I had to say something. Or get offended by their expressions.

"Just shocked to hear those words coming out of your mouth," Christopher said finally. "They sounded so mature and professional. Are you feeling okay?"

I shrugged. "So glad I appear to be a moron to the people closest to me. What you all choose to forget is that I have a degree in business, and one of my best friends happens to be a self-made millionaire many times over via entrepreneurship and the stock market both. I did pick up a couple of pointers along the way."

Everyone turned and looked at Chuckie. He grinned and shrugged. "I'm always so happy when I discover she was paying attention all this time. Kitty's right, it's a sound financial investment that will double as a great way to house your ever-growing menagerie without creating too much talk."

Jeff groaned. "You have to be kidding me, Reynolds. Richard, what do you think?"

White cleared his throat. "I believe listening to Mister Reynolds is in our best interests. As your wife so succinctly put it, he's made his money the American way, and we would be remiss if we didn't follow his guidance."

"Then that's settled." And it might mean I could move Bellie off into the other building, too. This was definitely a big selling point for me. "So, what did everyone else's gift cards say?"

"Ours said something similar to yours and Tito's card," Doreen said. "Congratulations on the birth of your baby, keep the birds around."

"Mine came with instructions for how to use the birds for security purposes," Walter said. He'd joined us, too, which was a rarity. I had the feeling Walter wanted his set of birds not only out of his Security Command Center but never returning.

"Richard?"

"My note was personal in nature, Missus Martini." White gave me a small smile.

I thought about it. I also noted that Nurse Carter was standing near White. And she'd sounded pretty calm. The only one who'd been calmer had been White. Because he'd understood how to handle the birds. And he'd been the one to tell me we had twelve pairs, when we really should have had thirteen, based on room occupancy.

"Magdalena, did you get a set of birds?"

She looked uncomfortable. "No, I didn't. At least, I don't believe I did."

"All the birds are here, Chief," Walter said. "I verified before I came up."

Chuckie looked like he was really trying not to laugh. I looked at Jeff. He looked surprised but rather pleased. Suspicions confirmed. "Safe to say you were likely included in the gift and the note, is that right, Magdalena?"

"Ah . . ." She looked up at White.

Who took her hand in his. "Yes, Magdalena was definitely included in the note."

Christopher looked shocked. "You're dating Nurse Carter?"

White rolled his eyes. "Pardon me."

Christopher's expression went to supershock. "You're kidding! You only knew her a couple of weeks before you left for Florida." He seemed borderline losing it.

"Some things move swiftly," White said, pointedly looking at Amy.

"But . . ."

I cleared my throat, and he looked at me. "Christopher, twenty-three years of mourning is pretty much considered about twenty to twenty-two too long. She wouldn't have wanted him alone this long. Why would she want him alone forever? Why do you want him alone?"

"I . . . I don't." He looked hurt and confused.

White sighed, kissed Nurse Carter on the cheek, dropped her hand, went over, and put his arm around Christopher's shoulders. "Son, let's go have a chat, shall we? Excuse us, please." He led Christopher out of our rooms.

Amy looked at me. "You are not allowed to die."

"Come again?"

She shook her head. "See how he is about his mother? He's that way about you, to a sort of scary degree. He's never gotten over losing her, and for whatever reason, you're one of her stand-ins. So's your mother."

"Ames, I told you. Mom and I look like Terry. Not a hundred percent, but enough."

Jeff jerked and stared at me. "I guess you do."

"You never saw it?"

He grinned. "No, not until this moment. Not with your mother, either." He laughed. "Terry thought like you, but she didn't act like you, or Angela."

"See?" I said to Amy. "I told you. Stop worrying. I don't need to have a jealousy chat with you, do I?"

She shook her head. "No. I just don't think he's ever dealt with losing his mother."

Jeff shrugged. "He didn't. My parents had to take us after Aunt Terry died. Richard was too heartbroken to be able to help either one of us. And my mother was still too jealous of Terry to deal with her death as well as we could have wanted. We both had to pretend nothing was wrong."

I hated hearing about their childhoods. Or rather, their brief mo-

ments of childhood interspersed with pain, horror, and adult responsibilities.

Jeff took my hand and gave it a squeeze. "No one's perfect,
baby. Other than you," he added with a grin. I snorted. "I've had
some long talks with my mother, and father. They've both talked to
Christopher, too."

"It hasn't sunk in," Amy said with a sigh. "He's still messed up
about it."

"The brooding types are always brooding for a reason, Ames."

She laughed. "Yeah. And I don't mind helping him through it.
But, seriously, you almost dying in childbirth? I know Jeff was a
mess, but Christopher was, too."

"It was going on five months ago."

"Seems like yesterday to me, baby." Jeff stroked the back of my
neck. I managed not to arch into his hand, but it did take some serious effort.

Nurse Carter sighed. "I should move back to Paraguay, shouldn't I?"

"That seems a little drastic. Christopher's just surprised, is all.
He'll get over it."

Amy put her arm around Nurse Carter's shoulders. "You're not
going anywhere. Those of us with no one else but the family we've
chosen to join have to stick together."

One of the birds, the male I was fairly sure had walked in with
White, went over and rubbed up against Nurse Carter.

"The bird says you're good to stick around." All the Peregrines
looked at me. They seemed remarkably pleased. The one that had
cozied up to Nurse Carter rejoined the flock. "Well, until we buy
the building next door, where are the Peregrines staying?"

All the birds continued to look at me. They now looked as
though they wanted to roll their eyes but were simply being polite.

"I'm scared of the birdies, Mommy," Rachel Lewis said in a
quiet voice.

One of the pairs looked at each other and went over to the
Lewises. Bird necks were extended, coos were given, bird heads
were reluctantly patted, then less reluctantly patted. Smiles and
giggles ensued. The birds cooed again, then rejoined the flock.
They all looked at me. Expectantly. Then sat down. En masse.

Reality dawned. "I'm going to have to keep these things right
here, aren't I? At least until their aviary is built. Wow, it sucks to be
me again."

Jeff sighed. "I'm just praying they don't have to sleep in the
bedroom with us."

CHAPTER 27

WE DISCUSSED IT AND DECIDED TO SEE IF, by chance, each set would go back to their original recipients. This sounded like a great plan, only the birds all looked alike.

To everyone else, at any rate. I could definitely see differences. I chose not to share this.

The others tried moving around and calling to the birds. They didn't budge. I had a sinking feeling about this. I got up and walked toward the back bedrooms. The Peregrines got to their feet en masse and followed me.

Two of them stopped and stood by Doreen, Irving and Ezra. Two more trotted over to the Lewises. The exact same two that had gone over to comfort Rachel and Raymond earlier. The others looked at me expectantly. "Oh, good. Doreen, you get to have your set with you. Feel lucky."

"Trying to."

"Failing like me?"

"Pretty much, yeah." The birds cocked their heads at her. "Oh, fine. But no being mean to our Poofs!" Everyone in the Embassy had their own Poof by now. We had plenty after all, and I felt it was a wise security measure. Besides, the Poofs were beyond cute. Who wouldn't want one? Well, the Peregrines, based on the looks they were giving said Poofs.

Who were quite unhappy, if their continued quiet growling was any indication. They'd gone back to small, but they were eyeing the Peregrines like nobody's business. The Poof that had attached to Jamie was perched on her, clearly ready to eat any Peregrine that came near.

"That's right, Peregrines. The Poofs were here first, and we love them. If you want us to love you, you have to play nicely with the Poofs. And the dogs and cats. And any other birds we happened to have around. Any animal that was here first is higher on our collective totem pole than any of you. So you need to leave them alone or protect them, depending. As well as be good birdies and all that jazz." I looked at the Lewises. "You guys okay with your new family pets?"

Kevin shrugged. "As long as they don't attack us again, sure. If they do, I'm going to start an interstellar incident."

"Should we be concerned that they've only attached to the families with kids?" Jeff asked quietly.

"No idea. At all. Naomi, Abigail, does your card give us any clue about that?"

"No," Naomi replied. "Our card said, 'While these birds will be most at home in the palace, they will help you control and stretch your talents while keeping you safe. Please enjoy them with our compliments.' So I guess either Sis and I are expected to leave 'our' Peregrine set here, or Alexander thinks we live here."

"Or that you should," Chuckie said slowly. "I've looked at the handwriting. The cards to Martini and White are in the same hand. All the others are in a different hand. King Alexander wrote the cards to his closest kinsmen."

"And Councilor Leonidas wrote the rest, didn't he?"

Chuckie nodded. "That would be my assumption, yes."

Nurse Carter looked at the card in Naomi's hand. "Yes, the card Richard received was in that handwriting."

"He let you see it?"

She looked embarrassed. "It was, as he said, personal. But for the two of us."

"Oh, one of those 'congrats on hooking up and welcome to the family' kind of messages." The Peregrines all cooed at me. It was as if they were telling me they loved that I was so intuitive. I didn't share this thought with anyone else either.

"What did everyone else's notes say?" Jeff asked.

Kevin pulled theirs out. "Captain, these birds will form the basis of the palace's defenses. While they can and should travel with the Royal Family and their other charges, always ensure at least two pairs remain present within the palace grounds." He shook his head. "They're really not clear on how things are here, are they?"

"Or they're being deliberately obtuse for reasons we still don't know." Alexander I could almost buy not being able to get his head around the whole "we aren't royalty" thing, but it was a stretch.

I was clear that Councilor Leonidas was Alpha Four's version of Chuckie and Winston Churchill rolled into one. Councilor Leonidas I knew for sure understood our position within Earth governments, probably better than anyone else in the Alpha Centauri system. I was positive he understood it better than I did. "And whoever wrote that clearly knows what the Defense Attaché position is all about."

Pierre nodded. "Mine reads, 'The Concierge Majordomo's position within the household is both honorable and perilous. These birds will assist you in your duties while protecting your person at the same time.' They certainly are focused on the whole attack bird idea, aren't they?"

Len and Kyle exchanged a look. "Our cards say almost the same thing as Pierre's, only they didn't mention job titles."

"Amy, make sure you grab Richard when he's done with Christopher and find out just what kind of jobs these birds are intended to do." Jeff's Commander voice was back on full. "I'm willing to give them the benefit of the doubt, but something that's entire job is protection isn't necessarily friendly."

The Peregrines gave him a group hurt look. A couple of them looked ready to cry. "Wow, you hurt their feelings, big time." Whoops.

"Excuse me?" Jeff said, very carefully.

Gave up. "I can see their expressions."

"What?" Jeff was clearly verbalizing everyone's question.

"Um, I feel like I . . . know what the Peregrines are thinking."

"It's like you're on drugs. They're birds. They have no expressions. I'm not convinced they have thoughts."

"Bellie's a bird, and you're convinced she has thoughts." The Peregrines all bobbed their heads. "See?"

"What does that prove?" Jeff asked. But he sounded nervous. "I think that's a bird behavior thing. Bellie does it all the time."

"Yeah? Well, I think it's because she's trying to nod yes." I looked at the Peregrines. The full flock bobbed their heads. "Can I get a bird amen?" Peregrine wings all flapped, there were several coos, and even a couple of hoots. "Can I get a *real* bird amen?" Peregrines hooted and flapped. They enjoyed the impromptu revival meeting.

I looked around the room. Apparently only the Peregrines and I were finding this amusing.

"Wow," Chuckie said finally, breaking the horrified human and A-C silence in the room. "You've become Doctor Doolittle."

CHAPTER 28

"I BELIEVE IT'S HER TALENT," White said as he and Christopher rejoined us.

"Excuse me?"

"Talent. Many A-Cs do have them, I believe you're aware." White seemed amused.

"True enough. But I'm not an A-C."

White coughed while everyone else looked slightly uncomfortable. "No, you're not. You're also not a human any more, either. And you've always been good with animals."

"Well, sure, but the cats and dogs have been my family's pets for years."

He pointedly looked at the Poofs. "And yet, the Royal Pets don't really obey anyone. Other than you. Supposedly Poofs will only obey their owners. And the head Poof."

"Harlie's the head Poof."

"True enough. However, I've seen Harlie do whatever you want, whenever you want it, unless you weren't phrasing your request in a way that would ensure Jeffrey would remain safe."

"It's a nightmare," Jeff said. "Fine, let's worry about this later, and by later I mean tomorrow."

"Wait, we haven't seen what Christopher and Chuckie's cards said."

Christopher looked as though his world was still spinning. Amy took the card out of his hand. "Congratulations on your recent nuptials. We wish you many happy years of fruitful marriage and hope these birds will serve you well as you take your place within Earth's hierarchy."

"That's nice."

Amy shook her head. "There's more. That first part was on the front of the card. This was on the back. 'As the Primary to His Royal Highness, we would like to warn you that we fear a threat against our mutual friend from a common enemy. Please take all due precautions.' It's not signed, but it's in different handwriting from what was on the other side. It matches the handwriting on Tito's card."

"The Primary?" This was a new one.

"It's an Alpha Four title," White answered. "Chief Councilor, which is Councilor Leonidas' full title, would correlate for Earth into a position similar to that of the British Prime Minister. The Primary, however, is different. Primaries tend to be a blood relation of some kind to the King, but the function is similar to that of the U.S. Vice President. It could also technically correspond to Christopher's role here, as Chargé d'Affaires."

"So, if Alfred had been crowned King of Alpha Four, the Primary might have been Stanley Gower?"

"Exactly. Well done." White looked pleased with my insightfulness. As did the Peregrines. Go me.

Amy, however, looked upset. "It's got to be my stepmother and Al Dejahl," she said to Jeff.

Jeff shook his head. "Why not just say that? They told Tito what the birds were for, they told Walter and Kevin and everyone else how to use them for security—why be cryptic to Christopher? Particularly about a threat?"

"What do you think, Christopher?"

He blinked. I got the impression that Christopher was still thinking about the fact that his father was romancing Nurse Carter. "Same as Jeff. I've got no idea why they do anything they do. I don't see any reason to be sending us hidden messages attached to attack birds."

"Possibly because they were worried about the birds or the messages being intercepted," Chuckie said. "If the threat to 'our mutual friend' means Martini, it wouldn't be out of the realm of possibility for them to be concerned that something would happen with the deliveries."

My throat felt tight. "Someone's out to hurt Jeff?"

"Possibly," Jeff said. He sounded irritated. And tired. "But right now, let's just get the last message to Reynolds and go back to bed."

Chuckie looked at his card. "Huh. You'd think they'd have said something similar on mine."

"What does your message say?" Jeff asked.

"Mine's like what Naomi and Abigail got. 'Please consider taking up residence with the rest of the American Centaurion diplomatic mission. Your skills will be needed within far more than without.' It's Leonidas' handwriting."

"Well, that's ominous." I looked at the Peregrines. "That's why they sent these birds now." Sure enough, the flock all bobbed their heads.

"I'm living in a zoo," Jeff muttered. "Fine," he said in his normal voice, "so we have a new threat. Nothing we haven't had before, I'm sure."

"Common enemy sounds like my wicked stepmother," Amy said for the third time. I hoped this didn't work like *Beetlejuice* and her mentioning LaRue three times meant she'd show up. I waited. No puff of smoke, no evil villainess standing in the room. I allowed myself to be relieved.

"Could be," Kevin agreed. "But we have other common enemies. And since none were named specifically, I wouldn't limit our thinking at this stage."

"Are you going to do what he asks, Chuckie? And by you, I mean you, Naomi, and Abigail. You've all stayed here before." If Councilor Leonidas thought we needed Chuckie and the Gower girls living here, then we probably needed Chuckie and the Gower girls living here.

Jeff and Chuckie looked at each other. "You're here so damn much anyway," Jeff said finally. "You already have your own room."

Chuckie laughed. "True enough. So do Mimi and Abby."

They nodded. "I think you need us right now," Naomi said. "So we're staying. Like Chuck, we're here a lot anyway."

"But it looks like the Peregrines are only going to go with those of us with children," Doreen pointed out. "I don't understand why, or how they're going to be protecting anyone if they're all with Kitty."

Considered this. As well as all the notes, the ones to Christopher and Chuckie in particular. "Maybe we have the majority of the birds because we have Jeff."

"Or Jamie," Denise said quietly.

"You think they're after my daughter?" Jeff said with a growl.

Denise shrugged. "Weren't they before?"

"Yeah, they were. And now we have more hybrids, too."

"Raymond and Rachel aren't hybrids," Kevin pointed out.

"But they're kids, in the Embassy. And, let's be honest—you and Denise are both great looking enough to pass as A-Cs. I wouldn't want to bet that whoever the Peregrines were sent to protect us from would ignore them."

I realized we were saying this in front of the children, and Raymond and Rachel were old enough to understand we were talking about scary people stealing them in the night. A quick glance at their expressions proved I'd indeed freaked them out. I wanted to do or say something to reassure them, and fast.

Before I could open my mouth, their two Peregrines both cooed. At the Poofs. Several Poofs growled back. The Peregrines squawked quietly. The Poofs mewed. This went on for a while.

Jeff sighed. "What's going on?"

I gave up and didn't even pretend I had no idea. "They're arguing. The Poofs don't want to do what the Peregrines are suggesting." The male Peregrine I knew was ours, specifically, looked straight at me. "Oh. Um, Poofies? I know you're all jealous. But the Peregrines are clear—Poofies were here first, and everyone loves the Poofies, so the Peregrines will be good. But my Poofies have to be good, too."

Several Poofs detached from the Poof side of the room and bounded over to the Lewises. "We already have our own Poofs," Denise reminded us.

The Poofs jumped onto their shoulders, purred, and disappeared. "Um, now I think you have more. So that Raymond and Rachel won't need to worry. They'll have their Peregrines and several Poofs. Nothing's going to get any of the kids, not with Poofs and Peregrines on the job, right?"

There was much head bobbing and wing flapping from the flock and a lot of purring from the Poofs.

"Well done, Missus Martini," White said. "Now, children, it's late and we were all awakened rather rudely. Let's deal with everything else in the morning, including moving new residents in more permanently and so forth."

"Dulce will continue to monitor the Embassy," Gladys shared. I'd forgotten she was still on the com. "Will alert Embassy personnel if the Peregrines attack. Or if any more show up."

"Great, Gladys," Jeff said. "Thanks. And good night."

"Dulce out."

Everyone took this as their cue to go back to their beds. Walter's Peregrines went with him, which was interesting. He wasn't a little kid, so I figured they were the flock's version of Security. Which potentially meant the pair with Walter were even more badass than the rest of the flock. Something to contemplate. Tomorrow.

Jeff, Jamie, and I walked down the hall to one of the smaller bedrooms, meaning it was easily as large as my entire apartment had been, back before it had been blown up by my first megalomaniac enemy, aka Ronaldo al Dejahl's father. The remaining members of the flock followed us.

"Peregrines, in here. You sleep in here. Don't destroy anything. Use the toilet. Flush. Or something." Jeff shook his head. "I'm reduced to giving orders to birds. How did we end up here, baby?"

"No clue. Can we go back to bed now?"

The Peregrines filed into the room, flew on top of the bed and settled down. All but one that was clearly on guard duty. Jeff started to close the door and the bird screeched.

"Huh." Jeff closed the door. All the birds started screeching. Great soundproofing or not, apparently a flock of Peregrines could be heard no matter what. He opened the door. Instant quiet. "Wonderful. If I find you've destroyed or messed on anything, you'll all be dinner."

We went back to our bedroom and checked on our Earth animals. They were all huddled together, other than Bellie, who was clinging to her perch. "Wow. The pets don't like the Peregrines, do they? I wonder why not. They're really just big birds."

Bellie looked up. "Bigger birds are coming! Bigger birds are coming!" She didn't sound happy about it. At all.

"Bellie, is that one of Daddy's secrets?"

"Daddy's secrets will help bigger birds! Bellie loves Jeff."

"Jeff loves Bellie," he said soothingly. He moved the Poof Condos back into our room, taking time to pet each Poof. While I held Jamie, Jeff got the cats and petted them, then put them into the biggest Poof Condo.

He ended up picking up each dog, too, even Dudley—and picking up a Great Dane was never for the faint of heart or weak of back—and putting them into their beds. I'd never seen my animals this scared.

Bellie's perch was the last to move. "You okay with her being in the room with us?" he asked me.

I didn't care much for her, but it was obvious the bird was still terrified. "Yes, it's okay. She's too scared to be out in the living room, and I don't think she should be in the nursery alone, either. I assume Jamie's going to spend the rest of the night in bed with us?"

"You know it." Jeff put Bellie's perch next to a Poof Condo. "Bellie needs to be nice to all the other animals," he said to her.

"I'm not positive the cats won't try to eat her, though."

Jeff coughed. "Ah, they tried that already. She's a lot like you—quite the fighter."

"So that's why the other pets got moved out of the bedroom?"

"Somewhat."

"You know, I'd argue about this, but since we have two dozen Peregrines, give or take, down the hall, I'm just going to opt for going to bed and hoping our Animal Kingdom remains peaceful."

We got into bed. Jeff put up a pillow barrier on one side so that Jamie couldn't roll off the bed. Then I wrapped around her and he wrapped around me.

"You know, this was an insane day and an even crazier night, but it's so nice to be snuggled together like this again that I frankly don't care about all the rest of the crap."

Jeff chuckled. "And here I'd thought you'd only missed the great sex."

"Oh, trust me, I missed that more than anything. In fact, I'm kind of bitter that tonight's events have ensured we can't fool around a little more right now."

Jeff kissed the side of my head. "That's what tomorrow's for."

CHAPTER 29

THE NEXT MORNING WAS PRETTY GOOD. The Peregrines hadn't destroyed too much in the bedroom. By that I mean they'd chosen to use the room's bathtub to do their thing and otherwise hadn't clawed up the furniture, drapes, or carpeting. Jeff wasn't amused, but we had nowhere else to put them yet.

Jamie was sleeping through the night now, but the disruption from the night before meant she was a tired, cranky girl when I woke her up for breakfast. We fed her, then Jeff rocked her back to sleep and put her down into her crib.

This enabled us to have yet more sex. I was great with this. Whoever was once again after my husband wasn't going to get him without a lot of pain from me. I'd spent a month without Jeff, I refused to spend longer without him.

Once all of us were up for the second time, we were able to really get up and get going. Jeff had work I couldn't know about to do, but that was fine. I had my own little team, and we had an investigative reporter to round up, a senator to grab, and some special K-9 cops to visit. My day was going to be plenty full.

Jeff put Bellie back into her enclosure. She seemed better today than she had last night. The cats and most of the Poofs stayed in the bedroom. The team Walter had assigned to take care of the dogs arrived, and the dogs practically killed them with love and excitement to leave.

The Peregrine situation was explained to the agents, along with their additional Peregrine cleanup duties. They looked as excited as we felt. I figured it made taking care of the dogs look better. Hey, I was all about the ridiculous optimism sometimes.

"I really hope the Peregrines and the pets get comfortable together. The dogs and cats had no issues at all with the Poofs."

"Don't know what to tell you baby. Maybe it's because the birds are large and not cuddly at all."

"And we have twelve breeding pairs—we could start the Attack Peacock Breeding Program."

"Maybe that's what Alexander wants. Who knows?" He kissed me. "Shall I take Jamie down to Denise on my way?"

"Nah, I'll do it. I may keep her with me today anyway."

"Don't take her into any dangerous situations."

"I won't. I'm just not sure she should spend all day with Denise right now. A few hours here and there when nothing much is going on is fine, but all I'm going to do is visit people who aren't going to attack her."

Jeff grunted. "I'll give you that Senator Armstrong isn't going to do anything to our child, at least not that we could prove."

"Right. We'll be fine, Jeff, I promise."

He sighed. "Fine, baby. Be sure to call or scream emotionally if you need me."

"You know I will."

"I know trouble finds you without any effort on your part." But he stopped arguing, gave Jamie more snuggles, me another kiss, then headed downstairs.

I finished getting dressed. It was springtime now, so it was nice out. I put on my Converse, a pair of comfy jeans, and one of my many Aerosmith shirts. Things were always better with my boys on my chest. I brought along my zippered Lifehouse hooded sweat jacket, because it could still get too cold for me here, and besides, I liked to ensure I had my rock bases covered.

I packed up what Jamie would need and got her stroller out. It was top of the line, a baby gift from Reader. He'd also had every known A-C bell and whistle added onto it, including a laser shield. That had saved not only my and Jamie's lives, but the lives of the boys and Mr. Joel Oliver, too. Operation Assassination had certainly been explosion-filled.

I settled Jamie into the stroller so that she was sitting up but protected by the sunshade. Hung the diaper bag on one strong hook, put my purse over the hook on the other side, draped my jacket over the sunshade.

I was ready to call for the boys when something cooed. It was right by my side. The male Peregrine I was pretty sure had been sent to me, specifically, was there. He looked as though he had every intention of accompanying us on our constitutional.

"You are staying here."

I got another coo and a hurt look.

"I'm going to pay a call on Capitol Hill. I think. But they don't let animals in."

Another hurt look, and a pointed look into the stroller to stare at the Poofs.

"They're smaller. They look like stuffed animals. No one notices. They also can disappear if necessary."

More pointed staring, at the Poofs and me. The bird for sure looked as if its feelings were being hurt.

"It's not safe out there for you."

Got a bird look saying if it wasn't safe for a Peregrine, it certainly wasn't safe for me or Jamie.

"Animal Control will take you away."

Really felt the bird was telling me Animal Control could feel free to "bring it."

"Oh, this sucks. Com on! Walter, can you connect me to Mister White?"

"Yes, Chief. Go ahead."

"Missus Martini, how goes your morning?"

"I have a Peregrine refusing to leave my side, Mister White."

"They are loyal."

"They are a problem. I'm getting ready to gather you and the boys so we can put our plan of talking to Mister Joel Oliver, Senator Armstrong, and our friends in the K-9 squad into action. I'm bringing Jamie along, and we have three attack Poofs with us. I think we're safe. Bruno the Peregrine Enforcer, however, feels otherwise."

White coughed. "Is, ah, Bruno standing there with you?"

"Yes. Why?"

He sighed. "Like the Poofs. . . ."

I looked down. "Bruno?"

The Peregrine bobbed his head, fluffed his feathers, and gave a manly coo.

"He likes it. Bruno it is. But Bruno has to stay here, guarding the manse. I can't go to visit Senator Armstrong to discuss faked dirty pictures with a humongous bird strolling alongside like it's a Labrador."

"Actually, you can. I'll be right up."

I eyed Bruno while we waited. He seemed quite pleased with himself. I wondered what his mate was called. "Your woman would probably prefer that you stay here with her."

Bruno gave me a look that indicated his woman felt the execution of his assigned duties was paramount. I wondered how I'd gone from no idea what went on in a bird's mind to having one-sided yet comprehensible conversations with a space avian.

There was a knock at the door. Bruno went with me to open it. Just like a dog. White was standing there. He looked ready to head out, too. That was good. Right now, nothing else was, so I was happy for any small victory.

"Richard, oh, my God. This is a nightmare."

Bruno ruffled his feathers and gave a quiet squawk. It was clear that I'd insulted him.

"Sorry, Bruno. I just wasn't prepared for your arrival."

Bruno nudged his head against my leg, indicating that he knew I was stressed and all was forgiven.

I looked back at White. "Richard, I'm losing it. I swear to you I'm having conversations with Bruno."

He nodded. "I'm sure you are."

"Oh, I hate it when I make an insane comment and someone says it's natural."

White shook his head. "Probably not natural. As I said last night, it's likely your talent."

"I know you said that last night. And it sounds as ridiculous this morning as it did then. I may be mutated, but how in the world would I inherit some bizarre Doctor Doolittle talent? I've never heard anyone mention speaking with the animals as an A-C talent."

He sighed. "It's not. Which proves my point."

"Not to me. At all. Clueless as to how you're making this leap."

"I realize you don't have what we'd call standard A-C talents. However, you have a natural affinity for animal sciences and an ability to control animal behaviors."

"Have you seen my dogs and cats? Because no one but my mother controls their animal behaviors, least of all me."

"A-C animal behaviors. You control the Poofs."

"They're guardians."

"As we also said last night, they normally only take direction from the head Poof. However, they all take direction from you, and have since they first arrived on Earth. Very rare, believe me. Why do you think Gladys doesn't feel the Poofs are safe? Under normal working conditions, the Poofs make the decision to, ah, eat or not."

I thought about this. When we'd taken on the old, nasty King of Alpha Four, I hadn't asked the Poofs to protect me when Adolphus had attacked me—they'd done it on their own, hence why Adolphus was no more. But they'd also done anything I'd asked them to, including eat up all the former Diplomatic Corps. Hey, I wasn't wild about people who took my men—all my men—and tortured them.

"Well, maybe they're just always in agreement with me."

"Maybe so. Perhaps they're in agreement with you, Missus Martini, because you talk to them in the right way."

"Wonderful. So, you're saying that because I've mutated, said mutation has increased my sensitivity or whatever to A-C animals, and so I can understand them and they can, therefore, understand me?" I thought about it. "Even better than they already understood me, since they understood me before. Right?"

"Well put. Yes, that's exactly what I'm saying. For all we know, it may extend to Earth animals as well."

"Fabulous, and we'll see. I'm more concerned with Bruno staying home. We need to get a move on."

White nodded. "Understood. Why don't you ask, ah, Bruno if he would be willing to go invisible?"

"Oh, no. Really? They go invisible? And this is normal on your planet?"

"Somewhat. These are Royal Guardians. I call it invisible, but it's more that they have the ability to blend in with whatever their surroundings are."

I groaned. "They're chameleons." I looked around. "How many of them are out here, hanging where I can't see them, pretending to be a chair or something?"

"None, since you're not in danger." White took my arm and started to push the stroller out of our rooms. Bruno cooed at him and trotted out with us.

"Bruno still looks like an attack peacock."

"Explain the situation to him."

I sighed. "Bruno, my man, bird, whatever, if you are going to force yourself upon me, then no one can see you, okay? We're not on Alpha Four. On Earth, humongous birds such as yourself live in zoos. They don't waltz around like pets. So, if you plan on waltzing, do it chameleon style."

Bruno bobbed his head, waited until I was looking right at him, and winked.

"Richard? He winked at me."

"Good. You and Bruno have clearly bonded. This is good." We

were in the elevator. Bruno flapped up onto the handle of the stroller.

"Bruno, um, hard to push with you here. And, seriously, if you poop or whatever on my Converse, my Lifehouse jacket, or, God help you, my Aerosmith shirt, you're dinner, bond or no bond."

Bruno fluffed his feathers to indicate he was more than house-trained. He also didn't move. He looked around, pointedly.

"Okay, fine. I understand. It's easier to see and be on guard. Fine, fine. If you'd prefer, you can perch on the front end, but if you poop on Jamie you are a dead bird."

Got the cooing and head bobbing. Bruno was fine with where he was perched, thank you very much.

"Richard, I don't think I can take this."

"Missus Martini, in my experience, there's nothing you are unable to handle. I already advised Len and Kyle to meet us."

The elevator doors opened. Sure enough, the boys were there, ready to go. They gaped at us.

"If you need to walk around with a pet, much as I hate to say it, the dogs are a better choice," Len said.

"I thought you said they could go invisible."

White sighed. "They can. Why would Bruno waste the effort while we're within the Embassy?"

"Oh. Good point."

"They can go invisible?" Kyle didn't sound like this was an exciting bit of news.

"Apparently. And Bruno here is coming with us. Look at it this way—we'll certainly be able to surprise Mister Joel Oliver. For once."

Len shook his head as we reached the front door. "I'm not worried about him. Or even the senator. I'm wondering what the K-9 dogs are going to do."

We all exchanged a look. "Wow. We are so screwed." I sighed. "Or, as we like to call it, routine. So, let's get going and see how bizarre today's going to end up."

CHAPTER 30

I WANTED TO WALK, because it was a nice day and we could use the exercise. However, Len felt we had too many places to go, and Kyle was concerned about using public transportation with Bruno along. Before this debate could turn ugly, White overruled us all, backed Len, and insisted we take a limo.

It wasn't always the best choice for us. The first time we'd tried it here, our limo had exploded. We had fun like that a lot.

I managed to refrain from asking why I'd bothered to get Jamie's stroller all set up nicely if we were going to drive, but before I could, my phone rang. I dug it out of my purse and checked the number.

"Senator Armstrong. It's been so long." Well, it had been in terms of experience. As I thought about it, though, I'd talked to and seen him roughly twenty-four hours ago.

"Ambassador, I heard there was trouble at NASA Base when you went there. Are you alright?"

"I'm fine. I'm rather touched that you're calling to check on my health and welfare." And suspicious. Very suspicious.

The senator was quiet for a few long moments. I remained quiet, too. Hey, I hadn't initiated the phone call. "I believe I need your help."

This was a new one. "I thought you were the one wanting to help me."

"I was and still am." He cleared his throat. "I . . . received new pictures today."

"Great. Who am I supposedly doing the nasty with this time?"

"Ah . . . me."

Well. Apparently I really got around. In someone's imagination, anyway. "You know what's funny?"

"Funny ha-ha or funny strange?"

"Both, I guess. We were planning to visit you today, anyway. To discuss the first set of dirty pictures. So, under the circumstances, do you want us to come to your offices or do you want to meet somewhere else?"

"Who is 'us'?"

"Me, my driver, my bodyguard, and my uncle by marriage." I decided not to mention Jamie, just in case.

"Your husband is still not taking this seriously?"

"Oh, I think he is. But he's a busy man. Busy, busy."

"Aha. You weren't able to take or pass the HSAC test, I presume?"

"I'll ignore the insinuation that I flunked it for now. It relates to the trouble at NASA Base. So, you haven't answered my question."

"I think it would be better to meet in an, ah, neutral location."

"Great. Sheridan Circle Park it is."

"That's hardly neutral."

"We don't own it. And it's nice and close. To me. I don't really care if you're inconvenienced right now. We *were* going to come to you. The mountain to Mohammed and all that sort of thing."

Armstrong sighed. "It's out in the open, where anyone could see us. Under the circumstances, neutral and out of the way of prying eyes would be best."

He had a point. I considered it. "Hang on just a sec." I muted my phone. "Richard, Senator Armstrong wants a meet, and he's asking for neutral ground that's private. I want somewhere we've got more backup than he does. Thoughts?"

"I believe our neighbors across the street should be amenable. Wait a moment." He zipped off at hyperspeed. I saw the Romanian Embassy's door open and shut.

Took my phone off mute. "We're lining up a safe location. Who's coming besides you?"

"No one."

"Not dragging Guy and Vance along for this particular visit?"

"No. Look, I brought them yesterday because I thought you'd want help in determining what to do and how to keep the pictures quiet. Guy and Vance had to hide their relationship for years, and they were willing to help."

Considered this. I was having to consider a lot on this call. Didn't care for it. "So, you're saying you thought the pictures were real?"

"I know your relationship with Mister Reynolds. The pictures look very real. It wouldn't surprise me at all if you two were having an affair."

"Wow, you rock the way with words."

He made the exasperation sound. "I'm not saying you *are*. I'm saying it's not hard to believe, and photographic proof makes it rock solid in most people's minds. And if you were having an affair, I wanted to help you hide it, as did Guy and Vance."

"For favors returned, of course."

"Good lord, you've heard the term 'politics makes strange bedfellows,' I'm sure. Where did you think that came from?"

"Yes, I've heard it. Doesn't mean I want to live it."

"Look, if you think anyone, anywhere, does something only out of the goodness of their hearts, then you're either the stupidest or most naïve person out there. You know as well as I do that there's always a quid pro quo. You're part of an elite group of people who are incredibly influential in certain circles. Of course I want to do a favor for you so you'll do one for me. It's how politics works. Surely someone briefed you about your job, didn't they?"

I'd been given briefing materials. Which I hadn't read. Not willing to share that with my strange bedfellow.

Before I could come up with a suitable retort, the Romanian Embassy door opened and shut again, and a moment later White walked in the door. "We're good."

"Great. Okay, Senator, we've found our neutral yet hidden location. Meet us at the Romanian Embassy."

"Excuse me?"

"Romanian Embassy. Across the street from ours. Lovely people, very secure, very secluded, ergo perfect for our illicit needs. It's there, the park, or my Embassy. Take your pick."

He sighed. "Fine. I'll take the lesser of the evils. I should be to the Romanian Embassy shortly."

"Enjoy the drive." I hung up. "Well, good thing we like Olga and Adriana."

"And that they like us," White agreed. "They're the only ones there today again, so we should be undisturbed."

"Oh, something will happen to disturb us. It always does."

"I believe it's wise that you're expecting trouble," White said.

"Trouble is my BFF, as near as I can tell."

Bruno squawked. I looked at him. He looked back. I got the hint.

"Bruno wants us to bring at least one more member of his flock along."

Bruno bobbed his head. Three times.

"He actually wants three more along. I guess one for each of you. He's not worried about Olga and Adriana, but Bruno prefers to be prepared."

Peregrine head bob, along with a coo indicating that I was the coolest chick on the planet and the smartest, too. I had to say this for the Peregrines—they were great for my self-esteem.

"Fine, but, Bruno, we're not clear on who's who. So, if I send someone upstairs, how will the right birds know?"

Got a look saying that I might be the brightest girl, but sometimes I was denser than dirt.

"Oh. Gotcha. Wait here guys, and Richard, keep an eye on Jamie, please. I'll be right back."

I took the stairs. I needed to practice hyperspeed control anyway. I went at the slow version of hyperspeed, which always sounded like an oxymoron but wasn't. Christopher had been working on this with me almost exclusively in the couple of weeks between the end of Operation Assassination and Jamie's teeth coming in, and I'd continued to practice while in Florida.

I was getting fairly good at the slow hyperspeed as long as there was nothing causing me to stress out and I could use all my focus on it. So I zipped upstairs safely and without any wall damage.

Entered our rooms. "I need three Peregrine Enforcers for a trip all the way across the street to spend time hanging around the Romanian Embassy while I have a meeting. It sounds boring. It'll probably be really dangerous. But there's more danger likely here in our Embassy. So, you know, choose accordingly. No fighting."

Three males and one female detached themselves from the group. I looked at the female. I was pretty sure she was Bruno's mate. "So, Lola, you're coming along too?"

She bobbed her head and fluffed her feathers.

"Ah. Gotcha. Nursemaid, just in case. We have Poofs with us, you know."

Lola shrugged and squawked as if to say that she was considered quite the nursemaid on Alpha Four and that while Poofs had their place, nothing said "your baby is completely safe" like having a Peregrine Enforcement Nursemaid along for the ride.

"Fine, I'm good with it. No crapping in the stroller, on Jamie, on me, and all that jazz rule applies. And definitely no destruction of any kind at the Romanian Embassy. They're our friends and I want to keep it that way. And that order goes out to all of you."

Got looks indicating that every Peregrine worth its badge was more than properly house- and potty-trained and I could stop acting like they were hatchlings.

"The rest of you, um, what should I, in reality, do with you? Everyone stays here?"

Much squawking ensued.

"Oh. Great. I thought only the Poofs could do that here one minute, gone the next thing."

A flock of Peregrines assured me they were able to do whatever and go wherever as needed.

"So why didn't you go with your assigned folks last night?"

Got a lot of "duh" looks. I'd had no idea birds could do that look, but our flock of Peregrines were up to the task.

"Oh. Yeah. Everyone was kind of freaked out. Good to know you'll probably be getting to know the gang as time goes by. Great. Um. Carry on. And all that."

I left, with my new avian friends tagging along. Eyed the three males with me as we headed for the elevator. Why use the stairs when I had this much company? Elevator arrived, we got in, I looked around, and the urge to name overcame me.

"So, boys, one of you is matched to Richard White, yes?" The Peregrine who inclined his head was quite big and studly looking. As Peregrines went. I considered it and realized I knew its name. Lucky me.

Stared at the other two as well. "You're with Len and Kyle, correct?" Bird heads bobbed to indicate that I'd guessed right again. "Neither one of you had better be named Tommy Trojan."

The Peregrines all hooted. Wow. They had a sense of humor. Unreal. And I was feeling pleased that they'd gotten the joke. If I hadn't just been gone for a month, I'd have suggested that I needed a vacation.

The elevator doors opened and we all stepped out.

"Wow," Kyle said. "We get to walk Peregrines instead of dogs."

"I didn't think this job could get any better," Len added with a very straight face.

Ignored them. "This is Lola, Bruno's girl. Richard, your birds are named Samson and Delilah. Kyle, yours are Fred and Wilma. Len, meet Barney. His mate's name is Betty."

The boys gaped. Continued to ignore them. The Peregrines, on the other hand, all hooted, to show how impressed they were with my insightfulness. I gave them each a scritchy-scratch right between their wings. They loved it.

Lola and Bruno wrapped their necks around each other, then she flapped up and settled into the stroller. I took a look. She was in front of Jamie, looking serene. And like a stuffed animal.

"Wow. You know, it's more than camouflage. Lola looks like a bird version of the Poofs."

"They've been bred for this for tens of thousands of years," White shared as he gave Samson a pat.

"Excellent. Well, let's get across the street, while we and our birds enjoy the fresh air for five seconds, and go wait for Senator Armstrong and his latest set of dirty pictures to join us."

CHAPTER 31

OUR SHORT WALK ACROSS THE STREET was uneventful. No one stared at us, which was amazing, since the four male birds looked exactly the same to me out here as they had inside.

"Why haven't they gone invisible?" Kyle asked nervously as we headed toward Romanian soil. "Someone's got to notice us with four big peacocks. I'm not sure it's legal to have animals like this in this city."

I looked around. If Buchanan was nearby, he didn't want me to see him, because there wasn't much going on in the way of activity. Which, all things considered, was unusual, even on a weekend. Maybe especially on a weekend.

"I'm not sure the Ambassadress wants us bringing animals into their Embassy," Len added.

Bruno looked at me and warbled. The complete insanity of me talking to the birds and them talking right back was becoming commonplace. How nice.

"They're visible to anyone they're assigned to, at all times, unless it's vital to said person's wellbeing that they aren't seen. So, right now, we can see any and all of our selection of the Peregrine Enforcement Squad, even if no one else can. Oh, and Bruno says that if they need to go, they'll let me know, but otherwise, everyone can stop stressing."

"Mister Joel Oliver is going to have a field day with these things," Len added.

Which reminded me. I stopped walking before we reached the Romanian Embassy's front door, dug my phone out, and dialed.

"Ambassador Katt-Martini. How lovely to hear from you. And welcome home."

I didn't ask how he knew. He always knew. For someone not working in covert or clandestine ops or possessing A-C talents, Oliver was the best-informed person around. In my experience there were only a handful of other people this aware of what was going on. I knew Olga stayed up on things in part by reading Oliver's articles. Chuckie did, too. I knew some of Chuckie's other sources, but did wonder if Oliver knew them, too—or if, rather, *they* knew *him*. Well, wasn't important at this precise time.

"Hey, MJO. Nice to be back, thanks. We've been planning to drop by to discuss dirty pictures with you."

"I didn't take any of those."

"No one took them. They're doctored."

"They looked very real. I tested them."

"I'm sure you did. Our tests, as I know you know, are better."

"True enough. I've blocked the *World Weekly News* from printing them."

"Wow, you have that much pull?"

"In a sense. I explained there was no way the Royal Family would ever allow me access again if our paper chose to take the low road. My editor understood and agreed. I doubt any other papers will be so discreet."

"I'm sure you're right. And thank you. I have a new scoop for you, too, that I need you to be discreet about."

"Oh?"

"But I don't want to tell you over the phone in case, as is so likely, our phones are tapped."

"I'd love a visit."

"I'm sure you would." I told him where we were and suggested he hurry it up, and we got off the phone.

"It's faster if he and the senator come to us," Len said. "I get that. But why do you want Mister Joel Oliver here right now?"

"I want someone with us who's likely to know what the hell is going on that no one can tell me about so he can let us know when the senator's lying."

"He's not an empath," Kyle pointed out. "So how will he know?"

"Empaths can be fooled, just like anyone else. But MJO has all the news that's fit and unfit to print, so he's got a really good BS meter." At least, so I hoped. "Besides, I think Olga will get a kick out of him."

"True," White said. "She *is* a fan."

As per her usual, Adriana opened the door and let us in before we could knock. Since White had been by already, she and Olga were briefed, at least somewhat.

The issue of what to do about the Peregrines turned into a moot point. I knew we were all waiting for Adriana to make a comment, but she didn't.

I left the stroller downstairs and took Jamie out of it. She held onto her Poof, and Harlie and Poofikins went into my purse, which I slung onto my shoulder. Lola hopped out of the stroller, leaving the rest of the Poofs with us on stroller guard duty. Adriana didn't see Lola, or if she did, Olga had trained her well enough that she didn't blink when a big bird jumped out of a baby's stroller.

Nor did she blink when four other big birds trotted upstairs right along with the rest of us. Clearly White was right, and Bruno hadn't overstated Peregrine abilities in any way.

Olga was in her study and Jamie squealed with joy to see her. I handed her over for snuggles as Adriana brought in refreshments. In addition to the usual lemonade there was also iced tea. The usual assortment of small cakes and cookies were complemented with some fresh fruit. Adriana clearly spent her downtime in the kitchen.

Once the goodies were up, Adriana went back downstairs to wait for the rest of our visitors. There were plenty of chairs in here again, so the rest of us settled down and made inconsequential small talk.

"Looks like Mister Joel Oliver's here," Kyle said. "At least I'm pretty sure that's him getting out of a taxi."

Considering the senator was likely physically closer and had his own driver, this was more than a little unexpected. I got up and checked the taxi driver out as well as I could from the study's window—no one I recognized. Oliver went to the door, the taxi drove off. Like normal. How refreshing. I went back to my chair, snagging another couple of cookies on the way.

Oliver was escorted upstairs and official introductions made, then Adriana went back down to wait for the senator. Olga was clearly quite pleased to meet Oliver. I wondered if she'd feel the same way about Armstrong, but knew I'd find out shortly.

Oliver didn't mention the Peregrines and I didn't bring them up. We were still waiting for Armstrong, but I wanted to get Oliver and Olga briefed so they'd have an idea of what was going on. However, it was somewhat embarrassing, and I really didn't know where to start. Back to the inconsequential small talk. "So, does anyone else think the foot traffic is a little light for a Sunday?"

Oliver shook his head. "It would be, but there's the huge event at the Mall. I'm sure most people from this part of town are there." Olga nodded.

"What kind of event?" White asked. "We haven't heard anything about it."

Oliver looked surprised. "I'd have thought you'd have been briefed immediately."

So whatever was going on at the Mall likely related to whatever I was now no longer qualified to hear. No worries. Oliver didn't know that. "We've been a little distracted. By the dirty pictures." Well, we'd been distracted by them yesterday, at least until Sandra the Android attacked, and they were the focus of my team's investigation, so it wasn't a total lie.

"You haven't heard about the International One World Festival?" Oliver sounded as shocked as he looked. "It's going on all week, but the President's kicking it off today." He checked his watch. "In about an hour."

"Don't tell me, let me guess. American Centaurion is helping the P.T.C.U. and whoever else with security."

"Yes. Well, Centaurion Division is. Not Embassy personnel, at least not officially. However, after the Titan Security disaster, the Office of the President requested that Centaurion Division assist the Secret Service and P.T.C.U. on this one. No one wants anything to go wrong, and in addition to the usual concerns, the current tensions between Israel and Bahrain have upped the threat levels."

"Meaning my mom's on duty, right?" And probably stuck in some awkward middle position politically, being former Mossad.

Oliver nodded.

It dawned on me that my parents hadn't called me at all this weekend. They'd called every day I was in Florida. I'd been too busy to register it before this moment, but they had to know I was back. And yet they hadn't come by to see me or Jamie. I'd have been hurt, but the reason was clear—Mom didn't want to lie to me and Dad couldn't.

Oh, sure, they'd lied to me for most of my life, but once I'd discovered aliens truly lived on Earth, they'd come across with a lot more information. Mom didn't have a problem telling me that something was above my security clearance normally, but since my HSAC test had ended up as a disaster, would anyone believe she wasn't telling me things? I hated Sandra and her creators and handlers just a little bit more.

"So, are we supposed to be there in an, ah, ambassadorial capacity?" Because if we were, I was going to be glaringly absent.

"Not so much, no. Though every diplomatic mission in the city is expected to provide some form of support and attendance. Most of the Embassies have had personnel over all this past week, setting up."

Olga nodded again. "That's where all of our mission was yesterday. And where they are today, as well. I confess to being surprised that no one has told you about it."

Wow. Our lack of intel had surprised two of the best-informed people around. Wonderful. "We've been a little distracted."

Oliver had stressed that it was Centaurion Division assisting. This meant Alpha, Airborne, Field, and Imageering would be involved, with Field teams out and about, doing their protect the world thing. American Centaurion was the political way of referring to us, and always indicated Embassy personnel and the Pontifex, when he was giving face time versus kicking butt. So Oliver's explanation made sense, but left something lacking. "MJO, what's American Centaurion's role?"

Oliver gave me a long look. "So, the story was true."

CHAPTER 32

"WHAT STORY?" WHITE ASKED PLEASANTLY.
"The story about the Ambassador no longer having a high-level security clearance."

Olga looked concerned. "I so wish this were not so. You being kept, as you say, out of the loop, is not a good thing."

"I'm not thrilled with it, either, but it lets us look into the dirty pictures business and hopefully get that put to bed. Bad pun totally intended."

"Ah, yes," Olga said. "Your plan."

"You sound as underwhelmed by the idea today as you did yesterday."

She jiggled Jamie, who giggled. "There is nothing wrong with your plan."

"Only you think more is going on. Maybe it is." I looked at White. "Should I catch them up on everything before the senator gets here?" This was a trick question. We were here to catch them up. But it seemed stupid to ask if we should mention our invisible birds or not, which was what I wanted his advice about.

White was nothing if not intelligent. He looked at the birds, which were nestled happily at our feet, then back at me. "Within reason, yes. Or we tell them nothing. But we did request this meeting."

I got his point. Keep the Peregrines our secret weapons right now. If a couple dozen big birds could really be considered either secret or weapon. Then again, Olga and Oliver seemed blissfully unaware of the birds in their midst. I sniffed surreptitiously. Like the Poofs, the Peregrines didn't give off much of an odor. I appreciated this trait in Alpha Four's animals.

"In for a penny, might as well toss over the whole checkbook?"

"So to speak. I believe if we want Madame Ambassadress and Mister Joel Oliver's assistance, we need to give them all the details."

Oliver nodded. "I'll keep everything in the strictest confidence. You have my word on that."

When we'd first met him, I'd have laughed my head off at the idea that a tabloid journalist was trustworthy. But Oliver had been a lot more trustworthy, helpful, and supportive than people who were supposedly our friends and on our side.

"Should Adriana hear this?" I asked Olga.

"I will give her the pertinent details." She smiled. "Securely."

"Never had a doubt about that." I brought Oliver and Olga up to speed quickly on the senator's visit in Florida, the "fun" we'd had at NASA Base and its ultimate HSAC Fail for me, the fact that I was actually now firmly out of the classified loop, and that Armstrong had new pics featuring him as my latest costar.

In addition to not mentioning our Special Delivery from the night before, I also fudged about how NASA Base had gotten damaged—per Chuckie and Reader, I was still supposed to be a secret weapon, and I wasn't sure how much either Olga or Oliver knew or merely suspected.

Finished up and took a deep breath. "Of course, yesterday, Malcolm Buchanan and Olga suggested that all of this was just for distraction purposes."

"It could be," Oliver agreed. "But it sounds like an effective distraction doing double duty." Olga nodded her agreement.

"So, distraction technique or not, Richard and the boys have chosen to remain clueless so we can actually still function as a team. And we have the latest set of dirty pictures coming for our viewing pleasure. If Senator Armstrong ever gets here."

Oliver closed his eyes, clearly in thought. "I'd assume the senator is having to extract himself from the One World festivities, which is why I beat him here."

"I don't get why he'd leave something like that just to bring the latest blackmail pictures by."

Olga snorted, and Oliver opened his eyes. "I'd assume because he's terrified his political career is about to be destroyed."

"He could never recover," Olga agreed. "It would not do you any good, either. Or anyone associated with you."

"Fabulous, not that this comes as a surprise." I didn't want to contemplate the reaction from the A-C community if anyone actually believed I'd been sleeping with both Chuckie and the senator. But a question shoved in and I gladly took my mind off the Scenario From Hell. "Is Armstrong eyeing a run for the Presidency?"

"Yes," Oliver said. "He has been for a while now."

"Okay, fine, I get why someone would want to blackmail a Presidential hopeful with potential to at least get his party's nomination." I might dislike Armstrong, but I was aware and astute enough to know he was a political animal and friends with many of the "right people." "But I don't understand why they'd choose me as his suspected affair. Especially since they already tried with me and Chuckie and got no reaction."

White cocked his head. "Did they, in fact, get no reaction?"

"Well, Jeff hasn't killed Chuckie, and the pictures haven't hit the streets yet. Armstrong came to warn me, at least that's what he said, and right now, I sort of believe him."

"So perhaps they didn't get the reaction they *wanted*," Oliver said.

Olga beamed at him. Oh, good. Another one racing to the head of the class. I'd have resented it, but at least I kept the smart ones close by. Besides, I was Questions Girl. At least right now.

"Related question. Why was Armstrong in Florida most of the time I was, especially if there was some big political event being planned?"

"Cover, maybe?" Oliver suggested.

"Or he wanted to enlist your aid," White countered.

"But I thought the pictures only showed up a couple of weeks ago, not four."

Oliver shook his head. "*I* only found out about them a couple of weeks ago. But I assure you, they were in existence before I discovered them."

"So maybe the senator had them for a lot longer than we know about." He'd been trying to see me for a month, after all.

"Limo approaching," Kyle, who was close to the window that faced Sheridan Circle, said before I could ask what kind of aid anyone thought I'd be able to give Armstrong in regard to my new career as an unwitting porno model.

Len looked out the window. "Looks like the same car that he was in yesterday."

"You're sure? Limos tend to look alike."

"I'm sure. We had to take a course."

"Len aced that one like he aced driving," Kyle added. "I did pretty well with it, too. And I agree. It looks like the same car. And it's got that 'drove all night and haven't hit the car wash yet' look. Parking down the street."

I decided to trust them on this assumption. It took about sixteen hours to drive up from Florida to D.C., but Armstrong had had more than enough time to do so. "Yesterday he left a briefcase with a bug in it at my in-laws' home."

"We'll assume he's recording us again, then," White said.

"Good call."

"We have detectors with us," Len said.

"We do as well," Olga added.

"Great, so if we don't like Armstrong's answers, he'll be on Romanian soil, and you can accuse him of spying or treason, or whatever your biggest crime is."

Olga laughed. "I love how you think. We must ensure you are not disgraced. I will be heartbroken if we should lose you as a neighbor."

CHAPTER 33

LEN AND KYLE WENT DOWNSTAIRS so they could scan the senator before he got past the foyer. Apparently he passed both the Romanian and C.I.A. Bug Tests because the boys brought him upstairs fairly quickly.

"You," Armstrong said by way of hello, pointing at Oliver. "Why are you here?"

"I was invited by Ambassador Katt-Martini."

Armstrong glared at me. "You want this to be trumpeted to the world?" He sounded angry and shocked. This was the first time I'd ever heard him really out of control of his Happy Politician Voice.

"No. I want whoever's done this stopped. And Mister Joel Oliver is far more on my side than you've ever been."

Armstrong opened his mouth. But Olga spoke first. "Don't say something you might regret, Senator. You're not on American soil."

Armstrong's mouth slammed shut. He glared at all of us. "This is ridiculous. Why do you want an audience for this?"

"Oh, I figure it's always wise to be sure they only print pictures of my good side. Like to have everyone vote on which shots we think are best."

"All your sides are good," Len said loyally. Kyle nodded his agreement. I was glad Jeff wasn't here—I was enjoying not having to have the jealousy chat with him.

"You can't be serious." Armstrong sounded horrified and a little repulsed. Charming as always.

"Dude, did I *sound* serious? Look, you're stressed. We all get it. Sit down, have some lemonade or iced tea, eat a couple of those little cakes, you'll feel better. Mister Joel Oliver is the only reason my first set of poses for Playmate of the Year haven't already hit the newsstands. Let's stop with the posturing and protestations and get down to business."

Armstrong didn't look as though he actually wanted to sit, but he did. He kept his briefcase in his lap. It was definitely not the same one he'd left at Martini Manor.

I looked at Len. He shook his head. "Clean."

"Of course I didn't bring any bugs with me," Armstrong snapped.

"And that would be the first time in our entire relationship when you haven't."

He had the grace to look slightly ashamed. "I can't be too careful."

"I know. You'd miss out on so many blackmail opportunities. Speaking of which, let's see the latest shots."

Armstrong looked pointedly at Olga. "I'm not sure that's a good idea."

Olga smiled. "Senator, I can assure you that I am the soul of discretion."

"Dude, Olga knows everything, all the time. I have no idea how she knows, mind you, but she does. Her Magic 8-Ball is never wrong. If it's relevant to her interests, she probably knows what you had for dinner last night. Stop being coy. She's our friend and we trust her. You're the one we're not sure about."

"Have it your way." He opened the briefcase and handed a folder to me.

I pulled the pictures out. "Huh."

"What?" White asked. "Oh, and when do the rest of us get to see them?"

"I want to show them to you in front of Jeff. It's so much more satisfying that way." I looked at Armstrong. "Was there a note with these?"

"No. With the set that showed you and Reynolds there was. But these just arrived this morning in that envelope."

It was an amazingly bland envelope, your typical manila that usually held boring documents for safe delivery. The address was Armstrong's D.C. one, no return address listed.

"Senator, did the other pictures go to you in D.C., too?"

"Yes."

I looked at the pictures some more. As with the set costarring Chuckie, I appeared to be having quite the good time. In fact, it was a very familiar time. I dug my phone out. "Hey, Christopher, are you anywhere close to home?" I could hear background noises that certainly didn't sound as if they were emanating from our Embassy.

"Ah, not really. Why?"

"We have new dirty pictures."

"Great. Need me to read them?"

"Yeah, but I need you to think back to the ones of me and Chuckie first."

"If I must."

"You must. If you can."

"Not hard, I read them yesterday." Nice to see he was at Full Snark Level.

"Goody. Look, is it possible for you to, I don't know, timestamp them?"

"Wow, a new Kittyism. Want to translate that for normal people?"

"Since when are you considered normal?"

"You know what I mean."

"Yes, I do. Okay, what *I* mean is—could you get a read on when each picture happened? As in, what day or month or whatever it was that my picture was taken from, and the same for when Chuckie's picture was taken from?"

He was quiet for a few seconds. "You mean, was each person photographed last week or last year, that sort of thing?"

"Yes."

"Hang on." He was quiet for a longer while. "Yeah, I think . . . I think your picture was from about a year ago. But Reynolds . . ." I waited. "Reynolds' picture was only from a month or so ago."

"Interesting." Very, very interesting. "Barring you killing a superbeing or saving someone's life, I think I need you at the Romanian Embassy five seconds ago."

Christopher sighed. "I'll clear it with Jeff and James and be right there."

"Use a floater gate or the really fast hyperspeed. Olga has refreshments." This wasn't said so much as a lure, since Christopher was, like Jeff, a very healthy eater. But when he used his Super Flash Level Hyperspeed, he needed to replenish, and he preferred food to sleep for it under most circumstances.

"Got it. Be there soon."

I hung up and looked back to Armstrong. "Senator, do you remember when you might have been doing whichever sexual positions you're photographed in?" I handed the pictures back to him.

Len, Kyle and White all got up and stood behind him. Oliver

smiled at me, then joined them. Wonderful. I looked at Olga. She was laughing quietly while she snuggled Jamie.

He thumbed through them and shook his head. "Not really. They're, ah, a little more, um . . ."

"Athletic?" Len suggested.

"Wild?" Kyle said.

"More like what I'd expect to see from Jeffrey," was White's quite insightful statement. "At least, based on my memories from when we were all housed at the Dulce Science Center."

Before I could reply or think up a suitable comeback, Adriana stuck her head in. "Excuse me, Ambassadress, but we have another arrival."

Christopher came in. A-Cs never sweated—even the hottest days in Pueblo Caliente were cooler than their home planet—but he wasn't breathing hard, either. Superpowers were where it was at.

I got up and grabbed the pictures. "I need you to read these," I said without any introductory preamble. Hey, things were going from weird to weirder by the second. "I know they're doctored. I know that's really me, though I was not, of course, having a fling with the senator here. I think the head is really Senator Armstrong's. I happen to believe the body is Jeff's, however. Only doctored. A lot."

Christopher took the pictures and put his hand on them and closed his eyes.

While he was doing this White studied the senator. "I realize he's built roughly like Jeffrey. But he's at least two decades older, and that shows in photographs."

"That could easily be achieved using age advancement techniques," Oliver said. "It's done for movies all the time, and law enforcement uses it regularly to catch criminals and kidnapped or missing children, among many other options."

"No one's going to look too closely. If the head doesn't seem wrong on the neck, then it looks real to ninety-nine-point-nine percent of the public."

Christopher opened his eyes. "It's you. From last night."

"That's what I thought. Can you tell a difference in the Armstrong makeup?"

"Yeah, but it's difficult. The brain and face are where we get most input from. And Mister Joel Oliver's right—the senator's body has been fiddled with a lot more than yours."

"Fiddled with? Is that a technical term?"

I was treated to Patented Glare #2. "It's very hard to read. The head is definitely the senator's. From a few months ago, I think. The body, though . . . it's hard to be positive, but I don't think it's his. It feels . . . familiar, so I'm willing to say it's Jeff's body."

"Thought so." I made another call. "James, I know you're busy."

"Like you wouldn't believe, girlfriend."

"Well, let me add a wrinkle. I'm calling you because I know if I call Gladys directly she'll ask me if I have your okay."

"On pins and needles."

"I actually figure you're on duty, but whatever. Senator Armstrong received new dirty pictures today. Only instead of me with Chuckie, I've branched out and am with the senator, having the time of my life."

He groaned. "Can it get worse?"

"Oh, yes. Yes, it can. This is what I pulled Christopher away for." As I said this Christopher made the "shut up, shut up" motions.

"What do you mean?" Reader sounded pissed. "He left his post? Why wasn't I informed?"

"Um, political emergency. And I'm claiming diplomatic immunity for us both. Anyway, snarl once you know the full details."

"Can't wait. Go ahead."

"The part of the picture that's me is from last night. And I think someone superimposed Armstrong's head onto Jeff's body and then did some really fancy photoshopping."

Reader was quiet for a couple moments. "How in the hell did someone get intimate pictures of the two of you from last night?"

"You've won Jeopardy's Daily Double! That's exactly my question. I'd love someone from Centaurion Division to give me an answer that isn't going to make Jeff pop a vessel, but I'm not betting any of us are going to like the answer."

"The Embassy was scanned several times last night," Len said. "Because of—"

"Circumstances," White interrupted quickly.

"Right," I said. "Len reminds us that the Embassy was scanned a lot last night. And these pictures are from, um, before that happened."

"Jeff said something about weird gifts from Alpha Four, but we've been too busy to get all the details."

"Not to worry, I'll fill you in later. So, aside from the fact that someone, yet again, is too cheap to buy their own porn and has decided to choose the American Centaurion Channel for all their video needs, what the hell do we do?"

"I have no idea."

"Great."

"I could try to turn straight and we could run away from all this."

"That, as always, sounds like such a wonderful plan. You never keep up your end of it, though."

"Oh, I keep my end up all the time."

"I knew you were going to say that, the moment the words left my mouth. So, going to make good on your teasing?"

"Nope, sorry, still gay."

"Paul's lucky."

"So's Jeff. At least, we were all lucky before. I'm not so sure about now. I wish to hell you'd passed that HSAC test. I need to run things by you like nobody's business."

"I'll bet. So, until you turn straight or I get another chance to take that test and see what happens, what do we do about these pictures?"

"I'll have Gladys run every scan we can do on the Embassy."

"Run Chuckie's place, too. I'd thought his picture was from a lot longer ago than Christopher says it is."

"Fabulous. Should we do the same for Senator Armstrong's places?"

I thought about it. "No. I'm sure they took his head from any number of sources. He's a public figure, plenty of pictures to use."

"Gotcha. And that makes sense. How soon will the pictures hit the street?"

"No idea. There was no note in the senator's Express Porn Package."

"Okay. I have no idea what our next move is or should be. We're very tied up here."

"At the International One World Festival?"

"Could be."

"Super. I'm going to figure out what's going on, you know. One way or another."

Reader dropped his voice. "Good. And do it sooner rather than later."

"Doing my best, James."

"Yeah? Do what you really do best, girlfriend. Ask a lot of questions, whatever pops into your mind, and don't stop asking."

"Why?"

"That's exactly what I mean. Love you, babe." And with that, he hung up.

CHAPTER 34

I CONTEMPLATED MY MANY OPTIONS and chose to look at the pictures again. Reader wanted me asking questions, and my bet was he specifically wanted me asking one question. "Why?"

"Why what?" Olga asked.

There were a lot of why's that what could be about. I tried to boil them all down to their most basic level. "Why is this happening?"

"Someone wants to blackmail me," Armstrong said.

"Yeah? Then why were the first pictures sent to you of me and Chuckie?"

"They wanted to blackmail Mister Reynolds," Len suggested, though he didn't sound convinced.

"Then why send them to the senator, not to Chuckie?" I missed being able to do this with Reader, Tim, the flyboys, Lorraine and Claudia, Chuckie. I was used to going through all the weird with them. I couldn't call Mom, Dad, or Jeff, either. I only had the people in this room and possibly Buchanan, who was who knew where and likely only able to drop hints the way Reader had.

"Is that the proper question?" Olga asked. Perfect. This meant she probably knew. I'd be annoyed about it later. If Olga knew, or had a really good guess, then we could hit onto the right idea, and she'd let us know it *was* the right idea.

A thought occurred. "Could Adriana come up and help with this?"

Olga looked pleased. "Why, yes. She is not aware of . . . everything."

"Good. I guess."

Adriana walked in the door. "You needed me, Ambassadress?"

"How in the world did you know?" Everyone looked at me. I thought about it. "Oh. Duh. Olga's confined to a wheelchair for the most part. You have an I've Fallen and I Can't Get Up button, don't you?"

Adriana laughed. "Of course she does."

Eyed Olga's wheelchair. It looked both sturdy and maneuverable. It also looked different from the one she'd had when we first met her; more like the sports-type chairs para-athletes used. There might indeed be a small keypad or similar in the armrests. Figured now wasn't the time to ask if Olga had joined a wheelchair basketball team and chose to get back to the situation at hand.

"Great, we're now all here. So, why send an android to kill me?"

"WHAT?" Armstrong looked freaked out.

"The 'trouble' at NASA Base was an android trying to kill me."

He looked shaken. "I heard there was a problem, but I had no idea . . ."

"Who did you hear it from?" White asked.

Armstrong rolled his eyes. "I'm a senator for the great state of Florida. Things that happen at NASA Base affect me and my constituents. I'm always informed when we have security issues." He shook his head. "But I was only told there was some structural damage."

"There was." I brought Armstrong and, technically, Adriana up to speed on all the goings on from the day before, again leaving out anything that could let them guess I'd become Wolverine with Boobs and that we now possessed the Peregrines, all of whom appeared to be snoozing. So much for that Alert Avian Guardian hype. "So, that sort of brings me to what I'd consider the ultimate question right now."

"Which is?" Armstrong asked, rather testily. Oh well, it'd been a long weekend so far for everyone.

"Why me?"

"Why not you?" Kyle said.

"No. We need to think and think hard." Reader had said why was the question. "Why is this going on? Why now, why me, why Sandra the Android? Why give me the crazy HSAC test instead of the real one? Why send dirty pictures of me and Chuckie to someone in politics who is not actually our friend?"

Len nodded. "It would make more sense if they'd sent them to Senator McMillan." McMillan was one of Arizona's senators, and therefore my home state guy. My sorority sister and bestie, Carolyn, worked for him, too, as his Girl Friday. I knew McMillan now, and liked him very much, and I knew he liked me.

Armstrong nodded slowly. "True. I hadn't thought about it. I assumed I was sent the pictures because I work closely with you and Reynolds, and I'm involved in a variety of committees and such that affect American Centaurion and Centaurion Division."

"So, I ask again, why me? I get that you work with me and Chuckie. But until this weekend, I would have never assumed you'd be on our side, ever."

Armstrong had the grace to look a little embarrassed again. "Politics, you know. I don't dislike you. Or Mister Reynolds, for that matter."

I snorted. "Right. Because you do so much for him."

He shrugged. "He's a brilliant young man and quite driven. Men like him can be very dangerous." I opened my mouth and he put his hand up. "I'm not saying he's a bad guy, if you will. But brilliant, driven people tend to muck up the works. Or they take over. Or both."

It was there. It was right there, tickling my mind. But I couldn't quite get it. I looked at Oliver. "You said earlier that you wondered if the reactions everyone had were the expected ones, didn't you?"

"Somewhat. I said that I wondered if the reactions your husband and the senator had to the first set of pictures were the reactions the picture takers and/or picture senders *wanted*."

"What would they want?" White asked. "Or, rather, what would they expect?"

"Normally, I'd have expected to see the pictures all over the newspapers or be asked for blackmail money," Armstrong replied.

"But neither have happened," Oliver pointed out.

"Senator, when did you get the pictures, the first set?"

"The day after you left D.C. for Florida. The note with them said there were things I needed to be aware of, and that was it."

I rolled this around in my mind. But it was me, so in order to have the rolling do any good, I had to run my mouth. Never a problem. "So, before I ask some obvious questions, let me ask one that's not so obvious. How did you and Esteban Cantu avoid being caught for Operations Confusion and Assassination?"

"Excuse me?" Armstrong sounded shocked out of his mind.

Christopher sighed. "There were major infiltration attempts when Kitty gave birth to Jamie, and then during the President's Ball."

"And you call them Operation Confusion and Operation Assassination?" Armstrong still sounded as though he couldn't believe his ears. No idea why. The names I came up with for things actually made sense.

"No," Christopher replied. "That's what Kitty calls them. They have no official names, because they weren't sanctioned actions."

White cleared his throat. "Well, the first one does have an official name—The Parisian Action."

"That sounds like an action movie starring Robert DeNiro and Matt Damon."

Len and Kyle laughed. I got Patented Glare #1 from Christopher. White went on as if I hadn't said anything. "I believe the other is referred to as the Titan Security Fiasco."

"Aptly put. My names are better, of course."

"Is now really the time?" Christopher sounded strained. Maybe he'd overdone it getting to us.

"Probably not. So, Senator, how'd you escape the P.T.C.U.'s net? Let alone the C.I.A.'s. And how did Cantu?"

"I had nothing to do with either one of those things. I have no idea what you're talking about in terms of Operation Confusion or The Parisian Action. As for what happened at the President's Ball, I was in as much danger as everyone else. I'd have been shot if an A-C agent hadn't saved me in time."

"Your wife wasn't along."

"She had food poisoning. I was thankful once all the shooting started, believe me. Even though she had to stay overnight at the Andrews hospital."

"Why did you have your wife go to the Air Force base?"

He gave me the "duh" look. How nice. "It's more secure. I'm a public official."

Christopher, Len and Kyle were all texting. I decided to forge on while they waited for the answers to the questions I knew they were asking. "So, why didn't Cantu bring a date?"

"I don't know. I don't ask him about his personal life. He's divorced and I don't share the female need to fix every single friend of mine up with anyone. Besides, he's more of a colleague than a friend, per se."

"Define the difference."

Armstrong shot me a glare almost worthy of Christopher. "Friends are people you choose to spend time with. Colleagues are people you work with and with whom you form alliances."

"Nice distancing."

Armstrong snorted. "Look, I'll say this to you again—politics makes strange bedfellows. Esteban and I are both hoping to . . . achieve higher offices than we have. We help each other whenever we can, but that doesn't make us friends. He'd say the same thing."

He appealed to White. "You, sir, as the former Pontifex, certainly understand what I'm saying."

"Oh, I do. I'm sure Missus Martini does, as well. Whether or not we believe you is the question of the moment, Senator."

"Well, he's not lying about his wife," Christopher said, looking at his phone. "She was held overnight due to a bad case of food poisoning." He looked at Armstrong. "It says you were sick, as well."

"Yes, but I recovered faster. And while I could excuse my poor wife, for me to miss the President's Ball would have been career suicide."

"Where did you eat? That gave you the food poisoning, I mean."

Everyone looked at me like I was crazy. Everyone but Olga. She looked quietly pleased. Nice to know I was on the right track.

"We had dinner with . . ." Armstrong's voice trailed off.

"With whom?"

"With Madeline Cartwright and Antony Marling. And Esteban and the others who we brought to your Embassy to meet you."

Or, as I called them, the Cabal of Evil. "Were you at a restaurant?"

"No. Antony's home."

"Interesting. So, she wanted you alive and out of it."

"She?" Armstrong sounded surprised.

"Madeline was the brains of the Titan team." I looked at his expression. "Seriously? You didn't know?"

"No."

I considered. Decided I needed to be really sure. Dug out the phone again. "Be right back."

Left the room and dialed. He answered on the first ring. "Hey, baby, what's going on?"

"Hi, Jeff. Intrigue and all the rest of the usual crap. Listen, can you do a long-distance reading on Senator Armstrong?"

"Uh, sure. I have to find him, though."

"He's not with you right now, he's with me. So, um, track on me and Christopher and Richard and you should find him."

"I'm not even going to ask."

"Because you're reading my mind?"

"No. Because I'm listening to the tone of your voice. Hang on." Jeff was quiet for a little bit. "Okay, got him. He's upset, feels incredibly betrayed, suspicious, and . . . frightened. He's very frightened."

"Of whom?"

"Of you."

"Me?"

Jeff chuckled. "You've apparently impressed him. I can feel him comparing you to Reynolds and not liking what he's coming up with."

"He thinks I'm as smart as Chuckie?" Maybe I'd consider liking Armstrong somewhere down the road.

"Something along those lines, yeah. He's also really angry with some people right now. So angry I can feel it directly focused."

"Can you tell who?"

"Yeah. The late Madeline Cartwright and Antony Marling, and Esteban Cantu."

"You're reading his mind, aren't you?"

"Not really." He sounded evasive.

"Explain the not really portion."

Jeff sighed. "You and Christopher aren't the only ones who've been working on managing your stronger powers, you know. I want to be ready for whatever Jamie's going to need and whatever new, frightening talents you're going to come up with. So I've been working on emotional refinement, by which, before you ask, I mean filtering the emotional threads into clearer images. It's like what I can do when I read your mind, but you're still the only one I can really do that with."

"Good."

"You don't want me reading someone else's mind?"

"No. You're not the only one with jealousy issues. I like that I'm the only one you can read that way. Not that I'd tell you not to try, since it could save our lives somewhere down the line, I'm sure. But still."

He chuckled. "Not to worry. You're still the only one for me, baby, heart, mind, and soul."

"I wish you were here, right now."

"Me too. But it doesn't sound like we could be alone."

"Sadly, no. So, can you tell if Armstrong is lying about not knowing anything about Operation Confusion or Operation Assassination?"

"I'll try." While he was quiet I basked in the glow of still being his main emotional focus. Hey, it had been a long month apart. "I've got . . . something. I can't be really positive, but I'd say that the anger at Cantu, Marling, and Cartwright is focused around confusion and strong feelings of being out of control and shoved aside."

"Sounds like he was telling the truth."

"Maybe. I wouldn't trust him."

"He needs us more than we need him right now. The enemy of my enemy is my friend. At least sometimes." Usually the enemies of our enemies ganged up and worked against us together, but hope liked to spring eternal.

"Okay, be careful. Keep Christopher with you. I'll cover what he was doing."

"That you can't tell me about, I know. You be careful, too."

"Love you baby. Don't get into anything with Jamie along."

"Love you, too, and I'll do my best, as always."

"That's what worries me."

CHAPTER 35

REJOINED THE OTHERS. "Okay, I'm willing to believe the senator for the time being."

"I'm telling you the truth, of course you should believe me."

I snorted. "You're a politician. Of course most of what you say is a lie, half-truth, or a statement filled with deniable plausibility."

Armstrong stared at me. "You're a lot smarter than anyone thinks, aren't you?"

"You're not really good with compliments, are you?"

"Whatever," Christopher said. "Where are we? Besides our usual nowhere, I mean."

"Are we expecting anyone else?" Len asked as he looked out the window that faced our Embassy.

"Not that I know of." Looked around. No one else indicated they'd invited anyone else to our impromptu party. I joined Len at the window. Most of the others joined us.

There wasn't a lot of legal street parking around here, so the several nondescript cars double-parking on both sides of our street were sort of obvious.

"They're purposefully dirty," Len said.

"No argument." These cars had either spent the last month off-roading—which seeing as none were SUVs seemed unlikely—had just driven through the biggest and wettest dust storm ever, or had gone through the dirt car wash. "It's amazing they can see out of the windows."

The dirt mobiles' passengers got out. Most were men, but there were some women, too. All were dressed the same way—jeans, sneakers, and long-sleeved, camouflage jackets with a lot of pockets. The jackets hung oddly on all of them, indicating there were things underneath the jackets. Potentially bulky things.

A tallish girl about my age with long dark brown hair appeared to be in charge. She was pointing, and people were moving, so that seemed to prove the "in charge" theory. "Anyone know the new girl? She looks vaguely familiar, but I don't know why."

Everyone peered out the window. Negatory replies given by all. Well, almost all. "She looks familiar to me, too," Christopher said slowly. "But I also don't know why."

"They look like suicide bombers," Kyle said. "How they're dressed, I mean."

As the words left his mouth, the brunette looked up and around, and I got a better view of her face, or rather the expression of burning hatred she was shooting around. Maybe it was the mention of suicide bombers while I stared at her fanatical rage, but I knew who was on our street.

"Oh. Crap. I think I know why Christopher and I recognize her. I'm pretty darned sure that's the stewardess from Operation Drug Addict, Casey Jones from Club Fifty-One, the one who was in charge of trying to blow our plane up." All the new arrivals started to fan out—not toward or around our Embassy, but around Romania's. The cars appeared to still be running, too. "Um, I'm getting a really bad feeling about this."

"What do you think their plan is?" Christopher asked.

I appreciated the fact that he wasn't asking me how Casey was here instead of locked up somewhere, in part because I figured he'd assumed what I had—our enemies had gotten her out of Guantanamo somehow, because that was exactly how our luck went. However, the answer seemed sort of obvious.

"I think they're here to blow things up."

"They're encircling this building," White said calmly.

"Why blow up this Embassy?" Christopher asked. "When ours is right across the street?"

Looked over at Olga, who was still holding and cuddling Jamie. "Oh. Double crap. Why do terrorists hit civilian targets? Because it makes the people they want to hurt feel even more awful, and it allows the terrorists to blame the murders they commit on their enemies." My parents had really trained me well. I hoped I'd be able to get us out of this unscathed so I could thank them yet again for their prescience.

"I believe it's catsuit time, Missus Martini."

"Right as always, Mister White. Len, Kyle, get the stroller, get it up here and activate its special features. Everyone else stay here and protect everyone." I ensured I made eye contact with the Peregrines, who'd deigned to wake up and pay attention, as well as any Poofs on Duty. All the animals seemed clear about my desires. "Christopher, let's move."

"What if they're trying to flush you out?" Armstrong asked.

"Then they get to feel successful." I grabbed White's and Christopher's hands, and we took off. Thankfully, we weren't going too far, because Christopher's Flash Level was hard on me and White.

We reached the street in about a second, and that included closing the Embassy door behind us. Even so, we were slow—Buchanan was already on the scene, and he wasn't alone.

There were three police officers accompanied by the same number of impressive German Shepherds. One dog in particular I recognized. He wuffed in a friendly manner as he raced past us and after one of the Club 51 goons.

"Heya, Prince." Nice to see that Buchanan had called in reinforcements in the form of Officers Moe, Curly, and Larry. They were better than the Three Stooges, but I was still partial to their nicknames. I'd wanted to talk to our personal K-9 cops, but under the circumstances, now didn't seem like a good time.

The street was chaos personified. There were many more Club 51 people than there were cops, dogs, and Buchanan. Some were running away from the dogs, some were running away from the cops. Buchanan grabbed a driver and pulled him out of his car, slammed him against the vehicle, flung him down, and cuffed him, all in about fifteen seconds. I was officially impressed.

"Focus on anyone around the buildings," White said. Christopher nodded and zipped off. "Missus Martini, I believe Mister Buchanan has the correct plan at the moment."

"Go for it, Mister White. I have a date with a former stewardess."

We separated, and I looked for Casey. She wasn't around. Ran around the Romanian Embassy. Lots of activity, much of it being caused by Christopher knocking people out, but Casey wasn't among them.

Did a tour of all the buildings on the street at hyperspeed. Was hugely impressed with my ability to run fast and corner without slamming into anything I didn't intend to. Was less impressed with my ability to find one chick, because Casey was nowhere around.

Rejoined Buchanan and White. They had all the drivers down.

Christopher had rounded up a lot of the general goons. So far, nothing had gone boom, and Buchanan and the cops seemed to be taking care of defusing whatever these people were wearing.

Got a bad feeling. Maybe Casey wasn't herself anymore and was, instead, an android. That would mean she was probably fast, and that also meant she might have slipped inside either our Embassy or the Romanians'. Neither idea was appealing, but my daughter was on Romanian soil.

Was about to run into the Embassy when something flashed out of the corner of my eye. Turned and looked to see Casey. I'd missed her because I hadn't looked up. She was on the roof of the building next to the Romanian Embassy, but on the other side from the Irish Embassy.

As near as I could tell, she had a rifle. And it was aimed at me.

CHAPTER 36

DECIDED I HAD HYPERSPEED FOR A REASON. I took off, running in a serpentine manner that probably didn't matter because someone I didn't like in the first place pointing a rifle at me had the ability to rev me over to rage without even trying.

As I had at NASA Base, I ran up the side of the building—I was becoming rather fond of this move—breached the top, and slammed into Casey. Confirmed she wasn't an android, which was kind of nice, all things considered.

The rifle flew out of her hands, and, thankfully, we both went down. Down on the roof versus down onto the ground three stories below. The fact that I'd inherited the A-C ability for fast healing was great, but broken, smooshed, and scraped parts still hurt.

The brilliance of hitting someone loaded with explosives didn't occur to me until after I'd hit up against her, but fortunately Casey didn't seem rigged to explode, and she either didn't have a kill switch or she didn't want to die, because we didn't go boom.

"What the hell is your damage this time?" I snarled at her as I reared up and prepared to hit her.

"We're trying to stop the invasion," Casey snapped right back. "If we get rid of you, the rest of them won't come and destroy us."

"You people are the biggest whack jobs going, you know that? How the hell did you get out of the hole the government tossed you into?"

"We have powerful friends. If you kill me, more will come to take my place."

"Yeah . . . but *you'll* be dead."

The logic of this didn't seem lost on Casey, at least if the panic that flitted across her face was any indication.

I was about to question her or hit her, or both, when I heard a sound I was familiar with, although I hadn't heard one for a while now. Looked up to see several helicopters coming toward us. People with long-range guns were leaning out of the sides. They were wearing camouflage that covered their heads and faces and sunglasses that hid their eyes. They would have looked at home in a war zone. In the middle of Embassy Row, they looked surreal, or as if we were in the middle of a Michael Bay movie.

Casey used my distraction to shove me off her and scramble to her feet. She started jumping and waving her arms. Apparently these were choppers she was expecting.

"We'll take it from here," a distorted voice said from the nearest chopper via loudspeaker. "Untie and back away from the prisoners or we'll shoot you where you stand."

Edged to the side of the roof and looked down. My guys were obliging, possibly because there were a lot of high-powered guns aimed at them.

The freed Club 51 folks bolted for their cars and took off. This left Casey on the roof with no ride. Contemplated my options. Had to figure that if the people in the choppers were friendly they wouldn't have had us let our enemies go. However, they weren't shooting at us.

All the choppers other than the one nearest to me and Casey flew off. The remaining one came closer and dropped a rope ladder down. Casey looked at me and smirked. "We'll take care of you, all of you, later." She grabbed the ladder and started climbing up.

"Bet me." One of the guns pointed right at me. I decided not to push my luck. "Guys, time to play catch!" I jumped over the side as the bullets hit where I'd been standing.

Happily, Buchanan was up to Jeff's standards when it came to catching me when I fell from a great height. I didn't want to contemplate Jeff's reactions as I landed in Buchanan's arms—I was just happy to not be going splat.

"Ooof! Missus Chief, perhaps it's time to lay off the Cokes."

"You're hilarious, Malcolm. Jeff never complains."

"They're still shooting," Christopher snapped. "We need to get inside. And the K-9 cops refused to get to safety."

Buchanan ran us into the doorway of the Romanian Embassy, then put me down. Christopher and White came with us. "The police officers said they were going to follow the helicopters," White said. "None of them or their dogs were hit."

"They were only aiming for Kitty," Christopher said. "Why?"

"I'm popular?"

"That kind of popularity we can do without," Buchanan said. He cocked his head. "The last helicopter's gone."

Christopher stepped away from the door and looked around. "Yeah, we're all clear. So, do we go after them?"

Buchanan shook his head. "I've called it in. It'll be handled, if at all possible, but it shouldn't be handled by any of you. So, since I'm sure to be asked, what was that all about?"

"We think our good friends from the supposedly defunct but clearly still in action anti-alien Club Fifty-One were trying to blow up the Romanians as a statement, because the Romanians are our friends. And Casey said they wanted to get rid of us to prevent an alien invasion."

We all exchanged the "what the hell?" look. "Are these people unaware that you're all here already?" Buchanan asked.

"Talk to Chuckie about them, but most of the Club Fifty-One loons aren't in the know. They think aliens are little green men with truth rays and anal probes, sort of thing. Most of the grunts have no clear idea what A-Cs can do, at least they didn't when we tangled with them before. So, did anyone tell Officer Moe that we want to chat with them about our other little problem?"

White sighed. "I did mention that we'd been hoping to meet up with the officers, but Officer Melville feels that they need to track down these Club Fifty-One terrorists much more than deal with faked dirty pictures."

"Can no longer argue with Officer Moe's logic."

Buchanan nodded. "Get back to whatever it was you were doing with Senator Armstrong. I'll stay on guard."

I thought about this. "If Len hadn't looked out the window, would we have even known this was going on?"

Buchanan grinned as he turned and walked away. "Guess that's one you'll never know, Missus Chief."

"Well, that was fun," Christopher snapped. "Can we assume Club Fifty-One's behind everything?"

"Hardly, though it's so 'nice' to know they're back in action, and with a lot better support than they had a couple years ago. No, we need to get back to the others and to what I wanted to do before we were so rudely interrupted."

"And that is?" Christopher's snark was at eleven and threatening to go for twelve, just to see if he could manage it.

"Establishing what's gone and going on. We have nothing else to work with, unless and until the K-9 cops track down Casey or her cronies, and let's admit it—that's a real long shot based on the firepower that came to back them."

"What was their purpose?" White asked. "They seemed to achieve nothing."

"Ah, but, Mister White, you fail to realize—that's the Club Fifty-One way."

"They flushed us out," Christopher said. "Just like Senator Armstrong said."

"And Malcolm, too. And the K-9 cops. I didn't realize Malcolm had them on speed dial."

"Mister Buchanan does seem to work in mysterious ways," White said. "Sadly, though, I'm inclined to wonder if this was a stalling or distraction tactic only."

"No. I think it was doing double duty." Something about that nudged at me. "We need to get back to the others. Whether or not Club Fifty-One was trying to blow the block sky high or just waste our time, we have a lot of questions that remain unanswered."

"I'm still questioning why we have those stupid birds," Christopher said. "They didn't do a damn thing during this incident."

"Missus Martini told them to sit and stay and guard," White said. "They obeyed, as far as we can tell."

"Have you told the others about the birds yet?" Christopher asked as he opened the door.

"Oh, no. They're still a super special secret just for the few of us."

He sighed. "I feel so lucky."

CHAPTER 37

WE HEADED BACK UPSTAIRS to find everyone calm and safe. Jamie was happy to see us and demanded kisses from all three of us to make up for our long absence. Then she demanded to go back to Olga while Christopher compared notes with the others about what they'd seen differently from us—nothing—and where we thought this put us—nowhere.

Christopher grilled Armstrong, but he seemed to know no more about Club 51 than the rest of us. He might have been lying, but we had more immediate questions and concerns, so I chose to believe him for the moment.

Jamie happily back in Olga's lap, I decided to get us back onto some kind of track. "So, Senator, enough about our good friends from Club Fifty-One. I'd like your thoughts about why someone would have given me a bizarre test in place of the real HSAC."

"How bizarre? You didn't give me many details before."

"It was a psychological profile."

"They all are."

"They aren't all like this. Every answer was set up to ensure I'd sound like a psycho, no matter how I answered. It was easily triple the length of everyone else's tests. And the questions at the end related to Chuckie and Cantu. Nothing relating to Club Fifty-One, by the way, for those keeping score."

Armstrong's eyes narrowed. "That makes absolutely no sense. Why didn't you question it?"

"Because she's Kitty," Christopher replied.

"Ah." Armstrong seemed to be considering. "Triple the length . . . you weren't done when the attack started?"

"I wasn't even close to done when the attack started." I thought about it. "I'd skipped ahead, though, and read the last page. That's what triggered Sandra, I think."

"Why did the android attack with witnesses present?" Armstrong was asking some good questions.

"Well, maybe she had to. I was supposed to be in a separate room, but the instructor found me and insisted I join the others."

Len jerked. "The weird test you got—that was Plan B. They wanted you separated from the rest of us to kill or capture you. But in case you were in the room with everyone else, they had Plan B in place."

"But why give her some bizarre test?" Armstrong asked. "Why not just give her the real one?"

"Because she'd have finished it along around the same time as the rest of us," Kyle suggested.

"That seems like a kind of . . . weak idea, really," Christopher said. "And hard to base your entire plan on what Kitty would do with a weird test."

I thought about it. "Maybe Plan B was only to delay things?"

"How do you mean?" White asked.

"An attack squad was sent to take out Chuckie, remember? Maybe they just wanted to be sure he'd be dead before I finished."

"Why?" Armstrong asked. "What would that do?"

"Piss me off more than you can possibly imagine." And the bad guys wouldn't want that. Any of them who'd gone up against me pissed off these days were no longer around to talk about it.

"That can't have been the goal." Armstrong shook his head. "To me, that test seems key."

"Maybe they really wanted her answers," Adriana suggested.

"Why?"

She looked thoughtful. "You said it was a psychological test."

"Yes, but it wasn't a normal one. Seriously, no one taking this test could answer in any way that would avoid sounding like a serious security risk and likely serial killer." Come to think of it, maybe they'd given me the entrance exam for Club 51.

"There's no way results from a test that biased would be allowed," Christopher said.

"True enough," Armstrong agreed.

"The last page was the weirdest, and that's saying a lot."

"That was the one asking you about Esteban and Reynolds, right?" Armstrong asked.

"Right. I didn't actually do most of the test and I didn't answer anything on the last page, so I don't see what anyone would get from it, other than a delaying tactic."

"No one goes to that much trouble to create something so specific without a related specific goal in mind," Armstrong said firmly. "It would have been easy enough to delay you. An official phone call, a requested high-level meeting, any number of other options. Why have a bizarre test that no one in their right mind would believe was the real thing?"

"Um, I believed. Sort of."

He gave me a rather derisive look. "For how long?"

"A few pages."

"And then?"

I sighed. "Yeah, and then I started reading ahead. Especially when everyone else was done so quickly."

Armstrong cocked his head. "What do you mean the others were done quickly?"

I looked at White. "Well, Richard was done fast. I figured you used hyperspeed."

"I did. And I rechecked my work three times. The test was very brief."

Armstrong sat up straight. "How many pages?"

"Twenty."

White considered twenty pages brief? Maybe so. Mine had had at least a hundred pages, after all.

Len and Kyle looked at each other. "Mine was thirty pages," Len said.

"Mine, too," Kyle added.

I dug out my phone and dialed. "Ames, have a second?"

"Yes, but I can't tell you anything about what I'm doing."

"No worries. How many pages was your HSAC test?"

"Excuse me?"

"Work with me here. How many, do you remember?"

"Yeah, around twenty-five pages or something. Why?"

"Usual crap. Talk to you in a few." I hung up and dialed again. "Malcolm, how many pages was your HSAC test?"

"Hi, Missus Chief. Great to hear from you. It's been so long and all."

"Dude, seriously, as if our skirmish from only a few minutes ago wasn't enough, we've got the standard DEFCON Bad stuff going on. Pleasantries later, after I choose to forget your crack about my weight. Just answer the question."

"I was only teasing, you're still a thing of beauty and a joy for-ever. Thirty-six pages, which is standard. Why?"

"Tell you later. I think. You okay?"

"I'm supposed to ask you that, but it's always nice to know that you care."

"I do. Don't be too far away, I think we're going to need you soon."

"My entire job now consists of not being far away from you. Trust me, I'll be nearby."

We hung up. "Okay, Amy's test was twenty-five pages. Malcolm's test was thirty-six, which he said was standard."

Armstrong nodded. "It is. Every test should have been thirty-six pages."

I looked at White. "You thinking what I'm thinking?"

He nodded. "I believe I am, Missus Martini."

"What's that?" Christopher asked.

"My test was indeed Plan B. If Sandra the Android could have taken me out where the others didn't know about it, that would have been better. They'd have gotten what they wanted anyway. But with me in the room, that meant that the others would know about her attack. And, since she wasn't trying to kill most of them, would survive."

"So?" Christopher asked. "I mean, glad everyone survived, my wife in particular. But I don't see where you're going with this, Kitty."

"No, you probably don't. At least, you haven't had to for a while. Think back to fugly fighting. When you were dealing with an in-control superbeing, what would you do to stop it? I mean before the tanks and artillery showed up?"

"We'd try to distract it away from any civilians and also try to limit the damage it would do. We did that with the newly formed ones, too, when needed. You know that. Why are you asking?"

I looked at Olga. She nodded. Nice to know I was right, at least about one thing. Looked at Armstrong. He nodded as well. "Your test was meaningless, in that sense."

"Yeah, I think whoever created it—and my money's on your 'associate' Cantu, by the way—was having fun." I looked at Christopher's expression and decided to be kind. "My test was the distraction. What they wanted, and have, were the answers the rest of the team gave."

CHAPTER 38

CHRISTOPHER'S EYES NARROWED. "You sure?"

"Malcolm's test was thirty-six pages, which Senator Armstrong verifies as the right length. Malcolm was also the only person taking the test who had ever taken it before. Therefore, he got a real test."

White nodded. "The rest of us were given different tests, I presume, anyway, based on length."

"Why were Len and Kyle's tests the same length?" Christopher asked.

"Because they're friends, went to college together, were on the same football team, are now doing the same job, basically, and they'll talk to each other. Boys, am I right that, if this hadn't gone completely haywire, you'd have compared notes?"

Kyle looked sheepish. Len shrugged. "We already did."

"But my father's test and Amy's test were different."

"Amy would compare with me. Your father wouldn't compare with anyone."

White nodded. "Very true."

"But how is it that the others passed?" Armstrong asked. "Those tests wouldn't have gone through the system properly."

"They didn't." Everyone stared at me, other than Olga, who gave me the Proud Teacher look. I was doing *great* with the finger painting. "The bad guys took the tests John nicely brought out of the room with him."

"Our teacher was clean," White reminded me.

"I'm sure he was. He got me out of the room where I was alone with Sandra, so he forced Plan B. I'm sure if he hadn't carried the tests out, none of us would have 'passed.' But he did, so whoever's in charge sent up dummy tests and had them rushed through, so no one would question."

Armstrong nodded slowly. "That makes sense. It would be easy enough to have prepared tests in advance."

"Paul requested they be rushed," Christopher reminded me. "And Reynolds probably asked for them to be processed quickly, too. He's been getting a lot of heat for the delay."

"Perfect set up, really. So, I get the crazy test. Everyone's focused on that, not on the fact that what our enemies got was answers to whatever they hell they asked the rest of our team."

Len and Kyle exchanged another look. "Our test was focused on questions about how we'd react in emergency situations," Len said. "What were Embassy procedures, how they differed from Centaurion Division procedures."

"What our chain of command was in case different personnel were incapacitated," Kyle added. "And what protective procedures we'd had in place in Florida. And which ones we didn't use, and why."

"My test focused a great deal on the Office of the Pontifex," White said. "But it did also ask a variety of chain of command questions."

Christopher dialed. "James, I need Amy brought to the Romanian Embassy immediately, under guard. Yes, it's about why Kitty called, only more so. No. No. Yes, a floater's fine, but I want her under guard at least until she's through the gate. I can and will come and get her myself if you don't want to help out. Fine, yes, thanks." He hung up and shot Patented Glare #4 at his phone.

"That sounded fun."

"We need a female from American Centaurion in attendance at the One World thing. It was supposed to be you, but without us able to tell you anything, Amy moved into the slot. But I think we need her here more."

"Have Doreen do it."

Christopher shook his head. "Jeff already forbade her to attend. Same with Claudia and Lorraine, only James did the forbidding on that."

"New mothers stay home and safe, right?"

"Right. And Serene's on Alpha Team and confined to Dulce right now on Tito's orders, so she's not an option, either."

I considered our options. Made another call. "Hey, Mimi, are you and Abby free?"

"Yeah, we are. Just hanging out with Denise since she and her kids have nothing to do today because Kevin's working."

"And he forbade them to attend the One World thing at the Mall, didn't he?"

"Yeah." Naomi laughed. "I knew you'd figure out what was going on."

"Oh, there's lots going on. I haven't even figured most of it out yet, but trust me when I say we won't like it when I do."

"I'm sure."

"Look, we need Amy at the Romanian Embassy. We also apparently need female Embassy personnel at the One World event. I'm officially announcing you and Abby as our Cultural Attachés. Go get 'em, tigers."

She laughed again. "I'm all for it. Sis and I are bored with our current jobs, which consist of letting Chuck run tests on us and smiling pretty. Besides, after last night, clearly our King expects us to live at the Embassy. What? Hang on." I heard her bring Abigail up to speed. "Back. Abby's on board, too. We'll go over to the One World thing now."

"Ah, expect your new . . . gifts . . . to want to come with you."

"Really? How will we explain them?"

"I don't think you'll have to." I looked around, and trotted out of the room again as the urge to name once again overcame me. "Your birds are named Posh and Becks."

There was a pause. "Oh, my God, I love those names for them! They're really perfect, too."

"Your birds are with you?"

"Yeah, they're hanging out with the Lewis' birds."

"Ken and Barbie?"

"How did you know that's what Rachel named them?"

"I didn't. Richard thinks this is my talent. Let's discuss my new level of bizarre later though, okay?"

"You got it. We'll take care of things. And I'll keep you posted on what's going on, probably via text."

"Isn't that a security breach?"

"Guess we'll find out. I'm kind of against not telling one of our leaders pertinent information, especially when the lack of that information could cause some or all of us to be killed."

"I like where your head's at." As we hung up, the air near me shimmered and I saw a floater gate appear. Amy stepped through a second later. She was alone. "Hey, Ames."

She blinked. "What's going on?"

"Oh, the usual crap. Only more of it."

"Oh." She shrugged. "So, routine."

"Yep." We joined the others. "Okay, so Amy's here. Naomi and Abigail, as our new Cultural Attachés, will cover whatever she was doing. Christopher, I'm assuming I know what you wanted her here for, but since you asked, you tell."

"You didn't run that appointment by anyone," Christopher pointed out.

"I see I need to remind you that I'm the Co-Head Ambassador. As such, I can assign anyone to do anything in our Embassy. If Jeff has a problem, he can whine to me about it. You, however, even though you're Monsieur Chargé d'Affaires, cannot."

He rolled his eyes, then gave Amy a quick peck. "Okay, I want Amy, Len, Kyle, and my father all writing down as many of the questions from yesterday's HSAC test as they can remember. Write down the answers you gave, too."

While Adriana went to get pads of paper and pens, we caught Amy up on what was going on. She looked slightly ill when it was done. "Kitty, I remember most of the questions."

"What were they about?"

Amy looked at Olga. No—she looked at Jamie. "About security in the Embassy and other Bases. And how well protected the hybrid children are."

CHAPTER 39

I WANTED TO GET MAD. But I knew I was going to need the rage somewhere down the line, and my bet was always for sooner as opposed to later.

"So, it's the old 'steal my baby' ploy." I looked at Armstrong. "What's your part in that?"

"I want nothing to do with it." He looked around and heaved a sigh. "You can all stop giving me your versions of the Evil Eye. Yes, there are people who want to get and control your children, particularly the hybrids. But I want, and therefore have, nothing to do with them."

"Any more."

"Ever. Look, I'm willing to do many things. But harming innocent children isn't one of them. I know you don't like me. I can understand why, in part because I realize none of you, except possibly your current and former Pontifexes, actually understand politics and diplomacy and how it all really works."

Amy's eyes narrowed. "I understand how it all works. I also understand that my father was a genius. And a lunatic. Are you insinuating you don't know anything about his various experiments?"

"Or Marling's? Or, frankly, any supersoldier program currently in existence?"

Armstrong looked trapped. Something my father had said to me chose to surface at this moment—a trapped animal will do or say anything to escape. You couldn't trust what someone who was trapped or defensive said most times.

I took a look at Olga. She was cuddling Jamie. And pointedly not looking at Armstrong.

I took a deep breath and let it out. "Let's all stop for a minute. Senator, despite how we all appear right now, we know we need to work with you. And we know you need to work with us. Let's declare a truce."

He looked at me suspiciously. "How do you mean?"

"I mean we tell you things, you tell us things, and neither side uses them against the other."

"Kitty, you're crazy," Christopher said. "You know we can't trust him."

I hit my speed dial. He answered on the first ring. That was happening a lot today. Had some guesses as to why, but none of them were concrete enough to share. Yet. "You're on the high priority line. This had better actually be high priority, Kitty."

"Hey, sorry I'm using the Bat Phone, but I needed to be sure you'd answer."

"When, in our entire lives, have I not answered a call from you?" Chuckie asked.

"Never, but you're in the middle of something with the One World stuff and I wanted to be sure I got you."

"You have me. What's going on? And where did White and Amy go? And," he sounded angry, "what the hell are they doing here?"

It didn't take genius to guess the Gower girls had just arrived. "They're our new Cultural Attachés. And Christopher and Amy are with me, because we're at DEFCON Bad and heading to DEFCON Worse at warp speed."

"What's going on?"

"Not sure I can explain it quickly."

"Try." He didn't sound like he was asking.

I gave it my best shot. While I did so, Christopher had the gang writing like fiends to get as much of what they could remember down as quickly as possible.

"Now that you know the latest bad news, let's get back to why I called. Do you trust Senator Armstrong? If yes, how much? If no, why not?"

Chuckie was quiet for a few moments. "I don't really trust anybody, Kitty, you know that."

"You trust me."

"You're different."

"You trust other people. I'd name them, but I'm not alone."

"I don't trust most people fully, let's agree on that."

"Fine. Back to the senator."

"I haven't found anything that proves he was involved in any of the various actions against us."

"Have you not found this because he's not involved or because he's just really good at hiding his tracks?"

"I'm honestly not sure. I realize you want a better answer than that. I can't give it to you."

"Fine. Esteban Cantu. Same questions."

"I guarantee that if Cantu could slit all our throats and not have it reflect badly on him, we'd all be dead. I can't say the same of Armstrong."

"When Operation Confusion started, Armstrong was one of the four having us do an unnecessary conference call." I watched Armstrong out of the corner of my eye, hoping he wouldn't really notice that I was doing so.

"Yes. Per what we found out then and you said Madeline Cartwright confirmed before she died, Cooper was in charge of that."

"Yeah, but she also said Cantu and Armstrong were involved." I watched Armstrong. He looked stressed and annoyed, but not overly worried. Had no idea what that meant. Found myself wishing Jeff and Chuckie were both here. "I wish you and Jeff were here, right now."

"We can't leave."

"I guessed. The President's about to kick the thing off, right?"

"Right. And we have no idea if there's going to be trouble or not."

"Trouble is a given."

"Why do you say that?"

"You have Alpha and Airborne involved. Before anything's happened. Meaning that everyone expects something *to* happen." Just like for the President's Ball. "So, someone got the head's up that something was going down at this thing, and you're all there trying to stop it."

"Right. And I can't really do my job while I'm on the phone with you."

"Oh, I have faith in you. I know you're not only the Conspiracy King, you're also the Emperor of the Multitaskers."

"Thanks. So, why are you asking me if we can trust Armstrong?"

"Because . . ." My voice trailed off because my brain was nudging me. "Who did you get the trouble tip from for this? Can you tell me?"

He sighed. "Not really. I'm sure you can figure it out, though, if you think about it."

"I can?"

"Yes."

I looked at Oliver. He shook his head. So he wasn't the one who'd tipped them about issues with the One World Festival. "I know it wasn't Mister Joel Oliver."

"Correct. Think, Kitty. Think about the name of the event."

"It's the International One World Festival." I looked at Olga.

She tossed me a bone. "Not everyone gets along with their neighbors as well as we do."

"Everyone's on high alert because of the break-in at the Bahraini Embassy and the resulting I Know You Are But What Am I between them and the Israeli Embassy, right?"

"Took you long enough. Yes. We have no idea if something's going to happen, but if we have some Middle Eastern countries who aren't happy campers, and we do, then this is a great opportunity to have a worldwide stage to present their displeasure."

"Gotcha. I'll let you get back to it."

"Great. Be careful, Kitty."

"You too, Secret Agent Man."

"And, Kitty?"

"Yeah?"

"Make sure Jamie's safe. Don't bring her into anything even remotely dangerous, and don't leave her with anyone we can't trust a hundred percent, and by we I mean me."

"Gotcha, Surrogate Daddy Chuckie."

He laughed. "Thank God your husband's not around to hear that."

CHAPTER 40

WE HUNG UP, and I calculated the odds that Armstrong was infiltrating us versus really in need of our help. They were fifty-fifty. Looked for some kind of sign from the cosmos about what to do. Because I needed to run the yap and ask some serious questions that would potentially give away a lot of information I didn't want a real enemy to know.

Bruno woke up and looked at me. I looked back at him. He looked around the room, stared at Armstrong, looked right at me again, then pointedly tucked his head back under his wing.

I decided my request of the cosmos had been answered. Prayed White was right about my new "talent." Looked at Armstrong. "What's your assessment of the actual threat level at the event the dirty pictures pulled you away from?"

"I'm not sure. I think there's reason to be alert and prepared."

"Yeah. Only, see, when Operation Assassination was going down, we were supposed to be alerted. So that the people who did the protection could fail that much more dramatically."

"Where are you going with this, Kitty?" Christopher asked quietly. "I'm not following you." But I could tell he was feeling the same unease I was, because he was neither snarking, snarling, nor glaring.

"Let's get back to MJO's question from earlier. I think it's probably the key point in all of this."

"You mean when I asked if either the senator or your husband reacted in the way expected?"

"Yes. Senator, why did you come to see me instead of, say, calling the *Washington Post*? Oh, and please give us the truthful answer, not the political spin. I think we need to have everyone's cards truly on the table for this one."

Armstrong seemed to be considering the question and his answer. "I didn't . . ." He shook his head. "As I said earlier, it was all too easy to believe you and Reynolds were having an affair. But I gain nothing from exposing that."

"So you were coming to blackmail me."

"Hardly. I involved Guy and Vance so you'd realize I wasn't trying to extort anything from you."

"Seriously? Why in the world would you think bringing them along would help?"

Armstrong stared at me. "You're friends with them."

"*Excuse* me?"

Armstrong shrugged. "They talk about you all the time. I mean, Guy's clearly smitten with you. Vance says he misses you in the Washington Wife class."

"And from that you deduced friendship?"

"They actually like you, so yes."

I decided to table my shock and horror, as well as ensure the Inner Hyena remained silent, so I moved back to the real matter at hand. "Okay, so you believed the pictures."

"Absolutely. They looked very real and it wasn't a relationship I would question."

"No one who knows you and Chuck would question it," Amy said, looking up from her scribbling.

I nodded. "Honestly, I agree." I looked at Christopher. "So, why didn't Jeff freak the hell out?"

"Because Reynolds was the one who brought the pictures to him," Christopher replied. "And *he* was freaked out."

"And Jeff can read Chuckie's emotions without difficulty." Lord knew, Jeff confirmed this all the time. I looked at Oliver. "During Operation Assassination the bad guys intended for you to alert us. How did you find out about these pictures?"

"I didn't use great deductive reasoning or any contacts. I insinuated I'd heard a tip so that Mister Reynolds wouldn't waste time or effort accusing me of setting it all up. But the pictures were sent directly to my editor. Because I've created a fruitful relationship with you, he showed them to me first. That's why they weren't published."

"That sounds like the sender expected you to alert Chuckie, though."

Oliver looked thoughtful. "Maybe. Or they don't understand how special some of your people are, your husband in particular."

"Or they don't realize that you have a positive working relationship," Armstrong said. "Frankly, until this meeting, I would never have actually believed you wanted him around. And no amount of money would have made me believe you would have stopped the rag you work for from printing those pictures," he said to Oliver, who shrugged and looked, all things considered, rather pleased and a little smug. I let him have his moment.

"Best investigative reporter in the country, perhaps the world. So, MJO, how badly did your editor want to print those pictures?"

"Badly. But he's smart enough to understand that we're getting access no one else is and how quickly said access would disappear if we printed something like this about you."

"Timeline is that the senator got the pictures the day I left. Then, MJO, your editor got them, what, two weeks later?"

"Roughly, yes."

"So whoever sent the pictures to the senator thought he'd do something with them," White said.

"And, clearly, what they expected wasn't that the senator would come down to Florida and try to show the pictures to me."

"I'd bet they expected the senator to go straight to Ambassador Martini," Oliver said.

"Why expect him to bring them to Jeff *or* Kitty?" Christopher asked. "The senator works more closely with Reynolds than he does with us. And we'd run anything to do with him through Reynolds first anyway."

It was there again. I could feel the answer throwing itself against the walls of my mind, trying to break in.

"I'm still amazed, and incredibly relieved, that Jeff acted like an actual adult," Amy said, not even bothering to look up from her writing. "His jealousy thing is so over-the-top sometimes, I'm amazed he didn't kill Chuck and then ask questions later, regardless of who brought the pictures to him."

And there it was.

CHAPTER 41

"A MES, I LOVE YOU. Keep on writing down the questions, but revel in the fact that you're totally on fire today." I dialed and he answered on the first ring. "I know what's going on."

"Baby, now's a really bad time."

"Don't let Chuckie out of your sight."

"I can feel your panic, and, as so often happens, it's centered around him. Why?"

"Because whatever's going on with the dirty pictures isn't being done to hurt American Centaurion. It's being done to destroy Chuckie and everything he stands for." I looked at Jamie. "And stands in front of."

"Mind explaining that?"

"Sure. They're after our baby, and all the other hybrid babies." Jeff growled. "Look, belay that for now. Chuckie has a lot of enemies, in no small part because he spends much of his time protecting Centaurion Division, our hybrids in particular. Senator Armstrong said it himself—brilliant, driven men cause problems, and many times they take over. We have a lot of enemies and the person who protects us from them is Chuckie. Take him out, what the hell happens to us?"

"You get Esteban Cantu running the Extra-Terrestrial Division of the C.I.A.," Armstrong answered. "It's considered a straight line to the top position. Antiterrorism used to be, but not since Reynolds took over as the head of the ETD."

"I heard him," Jeff said, voice tight. "I don't have eyes on Reynolds, but I'll get to him." He cursed quietly. "This event is a perfect place for an assassination."

"That's what you're all doing there, right? Ensuring that the International One World Festival isn't the President's Ball, Part Two."

"Yes. I need to get off the phone. There are too many people here—I need to focus to find Reynolds. So, on the plus side, he's not emotionally upset."

I refrained from mentioning that this could be because he was already dead.

Jeff sighed. "I'd feel it, if he died."

Good to know he was reading my mind. I reminded myself that I'd told him how much I liked that only a short while ago. "Why?"

"Because he's so tightly tied to you emotionally. It's an empathic thing, but if Reynolds dies, I'll know. And he's not dead."

"Good. Jeff, you be careful, too. Just because Chuckie's the goal, it doesn't mean they won't go for a double and try to get rid of you, too."

"Always nice to know you care, baby. I love you. I'll let you know as soon as I find him."

"I love you, too. Be safe."

I hung up and tried not to worry. Failed. I took Jamie from Olga and cuddled her. Made me feel a little bit better.

"So, the expectation was that Jeffrey would go into a jealous rage and kill Mister Reynolds," White said.

"Makes sense," Christopher said. "I was kind of impressed with how well he handled it."

"He was cut off from me and Jamie emotionally. I'm sure that had a lot to do with it. So he could tell how upset Chuckie was and read him correctly, without a lot of jealousy filtering required." I looked at Armstrong. "If you'd brought him those photos, though, I think it would have gone differently."

"So, why were you such a good friend to Kitty all of a sudden?" Amy asked.

"The truth," I added. "Not the political spin."

"They're the same answer—why upset your husband? That wouldn't do me any good politically. But if I could help you keep these out of the press, or at least help you prep for how to handle it when they hit the streets, well, I'd be your friend, wouldn't I?"

"And friends do favors for each other. Yeah. Same with Guy and Vance. And they told no one?"

"No. If we told someone, then we wouldn't be your friends, would we?"

"Since when did you want to become Kitty's friend?" Christopher asked.

Armstrong shrugged.

"No, it's a really good question, and you need to answer it. Because you haven't done anything the person who's sending the pictures expected you to. Meaning he or she knows you, and you've changed your game plan somewhere along the way. And they *don't* know that."

"They know," White said quietly. "That's why Senator Armstrong has new photos today. Because they know he's not doing what they expected and is, for whatever reason, choosing to align himself with us."

Armstrong sighed. "Yes, you're right. Look, Madeline Cartwright and Antony Marling are dead. I tied my horse to their cart, and it's only because I legitimately had no idea what they were doing that I'm still in office, let alone not in jail."

"How many supersoldier projects are active right now?"

He stared at me. I stared right back. He wasn't Mom or Chuckie—I had no worries that I'd win.

It took a while, but sure enough, he dropped his eyes. "Two."

"Based out of Paris and Paraguay?"

"Yes. You want to know the exact moment I decided it was time to change teams? When I found out that Cooper and Gaultier had been trying to use children as test subjects for the superdrug."

"So you did know about it."

"After the fact. Cooper didn't tell me because he was clear on where my line was. I had to read Reynolds' report to know the truth of what had happened."

"But you were still friendly with Cartwright and Marling."

"You don't discard people like that because someone they know did something insane and illegal. And if you want to know the moment I realized I wanted nothing more to do with any of the rest of the supersoldier programs, it was the President's Ball. Once it was all over, several of us who have the security clearances to know everything about Centaurion Division insisted on seeing what was going on down in that basement. I saw the 'perfect weapons' Marling had created. I saw things I'd thought of as people shown to be robots. I saw madness."

"You'd bought in before then."

"Yes. It sounds wonderful on paper—create an army out of the things from space that can destroy us without even trying hard. In reality, it was horrifying." He shook his head. "I've thanked God every day that my wife was too ill to attend. And now I realize they wanted both of us too ill to attend. I'd almost say they were my friends for that . . . only I know they didn't try to keep me away to keep me safe, but so that I wouldn't see what they were really doing. Until it was too late."

"Well, better late than never to the side of right."

He gave a bitter laugh. "My career will be over if these pictures of you and what everyone in the world will believe is me hit the newsstands. They're no longer after just Reynolds. I'm in their sights now. Whoever the hell 'they' are. The people I'd suspect are all dead."

"Other than Cantu."

"There is no way he's doing this alone. And I have no idea who he could go to who would have this kind of pull that I wouldn't know about already."

"And they picked a hell of a day for this, too," Amy said, still industriously writing, just as Len and Kyle were. White appeared done, so I assumed he'd once again used hyperspeed. He was the wise man. But Amy was my go-to girl right now.

"Ames, seriously, you're totally golden today. Why? James wanted me asking that. Why did the senator get the first set of pictures the day we left town?"

"My guess is that they truly expected him to take them straight to Jeffrey, which would have been simple because you were nowhere around to either intercept the pictures or protect Mister Reynolds from Jeffrey's wrath."

"Mister White wins the first round. So, the next question is, why did the senator get the next set of pictures today of all days? When the One World Festival is launching?"

"That," Olga said, looking straight at me, "is the proper question."

I knew my answer to this was going to mean I either flunked or got to join Oliver and Buchanan at the head of the class. I ran it all through my mind and it all added up. For once.

"Because it's not about the pictures. Everything that's going on—from the dirty pictures, to the mysterious-nothing-taken break-in at the Bahraini Embassy, to Sandra the Android, to Club Fifty-One's little show—is a diversion."

CHAPTER 42

OLGA BEAMED. "EXACTLY."

I didn't congratulate myself—we were too far away from any kind of positive outcome to get cocky.

"They may be diversions," Christopher said, "but people can still die from them."

"Oh, I'm positive they want people dying." Chuckie in particular. "But they're doing all this to distract us from what they really want—Chuckie out of the way and clear access to Jamie and all the other hybrid children."

As I said this, Amy finished up and handed her stuff to Christopher. He already had White's completed test recap. Len finished as Christopher glared at Amy's pages, with Kyle following shortly thereafter.

While Christopher perused their work and got more and more pissed off, based on the fact that he was running through Patented Glares #1-5 as if he were practicing for the Glaring Olympics and wanted to ensure the Gold in at least four out of five events, I went back to one of the diversions at hand.

"So, we still need to know how they got pictures of me and Jeff from last night."

White cocked his head at me. "Do we feel our current enemies, whoever they are, know us well?"

I pondered. "I think they know *us* well. They clearly didn't know Senator Armstrong as well as they thought they did."

"They didn't know Mister Joel Oliver as well as they thought, either," Len said.

"No," Oliver corrected. "They didn't know my editor."

"But our reactions are right out of our playbook. That's what you mean, right Mister White?"

"Yes, Missus Martini. I'd assume it's going to be catsuit time again shortly?"

"You never can tell, but I'd put money on that being a big yes. You know, since the Embassy was scanned several times last night, I have to assume that one of us brought whatever bug in. Either that or one of our personnel are working for the bad guys."

"Mister Reynolds has us scan everyone," Kyle said. "Regularly."

"Even me?"

"Especially you," Len said. "After all the bugs you carried in during Operation Assassination, he made it a daily task." The boys were the only ones who used whatever Operation name I'd assigned. I loved them.

Christopher snorted. "He was late on that one, because that sure as hell wasn't the first time Kitty had a bug planted in her purse."

He and I looked at each other. "Oh. *Snap*. Sandra was doing double duty, at least. Maybe she was supposed to self-destruct, maybe just run away. But, hell, I carried the bug in, didn't I?"

Len and Kyle exchanged a look. "Yeah, we didn't scan anyone yesterday," Kyle admitted. "At least, not after the incident."

"I don't think Mister Reynolds did, either," Len added.

"He didn't, because he didn't say, 'hey, Kitty, there's a bug in your purse.' So we still need to know what happened to it."

"I may know." Armstrong's eyes were narrowed. "Titan Security was working on micronized weapons and surveillance. They had some strong prototypes, including what they called the Tarantula."

"Let me guess, it's a metal thing that looks like a big ol' spider?"

"Yes. It can adapt to look like other things, as well. It 'sleeps' as a sphere."

"So, they took their cues from *Minority Report* and *Transformers*."

Armstrong shrugged. "What the mind can imagine, the mind can create."

"Excellent. Can't wait to see what the League of Really Crazed Super-Geniuses comes up with next."

"I'm going home," Christopher said. "I want to see if we can find the Tarantula."

Armstrong shook his head. "It's a gatherer, not a transmitter. It gets what it's sent to find and returns to its nest, so to speak."

"Let's be really sure." Christopher said. "I'll be right back."

"You could have Walter search, you know."

"I want him focused on security, not on searching."

"Oh. Wow. So that was the Club Fifty-One play."

Everyone looked at me. "Want to explain that?" Christopher asked.

"Sure. They were testing to see what our reactions would be, when most personnel are off site at an event, when a huge bunch of suicide bombers appeared out of nowhere."

"On the plus side, no one came out of the Embassy," Len said. "I kept watch, and the only people on the street were Mister Buchanan, the three K-9 cops and dogs, and the three of you."

"So we showed them we were hanging out with Romania in the off hours. But we showed them that we have people on surveillance of some kind, too. Meaning they did, as Christopher pointed out earlier, what Senator Armstrong said they were doing—they flushed us out of hiding." Jamie was in the room, so I resisted the impulse to curse.

"I'm still going to the Embassy," Christopher said. "I want to brief Walter and anyone else over there on what's going on."

"Fine. Call me before you come back."

"Why?"

"I may not want you returning alone."

I wasn't sure if Christopher was on my wavelength or not, but he didn't argue. He gave Amy another quick peck and zipped off.

"So, was the Tarantula sent to get new dirty pictures?" I wasn't thrown by spiders or bugs, only snakes, so the idea that some big metal thing made to look like the Godzilla of Spiders had been in my purse didn't freak me out all that much. It pissed me off to no end, though.

"Maybe." White looked thoughtful. "Maybe it was sent to get information on the interior of the Embassy and pictures of you two being intimate was a bonus, so to speak."

I wondered if it had seen the Peregrines' arrival or not. Bruno pulled his head out from under his wing and stared at me. Check. If an enemy Tarantula had been there, the Peregrines would have destroyed it. Good to know. I'd worry about my complete mental breakdown later. For right now, I was going to embrace the Dr. Doolittle and just run with it.

"Why use them, though?" Armstrong asked. "Doesn't it just give them away?"

"Only because you came to us, instead of going elsewhere. And only because we figured it out."

"And maybe they needed a better shot of Jeff," Amy said.

"Ames, again you bat a thousand. There are lots of pictures of the senator out there, I'm sure, but most of them won't be of him making the o-face. So the few that would work have to fit onto a specific body position. We gave them new options, they ran with them." Very quickly. Meaning they were either really good or had A-C traitors on staff. It was, like most of today's problems, a fifty-fifty bet either way.

"I believe the important question now is, what do we do?" Adriana asked.

"That is the question of the moment, isn't it? So, what do we know? Whoever's in charge wants Chuckie out permanently."

"Or to have him so disgraced that nothing he's ever said or done will be regarded," Armstrong said.

"I'd assume both," White added. "But they also want to steal our children."

"That cannot be allowed," Olga said, and I knew she wasn't saying it just because she liked us and didn't want to see Jamie hurt.

"True enough. Okay, so, what did we tell them about how the Embassy's set up, how we protect the kids, and all that jazz?" White handed me the papers he and the others had written. "Dude, seriously. It's me."

"She *can* read, you'd just never know that she does," Amy said dryly. "In addition to how we handled the children, with focus on dealing with their powers and how we protected them, my questions were about lockdown and how it worked, where we took people for lockdown, what we did when we couldn't get to a secured A-C facility, and things of that nature."

"Ours were similar," Len said. "Only with a lot more emphasis on actual tactics."

"Fabulous. So, they definitely know our playbook, or most of it, which is probably more than enough, since they most likely already had some of it. You know, whatever they didn't ask about." And they'd done a live test less than a half an hour ago, too.

That meant Dulce was out. So was NASA Base. Caliente Base was probably out, too. We always ran to these places. I ran through options in my mind. The last place we'd want to be was Euro Base, since it was in Paris. But I wasn't coming up with a lot of options. Decided to forge on. "Hiding here is out."

Adriana nodded. "Even if we hadn't been the test target, so to speak, we have none of the defenses your locations do."

"I believe hiding is the right answer," Olga said. "For some of us."

"Mister White, where is the last place you'd choose to hide someone?"

"I assume you mean other than 'in plain sight' or similar. And what you're asking is where could we go that would have all the security we'd need that, at the same time, our enemies wouldn't expect, correct?"

"As always."

He was quiet for a few moments while I tried to come up with not only who we should hide, but who should hide with them. I knew Jeff and Chuckie would both want me hiding, but that wasn't going to happen. However, someone had to be along who could and would kick butt. More than one, if possible.

"Are our phones tapped?"

"Mister Reynolds checks regularly," Len said.

"I would assume they are," Olga countered. "If not your Embassy's phone lines, or even your cellular phones, certainly some of the phones you wish to call will be."

I contemplated some more. Jamie had a full diaper bag, complete with bottles, formula, food, and change of clothes. I could ensure everyone else I needed to hide would be adequately prepped. But we were going to have to make it look like we weren't actually going into hiding and then hide somewhere effective.

"I believe I may have an option," White said finally. "It's not actually a Base."

"But it has the A-C bells and whistles on it?"

He smiled. "And then some. It has the added advantage of being the most secured place on, I believe, Earth. And yet, it's very easy for us to access."

I stared at him. "Wow. I think I know where you're talking about. And, yeah. It's perfect. And loaded with A-C Security dudes."

"The rest of us aren't so clear," Amy said.

"Probably not. But, um, just in case, I'm not going to say aloud where Mister White and I are talking about."

I looked at Bruno, who nodded his approval. Excellent. Now for the hard part—getting there. Well, in one sense, getting there was fairly easy. But we had to do it in such a way no one would be aware we were going there until everyone was safely tucked away.

I looked at White. "One big floater gate or do we all trundle over to the Embassy?"

"I believe a variety of jumps might be preferable."

"Makes sense." It did. If we were congregating in one area then jumping again, logic would determine that we hadn't left someone behind. Logic would be wrong, but it was worth a shot, and I didn't want to take too long to get things and precious cargo locked up and away.

My phone chose this moment to ring. "Hey Christopher, what did you find?"

"Nothing, which I suppose is a good thing. What have you come up with?"

"Oh, I think it's time for us to have a party."

He was quiet for a few long moments. "Is this you trying to pass along information in a way no one else would understand?"

"Yes."

He sighed. "I'm not James, Jeff, or Reynolds. I don't get your Kittyisms first thing out of the gate."

"And yet, there you are, right with me on the plan."

"No. I'm nowhere with you on the plan. I have no idea what the plan is, and if we continue on this way much longer, I won't have anything other than a migraine."

I had to accept that this was probably true. "I want to get everyone who's in danger and not equipped to properly protect themselves to safety. I also want to be sure said someones have others with them capable of kicking butt. And I want them hidden very safely somewhere that's still easy enough for us to access."

"Kitty, seriously, in the time you'll spend trying to get me to figure out your innuendos, they could launch their plan and kill everyone. Let's assume our phones aren't tapped and everyone in the room with you is trustworthy, and just tell me what the hell you want me to know."

"You take all the fun out of everything, you know that?"

"Not according to Amy. Seriously, what's going on?"

"We need to gather up every family with a new hybrid baby or one on the way, along with any Embassy personnel who aren't A-Cs or equipped to kick serious butt, and get them hidden safely where our enemies wouldn't expect."

"Where is that? We gave them all our responses to emergencies. They know everywhere we'd go, and in what order."

I rifled through the papers. Sure enough, no one had mentioned it. I could try to get him thinking along my lines but Christopher was probably right—I had to trust those with us and that our phones weren't tapped or we got nowhere. Nothing for it but to forego innuendo and tell the world of the genius that was me and White.

"Your dad and I want to get everyone out of Dodge and into the Dome."

CHAPTER 43

THE DOME'S FULL NAME was the Crash Site Dome. It was the real spot where the first aliens to visit Earth, the Ancients, had crash-landed on their second visit. So far as we knew, they'd done a lot better their first time coming around to say hi.

The remains of the Ancients' spaceship powered the Dome. Apparently their fuel cells had a half-life like nothing else in the galaxy. The Dome was the main gate hub for the entire world, and had the most Security of any A-C facility. It was, essentially, the A-Cs' version of JFK, LAX, and every other big airport rolled into one, without the mess and fuss most airports put you through, like parking garages and a zillion Cinnabon outlets.

It was also hidden from anything and everything human technology could discover. As far as I could tell, it was hidden from alien technology, too, because, so far, no one had tried to take the Dome out of commission. Maybe they couldn't, I didn't know. But I did know where it was and that it was going to be the last place anyone would think we were staying.

"Oh." Christopher was quiet. "That's a really good plan."

"Thank your dad, he's the brains of the operation. Anyway, I want everyone other than you, Tito and Walter out of the Embassy and over to the Dome. Tell them they're going to a tea party."

"Why?"

"Because I want the kids excited or acting like kids who don't want to go to a girly thing, not crying. Ask Denise to pack some extra clothes and diapers and such for Jamie. Ensure *all* the pets, including my dogs and cats, go along as well." I hoped he'd realize that "all" included Poofs and Peregrines.

"Can't wait," he muttered. "What about Jeff's bird?"

What about Bellie? Reality said I didn't like her and she didn't like me. Reality also said that if any animal was going to stress out the folks in hiding, it was going to be her. Of course, reality additionally said that if I left Jeff's bird to die, he'd never forgive me. Reality also said that if Bellie tried anything with me, she was going to be dinner.

"Keep her at the Embassy. I'll get her and take her with me. Have her stay with either Tito or Walter, depending on which one she likes best, until I get back."

"Why?"

Nice to see he was still focused on asking the big questions. "Because she has intel, and lord knows when she'll want to share it, but those of us in active roles need to hear it, and not filtered through from those in hiding."

"Whatever. She likes me better than Tito or Walter."

"Then you score Bellie-sitting duty. Get everyone, Denise and her kids and Doreen, Irving, and Ezra in particular, moving. I want Pierre with them."

"Why?"

"Because out of every adult I'm going to send over, Pierre's the one who's most likely to come up with things that will keep everyone calm and focused on the fun of the moment, versus the terror. If he wants to bring 'picnic' supplies, let him. I don't think we want them sending for take-out and such."

"Good points. Should I escort them?"

"Yes, then get yourself back to the Embassy. Leave Bellie in our room, in her cage, until you're back, and don't let anyone say anything about this in front of her."

"Why not?"

I resisted the impulse to give a sarcastic reply. "Because she's a freaking parrot, and the last thing we want is her blurting out where we hid everyone in front of the wrong people."

"Oh." He sounded embarrassed. "Right."

"Get moving. I'll meet you at the Embassy if we don't time out to go back together." We hung up, and I dialed again. "Lorraine, how goes it?"

"Fine. You sound stressed."

"Nice to see maternity leave hasn't slowed you down."

"I love my little Ross, but I'm also kind of bored." I heard Claudia chime in that she felt the same way.

"Awesome, you're together, and with the kiddos. I have just the cure for boredom, too. I need you two to pack up diaper bags for an extended stay of possibly a couple hours and possibly a couple days. Pack some extras for Jamie, please and thank you." Sure I'd told Christopher to have Denise do the same, but extra diapers, food, and clothes weren't going to be a bad idea.

"We're at DEFCON Worse?"

"And this is why I call you. Yes, we are."

I heard Claudia in the background. "Claudia wants to know if they're after our kids."

"You know, you two are so much smarter than the rest of us." Well, they were Dazzlers. Dazzlers had it all when it came to brains.

"We're not surprised, really," Lorraine said. "I'll tell you why later."

"Ross and Sean are already manifesting hybrid talents?"

"You're smart too. Okay, where are we meeting you, and who else, if anyone, should we bring?"

"Your mothers, if they're around, and your dads, if they want to go. Serene and Bryan, regardless of whether they want to go. Any other families with hybrids newly arrived or coming. Other than those in our Embassy, who are likely already there waiting for you."

"Gotcha. So, where is it they're waiting and we're going?"

I considered playing the innuendo game, but figured that time was really of the essence and decided to just go for it. "The Dome."

She was quiet for a moment. "You're really worried, aren't you?"

"Yeah, I am."

"Okay, I won't tell anyone else where we're going until we get there."

"Have Gladys do your gate transfer." I looked at White. He nodded emphatically.

"On it. I'll bring med kits, too."

"Always a good plan." Hung up and considered. There were four other hybrids out and about. Three of them I knew I needed and probably wouldn't be able to convince to hide out anyway. The fourth, however, I could get here based on the fact that I had cute girls who also needed protecting. Dialed again.

"Hey, Kitty, what's up?"

"Michael, are you in the middle of anything?"

"Just waiting for the One World event to kick off in a few minutes. It's dull waiting because nothing's going on until launch. And after that, it'll be hours of speeches. Basically, I'm in the middle of a long period of boredom."

"Great! I'm going to save you from boredom." I was saving everyone from boredom today, go me.

"I'm not supposed to leave my post."

"What is your post and who are you with?"

"I'm in the audience and I'm alone." He didn't sound happy about the alone part.

"Seriously? Look, I need you for a plan of higher importance."

"So you claim."

"I have cute human girls who need protecting, and you're the A-C for the job."

"You do know my weakness."

"I do. Zip over to the Romanian Embassy, will you? Use hyper-speed, please, not a gate."

"Be there shortly. What do I tell James or Paul if they ask?"

"Tell them you need to pee." He laughed and we hung up. I turned back to White. "We need a floater gate."

"Already handled. I have a Bat-Line to Gladys just like you have with Mister Reynolds."

"As always, you rock above all others, Mister White. Olga, Adriana, I'd really like the two of you to hide with the rest of our team."

"Why so?" Olga asked. I was clear she already knew, but wanted to make sure I knew. Not a problem.

"Because after they don't find us at the Embassy, they're going to come here to find us. For all we know, they'll come here first, just like the Club Fifty-One people did. Maybe *because* the Club Fifty-One people did. And if you and Adriana are here, they have hostages we care about. However, I don't want your husband or the rest of your diplomatic mission panicking and searching for the two of you, either."

Olga smiled. "Not to worry." She nodded to Adriana, who went to the desk in the room, dialed the phone, and handed it to Olga. Olga spoke to someone in what I assumed was Romanian, since I didn't understand a word. But she said one sentence very slowly and clearly. Then she hung up. "We are fine. None will panic when we are not here."

"Nice to see you and Andrei have a code phrase."

"If you do not, you should rectify that error immediately."

"Yes, ma'am. Just as soon as we ensure everyone's all tucked away safely." I looked around. They weren't going to like what I was going to say next. "Richard and Senator Armstrong will stay with me. Len, Kyle, and Amy, you're going with Adriana and Olga."

They gaped at me. "Why?" Amy asked. It really was the Question of the Day.

"Because none of you are A-Cs, and I need people with the children, my child in particular, who I know will protect her."

"Our jobs are to protect *you*," Len said.

"Nope. You're supposed to protect me *and* Jamie, and Chuckie said I was the boss unless he overruled me, and we don't have time for you to call him. Malcolm's around somewhere, he'll show up when needed as was proved such a short while ago. Otherwise, I can't do my job if I have to worry about my baby."

Amy nodded. "You're right. I'll be Team Lead on the inside."

The boys looked like they were going to argue. White and Olga looked like they were trying not to laugh. I decided to forestall both outcomes. "Works for me, Ames."

"Are we okay to keep our cells on?" Amy asked.

White nodded. "The Dome allows calls in and out but scrambles positioning. Even with the best GPS software, no one could determine where you were based on your phones."

"Awesome. If you find you need supplies while you're there, be sure to send one of the Security guys and have Len and Kyle scan them." I looked to Bruno, who bobbed his head at me. Good. Any Peregrine Enforcers at the Dome would be on the alert as well.

"What about me?" Oliver asked. "I don't believe you consider me a protector, but you haven't given me an assigned duty."

"Oh, you have a duty, MJO. You're going to be causing our distraction."

CHAPTER 44

THE DOORBELL RANG. I realized it was the first time I'd ever heard it. Either Adriana was slipping, or she was so engrossed in our planning that she hadn't noticed that we had someone arriving.

She, Len, and Kyle went downstairs. "Mister White, are you okay to take the senator over to our Embassy?"

He nodded, but Armstrong looked worried. "I don't know if it's a good idea for me to be seen going there."

"Look, they aren't releasing the pictures yet, are they? Because MJO's editor hasn't called asking him if the *World Weekly News* goes for it or not. We can spend precious time hiding you, or you can make life easy and just walk across the damn street."

"Why don't you want me at the Dome?"

"Because we still can't trust you," White said calmly. "For all we know, this is an elaborate ruse in order to get you positioned to hide with those our enemies want to kidnap."

Armstrong opened his mouth—to argue, I was sure—but then he slammed it shut and nodded. "You're right," he said after a couple moments of what appeared to be contemplation. "I understand why you'd be distrustful. I do know where the Dome is, of course, so you've already taken a chance there."

"Had to." Hey, Christopher was right—chances were good that I'd still be on the phone, trying to make him guess what I meant.

"Yes. And aside from keeping me in your sights and under your control, so to speak, I also have clearances you may not, which we may need."

"Good man, glad you're on board. So, I want the two of you

heading across the street now, so that Adriana can lock the door behind you."

"You haven't told Oliver there what you want him to do," Armstrong pointed out.

"It's *Mister Joel* Oliver, please," he said. "And the Ambassador is waiting until you're out of range so you don't know what my part off the operation is."

"And MJO shows yet again why I value his involvement."

Armstrong nodded and stood up. "Shall we?" he asked White.

White stood as well and gave Olga a courtly bow. "Madame, please excuse me from escorting you."

Olga smiled. "Just this once."

"I assume I shouldn't bother locking up our Embassy," White said to me.

"Oh, do it, if only to stop petty thievery and to slow down the Bad Guys du Jour for a minute or two."

"As you wish. I'll see if I can arrange some sort of harness for the parrot."

"A muzzle for preference."

White chuckled and led Armstrong out as Adriana and the boys returned, with Michael Gower in tow. Michael was a slightly smaller version of his older brother—big, black, bald and beautiful. He was also the A-C Player of the Year for, as near as I could tell, his entire life.

This was evident in the fact that Adriana was getting his standard "you so hot, babe" smile, which he gave indiscriminately to any woman between the ages of 18 and 98. The smile was expanded to include me, Amy, and Olga.

Adriana had a large duffle bag. Clearly, she was trained to plan ahead. "Supplies," she said with a smile, after Michael had been introduced to her grandmother. I assumed Adriana's supplies included weapons of some kind, but that was probably good.

The boys also had duffels, and Jamie's stroller was up here already, based on my earlier instructions. I checked—the Poofs were still in it, looking expectant. Had to figure Olga and Adriana knew we had special pets. For all I knew, they knew the Peregrines were in the room with us. And I couldn't send Oliver alone into danger without some kind of backup.

Reached in and took a Poof at random, handed it to Oliver. "Your Poof job is to assist Mister Joel Oliver here."

It mewled at me and jumped into Oliver's hand, where it mewled at him and purred.

"Well," Oliver said. "Aren't you a cute little button?" The Poof in his hands purred much louder.

"Ah, Kitty?" Michael asked. "Is that one attached?"

"Oops." Unattached Poofs bonded to the person who named them. "Um . . . Button?"

The Poof turned, looked at me, purred even louder, then jumped onto Oliver's shoulder and snuggled into his neck.

"Yes, Michael. It's attached now."

Oliver chuckled. "I didn't actually mean to name it Button. But it fits."

"Good. Okay, Button, you take care of MJO, and you report back to Harlie or Poofikins if he's in trouble." Button mewled at me and went into one of Oliver's pockets.

"So, what am I going to be doing?" Oliver asked.

"I've run some ideas around in my mind, but most of them end with you being arrested and possibly killed. So I'm not going to mention them."

"Good. I'm all for helping with the cause, but I'd like to see tomorrow, if you know what I mean."

"I do. So what I'm going to ask you to do has more to do with you confusing whoever's watching us more than anything else."

"You're sure we're being watched?" Michael asked. The entire room snorted at him. "Whoa, just asking."

Oliver nodded. "I believe it's the safest best we have right now."

"Me too. Okay, MJO, I want you heading over to Andrews Air Force Base. Demand to see the head man. Use whatever means necessary, but be sure that it's obvious you're trying to get into a military facility to warn them of an impending threat."

"That's a nice idea, but what makes you think I'll get past the gate?"

This question had occurred to me, too. Luckily, I'd come up with an answer. The Club 51 folks had been good for something. "Tell them you have proof an alien invasion is imminent."

He shook his head. "No one's going to believe me. I have a reputation, and it's not a good one."

"On the contrary," Olga said. "Your reputation is quite good among a select few." She nodded toward the desk and said something in Romanian. Adriana went to the desk, opened a drawer, rummaged through, and pulled out what looked like an old-fashioned writing kit, complete with a candle and small wooden handle with metal at the end.

"I have to ask—first, is that a sealing wax set?"

"Yes," Olga replied. "I do like to have some touches from the past at hand."

"Uh-huh, I'm sure. Here's my next question—what are you two doing?"

Adriana was writing industriously; she handed whatever she'd written and the pen to Olga, who nodded again and signed what I was pretty sure was her name at the bottom. Adriana folded up the letter, lit the sealing wax, let it carefully drip onto the envelope, pressed the seal into, and handed it to Oliver with a little flourish.

"Presto, old fashioned correspondence. Why?" Olga gave me her Disappointed Teacher look. I sighed and gave my best guess. "Sending something this way up to Andrews is some Diplomats of the Old Republic thing, right?"

"In a sense," she said with a smile. "It will help our friend to gain entry, which should assist in causing our enemies to watch the Air Force base more closely than . . . other places."

"What do I say when I actually gain entry?" Oliver asked.

"Demand to speak to the man in charge, only. That should take some time. Also insinuate that others will be joining you at Andrews. Hopefully it'll distract whoever the heck is watching us, at least long enough."

"I hear and obey," Oliver said with a smile. "Should I call for a cab?"

"Hail one, let it go by, hail another, you know the drill. Make it clear you think you're being followed and are trying to hide your tracks."

"I'll do my best." He nodded to all of us, then left. Adriana walked him down. I watched him from the window. He went to the Circle and started looking for transportation.

"So, what interesting thing do you have planned for me, Kitty?" Michael asked while we waited for Adriana to return and Oliver to score transportation.

Oliver had waved three cabs by before Adriana returned. "I locked the entire downstairs, drew all curtains, and generally made it look like we are hiding here."

Oliver finally got into a cab. "Great. Let's close the curtains in this room, too."

"Kitty, what's really going on, and what am I supposed to be doing?" Michael asked again as Adriana did as I'd asked.

I saw a shimmering in the air. "Tell you about it when we get there. Boys, please assist Olga through."

Jamie's diaper bag was still hooked onto her stroller. Amy

grabbed the stroller, Adriana and the boys had their duffels, I had Jamie and my purse. All set.

I looked at Bruno. "You first or us?" He fluffed his feathers, then all the Peregrines flew into the stroller and settled down with the remainder of the Poofs with us. "Fine, you're going in style." Thankfully no one asked me what or who I was talking to.

The gate looked big enough to take at least three at a time. "Michael, you take Adriana through first. Boys, you and Olga next. Ames, then you and the stroller. Jamie and I will bring up the rear."

Michael grinned at me, took Adriana's hand, and they stepped through the gate. Here one second, gone the next. I ignored the slow fade everything did going through a gate because nausea wasn't on my list of things to experience today.

The boys each took one side of Olga's wheelchair and lifted it, then they stepped through.

"See you over there," Amy said. She and the animal-laden stroller went through.

I steeled myself. I'd hated gate transfers from Day One with Centaurion Division, and gaining some A-C powers hadn't made them any better. Going through the gates was, for me, a nauseating experience at best. I didn't want to literally toss all the cookies I'd been scarfing down, and I really didn't want to toss them onto Jamie.

Took a deep breath, relaxed. Took another, relaxed more. Took a third—and heard a step behind me. In an Embassy that was supposedly locked tight and devoid of anyone other than me and my baby.

CHAPTER 45

I WANTED TO FREEZE, but instead I spun around. And let out the breath I'd been holding.

"What the hell are you doing, Missus Chief?" Buchanan asked.

"Malcolm, are you part A-C?"

"Not that I know of. Why?"

"You have an amazing ability to sneak up on me."

He shook his head. "Where's everyone else?"

"Um, where I need to go. But you can come, too."

"Oh. Great. Floater gate transfer?"

"Wow. Can you see the gate? I mean, I used to be able to see the gate, before, but only like a kind of faint shimmering."

"I didn't need to see it. Since you came inside, the number of people in the second floor study continued to increase and not all of the new arrivals came in through the front door. Mister White and Senator Armstrong went to the American Centaurion Embassy, but no one else has exited this building via conventional means. And now I'm in here, and the only people left inside this entire place are you and Baby Chief. It doesn't take genius to figure out that you've been using floaters for some reason. Are you worried about another attack?"

"Yes, but not from the Club Fifty-One lunatics this time. At least, I don't think so. Tell you the reason once we get to our next stop."

He sighed, took Jamie from me and held her in one arm as he put his other arm around me and headed us toward the gate. "You don't make this job easy."

"As near as I can tell, it's easy for you." I steeled myself. And hoped Jeff wasn't paying attention to me at this precise time.

Buchanan did a variety of things similarly to Jeff, and this was merely one of them. Whether Jeff would perceive this as being better or worse than Buchanan catching me I couldn't guess. I didn't really want Jeff and Buchanan to be forced to have the jealousy chat, in part because I didn't think Jeff was going to cut Buchanan even half the slack he cut Chuckie, and said Chuckie slack was essentially nil.

However, we stepped through, and my worries about Jeff's jealousy were wiped away by intense nausea. Buchanan's arm tightened around me, which helped a little.

I'd heard the gates' functioning explained as using a temporal warp filtered through black-hole technology or similar, allowing the fast, safe, movement of matter across a large physical space in a very short amount of perceived time.

That made as much sense to me as international politics, which so far had made almost no logical sense at all. Suffice to say that going through the gates felt like you were taking a very slow step while the world moved past you very, very quickly. I'd tried going through gates with my eyes open and my eyes closed. To date, the only way going through them had been even remotely pleasant was if Jeff was carrying me and I had my face buried in his neck.

Needless to say, since Jeff wasn't here, I was nauseated by the time our feet hit the terra firma of the Dome's interior.

Christopher was waiting for us and gave us a lovely shot of Patented Glare #2. "You took a while to get here."

"Oh, my God, did Jeff ask you to cover the jealousy stuff if he wasn't around? Malcolm got into the Romanian Embassy, God alone knows how, and found me and Jamie just before we were stepping through the gate."

"Actually, I found them while the Ambassador was stalling going through," Buchanan said as he let go of me and put Jamie in my arms. "I know how much she hates them—frankly, if I hadn't come inside, she'd probably still be there, prepping for the trip."

"You don't know me."

Christopher snorted, and Buchanan laughed. "Fine," Christopher said. "I think I have things under control here."

I took a good look around. The Dome looked as it always had—dull. It had gates everywhere you could imagine, some in differing sizes, meaning it was an airport metal detector enthusiasts' dream location, but otherwise it didn't scream "excitement."

What it did scream right now, though, was crowded. In addition to being the main hub of all gate activity, the Dome was used for larger transfers, like limo fleets or big machinery. What it wasn't used for, however, was housing. So while the Dome was quite large and rather spacious normally, right now it gave off even more of an airport feeling, complete with the accompanying noise and stress.

There were a lot more people here than I'd actually expected. Of course, interspecies marriage had been approved once Jeff and I had managed to get down the aisle without the world ending, though it had been a close call, both the generalized interspecies stuff and the specific world not ending. And I knew other A-Cs besides my friends had gotten married to humans. I just hadn't actually paid attention to the number of couples who'd tied the knot in the past year and a half or so. I'd paid less attention to what number of those couples had a baby on the way.

Apparently, that number was "lots."

The Dome was packed, and the Security A-Cs whose jobs were to hang out here didn't look happy. At all.

"We have a slight logistics problem," Christopher shared, winning the Stating the Obvious Award for this moment in time.

"You're not kidding," Buchanan said. "Are you sure this was a good idea?"

"It's Kitty's idea, so no, I'm not sure about it at all."

"Thanks for the vote of confidence, Christopher. It was actually your dad's idea. Besides, it's secure, and that's what matters right now."

"Security isn't happy." Christopher apparently wanted to ensure he won the Stating the Obvious Award at least once a minute.

"Yeah. I can see that." I could. The Security A-Cs ran big, bigger than Jeff usually, and that was saying something. These were men who, if they'd been humans and, therefore, not all totally gorgeous, would be working as bouncers for the likes of Jay-Z and Beyoncé and keeping the less cool out of all the really great clubs. Or starring as the barbarian hordes in epic fantasy films. Basically, they were all huge. And clearly unhappy.

"They're only doing this because Gladys told them to, and I'm here," Christopher said. "Without my father, Jeff, Paul, or James around, though, they're questioning what we're doing and why."

"Huh. I feel a revision of the plan coming on."

"I can't wait," Christopher snarked.

"Actually, you can. Which is my plan revision."

"What?"

"You're staying here. They're listening to you, because you used to be the Head of Imageering and so second in command. I'd imagine they're still not so sure how much they love taking orders from James and Tim. But they were great with taking orders from you and Jeff. So you stay, and the situation remains under control."

Christopher looked like he really wanted to argue.

"Your wife will be here. And your goddaughter. Who, let's be clear, is the likely focus for kidnapping."

Either my logic was overpowering or Christopher had done all the math I had and come up with the same answer: If we wanted to house civilians here, we needed someone who could shout the right commands at A-C speeds.

"Fine. But before we do this, are you absolutely sure this is necessary?"

"Happy to check."

"With who?" Christopher asked.

"On what?" Buchanan asked.

"Oh, ye of little faith." I handed Jamie to Christopher. "Entertain your goddaughter for a couple of minutes."

I sat on the floor and closed my eyes. Hopefully I wasn't going to disturb him at an inopportune time.

CHAPTER 46

ACE, **ARE YOU THERE?** I thought in my mind.

Yes, Kitty, ACE is here.

I know there's a lot going on.

Because ACE did its best to stay out of our affairs and so avoid becoming either a crutch we ultimately couldn't live without or an all-powerful despot, I didn't call for help as often as I wanted to. ACE was willing to break and bend the rules when the situation was dire, but it wasn't a good idea to push anyone all the time, and certainly not for things we could do ourselves. Since ACE resided in Gower, I was also careful to make contact only when it was necessary or I knew things were slow, because that way I didn't risk disturbing ACE at an inopportune time for Gower. While ACE was incredibly powerful, even the strongest entity out there could lose focus at a bad time.

I'd also discovered ACE could be, if not injured, then depleted in a way that was as bad for a collective superconsciousness as getting a major smack down was for any human or A-C. And I knew from experience that entities like ACE could be, if not killed, then destroyed in such a way that they wouldn't be "together" any more. So I did my best to word my conversations in such a way that they wouldn't stress ACE out. I didn't succeed all that often, but I did persevere.

Yes, Kitty. Much is going on.

Am I on the right track, feeling that all the things that have happened to me over the past couple of days are being done to distract me from the danger Chuckie's in?

Yes. But Chuckie is not the only one in danger.

Yeah, I know. Are Jamie and the other hybrids I have at the Dome safe here?

In a way. ACE sounded evasive. Great. Exact questions were always better.

Will having Christopher stay with them be a better choice than having him come with me?

Yes.

I pondered this. ACE usually preferred to give me longer answers, and often tossed out some helpful breadcrumbs, but only when I'd actually asked the right questions. ACE was a lot like my mom and Olga in that way.

Have I put the right people into hiding in the Dome? Am I missing anyone who should be here and be protected, or someone who should be coming along with me?

ACE was silent. Maybe I'd asked too many questions.

No, Kitty never asks too many questions. Right. ACE could "hear" my deeper-level thoughts, too. ACE enjoys speaking with Kitty. Kitty thinks right.

Sometimes you're the only one who believes that, ACE.

Chuckie always believes in Kitty, just as Kitty always believes in Chuckie. James will never give up on Kitty, just as Kitty will never give up on James. Kitty saved ACE, and ACE will never forget that.

You save us all the time, too, ACE.

Does Kitty still feel ACE is . . . correct to do so?

I stopped myself from giving a knee-jerk "of course" reaction. ACE only asked questions like this when it saw a big moral quandary ahead. So, why would ACE be asking me that question, right now? I had no idea.

Gave it a shot anyway. Well, if we put aside the fact that I like being alive and keeping all the people I love alive, I still believe you have every right to protect this world, and the people in it, ACE. This is your world. We're yours, you're ours.

Even though ACE is not like Kitty or Jeff or even Paul?

Yes. You're a combination of every A-C talent, but you were sent here to watch over us.

But ACE has done much more than watch.

True enough. But you were right to do it.

Why?

I thought about it. It's like Jeff's new bird, Bellie. You know about her, right? I didn't actually want to try to comprehend everything ACE knew, but I was fairly sure that if it had the slightest form of sentient thought, ACE knew about it.

Yes. Bellie belonged to Antony, who tried to destroy Kitty and Jeff and the others.

Yes. And my 'uncle,' Peter the Dingo Dog, sent her to me. But Jeff attached to her. Jeff loves her now, and Bellie loves Jeff. As she liked to share constantly. Jeff could have sent her to someone else, to a bird sanctuary, even had her put to sleep.

You mean killed.

Sometimes it's killed, yeah. Sometimes you're putting something you love out of its very real and painful misery.

If Jeff had sent Bellie away, it would have killed Bellie.

Then Jeff was right to keep her and take care of her, right?

Yes.

Well, it's like that with you and us, ACE. Jeff is much more powerful than Bellie. He's bigger, smarter, and, to her, probably very much like a god. But he takes care of her because she needs him to. And she repays that with her love.

Just as Kitty repays ACE.

Honestly, ACE, I don't know that I could ever repay you for everything you've done for us. But I love you for all you do. And for all you don't.

How can Kitty love ACE if ACE does not always do for Kitty?

You could have become this world's worst nightmare. You could have answered all our prayers. And both would ultimately have been terrible outcomes for us. Destruction of the world is easy to understand. But the achievement of all our hopes and dreams would leave us nothing left to aspire to, no challenges to meet. And humans, and A-Cs, don't do well with nothing to strive for.

Adversity helps humanity to achieve?

Yes. I knew ACE knew this. So why were we having this conversation right now? Um, ACE, are you not able to protect Jamie and the other hybrid babies?

ACE will guard the Dome.

The Dome. That seemed remarkably specific. ACE, are you saying you're only willing to guard the Dome and those in it, or are you saying that you're going to have to use a lot of power to guard the Dome and those in it?

ACE is never unwilling to watch over.

Watching over probably counted as guarding. I took this non-answer to mean that either ACE was being forced to guard only the Dome or that there was a lot of bad coming and ACE felt that he could only guard the Dome effectively. Neither option was really great. I was sort of sorry I'd asked.

ACE, are the supersoldiers going to be activated? And by that, I mean are they going to be attacking any time soon? Maybe at the International One World Festival, or somewhere else?

No. The supersoldiers are not prepared.

Oh. Good.

No. That is very bad.

It was? Why is that, ACE? They're destruction machines of the highest order. It took an incredible amount of power, teamwork and, frankly, luck to defeat the few we destroyed at the President's Ball. One of them could probably take out the Dome without issue, let alone more of them. Suddenly, the idea that ACE was going to focus on the Dome almost exclusively seemed wise, especially since my baby was going to be here.

Yes, the supersoldiers are machines. But there is thought inside the supersoldiers.

Fantastic. So, they're sentient? And do you mean all of them or just the ones we have under our control?

The few now under Chuckie's control are not like the others.

Well, Marling had told us as much right before he'd effectively killed himself. Do you mean the androids, like the one I fought yesterday? Or something else?

Yes.

Great, back to the one-word replies. ACE, am I okay leaving Jamie here without me?

No. The way he said it, though, made me think I had, yet again, phrased my question wrong.

ACE, will Jamie be safe if I leave her here with the others in the Dome?

Yes.

So, I was the one who wouldn't be safe. Well, that was, pretty much, the story of my life since meeting the gang from Alpha Four. I haven't figured out what you want me to, have I?

Not yet, ACE said politely. But Kitty will. Kitty thinks right. Kitty should think about what Kitty and ACE have talked about.

Fantastic. Oh, well, I needed to race off and make sure Jeff and Chuckie, not to mention everyone else, were okay, at least for the time being.

ACE, one last question.

Of course, Kitty. Kitty can speak to ACE whenever Kitty wishes or needs to.

Thanks, ACE, I appreciate that. My last question is this—have I figured out what's going on correctly?

Kitty has determined things.

Huh. Rephrasing time. Have I figured out what's really going on—not just part of it, but all of it?

No. The relief in ACE's voice was plain. Nice to know that ACE's issue had been that I hadn't figured out the full Bad Guy Plan of the Moment. But Kitty will. Kitty thinks right.

Thanks, ACE. You think right, too.

ACE thinks that ACE will protect Jamie and the others.

Thank you.

Or ACE will die trying.

CHAPTER 47

I FELT A SURGE OF WARM FEELINGS, which was ACE's way of hugging me in my mind, and then I felt him leave my mind. ACE certainly knew how to make an exit.

I opened my eyes. "Christopher, you're staying here. Prepare for something."

"What 'something' am I supposed to prepare for?"

"I have no idea, but I think it's going to be bad."

Christopher rubbed the back of his neck. "Really? That's it?"

"Yeah." I looked around. "Just how many people can the Dome actually hold?"

"Most of our people, if necessary."

"Really? It doesn't seem that big."

I was treated to something other than a Patented Glare—I got a Derisive Look. Nice to see he was branching out. "Kitty, you've been with us how long?"

"Close to two and a half years. Why?"

Buchanan sighed. "There are lower levels."

I stared at them. "There are? Seriously?" Truly, no one told me anything. I couldn't wait to discover what else I hadn't been told. I was sure it would be at a completely inopportune time, whenever the next surprising bit of information appeared.

Christopher shook his head. "Why am I surprised? At all? You were given briefing materials on every single A-C facility when you were made the Head of Airborne."

"Oh. Right. Those." The huge binders full of boring blah, blah, blah that I'd pretty much ignored this entire time. Well, we were all still alive and kicking, for the most part, so I decided the Binders of Boredom could wait a little while longer.

I took Jamie back and hugged her. "You be good for Uncle Christopher, Jamie-Kat. Mommy's got to go for a while, but she'll be back very soon."

Jamie looked up at me and gurgled. During Operation Confusion she'd been able to show us where all our kidnapped team members were, which was why they were still alive. I wasn't sure how much of that was Jamie and how much was ACE, but all I saw were her pretty blue eyes looking at me trustingly. I wasn't going to do anything to betray that trust.

Lorraine and Claudia came over, babies in their arms. Lorraine was a buxom blonde and Claudia willowy with brown hair a shade the hair dye industry would kill for. They were the perfect example of what Dazzlers were—gorgeous, brilliant, and really nice.

"You're leaving us and racing off?" Lorraine asked after we'd all hugged and exchanged baby kisses.

"Yeah, I am. I need you all here, safe and on guard."

"On guard for what?" Claudia asked.

"I don't actually know. But I think it's gonna be big."

The girls exchanged a look. "You've talked to ACE?" Claudia asked.

"Yes. I didn't get much. I mean, I got some, but not much." Not much I really understood yet, anyway.

Lorraine nodded. "For what it's worth, yesterday Paul said ACE felt more . . . absent than he ever has before."

"Yeah," Claudia chimed in. "He said it was as if ACE was really distracted by something."

"Did he say if ACE felt uneasy?"

They both shook their heads. "Paul's had a lot going on with—" Claudia slammed her mouth shut.

"With the high security stuff I'm not supposed to know right now, yeah, I figured."

Lorraine looked pointedly at Christopher. "Don't you need to help your wife or something?"

"You're so subtle. No, actually, I probably need to stay here and make sure Kitty doesn't hear anything she's not supposed to."

"What would it really matter?" Claudia asked. "I mean, it's never been bad for us to have Kitty in the loop."

"Half the time, she's the one who discovers the loops," Lorraine added.

Christopher shrugged. "To me? I don't really care at this point. I can't imagine how it would affect our diplomatic mission and she's already guessed half of it or more. However, if you all want to keep Reynolds in place, then Kitty can't hear it from any of us, because if she knows or, worse, we tell her, then his job's at risk."

"Fine," Lorraine said with a sigh. "We don't want Chuck out of the picture."

Claudia nodded. "He does too much for us."

This was the first time I'd heard either one of them use Chuckie's first name. "When did you two decide to get off Jeff and Christopher's Let's Hate Chuckie bandwagon?"

"We were never on it," Claudia said. "We just didn't want to get into an argument with Jeff, Christopher, or the other guys about him."

"You never said." At least, not to me. I hoped that someone had told Chuckie.

"We weren't Captains before," Lorraine said with a wink. "And after working with him, it's hard to understand why they're still acting like Chuck's anything but our friend."

"But then again, Jeff and Christopher tend to be a little slow sometimes." Claudia laughed, and I knew she was thinking about Operation Fugly.

"True enough." Lorraine grinned.

"I'm right here," Christopher said while reverting to form and offering Patented Glare #5 to all of us.

"Hey, I didn't call you slow. Right now."

"What restraint. Look, are you heading off or staying here?"

"Malcolm and I are leaving. You're staying. Pull in my dad and Jeff's parents if you're able to."

"I have a list," Claudia said. "We'll go through it and analyze who we can move in here when."

"I don't think it's a good idea for us to have a lot of people coming in with none going out," Christopher told her.

I opened my mouth, but Buchanan took my arm. "Let them figure it out. We need to go, Missus Chief."

"You're right." I looked around. I didn't see the Peregrines or Poofs. Oh, well, better they were here with Jamie anyway. I kissed her again. "Be my good girl. Mommy loves you and will see you very soon."

Christopher took Jamie, I hugged them all again, then Buchanan and I went to the nearest gate, which, in the Dome, meant we walked a couple of feet. "American Centaurion Embassy for two, please."

The A-C working this gate nodded and calibrated. "I couldn't help overhearing, Ambassador," he said as he spun the dial. "Should we be prepared for some kind of attack?"

"Honestly, I'm not sure. But being prepared is always a good idea."

He nodded. "I'll check with Commander White."

"Do that," Buchanan said as he took my arm and stepped us through the gate before I could mention that Christopher wasn't a Commander any more.

A few nauseating seconds later we exited in the Embassy's basement. "It's a good thing you had White stay there," Buchanan said as I let my stomach settle.

"Why so?"

"I don't know how happy your grunts are with the current chain of command."

"It's been almost five months."

"Yeah. That's not a lot of time to adjust to such a radical change."

"It wasn't that radical. Everyone who moved into leadership positions had been increasing in rank for a while."

Buchanan shook his head. "I know you had a hell of a time with transition to your current roles. So did the people who replaced you. Think about what that said to the grunts."

"They all dealt with my addition just fine a couple years ago."

"Yes, but you were added into what they could rightly consider the human section. None of them can fly, so a human being in charge of the new Airborne Division made sense."

"The new position holders make sense."

"Not to them, I guarantee it. You took your two strongest agents and moved them to face positions. You said it yourself to White a few minutes ago. Crawford replacing you? Okay, I'm sure they're okay with that. Reader replacing your husband, though? I'm sure they're not happy about that at all. And then, you put Serene Dwyer in as White's replacement *and* moved the two women you were just talking to into the slots Reader and Crawford had had? And this was right after the Pontifex retired, which was unprecedented, and put Gower in place."

"I realize some of the older generation are old-fashioned, but they do seem aware that women can vote and hold jobs and everything these days."

"It's not that, and it's not just the older generation. Their women *have* jobs, jobs they feel are vitally important. Their women do the brainwork. But they don't normally go out, guns blazing. It's one thing to intermarry. It's another to have no choice."

"There are a lot of times you remind me of Jeff. This is one of them. Look, there's nothing I can do about it now."

"Pat yourself on the back for keeping White there. You heard the grunt who sent us through—he called him Commander. He wants White back in charge, and your husband too, I'm sure."

"Fantastic. Let's get upstairs and you can share this with the man who actually orchestrated it all. I'm sure the former Pontifex will be happy to hear your doom and gloom take."

Buchanan shook his head again as we headed upstairs. "You hear but you don't listen, you see but you don't observe."

"Tell me, Holmes, how *do* you do it?"

"Training, attention to detail, and awareness of the big picture."

"Noted. After this is over, I'll take your class. I'm already signed up for one with Mister Joel Oliver. And as I said to him, your class has to be better than the Washington Wife class."

Buchanan sighed as we reached the first floor. "I learned all of this from your mother. You were raised with her, and I know she passed things along to you."

"Never draw to an inside straight was a biggie of hers."

"Now you're just being b—"

"Hey!"

He grinned. "I was going to say 'bratty.' "

"Sure you were."

CHAPTER 48

WHITE, ARMSTRONG, TITO, AND WALTER were waiting for us in the kitchen. Bellie was on a perch. I wasn't a great judge of parrot expressions, but she didn't look happy.

She saw me and squawked. "Bellie misses Jeff!"

"Yes, yes. Kitty misses Jeff, too. Busy times, Bellie, demand that we have to do our jobs."

"Security is job one!"

"Duly noted, Bellie."

"That was one of Antony's favorite sayings," Armstrong said.

"It's sort of a cliché."

He shrugged. "In many ways, Antony was a cliché. In others he wasn't."

Chose to not list Marling's fab personal traits at this precise time, so I looked at White. "Tell me you figured out how to keep her beak closed while we're racing off to try to figure out what's going on. And have a tonnage of bird treats on hand."

"We'll handle it, Missus Martini. Where is Christopher?"

"I kept him at the Dome. I think we're going to need him there." I looked at Bellie. "Let's leave her here and take this conversation to another room."

"I'll move her," White said. He took Bellie and her perch to the nearest room and shut her in it. "Now, what didn't you want the parrot to hear?"

Since Tito and Walter had missed it all and Buchanan had missed a lot, I filled them in on the high-level stuff, including what we'd figured out over at Olga's, what I'd asked Jeff to do, what Oliver was doing, my conversation with ACE, and what Claudia and Lorraine had told me as well. I was becoming the Queen of the Recap. Lucky me. "So, something's going on, and we for sure haven't figured it all out yet."

Walter looked worried. "I think I should be staying here, Chief." He sounded worried, too.

"Walt, I don't want you in danger, and we need your skills."

"But Security is supposed to leave only as a last resort."

"Fine, you can walk out last and lock the front door. We don't have a clear idea of what's going on, but I know we're going to need your help." And I didn't want Walter to be a sitting duck, all alone in the Embassy our enemies now knew how to get in and out of without issue. And who knew when Club 51 would come back with more bombs?

"None of our standard team with medical know-how are coming, right?" Tito asked, before Walter could countermand my orders out loud again.

"Right, they're at the Dome."

He nodded. "Fine. Be right back, I'm going to get my more advanced med kit."

"Probably wise."

Tito trotted off, which Walter took as his cue. "Chief, I know you don't want to hear this, but I need to stay in the Embassy." Walter sounded upset, worried, and more authoritative than I'd even heard before.

I studied his expression. He looked determined. "Why, Walt? Using words that aren't protocol, standard, or procedure."

"Because if we leave our Embassy unmanned and unprotected, then our enemies can come in and take it over, destroy it, put anything they want into it, and we'll have allowed that. My *job* is to ensure that this Embassy and all its personnel remain safe and protected. I'm not supposed to leave unless I have no choice."

"Gladys leaves Dulce all the time."

Walter shook his head. "She goes to another Base, where she can still monitor, and despite what you think, there are always Security personnel in every Base, even if you've been told that base is fully devoid of personnel."

"Mister White, is this true?"

"Yes. Security is the highest risk job after fieldwork. It's where our best and bravest tend to go if they don't have empathic or imageering talent."

Yet another thing no one had told me. I decided not to say this aloud, because it was probably in the Briefing Books of Boredom I'd never cracked.

"It's in your briefing materials, I'm sure," Buchanan said. "You know, the materials you've never looked at."

"I say again, you don't know me."

Armstrong cleared his throat. "I realize this technically falls under 'none of my business,' but I have to side with your Security Chief here. Leaving this base of operations with no protection at all seems rather foolhardy."

"Leaving someone to be used as cannon fodder, a hostage, or be killed sounds worse."

Armstrong nodded. "I agree. However, we determined earlier that whoever's in charge seems able to anticipate your reactions fairly well. Meaning they'd expect you to force Walter here to leave, ensuring easy access into your building."

I considered our dilemma and Armstrong's points. Sadly, he had some good ones. "Okay, Walt, if you're staying, you can't stay here alone. And I need Richard and Tito. I'm going to bring Malcolm along so I can trip him somewhere along the way and laugh as he falls flat on his face."

"In your dreams, Missus Chief."

I snorted, White chuckled, but Walter looked relieved. "I'll ask Gladys to send over Security support from Dulce, Chief. Thank you."

"No. Thank you. For still doing your job better than anyone else."

Walter looked proud. "Thanks, Chief." He nodded to the other men, then zipped off, presumably heading to his Mini-Command Center attached to his rooms.

"You sure this is okay, Mister White?"

"I'm sure that Walter's points were well made and accurate." As he spoke, a platoon of Security A-Cs trooped up from the basement. "Head to the third floor. Our Head of Security's there and he'll tell you what to do." They nodded and hypersped off.

As they did so, I felt someone watching me. Looked around to see several Peregrines, what appeared to be three mated pairs. And, while I hadn't really seen them outside of the full flock before, somehow I knew their names.

The two I knew were named George and Gracie did the head bob thing to me, then headed off. I knew they were going to join Walter in his Command Center. Han and Leia, who belonged to Chuckie, shot me very worried looks, then wandered off. I knew without asking they were on patrol. I also knew without asking they were worried about Chuckie and conflicted as to whether they should stay at the Embassy or go in search of him.

Tito rejoined us, big medical kit in hand. His Peregrines, Brad and Angie, followed him into the room. I managed not to ask aloud if they were coming along or merely guarding us while we were still on premises. It turned out I didn't need to speak. Brad gave me a long look and somehow shared that they were going to stay here once we left.

I didn't drink any more because A-Cs were deathly allergic to alcohol and I never wanted Jeff unable to kiss me. But right now, I really wanted to go to a bar and tell the guy behind the counter to make me a stiff one and keep 'em coming.

"Where are we heading?" Armstrong asked.

I thankfully pulled myself away from the contemplation of my mental breakdown and back to the matter at hand. "That, Senator, is the question of the moment." I pulled out my phone. I had no texts or missed calls. Specifically, I had no texts or calls from Jeff or Chuckie. I felt my worry spike.

Now that things were sort of handled and I sort of knew something of what was going on, taking a moment to think might be wise. This, of course, meant taking a moment to run my yap some more. Never an issue.

"You know, I want to ask one of Amy's insightful questions again. Why did Senator Armstrong get the new set of dirty pictures today of all days?"

"Because they're going to put whatever their plan of action is into effect today," Buchanan said without missing a beat.

"Right, no argument. But . . ."

"But, Missus Martini?"

Armstrong's eyes narrowed. "You're asking not only why today but when today, aren't you?"

"Yeah. They gave you time to get out of the One World Festival and get over to us."

Buchanan jerked. "Which they expected him to do."

"Right. They expected a different reaction for the first set of phony porno pics, but this time they knew he was going to come right to us."

"Right to you," White corrected. "You're who he went to before."

"So they've anticipated my actions well," Armstrong said. "But why send me away from the Festival?"

"Why did they try to keep you away from the President's Ball? My guess is that whoever it is still feels they can convince you to do what they want. Either because you have similar leanings anyway, are already up to your neck in it all, or because they can force you via blackmail."

"So, do we go to the Festival?" Buchanan asked. "Or do we go after Mister Joel Oliver like he's expecting?"

Considered the facts as we knew them. "Whatever's going on there, everything's been done to keep me and the senator away. I say it's high time we crash that party and see what's so special about it."

CHAPTER 49

"I SUPPOSE TAKING A GATE IS OUT," Tito said.

"I think we want to be able to get away. And I don't even know if anyone would give us a floater gate without Alpha Team's permission, especially since we're not in any danger we know of." And I was positive Alpha Team wouldn't give said permission.

"My car is down the street," Armstrong said.

"How trustworthy is your driver?" Buchanan asked.

Armstrong shrugged. "Yesterday I'd have said completely. Today, I have no idea."

"We could take one of our limos and be on our way." My worry about Jeff and Chuckie grew. I sent a text to Jeff, asking him where he was and what he was doing.

"I don't want to leave my driver," Armstrong said. "Not only is Evan unprotected, but we have no idea how long he'll be sitting in the street, waiting for me to return."

"And if he's loyal to the senator, or merely unaware of what's going on, he's in danger," White added.

"If you tell him to go home and he's working with our enemies, then it'll tip them off," Buchanan said.

"Mister Joel Oliver went off to do distraction duty." No answer from Jeff. Sent a text to Chuckie.

"That doesn't mean they followed him," Buchanan said patiently. "And it also doesn't mean there was only one person or team watching us. We have to assume we're still being watched."

"Fine. In that case, let me remind you that our limos have special extras installed."

"But the senator's limo will be less obvious," Buchanan countered.

"You want us in a car without a laser shield, Malcolm?" I wasn't sure I wanted us in a car without a laser shield. Especially since Chuckie hadn't answered, either.

Buchanan looked thoughtful. "Yeah, I do. Senator, please tell your driver to pull into the Embassy's parking garage so that we can all load in unobtrusively."

"If there's a bomb in that limo, then that's what they want."

"I understand why you're worried about that, Missus Chief. However, while we were in Florida, some special equipment was installed in the garage."

"How special?"

"Spot-any-and-all-of-the-bad-things-put-into-the-vehicles special. Some of it's experimental, but it's A-C experimental."

"How do you know about all this? You were in Florida with us."

He gave me a look I could only think of as pained. "Yes. I was. We weren't cut off from all communications."

"Oh. Good point. I'm distracted."

"Use whatever excuse makes you happy, Missus Chief. Senator, let's get your man into the garage."

While Senator Armstrong called his driver, Buchanan went upstairs to make sure Walter had all the new garage scanning equipment up and running, and I checked my phone. Still no reply from either Jeff or Chuckie.

"You look worried," White said.

"I am worried. I sent texts to Jeff and Chuckie, and they haven't replied. Now I'm wondering if I should call them."

"It might set your mind at ease," White offered.

"It might disrupt them at a bad time, too."

"And it might give you a chance to tell you not to go to the Festival," Tito added.

"Oh, Tito, good point. I'll wait until we're actually at the Mall to call in a panic."

"You work well under pressure," Buchanan said as he rejoined us. "Walter cleared the senator's limo—it's clean inside though he mentioned it could use a trip to the carwash. However, dirty cars aren't a crime, and there's nothing dangerous in the dirt, so let's get to the garage."

"We can test the dirt?"

"Amazing, isn't it? What *will* those crazy kids from Alpha Four think up next?"

"You're in an interesting mood." I looked at his expression. "What sneaky thing are you planning, Malcolm?"

"You wound me, Missus Chief. And disappoint me."

"You mean you're upset that I haven't already figured it out yet. Fine. Let's get Jeff's beloved parrot and get moving."

The temptation to leave Bellie at the Embassy and thus make her Walter's problem, regardless of Jeff's likely reaction to the idea, was strong. Despite the presence of some of the Peregrines, she'd clearly regained her nerve and normal personality.

Bellie refused to sit on my shoulder. She refused to let me touch her. She freaked out at Buchanan, screaming that she belonged to Jeff. She almost took Armstrong's hand off, even though she'd cawed his name out as though they were long lost besties—he escaped losing fingers to the Beak of Doom only because Buchanan pulled him back at the last moment. She tried the same with Tito, but he'd learned and kept himself far enough away that Bellie missed taking off his hand by a wide margin.

No, the avian beast only deigned to sit on White's shoulder. I took this to mean Bellie was aware of who the highest-ranking male was in whatever room she was in and, since she clearly had her standards, would only be with him.

Once our horrible parrot was taken care of, Buchanan headed for the stairway that took us down to the garage, which was not the stairway that took us down to the basement. Bellie was mercifully silent, no doubt because White was giving her a lot of attention and more than a few bird treats.

"So, Malcolm, what's our plan?"

"I'm thinking we go duck hunting."

The other men stared at him. I, on the other hand, was pretty sure I knew what he meant. "You want to use Armstrong's limo as a decoy."

"That's actually a good idea," Tito said approvingly.

"How does that prevent Evan from telling our enemies, if he's in fact a spy of some kind?" Armstrong asked.

"Oh, I don't care if he's a spy," Buchanan said. "Because we're going to give him an assignment. Senator, make sure you sell it in a way he'll believe."

"Sell what? I don't know your plan."

"Malcolm wants you to sell whatever he's going to say as truth in advertising."

"Actually," Buchanan said with a grin, "I want you to tell him, Missus Chief."

"Figures. So what am I telling him to do? Pretend he has all of us in the limo as a decoy and drive to the senator's offices so the bad guys think we're going there when we are, in fact, going to Andrews Air Force Base to warn of imminent alien attack?"

"See? I knew you'd figure it all out, Missus Chief."

"That could work," Armstrong said slowly. "Either he'll lead another tail off and away, or he'll tell our enemies that we're heading to Andrews. Either way, more of our enemies are somewhere other than around us and potentially more confused." Tito and White both nodded their agreement.

"Really? If I'd come up with this without Malcolm leading the way, right now, at this very moment, you'd all be telling me I was crazy and that it'd never work."

"Oh, we didn't say it wasn't crazy," Tito said.

"We also didn't say it would work, merely that it could," White added. "You know, Missus Martini—like most of our plans."

"And it really does sound like a plan of yours, Kitty," Tito added.

"Because it *is* a plan of mine. I just laid it out, Malcolm didn't."

Buchanan clapped me on the shoulder. "Great plan, there, Missus Chief. Let's see how it works."

I heaved a sigh as we headed for Armstrong's limo. "Malcolm, I'm seriously considering the benefits of hating you right now."

"Good. That'll make your husband happy."

CHAPTER 50

I COULDN'T TELL IF ARMSTRONG'S DRIVER was on his side or an evil bad guy, but Evan seemed clear on his duties and drove off as requested.

"How do we tell if he's doing what we want or not?"

"We don't care," Buchanan replied. "We need to focus on the important things, like what's really going on and where your husband and Reynolds are."

Buchanan went to one of our regular limos. We had several—enough to evacuate the entire Embassy via car if necessary. Buchanan chose one without a car seat in it; he got behind the wheel, Tito took shotgun, and the rest of us climbed into the back.

"Kyle always gets the door."

"I'm a doctor," Tito shared. "If you're hurt, I'll get the door for you. Otherwise, I thought you were an emancipated woman."

"I am. I'm also saying that shotgun gets the doors. It's in the A-C Limo Handbook. I mean, dude, Christopher got the doors when I first met these guys when he had shotgun, and he was the Head of Imageering at the time. You're saying you're too good to get the door?"

"No. I'm saying that Christopher was clearly trying to impress you. I'm not."

"He has a point," White mentioned.

I snorted. "I remember my first introductions to your son. His version of 'impress' and mine differ."

"Hence why you're happily married to my nephew."

"Speaking of whom." I checked my phone. Nothing. From Jeff or Chuckie. This boded. I couldn't believe both of them would ignore my "I'm worried, where are you?" texts, at least not willingly.

"Why aren't we moving?" Armstrong asked.

"We're waiting," Buchanan replied. "To give whoever's following your driver time to get out of range. Or to let him call and advise the bad guys that we're actually heading to Andrews."

"Should we have the laser shield on?"

"You're jumpy." Buchanan turned around and gave me a searching look. His expression softened. "We'll find them. I promise." He turned back and turned on the stereo. "Watching the Detectives" by Elvis Costello came on.

While we waited and Elvis crooned in his hipster way, I sent texts to Naomi and Abigail. They answered pretty quickly. "Per Mimi and Abby, there's been a lot of little skirmishes that our agents have controlled. The Mall's packed, so it's hard to pick anyone out. They're under orders to pay attention to assassination-type thoughts, and there are so many people there they can't actually spare the focus to look for Jeff or Chuckie."

Or, per Naomi, to fill me in on everything going on. She insinuated that my presence would be a good idea, though. At least if I took "you coming to find them probably would be a good idea" to mean she wanted me there. Which I did.

We had time for "Dirty Deeds Done Dirt Cheap" by AC/DC and "Round and Round" by Aerosmith to finish before Buchanan drove off. We left the garage to the sounds of Soundgarden's "Fell on Black Days." I really hoped the song wasn't going to turn out to be prophetic.

By now, my anxiety was such that I'd expect Jeff to call. I'd sent several texts to him, and he hadn't replied, so I wasn't trying to hide my emotions from him.

Decided to call Amy while we drove in an unhurried manner toward the Mall section of D.C. "Hey, Kitty, what's up?"

"I was just going to ask you the same thing, Ames."

"All quiet here."

"Really? I hear what I could politely call a commotion."

"I meant figuratively, as in nothing's happening, no one has attacked, and it's quiet and boring. And what you're hearing isn't a commotion so much as what it's like here right now, which is sort of like being in Grand Central Station at rush hour. What are you up to?"

"We're heading to the International One World Festival. Anything you want to tell me before we get there?"

"Yeah. Hang on." Amy was quiet for a few moments, but I could still hear the sounds of a lot of people around her. "Sorry, had to get away from Christopher without him noticing. Lorraine and Claudia and I agreed that whoever you called first would tell you about all the things that've been kept from you."

"Good. And thanks."

"It makes no sense that you're not told, and, frankly, while I get that Chuck's job is in peril if you know, I think more will be in peril if you don't know."

"Chuckie included."

"Right. So, anyway, while we were in Florida, a lot of terrorist threats were identified, focused on the Festival."

"Okay, we figured that out. And that's why the Bahraini and Israeli Embassies are extra hyper about the break-in and subsequent accusations."

"Yes, only . . . there's more. The terrorist organization that's popped the most is supposedly defunct."

My brain had the ability to move at lightning speed at times, and this was one of those times. "The Al Dejahl terrorist organization is back in action, isn't it?"

"Yes."

"And that's why everyone views this as a threat to me. Because I took out Ronaldo Al Dejahl and was the main reason Ronnie Junior had to take to the stars to escape." Which was why Claudia and Lorraine were set on telling me. Because they knew I'd be safer prepared.

"Right. Kitty, be careful. Remember in Paris—my dad and his insane friends thought Jamie could teleport herself to Jeff in order to save him. If any of them are behind this, they'll be willing to try that on you, too. And we don't know if they're right or not."

"ACE won't let Jamie do it."

"You *hope*. You don't know."

"True." I took a deep breath. "This helps, Ames, thanks. Is there anything else?"

"Yes. So far as anyone's told me, my wicked stepmother and her boyfriend aren't back on the planet."

"Do you believe that information?"

"I don't know. I find it hard to believe everyone would have left us in Florida with so little protection if LaRue was known to be back."

"Good point. Okay, we're almost there. I'll check in when I can."

"Do. I'll text if I learn anything else."

"You're the best Ames. Hang in there." We hung up as "M.I.A."

by the Foo Fighters came on. This song was definitely prophetic. Maybe we needed to focus on Boy Band Pop for a while, just to get things back to a more positive audio atmosphere.

"Did I hear you correctly?" White asked quietly.

"Sadly, yes." I contemplated what I could say in front of Armstrong and went with the plan that I'd worry about him being our main problem later. I shared Amy's intel. "So, the reason they don't want me here is to protect me. Sweet, isn't it?"

"You know our enemies know you," Tito said. "And the fastest way to get you out of hiding is to threaten Jeff, or Reynolds, for that matter."

"Any of you," Buchanan corrected as we reached the Mall area. "She's not good at hiding out when people she knows are in danger."

"It's a weakness they're exploiting," Armstrong said.

"They get to win this battle, then." But not the war. I'd never let them win that.

CHAPTER 51

THE NATIONAL MALL wasn't a big shopping center. It was a huge park with a lot of national landmarks and awesome museums bordering it. The Lincoln Memorial was at one end, and the Capitol Building was at the other, with the Washington Monument sort of in the middle. Aerosmith had played here, as well as a lot of other bands, and the International One World Festival was just the latest in a long line of events that had been held here.

Being Tourist Mecca for the D.C. area meant, in the weird way I was getting used to with the East Coast, that the Mall didn't have great parking as a general rule. On an average day it was hard to find parking. Today it was insane. "Malcolm, what are we going to do with the limo? Are you dropping us off and going back to the Embassy?"

"No. Just hang on." We were near the Smithsonian Metro station when he found what he was looking for—the entrance to an underground parking garage. It had a big sign stating that it was for Employees Only and that there was no event or Mall parking ever allowed. It also required a keycard for entry. Buchanan pulled a card out of his wallet, put it in, and the gate raised. We drove in.

"You don't work here for real, do you?" Maybe this was the P.T.C.U.'s hidden headquarters.

"No. The P.T.C.U. and the C.I.A. have all the cool toys."

"Works for me." Maybe I'd still check it out later, when things were quiet, to see if this was where Mom and her Gang of Cool Kick Butt Cats hung out during the nonengagement hours.

We parked. It was Sunday, so the parking lot wasn't packed, but

Buchanan still chose a section that was pretty isolated. We unloaded, parrot and all, and Buchanan hit the Invisibility Shield. The limo disappeared.

"Nifty. How will we find it again to ensure we can leave, let alone ensure it's not hit by someone else trying to park?"

Buchanan pointed to the sign above where he'd parked us—Reserved for Government Vehicles.

"Hope no one tries to come in to catch up on their work while everyone else is having fun."

Buchanan shrugged. "I have the laser shield activated, too. They'll bounce off. We can worry about the car or we can do what we came for."

"Good point. Again." We headed off for the real action while I worked on not allowing my stress level to affect my ability to look at the big picture. Wasn't impressed with my results.

Felt a nudge. Looked down to see Bruno walking alongside, like the best trained dog in the world. It was oddly reassuring to have him here, though. He looked up at me and gave me the "we'll handle it" look. He then craned his neck up so I could easily and surreptitiously pat his head.

"Shall we move at hyperspeed?" White asked me, with a smile for Bruno.

"Not sure the parrot can handle it, to be honest."

"We're not far from the main activity area," Buchanan said. I could tell he and Tito had noted Bruno's arrival, but Armstrong seemed blissfully unaware and I decided it was smarter to keep him that way. "Well, I mean where the main stage is set up. Frankly, the entire Mall is going to be packed."

He wasn't kidding. We'd parked in a building near to the Smithsonian's Castle, so that was the part of the Mall's middle section we headed for. As we reached our destination I took a good look around. The Festival wasn't overstating it about either being International or One World. It was like the biggest street fair ever, multiplied by a factor of at least ten. If you couldn't spot at least a dozen people from somewhere other than the U.S. in under a minute, it was likely you couldn't see. And if you couldn't spot at least two dozen people from the States in that same timeframe, you were blind and probably deaf as well.

Speaking of deaf, if I'd thought the background noise from the Dome was loud, the noise level here was intense. People were, for the most part, having a really fun time. There were booths aplenty, as well as what looked like roving street performers, in addition to several stages dotted all over. All of them had something going on, and every booth had lines at least four people wide and ten deep.

The smells from the myriad food stalls dotted all over happily overpowered most of the smell of lots of people in one place. I'd had two gate transfers recently, so the scents didn't make me even remotely hungry, though some of them were giving it a good run in the Smells So Good You Have To Eat It category.

It was easy to see why Naomi and Abigail hadn't been able to spot anyone using their eyes—our group got separated merely because we headed toward what Armstrong indicated was the main stage at the same time a swell of people headed the other way, and I had a couple moments of panic before I could spot Buchanan, who was the tallest, or White, who was wearing the Parrot Identifier.

We regrouped, and I put my purse over my head, after checking to make sure I still had Poofs on Board. I did, several unnamed ones in addition to Harlie and Poofikins. Good. Poof hitchhikers were never an issue.

"This is insane," Armstrong said. "I have no idea what we're going to achieve here."

"Do we get you to the politician's box or whatever it's called?" I straddled Bruno so he wouldn't get trampled.

"I don't relish the idea of letting the President know I didn't attend his speech." Armstrong looked toward the stage and squinted. "He's not on now. We've got a native song and dance going on, and I think it's from Venezuela, which was the third act for that stage after the President, presuming they didn't alter the program after I left."

I looked around again and concentrated, focusing on the inner me and my Wolverine abilities. I had to grit my teeth, but when I hit the Laser Beams From My Eyes level, I could see a variety of people moving much faster than anyone else around them. They were all dressed in the Armani Fatigues, not that this came as a shock.

"There are a tonnage of field teams here."

"Yes, there are," White confirmed. "But they all seem quite intent."

And they all looked alike. Oh, sure, they varied in height, body structure, and skin tones—we had pureblooded A-Cs who could pass for every ethnic type on Earth, because Alpha Four had varying skin colors and body types just like we did. But, as I was still shocked to realize, all that beauty tended to look alike after a while, especially if there was a lot of it on display. Clearly Centaurion Division had called in field teams from every Base worldwide, because I saw A-Cs who—if they'd been standing still and in native costume other than the Armani Fatigues—anyone would have sworn were from India, China, Russia, Africa and South America.

But none of them were standing still. They were, to an agent, looking incredibly busy, intent, and serious. They left hyperspeed to break up fights, return stolen wallets, take lost children to their parents, and generally act like the biggest bunch of Boy Scouts anyone had ever seen. Citizens safe, they went back to hyperspeed, looking for the next problem.

It was impressive in the extreme, but I got an uneasy feeling in the pit of my stomach. It wouldn't take much to turn the A-Cs into the world's police force. And while that had some good benefits associated with it, there were bigger downsides, starting with how fast the "police force" would be turned into the War Division. I gave it one big international incident. Like the one everyone was expecting to happen here.

One agent set managed to stand out—because it consisted of a guy and a girl. The guy was big, the girl was about my size. They were close enough, so I reached out and touched someone and managed to grab them both.

They stopped moving and stared at me in shock. They looked about Walter's age, early twenties. "I'm Ambassador Katt-Martini. We may have an emergency situation. Who are you and what are you doing here?"

They looked at each other, then at me and at White. "I'm Jeremy Barone, this is my sister Jennifer. We're policing the crowd."

"We actually have female field agents now that James is in charge?"

Jennifer smiled. "I'm an imageer, Ambassador. My brother's an empath. We work well together, and I'm not really good with math, science, or medicine, so I was approved for fieldwork."

Refrained from mentioning that the Dazzler version of "not good" at these pursuits was still probably Mensa material for the rest of us. Also didn't mention that I knew female imageers were rare, meaning Jennifer wasn't on fieldwork only because she wasn't good at normal Dazzler Duties. We had other things going on; I'd mention these points later.

"Okay, great. I need you two to try to find Ambassador Martini." They stared at me. "What?"

"You're right here," Jeremy pointed out.

"Oh. I mean former Commander Martini. Right, I was a Commander, too. I mean the other one. My husband, Jeff."

"Ah. Right." Jeremy looked at his sister. They both gave off an "I'm so uncomfortable" vibe.

"What is it?"

"We were told you might, ah, drop by," Jennifer said. "All of us, I mean, not just me and Jeremy."

"And what were you told, and who told it to you?"

They didn't speak. White sighed. "Children, are you aware of who I am?"

"Oh, yes, sir, Pontifex White," Jeremy said quickly.

"Then answer the Ambassador's question. Honestly and quickly, please." I noted he didn't correct them by adding "former," which, under the circumstances, I was A-okay with.

They exchanged another glance. "I'll do it," Jennifer said with a sigh. "That way you won't get in trouble."

"And Alpha Team's current Captains will be more than supportive," I added. "Time, guys. It's of the essence."

"We were told by Commander Reader that you'd probably try to help out, and that we should advise him and send you back to the Embassy."

"Great, I'd imagine he told you this during your prep meeting right?" They both nodded. "Super duper. Here's the deal—things have changed since prep time, and if someone doesn't help me find my husband and Charles Reynolds pretty much immediately, heads are going to roll in uncomfortable ways."

White cleared his throat. "We could very well be in a state of emergency. We can't confirm that until we can confirm where Ambassador Martini and Mister Reynolds are."

The siblings looked at each other and nodded. "We'll help you," Jeremy said. "But I'm not sure how, other than being two more people looking for them. There are too many people here for me to be able to pick anyone out specifically based on their emotions."

"And a picture won't tell me where they are right now," Jennifer added.

I had to remind myself that Jeff and Christopher had always been the most talented and that their Surcenthumain boosts had ensured no one was going to catch up any time soon.

Serene could find Chuckie and Jeff, if they were within fifty miles of her. Since I'd sequestered her at the Dome, which was in New Mexico, that option was out. Jeff had told me earlier he couldn't find Chuckie emotionally because of all the interference at the Festival, so Jeremy being unable wasn't a surprise.

Christopher might be able to tell, but pictures told him about a person, not necessarily that person's location. Then again, part of Christopher's Surcenthumain Talent Extension meant he could see anyone, externally and internally, to the point of being able to assist Tito in performing brain surgeries. He also had the best range around, to put it mildly.

I sent him a text asking him to use his Heavy Duty Searching Powers to find our missing men. Got a snippy text back sharing that he was already on that case, in between policing pregnant women and keeping the Security guys feeling important, and so far had nothing, but wasn't even close to being done with his search because he'd started at the Festival and searching through that much interference was a slow process.

It dawned on me that if someone wanted to kidnap pretty much anyone, this Festival was an awesome way to neutralize the people most likely to be able to stop said kidnapping. I had a sinking feeling I'd finally tuned to the Bad Guy Radio Channel, only I'd missed some important programming updates.

But before I could remark on how our luck was always consistent, in that it always sucked, Jeremy stiffened. "It's not the Ambassador, but someone's in real danger."

"Let's go, kids." I grabbed White with one hand and Buchanan with the other. "You run, we'll keep up."

CHAPTER 52

BUCHANAN GRABBED TITO and White took hold of Armstrong, and then we were off at the slower version of hyperspeed. I could see Bruno flying just above us. He was having no issues keeping up, even with Bellie in his claws. He was obviously carrying her versus trying to kill her. I decided to table my emotions about this for later.

We could have gone faster, but Jeremy and Jennifer weren't going all out, presumably because there were so damn many people here they couldn't go to full hyperspeed without bowling everyone around over.

I'd done the daisy-chain thing a few times before, but no one else with me had. It was interesting. Buchanan and Tito adapted fairly well, but Armstrong kept on knocking into people. White stopped, shoved Armstrong in between us, we each held one of the senator's hands, and we were off again.

Happily, this meant we were controlling Armstrong and so kept him from slamming into other people. Unfortunately, this delay meant we'd lost the Barones.

However, Bruno hadn't lost sight of them. He was ahead of us, but we could see him to follow him, and we did.

With Armstrong between us, it was also easier for White to lead and control the daisy chain, and we caught up to Bruno, and then the Barones, in short order, massive number of people to wade through or not.

They headed through the crowd toward an area with a lot of foliage. As we drew near, I could hear the sounds of struggle and fighting.

We stopped, and I dropped Armstrong and Buchanan's hands. They and Tito were busy retching anyway. White and I trotted after the Barones.

A part of me was hoping we were going to discover Jeff and Chuckie here, maybe fighting for their lives or protecting someone, but here, nonetheless. Those hopes were quickly dashed—I didn't know the people fighting in the foliage.

There was a woman about my mother's age. She had shiny, black hair, light olive skin, and was dressed nicely in expensive-looking clothes with even more expensive-looking accessories. She didn't look American; I put her from somewhere in the Middle East. There was a younger man, late twenties probably, who had the same coloring, but he didn't look like her, other than clearly being her countryman.

There were also two other younger men, about the same age. One was taller with curly light brown hair and glasses. The other was average height with straight brown hair. They were both wiry and muscular, and they also looked Middle Eastern, but not from the same country the woman was from. And they, and the black-haired man, were all surrounding the woman, fighting nothing.

At least, it looked like nothing. But from the way the men were reacting, either they were all crazy, or they were fighting something they couldn't see.

"Whatever it is, it's moving too fast for us to see," Jeremy said as I came up to him.

"That's the Bahraini Ambassadress," White said as Jeremy lunged toward the clutch of people fighting the nothing. I took a closer look at the men. The one who looked like the Ambassadress was in uniform. The other two weren't. Based on what had been going on and their looks, I took the leap and assumed they were Israeli.

Whatever these men were fighting, it was strong enough to hit Jeremy and send him flying toward us. White managed to catch him, but they both slid back.

This wasn't good and was probably going to get worse. Well, Jeremy and Jennifer were agents, so they probably had the gas manipulation chips in their brains. And even if they didn't, I'd worry about it later.

I opened my purse. "Poofs assemble!" I looked up. "Bruno, my bird, drop the parrot and let's stop whatever or whoever, right now."

Bruno released Bellie, who flew to White's shoulder. She was screaming. "Tino! Tino! Tino!" I decided to table Bellie's inability to say Tito's name correctly for later. Because Bruno gave the loudest bird shriek I'd ever heard as the Poofs jumped out of my purse and went large and toothy.

"Poofies, surround those people and don't let whatever or whoever's attacking them get away!"

The Poofs did as requested. Bruno, meantime, was flying in a circle, and he was going faster and faster. I got the impression he was trying to catch up to and then match the speed of the invisible assailant.

During Operation Fugly I'd had to stop an A-C racing around Jeff at hyperspeed with a needle full of badness in her hand. I'd had a baseball bat to work with at that time. I didn't have a weapon like that on hand, and I wasn't stupid enough to use my Glock.

However, I'd shoved my sweat jacket into my purse before we'd left the Dome. I pulled it out now. I so frequently had no options other than the crazy, I just went for it naturally now.

Flipped my jacket out as I shoved in between two of the Poofs. I watched Bruno, who was going incredibly fast. But I could see him. Couldn't see what he was following, but Bruno was a really clear bird-blur.

I needed the hyperjuice, and it wasn't hard to rev up to rage—rage was easy to get to once I'd already hit high anxiety and stressed confusion. All it really took was to look at the expression on the face of the Ambassadress—she was terrified—and to see the three guys getting punched repeatedly. This really pissed me off, because I was damned sure she hadn't done anything to deserve terror today, and protectors being beaten up in an unfair fight was far too close to what my guys went through every time some lunatic decided to try to go global and take over the world.

Based on the hits the dudes were taking, however, I judged that they were being attacked by something taller than me. I timed it, and the next time Bruno went past me I flung my jacket out and up, high, keeping a tight hold on both of the sleeves.

I caught something and pulled. "Toro!" If only I had a spear to shove into this particular invisible bull.

As I pulled, Bruno dived, screaming nasty things in Peregrine, and landed on whatever it was I had my jacket around, dug his impressively large, sharp claws in, and held on. Something, or rather someone, shouted in pain. Couldn't tell if it was a person or a thing shouting, though.

We were all moving now, at the really fast hyperspeed Jeff and Christopher used these days. I should have been sick, but I was too revved, which was good. Then I realized my Lifehouse jacket was getting stretched out of shape. And that seriously pissed me off.

Whoever I had "captured" tried to pull away some more. I let his strength pull me into him and body-slammed him. It was definitely a him—my jacket was over and around his head, but he felt human-shaped. However, no human could be doing this, so I was fighting either an enhanced A-C or an android.

My body-slam staggered him. Bruno used that to press down and I did my best to help him. We ended up on the ground. "Oof!"

Human-sounding voice. Could still be one of Marling's super-androids. One easy way to find out. I was in a good position for it, too.

I rammed my knee into his groin. He bellowed. Trees didn't shake and leaves didn't plummet to the ground, so this wasn't Jeff. No one bellowed like my man. Which meant, happily, this wasn't my man gone insane.

White, Jeremy, and Buchanan arrived, just as whoever it was flipped us over. He wasn't trying to fight me, though. He was trying to get away. White caught one arm, and Jeremy was able to grab the other, as Buchanan tackled our mystery dude around the waist and managed to bring him back to his knees while I rolled out of the way and scrambled to my feet. This was an improvement, but three of them were barely able to hold this guy. I'd lost my hold on my jacket, but it was still over his head.

Wanted to call Tito for help, but I figured he was doing medical on the people who'd been attacked. Besides, we didn't know if this guy was working alone, so Tito and Jennifer were better off staying with the others.

Bruno was still attached to this guy's shoulders, and he did the bird scream thing again, but it wasn't directed at me. It was directed at Bellie.

She cawed and got into it, as she grabbed my jacket in her beak and slashed the guy's chest with her claws at the same time. Then she flew to me, dropped the jacket, and alighted on my shoulder. "Bellie wants a treat!"

I was too busy being shocked about who I was looking at to be shocked by the fact that Bellie was suddenly my Best Birdie Friend.

I'd been wrong. No, I didn't know the people being attacked. But I sure knew their attacker.

"Clarence Valentino, what an unexpected displeasure."

CHAPTER 53

"TINO! TINO! TINO!" Bellie cawed. It dawned on me that she didn't have any mispronunciation issues—she was calling him Tino instead of Valentino.

"Right you are, Bellie. Treats coming soon. Hold him, guys."

"Trying," Buchanan said through gritted teeth.

"So you've shot up with Surcenthumain, haven't you, Clarence?"

He glared at me but appeared to be using all his effort to get away from the guys holding him.

I dug around for my phone. "Where's Jeff and Chuckie?" I took a picture of him. It wasn't a great shot, but hopefully it'd give Christopher and Serene something to work with.

Clarence laughed one of those low, evil bad guy laughs. "You're never going to see either one of them again. Not that you're going to be around too long to mourn their loss."

I wanted to kick his face, hard, but that wouldn't get me information. "Blah, blah, blah. Heard that the last time you decided to tangle with us. Where are Ronaldo and LaRue? They *are* the ones pulling your strings, right? I mean, you're not smart enough to do this stuff on your own."

Probably untrue. All the A-Cs were bright. But Jeremy was an empath, so I wanted Clarence's emotions reacting, in the hopes we'd get something from them.

"You'll see them soon enough." The men were trying to get his hands behind his back, presumably to handcuff him or tie him up in some way, but they weren't succeeding. Clarence had clearly taken a *lot* of the superpowers drug.

"Just the three of you against all of us? I don't like your odds." I relaxed as much as I could and then sent what I hoped was a really loud, really screaming emotional signal that I needed help, and as many A-Cs as possible, pronto. It had worked before, but that was in the Dulce Science Center. I wasn't liking my odds here at the Festival.

"We'll have your baby. She'll provide all we'll ever need." He struggled to his feet, despite the fact that we had two big, strong A-Cs and a big, strong human all doing their best to prevent this.

I was going to hit him, but before I could move, Bruno flew off Clarence's shoulders and right at me, screaming. I managed to stop myself. My rage was high, but I had to keep it in check. Bruno had been clear—if I attacked Clarence right now, he was going to escape, possibly with me in tow. "You're not getting her, or anyone else." Bruno landed in front of me and faced Clarence.

"How'd you get one of those?" Clarence asked, obviously talking about Bruno.

"What's it matter to you? Where are Jeff and Chuckie? What's your evil master plan? Why are you such a raging jerk?" No external reactions, other than an increase in the level of dirty in the look he was giving me.

"You never shut up," he growled.

"Nope, never. Where are LaRue and Ronnie? Why did you start the problems between Bahrain and Israel?" He jerked. Just a little. "What take-over-the-world plan are you guys working on now? Why send dirty pictures of me around town?"

Interestingly enough, this got a real reaction. Clarence laughed. "Because they'll ruin everything you've all worked for. And my self-righteous brother-in-law will get what he deserves—the knowledge that you're a slut and always will be."

"Wow, you're all still clinging to that one? It didn't work on anyone in Paris, and it's not going to work on anyone here."

"Oh, it still works on some of us," Reader said, as he, Gower, Tim, and the flyboys, along with a good number of field agents, surrounded us. "As in it really pisses us off. Let's get our missing traitor under wraps."

"Can we beat him up while we do it?" Jerry asked.

"Save that for interrogation," Tim suggested.

Bruno screamed again as Clarence flung Jeremy at the flyboys. Jeremy knocked them over like a humongous bowling ball.

With a hand now free, Clarence was able to grab Buchanan, pull him off, and throw him at Alpha Team. He missed Gower, but took Reader and Tim down, which also knocked over Hughes and Walker, who had regained their feet.

"Richard, let go!" It dawned on me that the bad guys always had some form of "destroy the Pontifex" in their plan.

White tried to comply, but Clarence had him. I was going to try to tackle them, but before I could move, Clarence tossed White at me. We landed, hard. As we did, my brain chose to cheerfully remind me that White was no longer the Pontifex while also pointing out that Gower had no one near him.

Bruno took to the air, headed right for Clarence's face, while I heard Bellie in the near distance shrieking, "Help! Help! Help!"

Bruno slowed Clarence down to regular hyperspeed, but no one was close enough to Gower.

"Paul, run!" As the words left my mouth, I felt rather than saw someone race past us. Said someone tackled Gower to the ground, which meant Clarence shot past them, as Bruno landed in front of Gower and Jennifer.

Jeremy was up and concentrating. "He's angry and he's scared. He's not coming back, though, I don't think. It feels like . . . he has something . . . more important to do."

The rest of us got to our feet. Jeremy helped his sister and Gower up, while White helped me. I looked around for the Poofs. Didn't see any. Checked my purse. Harlie and Poofikins were in it, looking cute and also alert. Very alert. But none of the other unnamed Poofs were around.

Bruno strutted over. "You were my big, brave bird, weren't you?" I gave him a nice scritchy-scratch between his wings, while I checked him for injuries. Bruno warbled at me, sharing that he liked the scratching, and the only injured party was Clarence.

"What are you petting?" Reader asked.

"Um, they're invisible. Sort of."

"Not any more," Gower said. "Thank the big bird for me, will you?"

"Bruno can hear. Quite well. So, you can see him?"

Reader coughed. "Did you hit your head when Richard got tossed onto you? It's a huge peacock, girlfriend. We can all see him."

"You couldn't before. I'll explain Bruno and his flock later." Besides, Bruno seemed agitated, as if he wanted to fly off but couldn't. I checked on Bellie. She was perched on White's shoulder, getting treats, and seemed calm. "We need to check on the Bahraini Ambassadress and the guys with her."

"I'm fine, thanks to all of you," she said as she and the others joined us. "My name is Mona Nejem. This is my driver, Khalid."

No last name given. Not a surprise, really. The younger man who looked like he was also Bahraini nodded.

"You're with the Bahraini Royal Army, right?"

Khalid looked impressed. "Yes."

"Dude, you're in uniform. It wasn't that hard to guess." I looked at the other two with them. "You two, however, aren't Bahraini. You're Israeli, right?"

They nodded. "I'm Oren," the smaller one said. "And this is Jakob," he indicated the guy with glasses. No last names here, either. Again, not a shocker. Despite the bruising they were both starting to show from being used as two-thirds of Clarence's punching bag set, an aura of readiness and competence radiated from both of them. They didn't look distressed—they looked quietly pissed off, and like they were both plotting how to rectify what had just happened.

"They were trying to help us," Mona said. "When they saw me being dragged away from Khalid."

"Mossad isn't always working against you, in other words." All four of them, not just Oren and Jakob, jerked, and all four of them looked a little panicky and a lot guilty. "You're all pals, aren't you?"

"In a sense," Mona allowed. "While our countries rarely get along, as I'm sure you're learning, being here is different from being at home. There are many times when we who do these kinds of jobs have more in common with our counterparts from other countries than we do our own countrymen."

"Not that the Ambassadress is in any way giving Israel even the tiniest bit of classified information," Oren said quickly. "Or vice versa."

"Our relationship is more friendly than antagonistic," Jakob added. "Though not friendly in an inappropriate sense."

"Do either the Israeli or the Bahraini Ambassadors know about this friendship?" White asked.

Oren, Jakob, and Khalid all put poker faces on. Mona smiled. "I don't have to share every minute of my day with my husband."

"In other words, Bahrain likely doesn't know, and Israel might, but if either one does know, they're pretending they don't because it never hurts to have friends among your enemies."

"Well put," Khalid said.

While we'd been talking, Tito had done quick inspections on those who'd gotten manhandled, including me. "Everyone seems okay, but I really think we should have the Ambassadress and her guardians checked out a little more fully, due to who was hitting them and where. Internal injuries are possible, and I don't have the equipment here to be able to confirm one way or the other."

"I don't think it's a good idea to go back to our Embassy," White said.

"Or any other Base."

"Andrews," Armstrong suggested.

"I agree," Buchanan said. "It's secure and has more than one gate, if necessary."

"Really?"

I got a lot of sighs and "when will you read the briefing books" looks. Buchanan just grinned. "Yes, really. Every U.S. military facility has at least one gate, some have more. Most friendly nations have them too. And by friendly I mean friendly to American Centaurion."

Truly I was the last to find out anything. Oh, well, the excitement of regular surprises overruled the "fun" associated with the briefing books. "Super, so Andrews it is. We have a limo nearby, hopefully it's safe."

"We have limos too," Reader said patiently. "Or did you forget that?"

"I'll hurt you later, James." Now that the adrenaline rush was dying down, I knew I needed to focus and think. The first thought that came to me was the fact that I had AWOL Poofs. I used to think the Poofs ran off when they felt outgunned. But experience had shown that they tended to run off when they felt they were more urgently needed elsewhere. So, that begged a question. "Where are the other Poofs?"

"Do you mean the big fluffy animals with huge teeth?" Mona asked carefully.

"Yeah. I sense a major debrief coming on, but guys, before we do that, I think it's an important question."

Reader shook his head. "Worry about the Poofs later; they can take care of themselves. We have a known traitor who's working with known terrorists on the loose. We need to track him down and confine him."

"That didn't work last time."

"They used specialized equipment then," Gower said. "Alpha Four disabled it."

"Disabled and unable to be reconnected aren't the same thing." The nagging grew stronger. We were missing something. *I* was missing something, and it wasn't just Jeff and Chuckie. But they were a part of what I was missing, in that sense. And, as so often happened, I knew I had everything I needed to put most, if not all, of the puzzle together.

"Let's get everyone to a hospital or some semblance of safety," Reader said. "And then we can worry about your theories."

"No. James, we need to stop and think. Someone went to a hell of a lot of trouble to prevent me from knowing anything and, therefore, to prevent all of you from talking about it with me."

"Missus Martini is correct," White said. "And she's considered number one on our enemies' hit list, meaning we need to stop pretending security clearances matter right now."

"Oh, they matter. They just don't matter in terms of all of us at the moment."

Armstrong cleared his throat. "If it helps at all, I firmly support Ambassador Martini being briefed on anything necessary. We have proof the HSAC test she was given was falsified, meaning our enemies wanted to keep her out of the loop. Let's not allow that any longer."

Had to hand it to Armstrong. He'd moved himself into our camp with ease, and he'd done it without coming off as a total jerk.

However, the senator's ability to be a good politician wasn't the issue of the moment. It was part of it, of course, but not what mattered right now. Think, think. I needed to think. Took the time while my brain was coming up with nothing to send the picture I'd taken of Clarence to Christopher, with an urgent request for him and Serene both to read it.

The key was probably ACE and what he'd been trying to get me to figure out. "Paul, is ACE uncomfortable?"

"No. He feels . . . distracted."

"Wonderful." Had a feeling ACE was being distracted by the real problem, not the fake ones. Got a fast reply from Christopher. "Well, this is interesting, in that 'oh crap, this sucks' sort of way. Christopher can't read the picture of Clarence I took."

"How can that be?" Tim asked. "Isn't it almost impossible to hide anything from him? Pictorially, I mean."

"No. Not with a major Surcenthumain boost. Christopher can hide his emotions from Jeff now, so can Serene. And the bad guys knew Christopher would be a threat, so they figured out how to block him."

"Kitty, we're wasting time," Reader said. "Richard, I want you sequestered somewhere."

"Why?" Jennifer asked.

Everyone stared at her. Other than me and White. We shared the

We Got One! look. It was nice to find someone who was on our wavelength.

"Because they're always after him," Jerry replied.

"No," White corrected. "They're always after the Pontifex." He looked pointedly at Gower. "Paul, I was tossed aside by Clarence."

"And it was only because Jennifer and Bruno got you away from him that Clarence didn't grab you, Paul. How'd you know what to do?" I asked her.

She shrugged. "The parrot was screaming for help, so I figured you guys needed me. I took in the scene, and it was clear the target was the Pontifex. The current one," she added.

"We need to get Paul to safety."

"I'm fine, Kitty. I have ACE."

Part of what was going on dawned on me. "No, Paul. If they can kidnap you, then *they* have ACE."

CHAPTER 54

THERE WAS MORE TO IT, but getting Gower to safety was probably Job One. "We need to get Paul to the Dome."

"I need to be here," Gower argued.

"No, you don't," an authoritative female voice said. It was an authoritative female voice I knew really well.

My mother strode onto the scene. She was dressed for action—black pants and shirt, bulletproof vest with Federal Agent on it, and black cap with P.T.C.U. embroidered. She was also armed to go bear hunting.

Kevin was with her, decked out in the same garb. Between the two of them, I was fairly sure they could take on a small nation. Buchanan seemed to naturally fall into line next to Kevin, so both of them were behind but flanking Mom. With him along, I knew they could take on that small nation and win.

I trotted over and gave her a hug, weapons or no weapons. "Mom, I'm so glad you're here."

"Malcolm called me, kitten." I got her breath-stopping bear hug. "Your father and I missed you and Jamie."

"We missed you guys, too. A lot."

"We'll do a family reunion soon, but not now," she said as she released me. "Anyway, Malcolm said we had multiple situations that were going to require authority to resolve." She looked around and took in the scene. "Mona, how did you get involved in this?"

I wasn't even surprised that my mother knew the Bahraini Ambassadress. She probably knew every person involved in D.C. politics including the janitors who cleaned the office buildings and the guys who drove the street sweepers.

She also knew Oren and Jakob, because I saw them pass a tiny sign to her, and she passed one back. I'd been looking for it, because I figured the Mossad had their own version of the Secret Handshake. What was really interesting was that Khalid passed a sign to Mom, too—a different one—and she passed a different counter right back.

"It's a long story," Mona replied. "But I'm more interested in the one your daughter is trying to tell."

Great. Time to table my interest in my mother's various kick-butt connections—I needed to pull it all together for everyone. If only I actually knew what "it" was. Oh, well, this meant that it was really time to do what I was good at—wing it while honing my Recap Girl skills.

"Okay, there's lots of crap going on, but most of it, if not all of it, is being done to distract us from what the bad guys are really doing."

"Which is?" Mom asked.

"I'm not totally sure. Yet. But I know Chuckie's a target, and so is Paul." So was ACE, but I didn't want to say that aloud right now.

"Kitty, we need everyone focused on this event," Reader said.

"No, we don't. Well, we did . . ." I looked at Mona and her retinue. "You know, Clarence is enhanced."

Buchanan was murmuring to my mother, so I assumed he was catching her up on everything that had happened so far. Fine, I was starting to rock and possibly roll as well.

"We know," Tim said. "But that just makes it more imperative that we catch him."

"So, we have a superenhanced A-C, one with no talents originally, I might add, who's good enough now to block Christopher. For all I know, he blocked Jeremy, too."

Jeremy shook his head. "Not really. I read him. He was emotionally clearest to me when he was running away from us, by the way. But I have to be honest—if he's good enough, he might have been able to fool me. You know, focus on one emotion to hide another one."

"Mister White, make a note—I want Jeremy and Jennifer assigned to us somehow. Moving on, my point is that Clarence is now definitely an evil supervillain, and he's more on the Juggernaut side of the house than, say, the Lex Luthor side—the big muscle carrying out plans versus the guy creating said plans. He's strong enough to toss Jeremy like he was a rag doll—when he wanted to. But when we arrived, what Clarence was actually doing was playing around."

"I wouldn't call getting hit constantly playing," Jakob said.

"Trust me. I don't care how well trained you guys are, and I know you're the best of the best, so to speak. But Clarence is enhanced." I turned back to my guys. "Remember Moira, James? She almost killed you with one punch. I can't believe that Clarence isn't able to do that these days, especially since he was moving so fast they couldn't see him, meaning he's taken a lot of that drug so he's closer to Jeff and Christopher's levels."

Reader's eyes narrowed. "Go on."

"He was moving at the fast hyperspeed, but we were all able to catch him and stop him. Richard, Jeremy and Malcolm all had him, but he still got away. And yet he struggled like two big A-Cs and one big human on him were difficult to manage—right up until what he wanted happened."

"Which was?" Tim asked.

"You guys showed up from wherever you'd been. He wants Paul, because Paul's the Pontifex and because of ACE, I'm sure. How did you guys know to show up?"

I got "really?" looks from all of them. The flyboys laughed. Reader sighed. "You broadcast a 'help me' emotional signal. The empaths with us mentioned that this was even better than the one you did when Mephistopheles was going to town in the Science Center, much more refined, clear, and accurate."

"Funny you mention that, because you know LaRue and Ronnie Junior still want to follow in Daddy Mephs' footsteps."

"Playbook," Buchanan said. "You've done it before and they know about it, so they knew you'd do it again."

"I agree," Armstrong said. Tito nodded.

"I as well, Missus Martini."

"Okay, great. So they've been anticipating our moves because they know us. Clarence was a traitor from at least the time I showed up, probably longer, and he's part of the extended Martini family and used to work for the Diplomatic Corps, so he knows all they did, too."

"Your moves," Tito said. "They're anticipating you more than anyone else."

"Maybe so, but I'll bet cash money they're busy anticipating as many of the rest of you as they can."

"So, maybe they anticipated you'd call for help in some way and we'd come running, but why pull us all away here?" Tim asked. "I mean, if Paul was the only goal, why not do something to make you want to get him to you alone?"

I could feel it. Tim's question was dead on for what was happening. But I didn't have answer yet. "What were you all doing, before my emotional cry for help rang out, I mean."

This question made them all uncomfortable, and some of them looked downright worried, my mother included. I took the logic leap. "You were trying to figure out where Jeff and Chuckie disappeared to, weren't you?"

Reader nodded. "Trying to determine how long they'd been gone, who'd seen them last, where we could look to determine if they were okay or not."

"They've been gone longer than you realize, they saw Clarence last, is my big guess, and I doubt they're okay, in that sense." They all looked uncomfortable, still, and none of the flyboys were making eye contact with me. Whatever news they had clearly wasn't good. "What?"

Silence.

"I want to know. I'm a big girl, and I've been aware that they were in danger and missing longer than any of you. Tell me whatever it is you don't want to tell me."

"Do it," Mom said quietly. The news moved from not good to potentially catastrophic. I steeled myself.

Reader came closer to me and took my hand. "Kitty . . . once we realized we couldn't find them, I called Christopher. He filled me in on what he was doing and said he'd been spending his spare time at the Dome searching for both of them."

"And?"

He swallowed. "He can't find any trace of either Jeff or Reynolds. And by any trace, I mean he's looked to the extent of his range."

Unlike Serene, Christopher's range wasn't fifty miles. His range wasn't even Planet Earth. Christopher's range went to the outer reaches of the Alpha Centauri system.

Meaning Jeff and Chuckie were really gone. Or they were dead.

CHAPTER 55

"OKAY. Back to the current situation."

I could tell I shocked everyone. "You're handling this . . . very well," Reader said.

"Look, I want to freak out, but I'm trying to think ahead here. Malcolm's right, and those of us on my team all discussed this earlier—they know us, so they're anticipating what we'll do. My natural reaction is to move Heaven and Earth to find Jeff and Chuckie. But if I do that, I think we all lose. And by lose, I mean likely die."

"She's right," Mom said. "Well done, kitten. So, what's your next move?"

"Well, what were you guys doing to find Jeff and Chuckie, since Christopher was out?"

"We were with Naomi and Abigail," Paul said. "Now that most of the major political players are gone from the Festival we can have them use their talents to search."

Reader stared at me. I stared at him. "Oh, *snap*." We said it in unison. I'd worry about the unison thing later.

"Where are they now, right now?" I asked as Reader dropped my hand and got onto his phone. So did the others.

"No answer from Abby," Jerry said, looking worried. The other flyboys were texting. "Trying Naomi now." He shook his head. "No answer."

"I've checked with the main field team contacts I had assigned under me for this," Hughes said. "None of them have eyes on either of the girls." The rest of the flyboys confirmed that their field contacts were also without Gower girls visual, audio or physical.

Reader cursed. "We have a problem. Superbeing formation in rural France. Because of this event we're short-staffed, Dulce had to send support to Euro Base, and Gladys can't spare the focus to find the girls."

"And the girls don't have trackers installed," Tim said.

"What? Why the hell not?"

"They're not Field agents," Reader said. "And they're not supposed to act in Field capacities. Reynolds has never pushed for it, either."

Meaning Chuckie hadn't wanted anyone to know where he did a lot of tests with the girls. Not a surprise, really, though it was proving to be a really bad idea overall. I chose to refrain from mentioning that the Gower girls had acted like Field agents a lot, including today. It wouldn't change things.

Time to go for the crazy. I opened my purse. Harlie and Poofikins were still there and still looked alert and ready to go. "Harlie, did you send the other Poofies to help Naomi and Abigail?"

Both Poofs purred at me.

"Can you take Kitty to them to help keep them safe?"

More purrs ensued. Good enough for me.

I looked down. "Bruno, my bird, I need whatever part of the flock that's free and able to get to Naomi and Abigail." Bruno gave me a look that said it was about time I was focusing on the big picture.

"Richard, hand Bellie off to someone she won't try to kill. James, do you trust me?"

"Yes."

"Then trust me right now and don't ask questions, don't argue, just do what I tell you. We need to get all of the people here out of range and to safety. Paul *has* to go to the Dome, and once in he's not coming out. ACE is guarding it, and only it, from what I've gathered. Get Paul safely into the Dome, get everyone else to Andrews and get Andrews onto some form of high alert, and tell Gladys that we need all we can get on Diversion Superbeing, because I think those are actually supersoldiers out for a playdate. Oh, and tell her to watch Paraguay, all of it, but the Chaco in particular, for the same activity."

"What are you going to be doing?" Reader asked.

"Getting to the Gower girls. Jeremy, Jennifer, you're with me and Richard. Malcolm, I need you to make sure they do what I just said. Mom, see you shortly."

I grabbed White's hand as Harlie and Poofikins jumped out of my purse and onto Bruno's back. I decided to accept that politics and danger both made strange bedfellows for all of us, Peregrines and Poofs included, and just go with it.

Bruno took flight, and we followed.

Bruno was flying at hyperspeed. I could tell based on how fast the four of us on the ground were moving. He led us on an erratic path, not straight the way you always hear the crow flies.

Of course, Bruno wasn't a crow. He also wasn't stupid. He was spotting the best path for us to take to avoid running into people, booths, and buildings and leading us on it accordingly.

We ran past the Washington Monument, around the World War II Monument, and alongside the Reflecting Pool. Either we were headed for the Lincoln Memorial or we were headed for the Potomac.

"Please, not the Potomac again."

White chuckled as we ran on. It was less crowded by the Lincoln Memorial, but that merely meant everyone who wasn't attending the International One World Festival was here instead. Or maybe it just seemed that there were hundreds of people around.

The Lincoln Memorial wasn't secluded. In addition to all the tourists, a road ran around three-fourths of it, and there were other roads leading to it, some that ran through the Mall and some coming from other directions. However, it also had clumps of big, dense foliage around it.

Sure enough, Bruno headed for the biggest, densest clump of trees and bushes, which was around the side and toward the back. He dove into the trees, and we lost sight of him. No problem, we ran into this little forest, too.

After the way the rest of this weekend had been, I wasn't really sure what we were going to find. My only hope was that we wouldn't find nothing.

So that worked out for me.

CHAPTER 56

OF COURSE, I'D EXPECTED TO SEE some Poofs and
Peregrines mixing it up with Clarence or even LaRue and
Ronaldo. What was there, however, was the Gower girls. They had
their backs to us and were facing . . . something.

I mean, I had to assume from their body language—which said
"we've been at DEFCON Worse for a while now"—that they were
facing something other than the trees around the Memorial. But
there was nothing I could see.

Well, that wasn't quite true. As with Mona and her under-
cover bodyguards, something was going on, based on the fact
that the trees and bushes were moving in the way they would if
someone or something was being thrown into and against them.
Either that or we'd found the Living Apple Orchard from the
Wizard of Oz. The way things were going, I didn't rule that possibility out.

The Gower girls were holding hands, which was normal for
them when they were really focusing their talents. However, it
looked as though Abigail was holding onto Naomi and trying to
pull her back, rather than them doing their Wonder Twins thing.

White and I ran to them. I grabbed Abigail around the waist, and
he did the same with Naomi.

"Let me go!" Naomi shouted. "They're going to die if I don't go!"

Ah, so it was the Bad Guy Go-To Plan for All Occasions. The
Evil Overlord types really revered the classics. "Jennifer, you help
hold Abigail. Jeremy, you help Richard with Naomi."

Once Jennifer had a hold of Abigail and was helping her stay upright, I went in front of Naomi. "What in the world do you think you're doing?" I put my hands on her shoulders and pushed her back. She was really trying to get free, not that this surprised me all that much.

"They have Chuck. And Jeff. And they're going to kill them if we don't go." Naomi was practically crying. I'd never seen her this out of emotional control before. Then again, I could understand, and relate, to the feelings she was having.

I shook her, hard. "Look at me!" I shouted it, in the same tone of voice I'd used when giving orders as the Head of Airborne.

She blinked and looked at me, really looked at me. "What are you doing? Why are you trying to stop me?"

"Let me rephrase. Shut up and look at me!"

Naomi gaped at me, but I definitely had her attention.

"I don't know what Chuckie's taught you in all this time he's been working with you, but I'd bet all the money in the A-C coffers that it sure as hell wasn't to trot over and give yourselves up to the bad guys when they have a hostage."

"He didn't," Abigail said. "He told us if and when we were put in this situation to run like hell in the other direction. And to find you, I might add."

"And here I am. Isn't that nice? So, why, Mimi, when he needs you to listen to him the *most*, are you ignoring what Chuckie taught you?"

"But . . . they're going to kill him."

"Yeah? Like they didn't manage when we were in Paris? I mean, clearly it's time for the two of you to get some actual official field training and experience, because right now you, Mimi, are acting like the biggest noob on the planet. And you will *be* the reason they kill Chuckie and Jeff."

"What?" She sounded shocked. Naomi was far too smart to be falling for any bad guy's line. But she wasn't thinking with her head.

"Get it together, and get it together right now." I was snarling. Quietly, but still, snarling. Sometimes being nice didn't work. This appeared to be one of those times. "You and your sister, along with your eldest brother and my baby, are what these bastards want. They have Jeff and Chuckie as bargaining chips. As long as we don't give them what they want, then Jeff and Chuckie's odds of living stay at least fifty-fifty."

"Those aren't good odds."

"No. But if you go with them and hand yourself over on a freaking platter with a big bow wrapped around you? First they will torture them in front of you, so you do every evil thing they want you to do, which I guarantee will involve kidnapping your sister and brothers, my baby and all the other hybrid babies, and that's just for starters. Then, after you've stupidly done exactly what they wanted and expected you to do, they will kill Jeff and Chuckie in front of you and laugh while they're doing it. Or have you forgotten everything that happened in Paris?"

I made eye contact with Abigail. "Who's they? Clarence, someone else, Clarence and someone else?"

"Just Clarence," Abigail shared. "He's enough on his own right now."

"What's pulling Naomi toward him?"

"Just Naomi," Abigail said. She sounded disgusted. "You know, because she's decided that you, Jeff, Christopher, and Chuck are all morons."

"I don't think that!" Naomi sounded indignant. "I just—"

"You're just reacting emotionally instead of with any form of logic or sense. Yeah, I get it."

"You race off like this all the time," Naomi said. Only she sounded a little truculent . . . and a lot less frantic.

"Yeah, I do. Here's the key point, and I'd like you, in particular, to pay close attention to the next things I say. Per the very enemies we are fighting right now and my track record, when *I* do it, I'm right. Per the track record the rest of *you* have when you all run off like idiots, you're almost always wrong. Trust me, you're worse than wrong right now."

"But . . . they'll hurt them."

"No duh. You think I like this any more than you do? Or that Richard does? Or anyone else? This isn't the time or place for self-sacrifice. This is the freaking time to prove that all the damn time and effort Chuckie's put into training and prepping the two of you hasn't been a complete and utter waste of his time."

"Charles wouldn't want you to sacrifice yourself for him," White said gently. "He's not that kind of man. And you know it."

"But what if they do kill him?" Naomi whispered.

"Then he dies so you live. I've known him more than half my life. He's been my best friend since we were thirteen. And I guarantee I still know him better than anyone else does, even you. And I promise you this—you doing the exact opposite of what he's trained you to do and, I know, told you to do will be the real thing that kills him, physically and emotionally."

She looked almost convinced, but not quite. Time for the big gun. "Unless, of course, this is all an act and you're really in league with the bad guys and want to go with Clarence so you can watch him hurt Jeff and Chuckie."

CHAPTER 57

NAOMI'S EYES FLASHED. "You know that's not what I want."

"Yeah? Prove it."

"Sis," Abigail said quietly, "you need to calm down."

"This from the person who's affected by emotions, I might add."

"Yeah, and Sis? Kitty's ready to beat the crap out of you if you don't pull it together. And she can do it. Let's not fight with the person we're supposed to go to for guidance and leadership in this state of emergency." It was clear Abigail was reciting something Chuckie had drilled into them.

Naomi took a deep breath and let it out slowly. "Okay."

"Don't let her go," I said to White and Jeremy. "Just in case she's faking us out and wants them dead."

Naomi glared at me again. Good. Anger was a better emotion for her than fear and panic right now. I turned my back on her. Let her stay pissed off. And focused on me instead of Clarence's threats.

Still couldn't make out anyone visually, though the trees and bushes were really taking a beating. This was a National Park—I was sure Clarence was amassing a host of major fines, but a park ranger arriving, or whatever division patrolled here, wouldn't help the situation.

"So, Abby, what actually happened?" If I squinted, I could just make out several Peregrines and some Poofs, large and in charge. They were definitely not fighting with each other.

"We were finally done with our version of patrolling the Festival when James told us we could start looking for Jeff and Chuck. Then we all got a big emotional message from you, the guys took off, and we searched." She was quiet for a moment. "We couldn't find them. So I think Clarence is lying."

"No, they have them. And I'm sure they're still alive." I was. They had no bargaining power if Jeff and Chuckie were dead. And, as Naomi was demonstrating, hostages were a strong incentive to be stupid.

I hoped ACE was going to keep Jamie safe and prevent her from time warping to Jeff in some way. That they were likely hurting Jeff and Chuckie both was, sadly, a given. I shoved the fear and heartache this knowledge gave me aside and added it to the rest of my anger. Anger I was stoking and saving for later.

"Okay, well, I hope you're right. Anyway, Sis and I were still searching when Clarence showed up out of nowhere. He said he'd come back to help us."

I snorted.

Abigail chuckled. "Yeah, neither one of us fell for that one. So he said he knew where Chuck and Jeff were. We followed him at a distance, he led us here. Then told us to come with him so Chuck and Jeff wouldn't be killed. Sis was ready to go, obviously. But then our Poofs went into attack mode, and they were joined by other Poofs, and then Peregrines. That's what Clarence is fighting."

"Thanks for the recap, Abby. So, can I not see any of them because they're invisible or because they're going so fast?"

"Speed, mostly. That and I put a protective layer around this area."

"Wow, even while holding Mimi back? I'm hella impressed."

"Despite how Sis is acting, we've been working with Chuck on a lot of things."

"Things I'm just betting we're going to have to put into action sooner as opposed to later."

"All well and good, Missus Martini," White said. "But how do we stop Clarence right now?"

"I'm wondering if the Poofs can eat him, or if that would end up being bad for us in some way. Or if it would give the Poofs heartburn."

"I think if they could eat him, they would have already," Abigail said. "They weren't happy, believe me."

Potentially the smart thing to do would be to take off and let the animals handle it. Only, they might get hurt, and if that happened, they'd need me.

Tried to look at this situation the way Chuckie would. There were pros and cons to capturing Clarence as well as to letting him go. If we caught him, great, we'd have him, and maybe we could break him. And we'd keep him off the streets, so to speak, and unable to lure someone else, like his wife or children, to the Dark Side or Hostage City, depending.

Letting him go had merit if there was a way for us to track him. If we could actually follow him, then we had a good chance of finding the Evil Genius Lair du Jour. If we could track him, in a way that would both work and not be something he could find and destroy.

"Any ideas, Missus Martini?"

"Breadcrumbs are out."

"Excuse me?" Jennifer said.

"We need to get a tracker into Clarence. I'd love to tag him like a wild boar, but I don't think we have the right equipment handy."

"Doesn't he already have one?" Jeremy asked.

I turned around to look at him. Everyone else was looking at Jeremy too. "Say that again, please."

"We all have tracking chips in us," Jeremy said. "If you have a job that puts you into any kind of danger, the chip is installed."

"The girls don't have trackers. Clarence was a diplomat's assistant. That hardly seems like a job that screams 'dangerous situations.' "

Jennifer raised her eyebrow. "You're a diplomat."

"Excellent point. Mister White?"

"Naomi, may I let go of you, or will you try to heroically yet stupidly do exactly what our enemies want if I release you so I can call Gladys?"

Naomi looked sheepish. "I'm sorry, Uncle Richard."

White kissed her forehead. "All is forgiven." He let go, though Jeremy held onto Naomi's arm. Abigail still had her hand, but Jennifer let go, though I could tell she was ready to lunge at either sister if needed.

White made the call. "Yes, Gladys, I do apologize, but this is actually of the highest need. Yes, superbeings attacking? Amazing, right where Ambassador Katt-Martini said they would. Yes, she *is* right here. No, not looking smug. She is, however, looking worried and impatient. I share those feelings. Why yes, I'd love to tell you why I called. I need you to verify the current whereabouts of Clarence Valentino. Yes, I am serious. Deadly, if you catch my meaning."

While White verbally wrangled with his half-sister, I tried to come up with another option if Clarence had no tracker or it was disabled. Really wasn't coming up with a lot. The other problem, of course, was what to do if Clarence was still tagged and traceable.

"Wonderful. Please continue to monitor, paying special attention to whenever and wherever you lose the signal. Should the signal be lost, continue to monitor, I believe it will come back, at least periodically. No, please don't advise Sylvia, but do put her and the rest of Alfred's family under a high and efficient level of protection. Oh? Interesting. Tell them we'll be there shortly."

White hung up. "Much is going on. The good news is that Clarence does indeed have a tracker. It's quite old, from when he first started working for Centaurion Division in an active role. When he transferred to the Diplomatic Corps, the tracker was kept on in case of international incidents, so to speak."

"Think he remembers he's got it?"

White shrugged. "I have no idea. However, it's not just you—most of us don't think about it on a regular basis. As with your wild boar analogy, once the initial shock of the tagging has passed, why think about it if it's not bothering you?"

"Okay, we'll vote for the side of things actually going our way for once. I'm sure we're due for one lucky break." It was kind of nice to know it wasn't just me and that others forgot about the trackers, too.

"So, are we going to run away like Chuck wants, then?" Abigail asked.

"Yes, but we have a problem."

"Only one?" Naomi asked dryly. She sounded more like her normal self. Good.

"If we just leave, won't he wonder what's going on?" Jeremy asked.

"And if he wonders, then he might remember the tracker," Jennifer added.

"I love you two! Mister White, another note—we not only are keeping the Barones, I want them on staff at the Embassy."

"Duly noted, Missus Martini. So, do you have a plan for how we extract the animals and make Clarence run away without alerting him to the fact that we actually want him to run off?"

I heaved a sigh. I'd come up with something no one was going to like, me least of all. "A plan? No, not really. I've only got the crazy right now, Mister White."

"Ah. So, routine."

CHAPTER 58

I PULLED MY GLOCK OUT OF MY PURSE. "Okay, you'll
know when to run away, I promise. Jeremy and Jennifer, once it's
obvious that it's time to run like hell, get Naomi and Abigail . . .
somewhere."

"Take them to Andrews Air Force Base," White said. "Per
Gladys, we apparently have a situation there."

"Works for me. And do that regardless of what I say once I roll
my offensive plan here, such as it is."

"What about you and Uncle Richard?" Abigail asked.

"Oh, Mister White and I will catch up. We're good at that."

I took the safety off. No need for caution at the moment. Then I
trotted toward the fight while I focused as much as I could. Got
myself to Laser Beams From My Eyes level again and was able to
make out where the Poofs and Peregrines were. They were slowing
Clarence a bit, which was helpful.

"Yo! Clarence! Get away from my pets!" I aimed and fired,
high, toward one of the trees near him, but above where any of the
Peregrines were. "Poofies, Peregrines, get away from him so Kitty
can shoot him!"

Interestingly enough the Poofs instantly went small and bounded
over to leap into my purse. The Peregrines all went to the ground;
they were between me and Clarence in a semicircle, blocking him
from me. However, he did have an escape route, heading toward the
Potomac. I aimed for another tree closest to where I thought
Clarence was and fired again.

I turned my head so I could still see where Clarence was, so to
speak, but project my voice to those behind me. "Get out of here

and get them back to the Embassy!" I shouted. "Send some Field teams. I'll take care of him until they get here."

Clarence gave it a shot to run toward me. I could tell because two Peregrines flew up and slammed themselves into his legs, beaks and claws first. He stopped running, because he was shouting in pain as the birds disengaged.

I aimed for his head. Happily, there were a lot of trees behind him, so if he dodged the bullet as I expected, it would again hit a tree. "Where's my husband?"

He gave me a dirty look. "You'll never see him again." And if Clarence didn't dodge the bullet, I was reminded that this would still be a big one in the win column.

"Then you're going to die." I pulled the trigger.

Happily or un-, depending on which viewpoint you took, he dodged as anticipated. I fired again, lower. He had to leap out of the way. I moved closer and fired again. He dodged and backed up.

"I want my men back, alive and unscathed."

"Too bad."

I did a rapid-fire technique Mom had taught me, and this time I hit him. It wasn't a fatal shot in any way, but his side was bleeding. He shouted in pain. I tried not to let that give me a feeling of satisfaction. Failed.

"I want them back, or I'm going to kill you, Clarence. This is a fifteen-shot clip, and I have a ton of extra clips in my purse. The Peregrines will keep you within range. So, tell me where Jeff and Chuckie are or prepare to bleed to death."

I did another rapid-fire technique and winged his arm and thigh. Mom was an awesome teacher, and apparently I was an apt pupil.

Clarence looked shocked that he was hit again. "How are you hitting me?" The pain was clearly shocking him into moving at human speeds, which was helpful.

"I'm good that way. And you're going to be dead. Soon." I fired at his head again.

This time he dodged, turned, and ran. He was limping, so running at human speed.

I ran after him. "Come back here, you coward!" I fired again at a nearby tree. I felt bad for the foliage, but hopefully Mother Nature would forgive me.

Apparently the sound of my Glock going off again spooked him sufficiently, because Clarence flipped it up to hyperspeed and disappeared. I stopped at the edge of the trees and put my gun back into my purse, being careful to not let it touch the Poofs. Didn't bother with the safety because, hey, why mess with my normal theme? Something nudged against my leg. "Bruno, my bird, is he still running?"

Bruno cooed and warbled.

"Oh? Good. Over the bridge already and not looking back. Excellent. A big well done goes to you and your flock, by the way."

I heard a lot of bird cooing and turned around to see about half the flock there, looking proud. "My Peregrines and Poofs rock." Han and Leia were among the group. "Can you two find Chuckie?" I asked as White joined us.

Much distressed warbling from them and the others.

"What's the status, Missus Martini?"

"Clarence has done a real runner and is long gone. Hopefully Gladys can track him."

"I'm sure she can, at least for a while. Nice shooting, by the way."

"Thanks, I do my best. Han and Leia can't find Chuckie, and they're freaked. I think we need the Peregrines to go back to the Embassy, though."

"I agree. I believe that will be the likely next point of attack."

"Yeah. Clarence has confirmed none of us are there, and I supposedly had the Gower girls sent there. So," I said to the flock, "you all need to go help George and Gracie protect Walter and the rest of the Security guys who are there. And maybe call in more. Bottom line—don't let them take the Embassy."

There were warbles, coos, and caws. Several bird chests were puffed out, and not just by the males.

"That's right! We're not gonna let them take *our* nest!"

More caws and a variety of hoots.

"Can I get a bird amen?"

All the flock hooted and flapped their wings.

"Can I get a *real* bird amen?"

They hooted, flapped up into the air, and cawed all the way back down.

"That's what Kitty's talkin' about! Now, go get 'em. And be careful out there!"

The Peregrines all flew around our heads and then disappeared. Other than Bruno, who nudged up against me and cooed in a questioning way. He sounded a little worried. "Oh, I know, Bruno. You're my main bird man. I want you with me, so you did the right thing, as always. And you led an awesome and successful defensive maneuver."

He didn't seem convinced I was pleased. I gave him a scritchy-scratch between his wings. He liked it, but it wasn't enough, I could tell.

"Gimme feather, down low." I put down my hand, Bruno hit it with a wing. "Other side." Did it with the other hand and other wing. "Victory salute, real slow." Put both hands up, he flapped both wings against my palms. "That's how we do it down in bird town!" Bruno looked pleased again, so all was back to right in the Peregrine World.

I finished this to see White both looking pleased and like he was really trying not to laugh his head off. "Well done, Missus Martini."

"Yeah, yeah. Just don't tell Jeff about this."

"I sincerely hope we can find him so that I can keep this secret from him."

"Me too." I heaved a sigh. "Andrews?"

"With all haste, yes. However, I believe the streets, rather than the Metro track or the Potomac, will be our best choice."

"It's like you read my mind."

White chuckled. "I'm good that way."

CHAPTER 59

WHITE TOOK MY HAND, AND WE HEADED OFF.
Hyperspeeding through the streets was always interesting. The
cars and people seemed to stand as still as the buildings, even
though I knew they were moving.

Field agents had to be able to run twenty-five miles without
issue. The better ones did fifty. Jeff and Christopher, of course,
were at the fifty-or-more level. So was White, and he always had
been, since I'd first joined up with the Gang from Alpha Four.
That none of our enemies still seemed to consider him a legitimate threat meant he remained our secret weapon. God knew we
needed one.

I'd been a sprinter in high school and college, so the distance
was something I'd worked up to before Jamie had been born. Okay,
I'd worked up to ten miles at a time. But that's good for a sprinter.

After Jamie, you'd have thought reverse-inheriting A-C powers
would have meant I could do the fifty miles, easy. You'd have been
wrong. No, I still struggled with distance. Fortunately, I was able to
lean on White's abilities and let him do the heavy-mileage-lifting.
I assisted by not running out of breath and not barfing when we
stopped. I was cool that way.

We stopped at the main gate of the air force base. I had no idea
why. When I was doing fieldwork with Jeff, we never let something
like human security people and cameras that weren't good enough
to catch anyone using hyperspeed stop us. But here we were, being
all polite and official. I wondered about White sometimes, and now
was one of those times.

Bruno was with us. I had no idea if he'd flown, run, or done some Peregrine Time Warp thing, but he looked remarkably un-ruffled.

"Ambassador Martini from American Centaurion to see the Base Commander," White said to the guards, who were looking completely freaked out by our arrival. Happily, they didn't seem to notice Bruno, so that was one for the win column.

"Where did you come from?" one asked while the other managed to use the phone in their gatehouse to share our request with the Powers That Be On Base.

"The Mall." Hey, it was true. "Great party going on down there. You guys should really be there. Our driver dropped us off," I added, for the sake of not being detained in the wrong way and by the wrong people.

"Oh." The airman didn't look convinced, but his gatehouse buddy shared we were cleared. "Walk on up. It's a ways. You should have had your driver take you."

"He was late for an important meeting. Just like we are." I hoped the hint would work.

The guys on gate duty had apparently recovered from our surprise arrival. They looked at each other, and the one inside used the phone again. "Transport's being sent for you."

"Thanks, you guys rock." I leaned up and whispered to White. "Why did you stop us here? Aside from it being fun to freak out the guys on guard duty?"

"I have no actual idea where on the base our team is," he whispered back. "We could have run through the entire place and every room, but this way seemed more expedient."

I couldn't argue with the logic, so I stayed quiet. Which wasn't so hard, since our ride arrived fairly soon. A Jeep pulled up with two airmen in it. White and I were escorted into the back seat, Bruno settled himself on my lap, and we took off at a rapid rate of speed. This was great in that we were in a hurry but bad in that the Jeep was an open-top and the resulting breeze was having a field day with my hair.

We pulled up somewhere—I couldn't tell where because my hair had spent this drive flinging itself everywhere, but mostly in my face. I dug my hairbrush out, brushed my hair as quickly as I could, and pulled it back into a ponytail. All the better to see that our driver and his companion had their guns pointed at us.

"Interesting. Mister White, what have I missed?"

"You arrived under suspicious circumstances," the driver said before White could reply. "Among other reasons. After you." He indicated with his gun that we should get out and head inside the building, which had "Headquarters" emblazoned on its exterior.

I put my hands up, but the other airman shook his head. "You're not prisoners. Our orders are to watch you with guns drawn, but you can keep your hands down."

"You know, this isn't the most diplomatic way for us to meet your main dude." Who, memory reminded me, Chuckie had said didn't like him or us, which viewpoint Cliff had confirmed as being true.

They both shrugged. "Orders are orders."

White climbed out, Bruno hopped out, and White helped me out. So far, no bullets had been fired, so I decided to buy the "we're just being cautious" line. For now.

We went in, the two guys from the Jeep behind us. A few feet inside the doorway another airman met us. This one was clearly an officer, and he was standing in that relaxed form of attention soldiers do to impress upon you that they're both soldiers and, though relaxed, ready to gun you down if at all necessary. He had a gun, but it was in its holster.

"Thank you," he said to the guys from the Jeep. "I'll take it from here." They left, and he nodded to us. "Ambassador Katt-Martini and Former Pontifex White?"

"Yes. Who are you?"

He smiled at me. "Captain Morgan. Here to escort you in to see the Base Commander."

"No gun?"

Morgan shrugged. "Things are a little . . . tense. If you would, follow me." He turned and walked on, before we could ask questions, I could make rum jokes, or lift my leg up to the side.

Morgan led us down a hallway. We made some turns and ended up at an office with "Base Commander" on the door. I didn't have to ask who was behind the door. He escorted us inside.

The office was fairly large and rather well appointed. Big desk, flags in stands, couch, chairs. All just a little sterile, but otherwise nice. I looked at the nameplate on the desk—it wasn't the name I was expecting. Instead of Marvin Hamlin, who I'd been told only yesterday was the man in charge, the plate on the desk declared the man behind it to be Colonel Arthur Franklin. The name rang a bell, but I couldn't place it.

The man behind the desk stood up and nodded to Morgan. "Thank you, Gil. Please stay here, at ease." He walked around the desk. "Missus Martini, no matter what you do, you do it with speed and style. I understand you've been having quite an eventful week-end. Hopefully it won't be as exciting as your high school reunion ended up, but I can't make any promises."

Recognition dawned. "You're the Air Force colonel who showed up at the end of Operation Drug Addict!"

He grinned. "Nice to be remembered. Your uncle asked me to ensure you were looking well."

"When did you talk to my Uncle Mort?"

"Yesterday." The smile left Franklin's face. "I understand that you were the one who sent the reporter, Joel Oliver, to us?"

I decided Oliver could insist that the military add the "Mister"—I wasn't going to, at least not right now. Franklin didn't look like he wanted to indulge civilian whims at this precise moment. "Yes. I'm sorry, but we're in the middle of . . . something. And we needed him to get some attention focused away from us." This sounded even lamer said aloud than it had in my head.

Franklin didn't seem to notice. Or care. He nodded. "Oliver said that you had news of an impending alien invasion."

"Right." I wondered how best to apologize for wasting military focus on our diversionary tactics. Hoped the fact that something bad was going on and that we'd averted another Middle Eastern incident by rescuing Mona and her men would help.

But I never got the chance to launch into what was likely to be my most amazingly confusing explanation yet, because Franklin and Morgan exchanged a very worried look. Then Franklin looked back to me. "Just one question."

"Okay."

"How do you know about it?"

CHAPTER 60

I RESISTED THE VERY STRONG URGE to share that I'd made it up based on "intel" from someone from Club 51. The expressions of the two military men in front of me indicated they weren't laughing now and wouldn't be laughing if I said "just kidding!" either.

My father's advice of answering an uncomfortable question with another question was, once again, my go-to reaction. "Not that I'm unhappy to see you here, Colonel Franklin, but why *are* you here? I was under the impression that the man in charge of Andrews was a Colonel Hamlin. As late as yesterday I was under that impression. So, what's going on?"

Franklin sighed. "We have no idea what's happened to Colonel Hamlin." Apparently not everyone's father had shared wisdom of the ages with them. Which was good for me.

"I know I speak for the Ambassador when I say we'd like more information," White said.

Franklin nodded. "My move to this position has been in the works for the past few months because the Top Brass feel that someone who is more . . . positively disposed toward Centaurion Division would be a better choice than someone who is somewhat . . ."

"Xenophobic," Morgan finished. "I've gotten intel from my former counterpart. Colonel Hamlin is not a fan of Centaurion Division."

"That former counterpart would be Cliff Goodman?"

"One and the same," Morgan said. "Cliff stressed that Colonel Hamlin is a good man, but he's also not pro-alien. Because of the variety of circumstances that have happened over the past few months, moving Colonel Franklin to Andrews was the best choice, even though that leaves us with a new commander in New Mexico." I managed not to ask if the circumstances had been the fact that we'd moved in as the American Centaurion Diplomatic Corps. Mostly because I was fairly sure the answer was a big yes.

"Not that you're biased, Gil," Franklin said with a grin.

"Wait. You ran Area Fifty-One?"

"Yes. And I loved it. This wasn't a post I requested, but it was impressed upon me that it was necessary. However, the transition has not been smooth."

"Hamlin didn't want to leave?"

"Our information was that he was happy to go to another post," Morgan said. "He was moving to the Department of Defense in an important role."

"Was?"

Franklin shook his head. "We have no idea where Colonel Hamlin is. Formal transition was to have been in a week. I was contacted yesterday, when no one could find Colonel Hamlin."

"A high-ranking Air Force officer goes AWOL and no one questions?"

"Oh, we questioned," Franklin said with a grimace. "However, the last time anyone saw him was Friday at thirteen-hundred-hours—he went off-base for lunch. No one's seen him since, and no one seems to have any idea what happened to him."

"Other than the suspicion that he ran away," Morgan said.

"Ran away? What from?"

Both officers stared at me. "The impending alien invasion," Franklin said finally. "You know, the one you know about but haven't yet told me *how* you know about it."

"Ah." I cleared my throat. "Any chance you know what's happened to my husband and Charles Reynolds?"

I got another long look from both of them. "What are you talking about?" Franklin asked carefully. Then he jumped. "Where the hell did that come from?"

Looked where Franklin was pointing and Morgan was staring. Bruno looked back at me. I did some fast thinking. "You let Malcolm see you." Bruno bobbed his head. "Because I can trust him completely, right?" Another head bob. "Ergo, if you've gone visible to the colonel and captain here, it's because you feel we can trust them, too, right?" Another head bob accompanied by a feather fluff.

"You're talking to the peacock?" Morgan asked carefully.

"Bruno's actually a Peregrine from Alpha Four. Royal birds, totally kick-butt fighters, too. And they can go invisible, so to speak. Bruno says that any good friend of my Uncle Mort's is a good friend of mine, sort of thing."

"Oh, good," Franklin said weakly. "There's nothing in my briefing papers about—what did you call them?"

"Peregrines, and no, they don't look like falcons, I know. And there wouldn't be because they just arrived last night, and Chuckie hasn't had time to do an update because he's been kidnapped by our enemies along with my husband." I looked at Bruno. "Mind reading or empathy?"

Bruno did some feather fluffing and head bobbing.

"A limited form of empathy combined with keen animal senses. Okay, works for me." Who was I, the wife of Mr. Empath Extraordinaire, to argue?

"I really want a full explanation," Franklin said. "Now."

"Mister White?"

"I believe Bruno's given you the go-ahead for full disclosure, Missus Martini."

Chose not to marvel about how we were now taking our cues from a space avian, studiously avoided contemplating my latest Dr. Doolittle moment, and just went for what I was becoming the best of the best of the best at—the High-Level Recap. Started with Armstrong's visit and carried on right through my audition for Crazed Shooter #2.

"So," I finished, "I have to be honest when I tell you that alien invasion was just me spitballing it, because Casey gave me the idea. Besides, there's no way in the world I can believe that anyone in Club Fifty-One is in the know about anything other than how to be conspiracy theorists."

"Maybe not, but whether they were guessing or actually know, they're right," Morgan pointed out.

Franklin looked worried. "They had high-level assistance the last time they surfaced."

"It's safe to assume they do now, as well," White agreed. "However, unless you have Club Fifty-One personnel identified on base, we'd now like information from you, since, one way or the other, Missus Martini and her Club Fifty-One contact are correct and we're being invaded."

"And, I'd like to know what you did with Mister Joel Oliver and the other people we sent here for safekeeping." We'd already lost

Jeff, Chuckie, and, apparently, a colonel. I didn't want to lose anyone else.

"They're here, at least most of them," Franklin said. "I'm just not confident we can or should share this with them."

"Well, all of them are aware that there are aliens on Earth. If they weren't aware before this afternoon, they're sure aware now. And I think they all may have information we need, even if they don't realize they have it."

All three men looked at me. "Even I'm having a challenge with that one, Missus Martini."

"They've seen things, and maybe they don't realize they're important things, but we know the questions to ask, or at least, I think I do. Can we do this with the others, though? In part because I want to reassure myself they're all alive and well and actually here."

Franklin rubbed the bridge of his nose. "We have a security failure if I simply read anyone and everyone in on what's going on."

"Colonel Franklin, that 'security issue' wheeze is what got us into at least half of this mess already. I promise to swear that I threatened you with Decapitation by Peregrine in order to make you speak, should, you know, any of us be alive tomorrow for anyone to care about it."

"Good point. Considering what's heading for us, I'm more concerned about someone leaking what's coming and causing mass panic."

"Mister Joel Oliver will keep whatever we ask him to in confidence."

"He's not my main worry," Franklin said. "Your Club Fifty-One people are a much bigger concern. But, fine. Why not end my career in a spectacular way and have the shortest command of this base in Air Force history?"

CHAPTER 61

WITH THAT EXCITING Pronouncement of Doom, Colonel Franklin led us to a door opposite the one we'd entered his office through. This door connected us to a larger room that had clearly shared the same decorator as Martini Manor.

The room was filled with nice, comfy-looking, and also expensive-looking furniture. The art on the walls was tasteful and only somewhat military. While this room had no windows, there was a fully stocked wet bar with nice crystal. A big door leading to another room was emblazoned "Executive Washroom."

"This is where the President hangs out when he has to visit, isn't it?"

"Yes." Franklin sounded mildly impressed. "I've been given to believe you haven't read any of your briefing materials, Missus Martini. Or should I be calling you Ambassador under the circumstances?"

"Oh, Colonel, under these circumstances, feel free to call me Kitty. And I haven't read the Briefing Books of Boredom. I'm just a really good guesser."

I took a look at the room's occupants. Happily, the Gower girls and the Barones were here, as were Tito, Armstrong, and Oliver. Sadly, Bellie was also here, perched on, of all people, Oliver's shoulder. Mona and her men were here as well, as was Buchanan, who looked relieved to see me. We even had a newcomer to today's festivities—William, who was Walter's older brother and the best imageer we had after Christopher and Serene.

"Nice to see you, Will."

"Happy to be here, Ambassador. Commander Reader pulled me

from the Festival and assigned me to your team for the duration of this situation."

"Works for me." There were, however, a few key bodies missing. Bodies I'd sort of hoped would still be around. "Where's my mother, James, and Airborne?"

"Chief Katt went back to the White House," Morgan said.

"To lock the President into the bunker or to keep him updated?"

"Yes," Franklin answered. "Commander Reader went to Paris, Commander Crawford and the rest of Airborne went to Paraguay."

"How?"

Everyone, even the Middle Eastern Contingent, gave me a variation of the "duh" look. Buchanan pointed to the Executive Washroom door.

"Seriously? There's a gate here?"

White cleared his throat. "It's an air base."

"There are gates in every U.S. military compound, as well as in most compounds that belong to friendly nations," Franklin said. "I see your good guessing skills only extend so far."

"Wow, I just realized how you and my Uncle Mort must have bonded—shared sarcasm. Moving on, why wasn't Senator Armstrong taken to safety?"

"I refused to go," he replied. "And before you ask, I'm staying because I may have information that we need, and you may also need my help."

"The senator's already in the know?" I asked Franklin.

"Yes. He noted some . . . things."

"That Commander Reader never had to tell anyone here to go onto full alert—the entire base was on full alert before we arrived. And when I mentioned I was looking for our friend the reporter, we were instantly taken into a polite form of custody."

"MJO, I see you're making friends everywhere."

"Truly. I must confess I was overjoyed to see the good senator here—he's the only reason I'm not still confined to a very small room."

"Nice to know it's the start of a beautiful friendship for the two of you. Where's the Pontifex?"

"Sent to the Dome, per your orders," Franklin said, sounding mildly worried.

"Just checking." Decided to check further and got my phone out. He answered on the first ring.

"Kitty, what's the status?" Christopher asked.

"Is Paul with you in the Dome?"

"Yes. He's brought me up to speed."

"Thank God. Okay, you still can't find Jeff or Chuckie, right?"

"Right. I had Paul talk to ACE, who, per Paul, is distant and distracted like you wouldn't believe. ACE is happy that Paul's in the Dome and said I've been looking the wrong way. So I've been thinking—"

"That maybe they're on Earth but in one of those rooms that's made to block out everything, including you and Jeff?"

"Yeah." He sounded kind of pissed that I hadn't let him do the big reveal. Oh, well, it'd been a Day of Suck for most of us. "Not that this helps us at all."

"I think it might. There's got to be a reason they've been trying to get us out of the Embassy."

"Not following you. What?" Christopher sighed. "One of those stupid birds is standing next to me. Making noise."

I hated what I knew I was going to have to say next. "Please put the phone down to the bird. Boy or girl, by the way?"

"Male, and did I just hear you right?"

"Yes."

"How did our lives get this unreal?"

"No idea. I need to talk to Bruno's rightwing bird there, okay?"

"I refuse to ask any more questions. Shout when I get to talk to you again." I could tell the phone had moved. I heard urgent cooing, some feather rustling, and what I felt was just this side of screeching.

"Thanks, got it. I'll take Christopher again."

"The bird tried to bite me. Was that the signal to talk to you again?"

"Yes." It worked, so that meant yes in my book. "Your bird feels things are secure at the Dome, at least for the moment, but would like you to ensure that all of the Security force is prepped, and by all of Security I mean Gladys and anyone who even sort of reports to her."

"Why?"

"Because the Dome is going to be the focus of an attack like we've never had before."

"You know this how?"

"Aside from some information I have that you don't, the bird, ah, told me." Felt the overwhelming urge to name the bird. "Harold's a little stressed. Stop kicking at him."

Christopher was silent for a few long moments. "You're calling this thing Harold? And you know it's stressed? How? Why? And if it would stop pecking and clawing at me, I'd stop kicking at it."

"He. Harold. Call him Harold and he'll be nicer. His mate's name is Maude, and she doesn't like being kicked at either. And Harold's stressed because we're about to be invaded."

"By whom?"

"I have no idea, other than that they're from space. I needed to call you to make sure Paul was there before we got the full details."

"Lucky me. Why didn't you send my father here along with Paul?"

"I need my partner. It's action time. Besides, he and I were busy."

"I heard. Why do you want my father doing the action stuff and not me?"

"Because I want you safe, a Commander everyone will listen to guarding everyone the bad guys want to kidnap, my baby's A-C godfather watching over her, and to keep you where I can reach you without worry."

"But you're okay with my father not being safe?"

I coughed. "Dude, he's the best field agent we have."

"According to you."

"Yeah. And also according to his track record."

"I understand you also commandeered the Barones right out from under James."

"Head of Recruitment now, remember?"

"You never let me forget."

"Jeff and Chuckie still missing and likely in life-threatening danger. Space invaders coming. Superbeings and supersoldiers popping up all over the place. You handle internal affairs, I'll handle external."

"Wow, the ambassador-speak is starting to rub off on you. In another decade we might be able to take you out in public."

"If Bruno weren't here, you'd be sorry you said that."

"I'm sorry already. Harold just pooped on my shoe."

"I love my Peregrines."

CHAPTER 62

HUNG UP AND TURNED BACK to Franklin. "Ready for that debrief now."

Franklin's eyes were narrowed. "Why did you call to verify that your Pontifex was where I said he'd been sent?"

"Because I'm getting used to people I care about disappearing without a trace. It wasn't a reflection on you, Colonel."

"No offense taken." Franklin still looked worried.

"What is it?"

"We have too many disappearances, too close together, and all of those missing vanished without a trace. Humor me, and let's be certain the rest of your people are where we believe them to be."

"Okay, Paul's where he's supposed to be, but I'll verify the others are okay, too. Just give me a moment." Decided not to call, so sent texts to Reader, Tim, and all the flyboys.

Franklin grimaced. "The Pontifex went to the Dome via a floater gate, per Commander Reader. But the two Commanders and their teams went to their locations using this gate. And, with my predecessor gone under extremely mysterious circumstances . . ."

"Right, it's a little worrying." None of them answered immediately. "We need to give them a little time to answer, since they all went to areas with active situations."

Franklin nodded and headed for the Executive Washroom. "Come with me for a moment, please." I could wait for texts and walk at the same time, so White and I followed him as requested. There were five stalls in here. Franklin went to the one farthest from the door. "Can you verify that this gate is in working order?"

"I can't. How do you even know there's a gate here?" I could see it because I was enhanced—airport metal detector standing around a toilet, never a thrill—but Franklin was a regular human, insofar as I knew.

Franklin shook his head and pointed to a tiny red disk on the back wall, right by the floor, behind the toilet. "That's the identifier for a gate anywhere in the world. I can't see that a gate is here, but I can see the disk."

"It looks fine to me, but I honestly have no way of truly knowing," White said.

"I learn something new every, single day." Why was I, truly, the last to know anything and everything? Chuckie undoubtedly knew about this. Hell, Amy probably knew about it. For all I knew, everyone other than me knew. The horrible truth was obvious—I was going to have to break down and look at those briefing books. One day.

But not right now. Right now, we had a situation, and I hadn't heard back from any of the guys.

Just before worry could take over, I got a reply from Reader. "James is fine, situation in France is not. It's not superbeings they're fighting but supersoldiers, and rural France meant just outside of Paris."

Another text came in, then another. "Tim and Jerry are also fine, and confirmed that the rest of the flyboys are okay, too. They're getting into the air, though, because it's worse in Paraguay than in Paris right now. They're dealing with superbeings in Paraguay but more than James has in France."

"Convenient," White said dryly.

"Truly. Between the Festival and this, all of our Field teams are tied up."

"This situation is going from bad to worse," Franklin said.

"Undoubtedly the bad guys' plan. Look, Colonel, let's get back to the others, and you tell us what's going on so we can figure out what to do."

We rejoined the others. Oliver was looking rather pleased. "Colonel, you'll be glad to know everyone in the room has been declared a safe security risk." Oliver's eyes twinkled. "Including me."

"Excuse me?" Franklin said.

"I took pictures of all of us, myself included," Oliver explained. "Captain Ward read them."

"Captains of industry!" Bellie said.

I ignored her. "Captain Ward?"

"Captains of military!"

"Hush, Bellie. Not now."

"I got a promotion," William said with a grin. "I had Jennifer read them, too, though, because everyone reads differently."

I managed not to share that, in all this time, I hadn't actually bothered to find out what William and Walter's last name was. I felt remarkably thoughtless, but fortunately William was an imageer, not an empath.

Speaking of empaths, though, I turned to Jeremy, whose last name I actually had learned right off. Go me. "Jeremy, you need to read everyone, too."

"We're ahead of you, Ambassador. Senator Armstrong already suggested it, and Captain Morgan approved. Each of us asked a question of the others, and I read reactions."

"Call me Kitty. And that's great news. But, what questions did you ask?"

"All along the lines of 'which one of you is trying to kill or betray us,'" Oliver said.

"Did anyone ask about the alien invasion?"

Everyone sort of stared at me. "Excuse me?" Mona asked finally, clearly voicing most of the room's views. "What are you talking about?"

I looked at Jeremy. He wiped the shocked look off his face. "Confusion, annoyance, amusement," he indicated Buchanan as the one who was finding this funny, "shock, fear, some anger. Feelings of being out of control and in danger. Boredom, stress, the standard stuff."

"No one focus on a single emotion?"

"No. Just the typical panicked attempt to hide that everyone does. Well, most everyone."

I took a guess. "Malcolm, Tito, the senator, and Mister Joel Oliver didn't do that, right?"

"Right."

"Makes sense." I turned to the Gower girls. "I sincerely hope I didn't have to tell you that I expected you to be paying attention, too, did I?"

"Nope," Abigail said. "Now that Sis has calmed down, we're able to focus. I got what Jeremy got—no one knows anything about the invasion, other than you, Uncle Richard, our two military men, and Mister Buchanan, but he guessed, and your question confirmed his suspicions. I don't think anyone here is actually working with our enemies, either."

Naomi looked at Armstrong. "Any more."

He rolled his eyes. "That's so five hours ago, young lady."

"Senator, you have a sense of humor we've been unaware of. How refreshing. William, Jennifer, your thoughts?"

"All clean, so to speak," William said. He smiled at the Middle Eastern Contingent. "Your secret will be safe with us, by the way."

"Secret?" I looked at the four of them. Khalid was on a couch next to Mona. Jakob was in a chair near him, and Oren was in a chair near Mona. I studied their body language and expressions. Mona looked protective. So did Oren. Jakob and Khalid, however, had poker faces on. And, as I judged the body language, they were leaning toward each other, just a bit. I had a feeling Mom somehow already knew what the secret was. "Ah. Interesting. We're really a very open principality. Or country. Or whatever you think we are."

Jeremy cleared his throat. "You just raised their anxiety levels, Ambassador."

Abigail laughed. "You met my brother, didn't you? And his husband, Commander Reader. It's not exactly a secret. Our people don't have any issue with who someone else loves."

I saw the human males catch up, other than Buchanan, who looked as though he'd already known. Mom's training, most likely. My strong impression—based on him flirting with me and sometimes seeming to live for making me blush—was that Buchanan was straight, at least if Jeff's jealousy meter was any indication.

"It's a tremendous security breach, not to mention culturally frowned upon, so I can understand why the four of you don't want it shared with the world. But since the secret you're trying to hide isn't related to interstellar security and the fate of the world, the four of you can relax."

"Interstellar?" Jakob said. "Did I hear you correctly? You were serious about an alien invasion?"

"Yes," Franklin said. "Based on everything that's happened, much of which has involved all of you, I'm prepared to break any number of protocols and bring you up to speed. Because I think we need to focus on saving our world more than my career."

CHAPTER 63

"ON SATURDAY AT OH-FIVE-HUNDRED HOURS we intercepted an extremely long-range transmission from space," Franklin said. "From what we can determine, the message was sent to someone here on Earth."

"Clarence Valentino."

"Tino! Tino! Tino!"

"Thanks, Bellie. Hush."

Franklin nodded. "It's a reasonable guess," he said after Bellie quieted down. "Especially since the transmission was coded, but it was in a language we're actually able to translate."

I took a guess. "In the native language of Alpha Four?"

"Yes. At first we thought it was meant for someone in Centaurion Division, but decryption proved this to be untrue."

"Who decrypted, my father?"

"And his team, yes."

My dad had a team? I tabled asking why I never knew anything. If we survived the latest world-ending events, I'd read the damn Briefing Books of Boredom.

Franklin went on. "The message was fairly simple: Forces ready, put plan into action."

"That doesn't really scream 'alien invasion' to me."

"Nor to anyone else. However, we have some long-range probes, and due to our relatively new relationship with Alpha Four, we've been able to launch the probes farther and get readings back from them much more quickly."

Morgan brought over a folder and handed it to Franklin, who opened it and showed us the pictures inside.

"That looks like a whole lot of spaceships." So many spaceships that I didn't try to count them. They didn't look like any of the ships I'd seen from the Alpha Centauri system. They looked a lot like the space ships from the Space Invaders game—sort of inverted bowls with legs, with what appeared to be blinking lights. Very Hollywood. Meaning they might be faked. Or our alien invasion stories had a basis in fact. I was married to a space alien, so I voted for the latter.

"Yes. And they weren't there two days ago."

"Well, where are they? I mean, that looks far, far away."

"They were within a few thousand light years of us when this picture was taken."

"We can take pictures this good from that far away?"

"We can with Alpha Four's help, yes."

"So why are we panicking? I mean, it's going to take them forever to get here. By the time they arrive, we'll probably have built a space wall around the solar system."

Franklin handed me another photo. Same spaceship armada. "This was taken by a closer probe at twelve-hundred hours yesterday. We aren't sure how they're moving, but they moved a thousand light years per hour."

"That's impossible," Oren said. "Nothing moves like that."

"We do. All the time. Because of the gates." I looked more closely at the picture, then handed it to William. "Feel free to check out the space ships, but I'm more interested in what's sort of in front of them."

"Looks like space dust," Morgan said.

"I don't think it is." It looked rather gelatinous to me.

William touched it, hissed, and dropped the picture. Jennifer retrieved it and carefully touched the spaceships. She seemed fine. Then she moved her hand to the area I was most interested in. She dropped the picture, too. Sadly, this was typical behavior. It was a behavior I'd hoped I wouldn't see, but it didn't surprise me all that much.

"You two mind sharing what you just read?" Tito asked. "Kitty looks like you just confirmed her suspicions, but I think I speak for the rest of us when I say we have no idea why you both just freaked out."

William looked shaken. "That's not space dust in front of the armada. It's an inordinate number of parasites."

CHAPTER 64

JENNIFER LOOKED PALE. "What's in the spaceships isn't a life form we're familiar with, but I think there are more parasites than there are spaceships."

This hadn't shocked me because their reactions had been textbook for an imageer or empath touching the image of a superbeing. Jeremy pulled some wipes out of his pocket and handed them to William and Jennifer, which was the textbook response from any other A-C around someone who'd touched a superbeing image.

Parasites was the name given to the jellyfish things from outer space that attached to mammals on Earth and turned them into horrific superbeings. My introduction to my new life happened when a superbeing formation occurred right in front of me.

The parasites were attracted to rage, meaning they tended to attach to humans. Superbeings were just that—super, but in a bad way for the Earth in general and humans in particular. Most of them turned into enraged killing machines at the moment of transformation.

They were stoppable, but it took a whole lot of firepower to do it. If the invaders were bringing or driving more parasites toward us, we were in worse trouble than anyone could imagine.

"I thought we'd gotten rid of most of the parasites," Tito said. "Based on what I've learned since joining Centaurion Division, we've destroyed hundreds of thousands of these things."

"They came from a world whose sun went supernova. We have billions of people on this planet—why assume their planet had any less of a population?" Based on the number of parasites heading toward us, I felt confident they'd had a population to rival, or even beat, ours.

"Has anyone contacted Alpha Four?" White asked.

Franklin laughed mirthlessly. "Oh, yes. This is the answer we got back: 'Until you verify via the proper protocols, we cannot trust your transmissions.' Signed by King Alexander and Councilor Leonidas."

"But they sent us the Peregrines." I looked at Bruno, who looked right back. "Because they don't trust Earth, necessarily, but they do trust us." Bruno bobbed his head. "Why don't you have the proper protocols?" I asked Franklin.

"We aren't the ones who normally contact Alpha Four."

The light dawned in a big, bright way. "Oh, crap. The notes that came with the Peregrines—the 'mutual friend' Christopher was being warned to protect wasn't Jeff, it was Chuckie. He's the one that Alexander and Leonidas trust. So if you take him out, then Alpha Four no longer knows who to talk to."

"And they've been fooled before," Naomi said.

"Exactly, and by those most likely involved right now. For all they know, Earth has called this invasion force out to take over the Alpha Centauri system."

"Interesting that you say that," Franklin said. "Because as of right now, we can't be sure where this armada is headed. The direction they're coming from indicates they're headed for us, but they could easily branch off and head for Alpha Centauri, or even divide and attack both solar systems."

"If the message was sent to Clarence, then somehow LaRue and Ronaldo have made new friends, and they're the ones dropping by for a visit."

"We need to be able to prove that," White said. "Because if it's not them, then there's another action being taken against Earth, and that complicates the situation even more than we suspect."

William and Jennifer were talking quietly, and he had the picture again. He nodded. "Ambassador, we've both read the beings inside the ships. It's difficult, from this distance, because in addition to the distance, what we have is a metal of some kind that we have to read through. So we can't identify any individuals."

"But we can pick up generalities," Jennifer said. "So I can tell you that the minds aren't mammalian."

"They feel somewhat familiar," William said. "But not like anything I'm really used to reading."

"You two can't read through these ships, but I know someone who can, especially if he knows where to look and what to look for. We need to get these pictures to Christopher White, faster than immediately."

"I can't let these out of my control," Franklin said. "You'll have to bring him here."

"No way. He's all we've got right now. They took Jeff, who Alexander and Leonidas might listen to. If we lose Christopher, then we have no one who's able to work at the super levels." And I knew in my gut they'd be after Christopher. The Peregrines had arrived just in time, presumably at the exact moment Alpha Four had determined that the space invaders were absolutely heading for Earth.

"It might not be related," Abigail said.

"It is. I know it is." I did. What Jeff called my feminine intuition and my mother called gut reactions said this was all part of LaRue's plan. She'd been the brains of Operation Confusion—the massive number of distractions that had been doing their evil double duty were classic LaRue. And when they'd escaped in the FTL spaceship they'd conned Alexander out of, they'd gone out of Christopher's range, meaning far, far away. Who knew what, or whom, they'd found to help them?

Ronaldo was part Yates and, as we'd determined, he was Serene's older brother, meaning his mother was an A-C, too. But Yates had been a player of the highest order, so there could be a ton of his kids, most likely hybrids, out here. They could be organized—after all, the Al Dejahl organization was back in action.

Yates was also one of the few who'd managed to remain in control of his human side once he'd joined with the Mephistopheles parasite. Meaning Ronaldo probably had that ability, too. For all I knew, White, Lucinda, and Gladys might have it, as well. They were all Yates' offspring, after all. But whether or not this meant Ronaldo had joined with the parasites or just knew how to control them, I didn't know. But only someone with experience in controlling them somehow would be able to use them as a strike force.

"What about ACE?" Naomi asked quietly. "He's connected us to Alpha Four before, and that means of communication has been trusted."

"This is why he's been distracted. He can't help us—he's already torn." And ACE had told me as much. ACE was going to guard the Dome. Or die trying. That statement had a lot more impact now that I knew what was coming. "We can't rely on ACE for this. He's protecting the only area of the world he can."

I took the leap, but I took it silently—ACE was protecting what the invaders were after. We were making it easier on him by moving all the goals into one place, but that meant we were focusing more firepower at ACE, too.

Operation Assassination had been a good trial run, but I knew that Reader and Tim were still too untried for the magnitude of what was coming. So was I. We needed the guys who'd managed enemy attacks for over a decade and knew how to do it in their sleep. We also needed the guy who'd likely planned for this eventuality. The bad guys knew it, too, which was why Jeff and Chuckie had been kidnapped.

"How did Valentino get here?" Buchanan asked. "Without anyone noticing, I mean."

"Tino! Tino! Tino!"

"Yes, Bellie. Seriously, MJO, shut her up. Anyway, Clarence used a gate of some kind. They're using something like that to move as fast as they are through space. The Alpha Centauri system has faster-than-light travel and they use it, but they also use gate technology to move even faster."

"Something else works that fast," Tito said.

"True." Nothing moved you faster than ACE, and I knew that was what Tito meant—he and I had been part of the team that had taken the Time Warp Express over to Alpha Four during Operation Invasion, after all. "You think they figured out how to reengage their mini-ACE?" I asked him.

"I think it's a really strong likelihood, yeah. They could have sent Clarence here that way, too, which would mean we'd be unlikely to notice."

"And we weren't looking for Clarence," Naomi said.

"We were supposed to be," White replied.

"But why didn't ACE say something?" Abigail asked.

My conversation with ACE came back to me. "Because whatever it is they've got is also sentient and is trying to, I think, confuse ACE, turn him against us, something along those lines. At a higher level than we can understand. And ACE warning us goes against his 'observe and don't affect' programming."

"From what I've heard, ACE struggles with the decision every time he helps us," Tito added.

"True enough. Look, we have to get these pictures to Christopher. We need to stop flying blind."

White nodded. "I agree. I'll take the pictures to him."

"I need you here. Can't we just calibrate and toss them through the gate?"

"It's not a secure method," White admitted.

"And I say again, I can't let them leave our control." Franklin neither looked nor sounded happy. I couldn't blame him. "It sounds like it would be wiser for us to have him come here, in part because I'm sure we could use his help."

"We can't risk Christopher. Period. Right now, he's the most important person on Earth. At least, if we want to have an Earth left."

CHAPTER 65

"I'LL TAKE THEM, SIR," Morgan said. "That way, they remain in our control."

Franklin didn't look excited. "Are you sure, Captain?" Captain, not Gil. Meaning he was likely going to approve it officially somehow.

"Captains in place!" Bellie squawked. "Captain is good man! Captain can do!"

"Why is that bird talking about Cliff and Esteban?" Morgan asked.

"Excuse me?"

"We were told whose bird she used to be. And the names she just said—Goodman, Cantu. She's calling them captains. Why?"

The rest of us had heard it in syllables, but Morgan heard what, now that I thought of it, Bellie was probably saying. She called Clarence 'Tino,' after all. And, as I thought about it, she'd done Armstrong in two distinct squawks, not one, when greeting the senator.

"Chuckie trusts Cliff."

"But not Cantu," Buchanan said. "Rightly."

"And good man is too wide a term. Everyone keeps on saying Colonel Hamlin is a good man, for example."

"It's Hammy time!"

This time we all stared at Bellie. "I have to ask this. While I was in Florida, was Jeff listening to a lot of M.C. Hammer?"

"No," Tito said. "Not at all."

"Then Bellie's certainly heard someone talk about a Hammy."

"That's Colonel Hamlin's nickname," Franklin said. "At least among his peers and close friends."

Morgan nodded. "Cliff calls him that, too. When they're both at ease, I mean."

"I really want to question the parrot some more, because I just live for bird chats these days, but we have to get the damn pictures to Christopher. Like now."

Morgan and Franklin debated, but it turned out there were several sets of the pictures, and Franklin had another on hand. There was, of course, the standard, required angst about security breaches, as well as chain-of-command crap. Resolved by my pointing out that we actually were the only people likely able to do anything with the invasion information and the only ones with a prayer of getting Alpha Four on board.

Drama Llama Time over for the moment, I sent a text to Christopher to let him know what was going on and who was coming while White calibrated the gate.

Morgan stepped through. It was no less nauseating to see someone do the slow fade than to experience it. Christopher shared that Morgan was safely in the Dome and that he was calling a high-level meeting. He actually had more of Centaurion Division's top personnel in the Dome than not, so this made sense.

As we left the bathroom, I asked Franklin the question I should have asked Chuckie during Operation Confusion. "Is there anyone at the C.I.A. we can trust to help us, and help Chuckie, or is it literally him and Centaurion against the world?" It was a shot in the dark that he might know, but I had nothing.

Franklin looked pensive. "Well . . . his superiors like him."

"How superior?"

"Very superior. He's well thought of, for a variety of reasons, by those at the very top. Which probably means that anyone at a similar level is angling for his position."

This I already knew to be true. And Armstrong had confirmed that Chuckie was on the fast track to top levels; a track Cantu had been on before Chuckie had arrived at the C.I.A.'s doors.

"We need C.I.A. help, because we have to figure out what Chuckie's protocols are so that we can contact Alpha Four. I don't know if it's a good idea to call the head honcho, though." And I figured I'd rather have Mom do that than me. She was so less likely to screw that conversation up. But Mom was busy protecting the President, and, under the circumstances, that seemed vitally important.

Franklin headed for his office. I followed him. He went to his desk and rummaged around. "I was given a packet to review.

Haven't gotten all the way through it yet." He pulled out a binder that would have given Paul Bunyan a hernia.

"Dude, are you serious? They call that a packet in the Air Force?"

He laughed. "Yes. Hang on, I think there's something in here about C.I.A. contact." He thumbed through the Encyclopedia Centaurion while I fretted.

The rest of the gang joined us, Bellie and Bruno included. It was more comfortable in the other room, but no one wanted to lounge around. Everyone looked worried, which I assumed meant everyone felt scared or terrified but weren't willing to let it show.

"What are we doing to find Chuck and Jeff," Naomi asked me quietly while Franklin continued his search.

"I don't know."

Bruno warbled, and I heard mewling from my purse. Looked inside to see Harlie, Poofikins, and Fluffy, who was Chuckie's Poof. Bruno warbled again. The Poofs grumbled. Oh, goody, another argument.

I closed my eyes, took a deep breath, and focused on my inner Talk To The Animals Powers. I was able to understand the Peregrines without trying. But I'd had the Poofs longer, so that should count for something. Opened my eyes. "Poofies, may Kitty have a word?"

The Poofs poured out of my purse, settled at my feet, looked up, and gave me their totally focused, adorable attention. There was a blanket of cuteness in front of me, making me think that Harlie had called in reinforcements, and that they all hadn't been in my purse a few moments ago.

I knelt down. "Thanks. Harlie, does Fluffy know where Jeff and Chuckie are?"

The Poofs mewled and grumbled. Fluffy jumped up and down.

"I see. Can Fluffy *find* Jeff and Chuckie? It'll require regular animal searching, I think. But I also think I know where to start."

More Poof mewling. Bruno cawed derisively. Several Poofs growled.

"No fighting. Bruno makes a good point. We're well beyond DEFCON Worse. We're at DEFCON Oh My God, and even I don't know what DEFCON we're going to hit soon. We need Jeff and Chuckie, very much. We'd need them even if we didn't love them."

More Poof mewling and growling. "Yes, noted. But Jeff and Chuckie are more important. Kitty will work on that if you'll find them."

Poof purrs. Great. "Okay. Head to the tunnels under the Embassy. Start there and search. They could be farther away, but I think they're being held closer."

The Poofs cocked their heads at me.

"Feminine intuition."

The Poof heads straightened up. I received more purrs.

"Super. Search high and low, and report back as soon as you know anything that might interest Kitty, even if it's not about Jeff and Chuckie. You all be careful, too. Kitty doesn't want to lose any Poofies."

This earned me tremendously loud Poof purrs. All of them snuggled up to me, which was a lot of concentrated cuteness at one go. But I was fine with it and felt a little better afterward.

The Poofs disappeared, and I heard a throat clear behind me. "Ah," Tito said, "what are you working on for the Poofs?"

"They want me to figure out what's going on with the supersoldiers."

"Really." Tito's tone was very neutral. "Why is that?"

"Because the Poofs think we're going to need to use them." I stood up, ignoring the looks of horror, amusement, and concern on most of the faces looking at me. "Anything yet, Colonel?"

"Here it is," Franklin said. He was deep into the Encyclopedia Centaurion, so wasn't paying that much attention to my Dr. Doolittle impersonation. "It's sort of hidden, but it appears that I've found the hierarchy of command for dealing with Centaurion. In all cases, first point of contact is Charles Reynolds. If he's incapacitated or unavailable, next options are to contact. . . ." His voice trailed off.

We all looked at him. "Who?"

Franklin shook his head. "This can't be right." He thumbed through a few more pages in the Book of Bigness. He shook his head again. And looked worried.

"Colonel, may I ask what you're concerned about?" White asked.

Franklin grimaced. "I expected to see official names or titles—P.T.C.U., head of the C.I.A., the President, even." Franklin seemed to be talking to himself more than any of us. "Possibly Reynolds' second in command or other underlings."

Chuckie had a second in command? I knew he had underlings—Len and Kyle were two of them—and he did make calls and have operatives do things like hunt down the Pontifex when he was in danger. But they never interacted with us directly. Ever. And I'd never heard him call one person specifically.

"But the names are not those names?" White asked, managing to sound both polite and unstressed, which was better than I was going to manage.

Franklin was still talking to himself. "Hell, maybe Mort's name, mine, even. This makes absolutely no sense."

There was a pointed silence. "Erm, Colonel? What name do you see?"

He looked straight at me. "Stryker Dane."

I couldn't help it. I started to laugh.

CHAPTER 66

"WHO?" THIS WAS CHORUSED by everyone in the room other than Colonel Franklin. Even by Naomi and Abigail. Interesting. Out of everyone, I'd have thought Chuckie would have shared this bit of intel with them. Apparently not. But then again, he'd told them to come to me in this type of emergency.

I got myself under control. "Stryker Dane is probably the most famous conspiracy theorist going. He's the guy who writes the *Taken Away* books. About his being abducted by aliens and taken to their world for experiments, that sort of thing. I think there are like ten books in the series, maybe more. He also runs a pretty popular website and an even more active blog. Kind of an underground celebrity."

"Oh, him." Tito nodded. "I think he's done book tours that came to Vegas. I never went. But why is that funny? I mean, you were laughing like a hyena."

"Pardon me. I just find Chuckie's sense of humor funny."

"How does this have anything to do with Reynolds, in that sense?" Buchanan asked.

"It's a message from him. I don't know why Stryker's down as the next guy on the list, but I have a guess."

"At the edge of our seats, so to speak," White said.

"Chuckie must have been able to influence what went into his part of this briefing book. And Colonel Hamlin wasn't someone he trusted or liked."

"So?" Franklin was stepping onto the impatience wagon.

I resisted the urge to sigh. "Stryker Dane is from Arizona." I waited. No looks of comprehension. "Chuckie's the Conspiracy

King." Still nothing. Maybe they were all too worried about Jeff and Chuckie and the impending space invasion to make the connection. "He knows Stryker. Very well. And trusts him, more than most of those he deals with on a daily basis."

"He trusts a nut job?" Oren asked.

I coughed. "Have you not been paying attention? I mean, I realize you all got dragged into this sort of unexpectedly, but still. Aliens exist."

Jakob shrugged. "We've heard certain rumors already, so finding out about what American Centaurion really is, that's not that much of a shock. But those *Taken Away* books . . . they're all full of sh—" He looked at Mona. "Untruths."

She chuckled. "I've heard the word. And used it. More than once. But Jakob does have a point, Ambassador. Those books are works of fiction."

"Yeah, they are. Because Stryker's a great fiction writer. But, ah, well, he's also not exactly wrong. And he's very pro-alien."

"You think." Buchanan didn't sound convinced.

"No, I *know*." More blank looks, other than from Oliver, who looked both like he believed me and that one of his greatest dreams was coming true. "Gang, really. I'll say it slowly. Chuckie's been my friend since ninth grade. My best guy friend since we were thirteen. We went to high school and college together." Blank looks that indicated annoyance was coming up fast. I gave in to the urge to sigh heavily. "I know Stryker. Personally."

"Great." Tito didn't sound as though he meant it. "So what are we supposed to do? Race to Arizona, dig out the head wacko, and ask him for help?"

"No. We're going to make a phone call and then probably drive over to see him." The blankness in the room was awe-inspiring. "He lives here now. He's made a good living off those books."

"You keep in touch with him?" Buchanan seemed to be trying to channel Jeff, just to keep me on my jealousy toes. Oliver, meanwhile, was salivating. I was sort of surprised that he didn't know Stryker personally, but then again, I knew Stryker, and Stryker trusted fewer people than Chuckie did.

I couldn't hold out any longer and rolled my eyes. "I keep in touch with Chuckie, to put it mildly. Chuckie keeps in touch with Stryker. The page our friend the Colonel is looking at is there solely for a situation such as this—why would anyone, ever, read that gut buster otherwise? Something's gone wrong, we don't know what to do, so pull out the big book and see what's in there. Chuckie wants

Stryker contacted either because he's briefed Stryker on something
or because said contact will alert Stryker to something he has to do
for Chuckie."

"You're sure, Missus Martini?" At least White didn't look annoyed.

"Pretty darned." I pulled my cell out of my purse and found the
number on speed dial. The number Chuckie had insisted I program
in right after Operation Confusion. I let the phone ring three times,
then hung up. Then let it ring twice and hung up. Then three, two,
four, and then one.

"What in God's name are you doing?" Buchanan asked.

"Secret ring code."

"So, Reynolds wants us to contact a lunatic. Great, just great."

"One man's loon is another man's head of the Extra-Terrestrial
Division of the C.I.A., let me just say." Dialed again. This time, I
let it ring.

Phone was picked up on the fifth ring. "Hello?"

"Eddy! How's it going, big guy?"

"Kitty? Is that you?"

"In the conspiratorial flesh, so to speak."

"What are you doing, using the secret password?"

"Chuckie gave it to me."

"Why are you using my real name?"

"Because I can. We're at DEFCON Worse, well, really,
DEFCON Oh My God, and for some reason, Chuckie's left instructions that when he's incapacitated, you're the man for the job."

"What's happened to Chuck?" He sounded suspicious and more
than a little scared. Some things never changed.

"He's disappeared. Along with my husband. And, no, they're not
gay. I think they've been kidnapped. Sort of."

"Taken from the solar system?"

"Not that we can tell."

He was quiet. "Is Chuck in danger?"

"Dude, what part of kidnapped and cannot find didn't register
the first time?"

"Are you in danger?"

"Currently in danger of freaking out about the whereabouts of
my husband and oldest friend. Otherwise, no. The moment I leave
this building? No guess." Now wasn't the time to mention the impending invasion. I knew Stryker far too well, and we clearly
needed his help.

"Am I in danger?"

"If you don't freaking tell me why Chuckie has you down as the go-to man, you're in danger of me coming over there and kicking your butt in a serious and nasty fashion. Otherwise? No clue. You still dating that chick with all the piercings?"

"No, we broke up. Years ago," he added resentfully.

"Good choice on your part."

"She dumped me."

"You never learned how to do the spin, did you?"

"Is this relevant?"

"Just wanted to know if I had to warn the people with me not to make eye contact with your, ah, lady friend."

"No current lady friend, so they're fine. What people?"

"Good friends. Eddy, I feel no closer to knowing why Chuckie wanted you contacted in this kind of emergency. Do you remember how I used to get when you would try to be all mysterious with me?"

He coughed. "Yeah. So, what's the plan, Kitty?"

"No clue. That's why I called you. You are listed as the person to call when we have lost Chuckie. Ergo, I am calling. Ball's in your court."

He was quiet again. I let him sit there in silence. Stryker was good at it, but I'd been trained in how to sell—and one of the top five rules of selling was that whoever talks first after the offer has been made loses. I just gave Bellie some bird treats that White had on him and gave Bruno a good scritchy-scratching between his wings. It took three and a half minutes by my random count, but he finally sighed. "Fine."

"Excellent. We coming to you or are you coming to us?"

"You know I don't leave the bunker."

"Dude, you write published books. You have an agent and so forth. You leave the stupid bunker all the time. Stop acting. Two of the most important men in my life are missing and believed to be in life-threatening danger. Stop making me want to take out my fear and worry on your person."

"You do and I won't tell you how to get here."

I snorted. "Dude, seriously. Ask yourself—between the two of us, who does Chuckie both like and trust more?"

He was quiet again for a long minute, then started cursing up a blue streak. "He told you where I am?"

Well, not so much, but I knew better than to admit it. "And gave me your number, and the secret code, and all that jazz." Stryker kept on ranting. "Eddy! Enough with the blah, blah, blah. Focus! You here or us there?"

"Where is your there, exactly?"

"Andrews Air Force Base."

There was a significant pause. And then an embarrassed clearing of the throat. And then another cough.

"Eddy, what don't you want to admit? Surely you know how to get to Andrews."

"Oh, yes. I know."

I looked at Franklin. He was flipping through another book, smaller than the Encyclopedia Centaurion. He felt me looking at him and looked up. "I don't find a Stryker Dane."

"Try Eddy Simms."

"Kitty, you're under oath not to reveal my true identity!"

"Eddy, dude, you are not Superman. But, just to make you feel better, I'm kinda Wolverine. With boobs, of course."

"Of course. They still nice and perky?"

"Dude, Chuckie and my husband both will break your neck if you ask me that question again."

"He always was jealous."

"My husband? Yeah, how'd you know?"

"I meant Chuck. Told me you were his and I was never allowed to make a move."

I managed to refrain from sharing that in the Possible Alternatives to Jeff Olympics, Stryker's chances were slimmer than the Jamaican bobsled team's and let this one go. Sent a mental thank you to Chuckie for preventing an embarrassing and beyond gross situation in the past. Figured I'd handle the upcoming one with more grace and style than when I was younger—I had a lot of extra muscle with me.

Franklin cursed quietly. "Here it is. Edward Simms. Christ." He stood up. "Let's go."

"Be there shortly, Eddy."

"Kitty, I'm not prepared to receive visitors!" He sounded panicked.

"Pity. 'Cause I'm coming right now." I looked at Franklin's expression and felt I had all the confirmation I needed. "With a bunch of tough guys . . . and your boss."

CHAPTER 67

I HUNG UP AND DROPPED my phone in my purse. "I'm assuming we can walk it, Colonel?"

He nodded. "Yes. The 'bunker' is close by." Franklin looked seriously pissed.

"Do we want everyone to go?" White asked.

I considered. "I think we can use the addition of the skills, experience, and mindset of the Bahraini Royal Army, and that goes double for Mossad. Ambassadress, are you up for it?"

"Absolutely, Ambassador. As long as you call me Mona."

"Works for me, and call me Kitty. Everyone else I feel is needed, Mister White. Unless you think we need someone protecting Colonel Franklin's office or the gate within."

"It's been secure all this time," Franklin said. "I believe we can leave it."

I wasn't so sure, but this was Franklin's call, not mine.

"I actually was wondering if you wanted to leave the parrot and Mister Joel Oliver," White said dryly.

"Oh. MJO, I'm betting wild horses wouldn't keep you away."

"Correct as always, Ambassador. I'll do my best to keep the lovely Miss Bellie quiet."

Bellie nuzzled up against him. "Bellie likes Mister!"

"Bellie, you cheap slut. What is Jeff going to think when he sees you cheating on him?" I hoped he'd think that Bellie needed to stay with Oliver, but I doubted my luck would be that good.

Franklin stalked out, and we all trotted after him like a flock of really big ducklings. We were headed up the road, so to speak, but on a path that led us behind some buildings. They all looked military and official to me, and I tried to spot landmarks, in case we had to run back to Franklin's office. However, all I came up with was that military bases really looked a lot alike—dull. If I got lost, I'd call Mom—she'd undoubtedly been here before and had the entire layout memorized.

Unfortunately, I had time to think but didn't feel that speaking aloud was a good idea when we were out in the open, so to speak. Which meant I stressed about Jeff and Chuckie. Interstellar invasions were the big picture, sure, but people I loved dearly were in much more immediate danger. This wasn't helping. Focused on getting to Stryker. If nothing else, I could take out the fear and worry by kicking him.

We reached a boring looking building, which was saying a lot, all things considered. Based on my Inverse Boredom Rule—which said the more boring a building looked, the more vital and secret its function—we were heading into Super-Duper High-Security Clearance Territory.

Franklin ushered us inside, then took us downstairs. Down a lot of stairs and a lot of levels. We walked it, instead of taking an elevator, which I found interesting. I knew Stryker well, and, frankly, the idea of him taking stairs, ever, was kind of farfetched. More farfetched than what was going on with the rest of the galaxy right now, as I thought about it.

"Colonel, why are we taking the stairs instead of the newfangled elevator?"

Franklin shook his head. "Stairs are safer."

"Security is breached," Oren said.

"How so?"

"You don't lose a colonel without something being wrong," Jakob replied. "Let alone everything else we now know about."

"It's easy to trap and kill people in an elevator—they have nowhere to go," Khalid added.

"We could get trapped on the stairs, too."

"We could. However, most of us have weapons with us, and from what we've seen, some of you appear to be living weapons. We have a far better chance of survival on the stairs than in an elevator." The way Oren said this, I figured that the Mossad had done various tests and studies, or the U.S. had, and they were all confident the results were accurate.

"He's correct," Franklin said.

"Fine, not arguing with my military advisors."

"Missus Martini, you're learning the diplomacy-speak so well."

"Mister White, be careful with the sarcasm or I'll start calling you Rick again."

White chuckled. "I expect that within fifteen minutes, regardless of whether I use sarcasm or not."

"Good point." I refrained from asking what attacks everyone was expecting. Better prepared for anything than caught unawares because we were prepped for nothing.

We reached the bottom, finally, and Franklin led us down a long hallway with no doors at all except in the far distance.

"Colonel, sorry to be asking and all, but this sure seems like a bunker to me."

"It is and it isn't." Franklin was great on the no information right now.

"How secure is it should, say, someone bomb the base?"

"Secure."

"So it's a bunker."

"Not in the classic sense."

"I love that we're already good enough friends that we can play verbal gymnastics while trying to thwart an alien invasion. Where, exactly, are we going?"

"To one of the most classified, and secured, areas on base."

We reached the doors. They had the usual "Authorized Personnel Only" signs and a lot of security doohickeys to get past. While Franklin slid his badge through the reader, typed in a series of codes on the keypad, and pulled out his keys, I listened at the door.

I could have sworn I heard the sounds of furniture being moved, quiet cursing, and similar. I'd have been worried, but it sounded familiar—I was pretty sure I'd sounded like this any time my parents had unexpectedly suggested they drop by for a visit when I lived in my old apartment. The A-C Elves ensured this scramble was a thing of my past, but I still remembered it vividly.

Franklin opened the door and we were greeted to an interesting sight. It resembled the Centaurion Command Centers—lots of computers, lots of TV screens, lots of official looking stuff. Lots of sound, too, coming from what looked like radio equipment and funky EKG machines.

But there were only a handful of guys in here, and none of them resembled military, let alone A-Cs. No uniforms, no neat and clean, no high and tights, no total hotness. Heavy emphasis on the no neat and clean, or at least not tidy. I wasn't interested in doing a white glove test, but the clutter factor in here was scary high.

Sniffed carefully. Someone had sprayed a ton of Febreeze around. Thankfully.

I'd been right; they were frantically trying to straighten up. Franklin's expression—barely controlled fury—told me they weren't succeeding. However, I had to figure they hadn't been hired for their military acumen or their ability to get a quarter to bounce on their beds.

White was taking in the scene as well. "Colonel, as Missus Martini asked, where specifically are we, exactly?"

Franklin didn't need to answer—I already knew. "Gang, welcome to Hacker Central."

CHAPTER 68

I TROTTED INSIDE, and there he was, furiously stacking old pizza boxes and Big Gulp cups. I did my best Columbia from *Rocky Horror*. "Eddy!" Long, squealing, and drawn out. Missed Chuckie—he'd have appreciated it and found it funny. No one else seemed to either get it or be impressed.

Stryker turned and gaped. "Kitty? You, ah, got here really fast."

"Dude, we walked over from Headquarters and down an unreal number of steps. Not my fault you live like a pig. You know, like you always have."

I did a quick study. Still an average-size guy if you ignored the gut and man-boobs, still wearing a "The Truth is Out There" shirt that I hoped was a newer edition than the one I'd become familiar with when I was in high school and college. Full beard, and it was still fairly unkempt. Hair still worn long and sort of curly. Stryker would have had beautiful hair if he ever took care of it. That was Stryker's only attractive physical quality, though if I believed him, he was supposedly lovely with his pants off. No amount of money in the world would be enough for me to want to find out, however.

"What in the hell are you gentlemen doing in here?" Franklin snarled.

Stryker stood up straight. Not much of an improvement. "Our jobs, sir. Supreme Commander Reynolds understands."

I couldn't control the Inner Hyena. "Oh, dude, did he really tell you to call him that?" I asked in between snorts of laughter. "God, I love Chuckie's sense of humor."

"Kitty, shut up," Stryker hissed at me.

I rolled my eyes. "Colonel Franklin, I know you know why

Eddy and the others are here in the 'bunker.' They're C.I.A. operatives monitoring all incoming data for security threats and breaks." I made eye contact with Stryker. "And I do mean *all*."

"No idea what you mean, Kitty," Stryker said, giving me the "shut up, shut up" look.

"Eddy? I'm married to a space alien, okay? Who, along with my oldest friend, is missing, snatched out of thin air kind of thing. Everyone with me knows about it. So stop with the ridiculous posturing. True believers here, okay?"

Stryker relaxed, a little. "Fine. Yes. We monitor all incoming and outgoing transmissions."

"All?" Buchanan asked. "You mean worldwide?"

"He means world and galaxy and potentially universewide, don't you Eddy? In fact, the information that has everyone in a tizzy was probably filtered to everyone from down here in the 'bunker'."

Stryker nodded. "We have the highest-level security clearances. And, yes, we've been monitoring the . . . activity."

"You're paid thirty thousand dollars a year," Franklin snapped. "No one at that salary level has these kinds of clearances."

I checked out our other bunker-mates, most of whom were, like Stryker, vacillating between looking at Franklin in a terrified manner and checking out Abigail, Naomi, and Jennifer while trying to pretend they weren't so checking and while also trying to hide their drooling. Dazzlers had that effect.

One of the nervous droolers was tall, skinny, and black but otherwise matched Stryker, including in his love of the *X-Files*. One was small, scrawny, bald, and Chinese and also one with the idea that the *X-Files* was the best show ever. One looked Indian or Pakistani, but with an actual normal body build, and also wore a shirt proclaiming his *X-Files* devotion.

The last one, who was the only one not staring at the gals, was actually rather boring, albeit very Slavic-looking, if you didn't notice the dark sunglasses and the fact that he looked as though he worked out. He was a big guy and normal for the regular world and therefore looked totally out of place here,. He was apparently also more open-minded, or else just held to the classics, because he broke the uniform and was in a vintage *Star Wars* shirt.

It was like entering the set of *The Big Bang Theory*. I refrained from asking why none of them were supporting that show, *Eureka*, *Star Trek*, *Warehouse 13*, *Fringe*, or *Men in Black*, let alone a host of other options. Maybe Sundays were *X-Files* days at the Hacker Central offices, and my big man in shades was just a rebel.

"They have those clearances if they're not doing this so much for the money—because they all already have their own from a variety of other pursuits —but because they live for this stuff, and they also probably like the benefits."

Stryker grimaced. "Yeah, so what? Government bennies are great, and we do a good job."

"I'm sure you do. Colonel Franklin, you see before you the top hackers in the world, and if they're not the top in some area, they know who is. Stryker Dane, aka Eddy Simms, resident U.F.O. expert and extraterrestrial languages expert."

I pointed to the skinny black guy. "Big George Lecroix, who is Europe's best hacker. Helps that Big George speaks, reads, and writes twenty languages fluently. And, no, I'm not making that up."

Our scrawny Chinese guy was up next. "Doctor Wu, otherwise called Henry. He really has a doctorate, several, actually, and his last name really is Wu. The fact that his name is the same as a cool Steely Dan song is just an added bonus. Covers all the languages that Big George doesn't, also a software expert. China's best hacker."

I pointed to our Indian. "Ravi Gaekwad, Indian, wait for it, their best hacker. He's also big into both the software and hardware sides of the house—if you need it made or unmade, Ravi's your guy." I chose not to share his nickname.

"Geekwad?" Tito asked. "Really?" Never mind. Tito figured it out.

Ravi glared at him. "It's a fine name where I come from. Particularly when pronounced properly."

"Tito, now isn't the time. Besides, his real nickname is Ravi the Geek, like Jimmy the Greek, only less flattering."

"That's not how I like to be introduced," Ravi said sulkily. "And I prefer my name pronounced properly."

"Oh, please. Like you haven't heard that one as often as I've heard the 'Hottie from Hot Town' jokes? Let it pass. Last but in no way least, meet Omega Red, aka Yuri Stanislav. Yuri wears his sunglasses at night because he's legally blind. So, really, they should have named him Daredevil, but he's Russian, so, you know, had to go with the fitting code name and all. Killer with the audio cryptology among other pursuits."

"You know all these guys but had no idea of what your parents did for a living?" Buchanan asked. I could tell he was trying not to crack up.

"Chuck could never keep a secret from you," Stryker fumed.

Sadly, I knew this to be untrue, since Chuckie had figured out what my parents really did when we were in high school and hadn't shared. But I chose not to mention it.

"Why do you have a parrot and a huge peacock with you?" Ravi asked.

"They'd better not crap all over our equipment," Big George added.

Bruno cooed. Bellie mercifully remained silent. "They seem pleasant," Omega Red shared.

"I don't like birds," Henry said quietly. "They scare me. Just a little," he added a touch too defensively.

"Whatever," Stryker snapped. "It's Kitty. Be happy she didn't bring her dogs."

"One party, Eddy, that's all. One party when I had to dogsit and you and Chuckie insisted I had to attend. They didn't break that much, anyway."

"They destroyed my entire collection of Happy Meal collectibles." Stryker sounded as though he'd had a collection of Ming vases on his shelf, not a bunch of kiddie toys.

"Not my fault they were covered with hamburger smell. Or that you left them just lying around."

"They were up on a shelf that was at head height."

"Give the bitterness a rest, Eddy, it was a decade ago. The people with me work with me in some capacity. In my current job, as Ambassador for American Centaurion."

I did a really fast first name intro of everyone with me. The fact that I had a lot of people with me registered at this point. This many people had probably never been in Hacker Central at one time, ever. Good, it'd be something for Hacker International to remember, a red-letter day sort of thing.

I had to figure Bruno had shown himself to one and all because they were trustworthy. Either that or Bruno wasn't a good judge of character. I chose to go with the former.

"Now, charming introductions over. Your new boss of less than a week and the good senator from Florida may want a more thorough review of your skills, but we don't have time right now. Two of the most important men in my life have been kidnapped with clear intent to do serious harm, and we have what appears to be the biggest alien armada ever on a direct course for little old Earth. As Chuckie likes to say, you're either part of the solution or you're part of the problem. So get to work."

The hackers all looked at each other. "Doing what, exactly, Kitty?" Stryker asked finally.

I sighed. "Dude, seriously. Colonel Franklin has the huge Encyclopedia Centaurion in his office. In it, it lists that when we have lost the head of the C.I.A.'s Extra-Terrestrial Division, also known as Chuckie, we are to, against all logic and common sense, come to Stryker Dane for the save. So, save."

"I need a protocol," Stryker said. I got the feeling he wasn't being contrary.

"A protocol?"

He gave me a look I was familiar with. The "you're giving me orders why?" look. "A protocol, a code phrase, something to indicate that I should trust you."

"I know what they are. But it's me, Kitty, remember? Known you almost as long as I've known Chuckie?"

Stryker shrugged. "You could turn on Chuck, be mind controlled, be a robot. I have to know I can trust you."

I'd managed to keep the anger and fear somewhat at bay. But every minute we wasted was a minute I could bet Jeff and Chuckie were suffering in some horrifying way. And my baby was in both the safest and most dangerous place right now, and the longer we delayed, the more danger Jamie, ACE, and everyone else were going to be in.

"Eddy? You either tell me, right now, why Chuckie has you listed as his immediate backup when things are beyond dire, or I will kick you in the balls so hard that you'll wish you'd never, ever, heard of the term U.F.O."

Stryker grinned. "See? That wasn't so hard, was it?"

I knew I wasn't the only one gaping. "Excuse me? That was the protocol?"

He laughed. "For you, yeah." Stryker shrugged. "What can I say? Chuck knows you really well."

CHAPTER 69

BEFORE I COULD COME UP WITH a suitable retort, Stryker was giving orders. All the hackers raced to their stations, easily spotted by the fact that they were the messiest parts of this particular high-security pigsty.

"How does Yuri not kill himself in here?" I asked as Omega Red lumbered to his station without incident, even though his path was scary cluttered.

Stryker shrugged. "Nanotechnology's good for a lot of things."

Bruno seemed to agree, or at least he liked the trash Omega Red had. He flapped up out of the way, settled into some of the mess like it was a nest, tucked his head under his wing, and, as far as I could tell, went to sleep. I chose to take this to mean I was safe and among friends.

"Whatever. Where are my men?"

"Geez, Kitty, give a guy a minute. I don't remember you this impatient."

"Do you remember me stating that my husband and oldest friend are missing?"

"You've checked the obvious places?" Stryker asked as he sat down at his console and started typing away on what looked like a megakeyboard. It had more than the standard qwerty stuff on it, by far.

"We've searched all the way to the Alpha Centauri solar system. There is no sign of Jeff or Chuckie. I think they're on Earth but in one of the many rooms our enemies have constructed that appear to be impenetrable via normal and alien means."

"Nice to know you think we can work miracles," Stryker snapped.

"The Supreme Commander's January report indicated that a number of subterrestrial locations that have been recently identified are priority one," Henry shared. "So that's where we've been focusing."

"Dudes, really, what's up with the Supreme Commander stuff? You're aware that Chuckie's laughing his butt off when he uses that title, right?"

"Sure," Ravi replied. "But he *is* our Supreme Commander."

Franklin cleared his throat. "Not if you're on the U.S. Air Force's payroll he's not."

I thought about the various chains of command I'd learned about over the past two-plus years. "Actually, Colonel, they might be right. But guys, really, lay off with the titles."

Big George shrugged. "If we must. However, Henry's right. There's a network of sub-terrestrial strongholds we have yet to map completely."

"Put them onscreen," Franklin snapped. "Speaking as the Supreme Commander in attendance."

Henry did some fast typing, and a map of the United States appeared. The map was hard to read since it covered all the U.S., but I spotted what I was confident were the locations of the Dome, the Dulce Science Center, and Caliente Base. Each was surrounded in red. "Why are those circled?"

"Chuck wants us to ignore them," Stryker replied. There was a lot of color in the area where NASA and East Bases were and even more in the D.C. area.

"And you do?" I found this hard to believe, knowing Stryker as well as I did.

"Yeah, we do, 'cause Chuck monitors every damn thing we do, and he's gotten really nasty in his old age." Stryker sounded annoyed. Considering Chuckie and I were ten years younger than Stryker, this was amusing.

Stryker zoomed in on the D.C. area. Sure enough, there was the Embassy and the Pontifex's residence, circled in red. Jeff and I were going to have a serious talk about this once I found and saved him and dealt with the people who'd, again, taken and most likely hurt my men.

However, there were a variety of locations marked in green. "Eddy, the green ones are the ones you guys are mapping?"

"The green circles are subterrestrial locations. The green lines are the access tunnels that connect the subterrestrial locations to each other and to upper-level exits and entrances. We're mapping the entire network." He zoomed out a bit. It was a rather impressive network of green lines. This boded.

"Trying to map," Omega Red added. "They're difficult for a variety of reasons."

"The rooms or the tunnels?"

"The subterrestrial locations are more difficult than the access tunnels, but both have their own challenges," Stryker said.

"Cloaking, lead walls, visual and audio disturbances," Henry clarified. "Very little computer activity we can track."

"Any more," Ravi added. "Fortunately, we monitor and save everything, and so did our predecessors."

"Predecessors?" Franklin sounded like he was going to get a migraine. "How many predecessors?"

Stryker shrugged. "Enough." He looked over his shoulder at Franklin. "You're in charge and this is a surprise?"

"These functions are not a surprise. Who's doing them is the surprise."

Stryker shrugged again. "You want the best for this kind of work? Accept that the best of our breed don't join the military."

"Yeah, most hackers aren't into the up at five a.m., run twenty miles with a full pack on, and do two hundred pushups lifestyle." They were into the sleep until noon, catch up on the latest internet porn, eat all the junk food they could manage, while spying on the world lifestyle. I looked around. Sure enough, there were some donuts. I checked them out. Fresh. Snagged one, took the box around and offered it to the rest of the gang. I got a dirty look from Stryker, but he kept his mouth shut.

"Glad you're making sure we have fuel," White said. "As always in these situations, I was a bit peckish."

"Donuts are nice," Tito agreed. "However, we're not much of anywhere, Kitty."

I looked at the map again. "I think we are. ACE said Christopher was looking the wrong way. Since he was looking all over the planet and in two solar systems, Christopher and I both figure ACE didn't mean that Christopher just needed to work harder and try to reach another galaxy. Oh, and note how many of the ones with green circles radiate out from the one with the red circle that happens to correlate to where many of us now live."

"Seven," Buchanan said. "Nice to see you're keeping on top of things."

"You're almost as funny as Chuckie and Mister White. Big George, how far are you into any of these?" I pointed to the green circles near the Embassy. There were others, dotted all over the globe, but these seemed the most likely targets.

Of course, "near" was a relative term, because maps always made things seem closer than they actually were. I assumed the circle nearest to the Embassy was the remains of the Secret Lab where Amy's father and his cronies had done their horrible and horribly successful experiments. The others were farther away, and none were in a straight line from the others.

"As noted, in the D.C. area, we've identified and located seven rooms," Big George said, rolling his pointer over different points of the map. "We call them rooms, but they could be a series of rooms, caverns, something else that has a general cube shape. But they're not tunnels, because we can actually enter the tunnels and confirm structure."

"We call them dead zones until we can confirm their structure," Henry added. "Because we can't read anything within them, so it's like they're dead to our equipment."

"Henry, I think everyone with me understood 'dead zone' without the condescending explanation. But it's nice to see you're still the fun party dude I remember."

"One of the D.C. dead zones, the one nearest to your Embassy, was declared destroyed by Chuck, but we mapped its area as best we could as well," Big George went on quickly, pointer on the green circle closest to the Embassy. He rolled the pointer. "We feel there's another one in this area, but haven't finalized mapping."

The one Big George's pointer was now on seemed to be within or near to the metro area of D.C. But in order to show the dead zones all on one screen, the map was small enough that I couldn't really make out city names or exact locations. However, the others were all farther away, and one, per the map, appeared to actually be in the Atlantic. I presumed under the ocean floor, but I put nothing past the Club of Evil Super-Geniuses these days.

"So, by mapping you mean what, exactly?"

"We send sonar, infrared, electronic, and other forms of probes and scanning through the earth," Omega Red explained. "Areas our equipment's unable to access in some way are declared dead zones. Some are just dense rock. But others are clearly structures or constructs of some kind, because their shapes are too regular."

"Because of the tunnel under the American Centaurion Embassy, we were able to begin exploration, which also allowed us a way to determine how to spot either a tunnel or what we're choosing to assume is a room," Stryker added.

"So, the dead zones you've mapped—have you entered any of them?"

"We haven't been able to determine how to breach any dead zones yet," Henry admitted. "Only the tunnels. They're easier. They're hidden from us, but not to the same degree as the rooms." He paused, a little too obviously.

"Okay, fine. Explain how they're not hidden in the same degree as the presumed rooms."

Henry looked like I'd just offered to have sex with him. Had to give Hacker International this—it was easy to make these guys happy. "The tunnels don't have the same level of blocking. It's more like what's around certain areas Chuck doesn't want us probing."

"Areas in, say, New Mexico and Arizona?"

"Among others."

"Okay, super." I'd ask about all the similar locations another time. "So the tunnels are cloaked in some way, but not like the dead zone areas. Fine, I guess that makes sense." In the Bizarro World I now lived in, of course this made sense.

"We haven't finished a full mapping of all the tunnels worldwide, either," Big George said. "And until we map, we can't send in agents to physically examine the system."

"Chuck's pissed about it, too," Ravi added. "He doesn't like the delay."

We'd only discovered the Embassy's secret lab four and a half months ago, so it wasn't as though they'd been working on this for years. Figured I'd better check. "When did Chuckie start you on this particular project?"

"January, like I said already," Stryker replied. I loved being right. "Four and a half months ago," he added, sarcasm knob positioned around six on my scale. "We were working on some high-level transmissions prior to that."

"How high level?" Franklin asked.

"Out of this world," Big George replied.

Stryker nodded. "From systems past Alpha Centauri."

CHAPTER 70

I LOOKED AT WHITE. "If we've heard them, then the folks on Alpha Four have heard them."

White nodded. "Which means our enemies in that spaceship which left the range of our two solar systems undoubtedly know there are other inhabited planets and headed to one of them."

"And found one, made friends, and are heading back for a really bitchin' homecoming party." I wanted to say we were screwed. I refused to accept it, though. "So, we prepare for another game of Interplanetary Risk. But all of this was set up well before LaRue and Ronaldo took to the stars."

"You think Jeff and Chuck are in one of those dead-zone rooms, don't you?" Naomi asked.

"I do indeed. Because I think one of the goals of all of the crap that's been going on was to get us all out of the Embassy so Clarence could get in easily." I looked at William. "Walter refused to leave. He's not alone, he's got plenty of Security A-Cs and Peregrines with him, and they're in full lockdown."

William smiled. "He's a good kid."

"Peregrines?" Stryker asked.

"Tell you later, Eddy."

"But which dead zone?" Khalid asked. "There are six available, at least."

"My bet is the last one, that the guys here haven't finished with."

"Feminine intuition?" White asked.

"Betting on how our luck usually runs is more like it."

"There's more than one pathway to that room," Mona said. "At least if the schematic on the screen is accurate."

"Yes, the tunnels are interconnected, at least the ones in D.C. and on the Eastern Seaboard are," Big George said. "The others appear to be interconnected as well, but we haven't been able to confirm fully yet. We've put security within every tunnel we've explored so far, with extra around where we'd say an entrance to a 'room' is. With even more security in the tunnel that leads to your Embassy. Per Chuck's orders." Walter had confirmed as much when the Peregrines had arrived.

"If the tunnels are also dead zones, how does the security work?"

"Well, as Henry said, they're not as dead. So to speak. Once we found them, it was fairly simple to put high-frequency equipment in them. NASA was helpful, so we have a variety of equipment used to look out into space broadcasting from within the tunnels."

"Fine. But if no one can get into these supposed rooms," Tito asked patiently, "how are we going to get them out? How are we even going to guess what room they're in? Or tell if they're really in one of these dead-zone rooms at all?"

"Tito, you're just batting a thousand on the tough questions, aren't you? I don't know. I'm hoping the Poofs can manage it. Somehow."

"I think if they could, they'd have done it already," Abigail said.

"Poofs?" Stryker asked.

"Tell you later, Eddy." There had to be more. Chuckie wouldn't have arranged to have Stryker as his backup for this reason only. "Eddy, how do you contact Chuckie?"

"He calls or comes by. Why?"

"You don't have some special way of tracking him?" I knew Chuckie had been tagged by the A-C Wildlife Association, just like the rest of us, not that this had helped. But maybe the hackers had something even better.

"Not really. He's the boss. He tracks us."

"How?"

Stryker sighed and showed me his left wrist. It had a watch on it. "Nice to see the time. It's only three in the afternoon? Wow, time drags when my guys are in danger."

I got the long-suffering look. "It's also a tracker, Kitty. We all have one." The rest of Hacker International flashed their wrists. "We can't take them off, either."

White cleared his throat. "A-C technology." The security stuff from NASA probably had a lot of A-C stuff in it too. Hoped that was a good thing.

"Gotcha. So, what level of testing has Chuckie done on those?"

I got blank looks. "I mean, how often has he tried to reach you, where does he check from?"

"No idea," Stryker said.

Omega Red cocked his head. "Chuck's been with the operative teams when they've investigated the tunnels we've explored so far, including close proximity to the dead-zone rooms."

"Yuri, you think Chuckie monitored you guys from there?"

"I think it's possible."

"Know where you're going with this." Ravi pulled off his watch and started doing some fiddling. "Going to take me a few minutes, though."

"I thought you couldn't take them off."

"Still in contact with my skin," Ravi answered. "As long as the contact is maintained, we don't, ah, have to deal with consequences."

"Consequences?"

Stryker gave me a long look. "You know him. What do you think the consequences are?"

I pondered. "Heads explode sort of thing?"

"Pretty much, yeah," Stryker said.

"And you agreed to that?"

"I'm not a traitor, and if someone got to me, considering what intel I've got, honestly, better I explode."

"Eddy, I had no idea you were hero material."

He shrugged. "It's a living."

"Where is he going with this?" Franklin asked.

"If it can transmit one way, it can transmit the other." I just hoped that Chuckie still had on whatever it was he wore that allowed him to track Hacker International. The memory of all my guys stripped to the waist and hanging in a Parisian dungeon flashed through my mind. I got the worried feeling again, since I didn't think Chuckie was going to carry this tracker in his underwear.

"What Kitty said," Ravi muttered. "Do need to concentrate, since I don't want my head to explode, if it's all the same to you."

"Carry on." While Ravi was occupied, I turned my attention back to Stryker. "So, Eddy, let's take the horrible idea that Chuckie's gone for good. What, in that case, does he expect you to do?"

Stryker looked uncomfortable. "We don't know he's gone for good, Kitty."

"We don't know that he's still alive, either. Let's say we presume Chuckie's dead. Share what, in that case, you're supposed to do, or watch me react as if Chuckie and my husband are truly dead and gone. Trust me, you'd rather tell us what Chuckie expects you to do."

Stryker didn't seem eager to comply, if I took him not moving and looking uncomfortable to be clues.

"Do it, whatever it is, or I'll have you up on charges." Franklin was really pissed.

Stryker chose discretion over valor. "Fine." He opened the lowest drawer on his desk and pulled out an envelope. It had "Contingency" written on it. I recognized the handwriting—I'd seen it since ninth grade.

Stryker opened the envelope. And stared at it. "What the hell?"

"Blank sheet of paper? If so, lemon juice and heat is the right thing."

"Thanks, Kitty, we're not starring in *National Treasure*. No, there's writing. It just makes no sense at all."

"Colonel Franklin had that same reaction when he saw your name, Eddy! Isn't that cool and all? What the hell does it say?"

Stryker sighed. "Tell Centaurion to activate the Avenger Initiative."

CHAPTER 71

I COULDN'T HELP IT, I laughed again. And got everyone staring at me like I was crazy again. "He's amazing, he really is."

"I'm confused, not amazed," Tito said. He was obviously speaking for everyone else in the room.

If only Reader were here instead of Paris. He would have gotten it immediately, but he was a comics geek like me. The A-Cs didn't go in for comics or science fiction movies and TV shows because they lived it in real life, though Jeff might have figured it out, based on the fact that he'd read a lot of my comics to be a good husband and share my interests. But Hacker International really had no excuse.

"Stryker, really, why is this hard to follow? You yourself mentioned protocols. I guarantee Chuckie has them."

More blank stares. Well, I thought better running my mouth, so I could look at this as getting a double. "Look, in the comics, the head dudes always run diagnostics on their heroes, so they know the pros and cons, strengths and weaknesses, in case said heroes go to the dark side. The baddies do this, too. In Marvel's "Onslaught" alternate universe arc Professor X had full rundowns on all the X-Men, focused on how to kill them."

"That was from a long time ago," Stryker said, a tad defensively.

"It wasn't 'Age of Apocalypse,' I'll grant you, but it's still kind of a classic. And don't even try to pretend you don't have every issue."

"You think Chuck wants to kill us?" Naomi sounded confused and a little upset about the insinuation.

"No. Geez, he wants to protect us. But he's thorough, and he has to be able to take any one of us out if we go all Crazed Evil Villain on him, right?"

"Right. And he wouldn't be the only one." Big George had, thankfully, joined the party. He tapped something on his keyboard, and a document appeared. "I've found the file on you, Kitty—Katherine Katt-Martini—Confidential." He opened it and started scrolling through, quickly. "There's enough here to make some good assumptions about what you'd do in a crisis," he said as he reached the end.

"Is that Chuckie's file on me?" He'd found it awfully fast.

Big George shook his head. "These are from the C.I.A.'s ultra-confidential files. Supposedly, no one in the EDT has access."

"So, asking the Hacker International guys this question—who's your loyalty to? The C.I.A., the U.S. Government?"

They all gave me the "duh" look. "Chuck Reynolds," Stryker replied. "Who the hell else, Kitty?"

"Hey, thought so, just wanted the confirmation." Wished Jeff were here to empathically confirm, but no such luck. Bruno pulled his head out of his wing and cooed. Right. They could see him. That meant they'd passed the Peregrine test. I hoped.

Abigail nudged me. "I can read the emotions, remember? So can Jeremy. Sis has checked, too—everyone here is working for the good of Earth."

"I've taken the liberty of snapping some quiet photos," Oliver added. "William and Jennifer have read them."

"Enemies are not present," William confirmed.

"Not even Senator Armstrong," Naomi added.

"I heard that," he said, though he didn't sound upset. "I believe, gentlemen, that what the Ambassador would like is for you all to do your jobs and find whatever protocols Mister Reynolds has hidden. Pronto."

Hacker International took the hint, other than Ravi, who was still busily reverse engineering. The rest of them typed rapidly on their keyboards, some, but not all, with more than two fingers. Bruno went back to sleep.

"I hate to ask this," Tito said. "But what good will finding Jeff and Reynolds do for us with a hostile force on the way to, most likely, attack and conquer us?"

Naomi and Abigail looked upset. "Girls, it's a good, legitimate question. As I said not too long ago, you both need real field experience. Here it is. So start thinking like leaders."

"We'll get assistance from Alpha Four if we can get Charles back safely," White pointed out.

"I think Tito's looking at the bigger picture, Mister White. Tito, what are you thinking?"

"I'm wondering why everything that's happened this weekend, other than Reynolds being kidnapped, has happened at all. It seems like a lot of work for, well, nothing, really. Earth isn't truly equipped to fight an interstellar invasion. So why bother with all the other stuff? Take Reynolds out, one and done, the fight's over before it can start, because we can't get any backup."

"It's a good point," Buchanan said.

Armstrong nodded. "Why bother with the naked pictures if none of it matters tomorrow?"

"Naked pictures?" Stryker asked.

"Later, Eddy."

"Promise?"

"No, I'm lying. Never. Get back to work." Armstrong and Tito had exceptionally good points. Time to stop being The Ambassador, run to a phone booth, and change into Megalomaniac Girl. "Per Tito's question, pretty much every distraction they've tossed at us has done at least double duty."

"But it's all pointless," Abigail said. "If the only goal is to get Chuck out of the way."

"So that means getting rid of Chuckie can't be the only goal."

"Makes sense," Buchanan said. "But, other than chaos and destabilization, what were your enemies achieving by everything that's happened this weekend?"

"Why say 'your' enemies?" Tito asked. "You've been under fire, too."

Buchanan shrugged. "Only because I'm assigned to watch over Missus Chief. Otherwise, honestly, I haven't been in any danger."

My brain nudged. "Maybe that's because the bad guys don't know you exist, Malcolm." He'd only been assigned to be my shadow six weeks ago, and he'd spent four of those weeks in Florida.

"I don't follow you," Naomi said.

"So few ever do, Mimi. I mean that Malcolm's right. Essentially he's been ignored, and considering his skill set, that's kind of stupid. And our enemies are many things, but stupid, sadly, is never one of them."

Think, think. Everything we needed was in front of us, just like always. I had to stop worrying about the impending invasion and the lack of Jeff and Chuckie and focus on what we knew for sure. "Okay, every action this weekend was focused on getting everyone else completely distracted and Chuckie out of the way. But each action also did at least double duty, so that if it failed in one of its missions, it didn't fail in the others."

"How so?" Franklin asked.

"Sandra the Android failed to kidnap or kill me, but she slipped a bug into my purse and ensured I'd be kept out of the high-level security briefings, presumably because I might see a pattern or make a connection the others wouldn't. Senator Armstrong didn't take the dirty pictures to the person they'd hoped he would, but he identified that he wasn't on their team any more by doing so. Him taking the new set to me today got him out of the way."

"Another set of dirty pictures?" Stryker asked. "When do we see those?"

"Never, Eddy. Get back to work."

"Why was getting me out of the way at the Festival important?" Armstrong asked. "It's not like I'd have been able to prevent anything that happened."

Mona looked pensive. "Actually, Senator, that's incorrect. My husband was supposed to spend time with you and some others this morning. Because you disappeared, the meeting was rescheduled."

"Meaning . . . what?" I asked her.

"Meaning Khalid and I were free to wander the Festival. If the Ambassador had been at the meeting, we would have been there as well, waiting."

"Why?"

"Political photo op," Armstrong said. "So they could show how nice they are."

"And impress everyone with how awful it was that the evil Israelis broke into their Embassy," Oren said, with no malice at all in his tone.

"But it wasn't Israelis who broke in, was it?" All of the Middle Eastern Contingent shook their heads. "So, who did?"

"Our surveillance cameras caught nothing out of the ordinary," Khalid said. "I had Oren and Jakob review them, as well. None of us could find anything."

"What was taken in the break-in? I know the papers said nothing, but clearly an alarm was triggered or something."

Mona shook her head. "No items of significance were taken, and no alarms were set off."

"Share what insignificant things were taken. I mean, how did you even know an unlawful entry had happened?"

"We had unimportant things missing. Food, mostly. Rooms not

under surveillance were in disarray, but it was slight." She shrugged. "It was strange, and a bit unsettling, but not necessarily criminal."

"So, why blame the Israelis?" I got "duh" looks from everyone. "Oh, come on. Seriously, you guys can't blame everything strange or bad that happens on Israel."

"True," Mona said with a laugh. "It was thought to be Mossad because of how cleverly it was done."

"Only Mossad doesn't break into other Embassies in order to steal food and make beds untidy," Jakob said.

"A-Cs moving at hyperspeed don't show up on human cameras. So Clarence was hanging out at your Embassy. When did it start, the weirdness?"

"Last week. It went on for several days before we brought it to the press. In an effort to get the intruder to leave."

"So, that's when he came back to Earth. Which, I suppose, makes some kind of sense for how the invading armada is traveling. Presumably he was either on a scout ship or they can move one individual even faster than they can the armada." The A-Cs used the Dome for the big transfers, after all, and they definitely took longer than sending one guy through a gate.

"But the first set of pictures arrived a month ago," Armstrong reminded me.

"Meaning they definitely have people in place who were advised to roll their part of the plan. Yuri, Eddy, take a look at any transmissions that may have filtered across your desks, or anyone else's, from a month ago."

"What are we looking for?" Omega Red asked.

"Something innocuous that still seems out of place." A random moment from earlier flashed through my mind—the way Olga had advised her husband that she and Adriana wouldn't be around for a while. "You know, as if someone were having a normal conversation and then said one line with a different kind of emphasis. Too casual, too well enunciated, things like that. Or one simple line that comes out of the blue, with no response. Sort of thing."

"Kitty, that'll take us hours, if not days or even weeks," Stryker said.

"Dude, I didn't mean every conversation on Earth. I meant every transmission from space."

"Oh, that's *so* much better."

"Cry me a river. I know you can come up with this faster than you want anyone to believe, Eddy."

Eddy grumbled about demanding females who only dropped by

when they wanted something while I went back to trying to make
sense of what the hell was going on. "So, why create unrest between Bahrain and Israel? Clarence could have ensured you had no
idea he was using your Embassy as his base of operations, and yet
he did things specifically to let you know he was there."

"Tensions are always high between Israel and the rest of the
Middle East," Franklin said.

"I can't buy that this incident would cause a war."

"They've been started for less," Oliver said. "Though I do agree
the break-in seems like a slim reason to break even an uneasy
peace. However, the kidnap and/or murder of the Bahraini
Ambassadress? That would start a war almost instantly."

CHAPTER 72

I CONSIDERED OLIVER'S STATEMENT. It made sense, but lacked something. "But why choose Bahrain? Over any other country? What is it about that country that would make it a target at all?"

Naomi cocked her head. "Their secret."

"Daddy's secrets!" Bellie shared.

"Yes, Bellie. Hush."

"Naomi is right," Oliver said to the Middle Eastern Contingent. "The four of you share a secret you don't want exposed. If a spy was hiding out in the Embassy, he would have found evidence of what you're covering up, wouldn't he?"

"But Clarence wasn't really trying to kill them. They were being used as a lure for all of us, so he could grab Naomi and Abigail."

"Your enemies know you." Buchanan's eyes were narrowed. "It's a safe bet that you wouldn't leave the four of them at the Mall."

White nodded. "Missus Martini is our Head of Recruitment for a reason, after all."

Henry spun in his chair, got up, raced to a different terminal, and typed like a madman. "Kitty, you're not going to like this. I just checked the news feeds. More than one news outlet is reporting that the Bahraini Ambassadress has disappeared, along with her body-guard. Foul play is presumed, and since the Israeli Embassy is missing two of their staff, too, it's presumed said staffers are the culprits."

"How fast are the tanks being assembled?" Franklin asked. He didn't sound like he was trying to be funny.

"Talk has moved from nasty threats into real ones," Henry reported. "And because this happened on U.S. soil, at the International One World Festival no less, the U.S. is also being held responsible and blamed."

I looked at Oliver. "MJO, what's the likelihood this means war?"

"High. Escalation will be easy to influence, and it will come out quickly that Oren and Jakob here are Mossad. That's all it will take."

"I hate these people. Though I'm hella impressed with how damned well they know exactly what I'll do."

"What you'll all do," Big George said. "I have all the C.I.A.'s confidential files on all of American Centaurion and Centaurion Division." He shook his head. "The expectation is that if World War Three truly happens, Centaurion Division will be forced to take an active role."

"I'll call my husband," Mona said. "This must be stopped."

"Wait," Franklin said. "If you do that, you let him know where you are."

"Why would that be a bad thing?" she asked. Several of us, myself included, nodded in agreement.

"What will the immediate reaction be, if you call and say you're at Andrews Air Force Base?" Franklin asked in return. So he had been given that sage advice and just hadn't used it earlier. Good to know.

Mona took a deep breath. "I'll have to explain *why* I'm here."

"And?" Franklin prodded.

"I would say I was attacked, Mossad came to help us, and they took us to Andrews for protection."

"Does that sound believable?" Buchanan asked. "I mean, we know it's essentially the truth, but will your husband, or anyone else, believe it? It sounds fishy to me, and I'm intimately involved in the situation."

"And, attacked by whom?" Franklin asked. "If my wife disappeared, then called to tell me she'd indeed been attacked and almost kidnapped but *not* by the people I thought, I'd damn well want to know who she'd actually been attacked by and who was trying to kidnap her. So I could send my tanks and missiles toward them."

"I'd want to know why you were taken to the Air Force Base, not your own Embassy," White added.

"Oh. Well, then I would explain more fully." She looked around. "And that would mean an explanation no one will believe."

"Some will believe it. Oh. Crap."

Franklin nodded. "Some *will* believe it. And they'll really believe it when an alien armada arrives."

"But Clarence is the one who did the attacking," Abigail said.

"Right. And he's an A-C. If we say Clarence is a terrorist, the instant assumption will be that you're all terrorists. It's not necessarily the logical view, and as individuals not everyone would believe it. But people as a whole will assume the A-Cs are here as enemies, not protectors. And all those fears will be instantly confirmed when we're attacked from space."

I could see it—world war, us fighting each other instead of the space invaders. Us fighting each other *and* the space invaders. Earth being taken, easily, because we had high-level influencers along with people in strategic positions within the world governments who wanted it that way and were doing their parts to ensure this happened. And despite everything we'd tried to do to avoid it, we'd still ended up playing right into their hands.

"Can one person really be this important?" Jeremy asked.

"I would be a symbol," Mona said. "It wouldn't be about me but about what I stand for."

"Assassinate Archduke Ferdinand, have yourself a world war. Yeah, one person can be this important. Chuckie, for example. Without him, we apparently have no allies."

"Like England during World War Two, at least for a while," Franklin agreed.

"England had Churchill leading them, at least." I always thought of Councilor Leonidas as Alpha Four's version of Churchill. Chuckie had agreed with that assessment. I realized I was thinking of him in the past tense. That had to stop. If we gave up now, the bad guys won for sure. "Never give up."

"Some countries will surrender to the invaders instantly," Oliver said. "There's too much historical precedent to assume otherwise."

"Never give up." That was Churchill's famous line, after all. So, if we were England, what did that make Alpha Four and the rest of that system? "The U.S. didn't get involved in World War Two until they were attacked. We had servicemen and -women going to help the cause, but Pearl Harbor was the official entry point. Something big and unavoidable."

"Where are you going with this?" Tito asked.

"Not sure yet." I was almost there, though. A strong suspicion niggled. "Eddy, I need Chuckie's files on us, and I need them yesterday."

"Working on it," he snapped. "And the ten other things you want immediately, too. I'm only human."

"True enough. Mister White, why were the Peregrines sent to us?"

"Ostensibly because the flock was ready and they're a traditional gift."

"Uh-huh. A traditional gift that came with gift cards strongly suggesting Chuckie, Abigail, and Naomi needed to take up residence in the Embassy. A traditional gift that warned us to keep an eye on Chuckie. If we know what's coming, they know what's coming. We're England, they're the U.S. They have more troops, but they're waiting for proof that they need to get involved."

"An entire space armada isn't proof?" Franklin asked.

"Colonel, how fast does the U.S. commit troops when our allies get pissed off at each other and take their familial disputes out of the private arena and into the public one?"

"We're slow to commit," he admitted.

"Right. Because we don't want to back the wrong side, make the problem bigger than it is, be accused of trying to take over. We want to see if our allies can figure out what to do on their own. If they can't, and it looks bad, and they beg us, then we come in."

"That's standard for most of the superpowers," Oliver said.

"Most countries, really," Franklin added.

"Right. Well, as far as superpowers go, the Alpha Centauri system has way more of them than we do."

"But what are they waiting for?" Tito asked. "Reynolds and Jeff are gone, we have superbeing clusters all of a sudden, international unrest of the highest order, and a huge war looming."

"I don't know what they're waiting for us to do. But until we do it, they're staying out of our affairs."

"Speaking of surrender," Armstrong said quietly, "you do realize that the moment the head of the C.I.A. and Department of Defense realize Mister Reynolds is missing and presumed dead, they'll move Esteban into his position. And if your suspicions are correct—and I'm sure they are—he'll suggest the U.S. broker a surrender to the invaders."

"Wow, Senator, I can't believe I'm saying this, but I'm glad you're with us on this one. Right you are, and the Bad Guy Scheme du Jour falls nicely into place." We needed help. I needed help. "I need to call James. Or my mom. Or James and my mom."

"Wait," Stryker said. "I think you need to see this."

CHAPTER 73

STRYKER WAS BUSY AT HIS KEYBOARD. I trotted over. "It's a computer screen with what looks like code on it. Why am I looking at it?"

"Okay, I meant I need to tell you what it says. I'm decoding in my head, because I want to make sure I'm on the right track. Chuck's not above installing a kill switch."

"You mean, you guess the decode wrong and it all disappears?"

"Right. So . . . who's Captain America?"

I took a moment and refrained from a variety of snappy comebacks. "I assume you mean, do I think Captain America is a code name for someone, right?"

"Yes."

Considered the options. "Got to be James."

"He's not a Captain any more," Naomi said.

"No, but Captain America is like the perfect man, and he's also the leader of the Avengers."

"Whoever it is, he's supposed to take control of these files if he's not incapacitated," Stryker shared.

"See? I'm right, it's James. He lives for the light reading."

Stryker nodded. "Makes sense. But let me run the others by you. If you can figure them out without too much trouble, I can feel confident I have it all right."

"I'm flattered."

"You're the protocol, Kitty. The first thing I decoded said 'Run this through a CAT scan.' It's not flattery so much as doing what Chuck said to do."

"You say tomato, I say whatever."

He sighed. "So, Wolverine, that's you, right?

"Right.

"Professor X?"

"Mister White." I'd called White that during Operation Confusion.

"Cyclops?"

I was tempted to say Jeff, but thought about it. "Betting that's Christopher." Based on the glaring, which I was sure Chuckie had noted as I had, and Christopher's ability these days to see far, far away in his mind's eye.

"Incredible Hulk?"

Nice to be right. "Jeff."

"Wonder Twins?"

"Naomi and Abigail." They weren't actually twins, but I called them that all the time and I knew Chuckie did, too.

"Thor?"

"Paul Gower, our Pontifex." He wasn't a blond god from Asgaard, but he was carrying a godlike consciousness inside him.

"Beast?"

"Tito."

"Huh?" Tito asked. "Why would I be called a beast?"

"You're the doctor, you take out A-Cs with your fists alone, blah, blah, blah. It's not an insult. Beast is a cool, kick-butt, genius doctor in the X-Men, Tito."

"Okay. I guess."

I decided not to tell him that Beast was also covered in blue fur. Why spoil the moment?

"Wow," Stryker said. "One that's not actually a comic book character. Joe Montana?"

"Kevin." I was good. Then again, I knew my source and he knew me. "Good thing I'm around to figure this out."

Big George nodded. "Your C.I.A. file indicated you would be. 'Subject exhibits extreme random tendencies.'"

"What's that mean?" Jeremy asked.

"Means luck," Buchanan said. "And they're not wrong."

"Your C.I.A. file also indicates a strong likelihood to contact the head of the P.T.C.U. for advice and counsel," Big George shared. "It also indicates that you listen to and tend to abide by that counsel."

"Just call me a Mamma's Girl and proud of it."

"Weapon X?" Stryker asked, getting us back on track.

"My daughter, Jamie."

"New Mutants?"

"All the rest of the hybrid babies coming."

"Gambit?"

"Tim."

"You're sure?" White asked.

"If we didn't have Captain America as the guy who's in charge of the files, then I'd say Gambit was James. But considering what Tim did during Operation Confusion, I'm really damned positive."

"Works for me," Stryker said. "You don't have to be right for all of them, but you have to *think* you're right."

"I'm not even going to ask you to explain that."

Stryker shrugged and went on. "S.H.I.E.L.D.?"

"Claudia, Lorraine, and the flyboys. Len and Kyle. Malcolm. All the people who kick butt with us who aren't the official leaders or extraspecial mutants."

"X-Factor?"

That one I had to consider. Unless I was wrong about my code name being Wolverine, and I really found that hard to believe, I had no clear idea. The X-factor was the unknown, really. Oh. Duh. "Serene."

"Ma and Pa Kent."

"Alfred and Lucinda."

"Indiana Jones."

"My dad."

Stryker snorted. "If you say so."

"My dad's cool, and I do say so."

"Black Widow."

"Speaking of the head of the P.T.C.U. My mom."

"Really? Your father's still alive."

"Yeah, because of my mom, trust me." Black Widow had no real superpowers, she was just totally badass and beyond impressively trained. Just like Mom. Who I desperately wanted to call but now refused to, lest Hacker International get to feel even slightly superior.

"Last one's Nick Fury."

I laughed. "Chuckie."

"He kept a file on himself?" Armstrong asked.

"He's thorough, and he pays attention. And, let's face it, Nick Fury's the Supreme Commander of S.H.I.E.L.D., isn't he?" Of course, I thought of Jeff as Superman, Christopher as the Flash, and Chuckie as Batman, and I was fairly sure Chuckie knew it, because I'd said so in his presence at least once. But this was his code for me to understand, not mine for him.

"Okay, good enough. I'm going to hit the decode. Let's all hope Kitty's right." Stryker hit something on his keyboard. A nearby printer started making a lot of noise.

He got up, raced over, and took a page out of the tray. His whole body relaxed. "That was it. There's a lot more than the ones we went over, Kitty. He might have done everyone in your Embassy; maybe all of Centaurion Division."

"Nice to know he has a hobby that keeps him off the streets. Where is the information on the Avenger Initiative?"

"Waiting for it to print out."

Big George went to another printer. "Who do I give these to?" He had a thick stack of pages in his hand.

"What are they?"

"These are C.I.A's confidential files on all of you."

"Why'd you print them instead of give us to them electronically?"

I got the "duh" look. I was really scoring with that one this weekend. Oh, well, it was probably better than the "you so crazy" look. "I'm ensuring the electronic trail ends here."

Before I could ask about that, I heard a soft mewling and looked into my purse. There was a Poof there. Not Harlie or Poofikins. I was fairly sure it was Jamie's Poof. "Why are you here? Is Jamie alright?"

The Poof purred, so I belayed panic on that front.

"Did Jamie send you?"

Another mewl. Might mean yes. Might mean no. Might mean the Poof was hungry. I couldn't tell.

The Poof jumped out of my purse and onto my shoulder. It nuzzled me, which was always nice. Bruno woke up and came over to stand next to me in that "this one's mine" way all animals seem to have.

"Um, a cuteness break is always appreciated, but we're kind of at DEFCON Universal Soldier here, so if you're here to pass on a message, Kitty needs some help."

The Poof jumped over to White and mewled at him. "I'm no clearer than Missus Martini. Are you requesting reinforcements?"

The Poof heaved a Poofy sigh. It jumped onto the floor in front of Bruno and mewled rather pitifully. A Poof appealing to a Peregrine for help? Apparently wonders never ceased. Or this Poof had no ego attached to asking for assistance.

Bruno warbled nicely at the Poof, then looked at me. Then back at the Poof. Then at me. The Poof. Me.

"Okay, stop giving yourself whiplash. You're right, I forgot something."

"You talk to the giant peacock?" Stryker asked. "And it talks back to you?"

"Later, Eddy."

"What did you forget?" White asked.

"The Poofs asked me to do something for them when they went to find and help Jeff and Chuckie."

"You talk to the Poofs, too?" Stryker asked. "For real and not pretend?"

"Later, Eddy. Like when this is all over later."

"You said you'd try to find the supersoldiers," Jennifer supplied.

"Supersoldiers?" Stryker asked. "You mean Chuck wasn't kidding, they're real?"

"*Later*, Eddy. Shut up or die, Eddy."

"Are you supposed to find them to stop them from attacking?" Jeremy asked.

"No. To keep them from being destroyed."

CHAPTER 74

"WHY WOULD THE POOFS want the supersoldiers protected?" Buchanan asked. "They're killing machines of the highest order."

"Killing machines that can help us fight whatever's coming."

"How?" Franklin asked.

"There's a controller for the twelve that attacked us at the President's Ball. We destroyed three of them, but it was amazingly difficult." And had only been achieved because Jeff was high on adrenaline, he and Christopher were enhanced, and Chuckie had figured out how the remote control worked.

"Difficult enough to face space invaders?" Stryker asked.

"I hope we're able to find out." After all, ACE had insinuated that the supersoldiers not being ready was the concern, not that they existed. "Problem is, Chuckie is the only one who currently knows how to control the nine we captured. He may be the only one who actually knows where they are."

"I guarantee James knows," Abigail said. "He's the Head of Field."

"Good point, Abby. Ravi, I need you to multitask."

"Kind of hard, Kitty."

"Ravi, it's the end of the world as we know it if you're actually less good at what you do than what you were when I was in college."

He sighed. "What miracle is it you want me to perform while I continue to try to avoid my head being blown off?"

"I need you to connect with the Dulce Science Center. They're reverse engineering an android we managed to capture yesterday.

See if you can help them. More to the point, see if you can figure out where said android called home and where it was 'born' if they're different."

Ravi heaved another martyred sigh. "I need someone to help me with the headset and the phone."

"I'll do it," Jennifer said. Ravi visibly perked up.

"Thanks. So, Eddy, the printer's stopped printing. What does Chuckie actually want us to put into action?"

"Kitty, there's nothing," Stryker said, sounding stressed. "I mean, there's all the data on all of you, but when I get to the part about the Avenger Initiative, all it says is 'go with the crazy.' "

Jamie's Poof jumped up and down. Bruno warbled and flapped his wings.

My brain nudged again. "Nobody say anything. Don't forget whatever it is you're thinking, just don't say anything right now." I took a deep breath, let it out, and focused on the Inner Me. "Big George."

"Yes, Kitty?"

"There are superbeing clusters in Paris and in the Chaco area of Paraguay. I'm sure they passed some form of electronic information. We need it."

"Why?"

"Because we need to find the supersoldiers and the androids and reprogram them."

No one spoke. Waited for the sounds of crickets. Got electronic beeping instead. Same thing, really. Finally Tito, who'd apparently been chosen as Group Spokesperson, opened his mouth. "How?"

"Um, we're standing in the middle of Hacker International. What do you mean 'how?' Will Smith reprogrammed an alien craft in like five minutes in *Independence Day*."

"Kitty, you do know that's fiction, right?" Stryker asked.

"I point to the alien armada coming to destroy us, my missing husband who happens to be an alien from a different solar system, and the fact that we can travel via the subspatial time warp filtered through black hole technology that is the gates—just for starters, mind you—and say that *Independence Day* strikes me as more of a blueprint written by someone in the know than a fictional piece."

"She has a point," Franklin said dryly. "I'd also like to mention that we don't have time to nurture the idea of failure. Do what she wants, and do it now."

"Colonel, don't you have to take all this up to higher authorities?" Buchanan asked.

"I do, when I have a credible idea of what to tell them. They know about the impending invasion, believe me."

"Then why did they let the One World Festival go on?"

Franklin shrugged. "To avoid mass panic, among other reasons. If we can avert the invasion, we don't have to let any civilians know about the danger."

"Ah, the *Men in Black* theory. It's sound, I'll give you that." But it lacked a certain something, which was any plan for what to actually do to avert the armada. Possibly because there was no way to avert it. Negative thinking. Had to stop that. "Can we somehow get visuals on Paris and Paraguay, where our teams are?"

There was a lot of muttering from Hacker International, but two of the smaller screens in the room came to life. On the left we had lush French countryside and on the right we had the wilds of the Chaco. On the left we had a lot of huge, scary, metal-encased monsters going wild. On the right we had a lot of huge, scary, non-metal-encased monsters trying to outdo the ones on the left.

We watched a number of jets flying around all of them. I was pretty sure I could spot the jet Reader was flying based on the fact that it was the one doing the most awesome job avoiding getting hit, which was, from the amount of firepower the supersoldiers were sending out, impressive. But the team in France wasn't slowing the supersoldiers down.

Same situation over in Paraguay. I could spot Tim and the fly-boys based on skill and flying signatures. And while the superbe-ings weren't as weaponized as the supersoldiers, they had their own naïve charms in terms of horrifying appendages and bodily fluids and such, all aimed at our team.

However, it was only going to be a matter of time before some-one on our side managed to break through. Or until we'd blown up both countries to tiny bits. Or worse.

A jet was batted out of the sky by a supersoldier, and we all gasped. It crashed into the earth, but its pilot made it out. Only to be slammed into the ground under a different supersoldier's feet. More gasps, and I heard a couple of sobs, too. Another casualty. We needed to stop this. Part of me wished I hadn't asked to see what was happening, but we needed to know. I needed to know. I worked better seriously pissed off.

"What is the crazy you're going for, Missus Martini?" White asked quietly. "I believe we need to get whatever it is into action."

He was right. And I needed to get back into the frame of mind to give orders and keep people going. Took a deep breath, let it out, and turned away from the screens to face the others.

"We're going to show a united front, Mister White, and do the one thing I think the bad guys aren't expecting."

"What's that?" Oliver asked.

"We're going to use their weapons against them."

CHAPTER 75

"HOW ARE WE GOING TO DO THAT?"** Naomi asked.

"Great question! You and Abigail are going to be doing a lot of it, so glad you're eager and all that."

Reader had once said that Naomi and Abigail could probably move solar systems if they took Surcenthumain. It was a joke that was likely more true than funny. Chuckie hadn't liked this, and the incident was what had allowed Christopher to get fooled into becoming a Surcenthumain junkie.

I wasn't sure that I wanted to toss drugs at anyone, but I was sure that the Gower girls had a tonnage of untapped power and potential. Chuckie wouldn't have spent as much time working with them if that weren't the case.

"I'm almost afraid to ask," Abigail said.

"Good, because I need you to call Tim while I call James. We need them corralling, not destroying, all the supersoldiers and superbeings and whatever else they may be fighting. And then, once the evil monsters are corralled, we need to find where they call home. Pronto."

"Gotcha." Abigail pulled out her phone while I pulled out mine. We both stepped away from the others, the better to have fun conversations without interruption.

The phone went to voicemail three times before Reader picked up. "Girlfriend, this had better be life or death important."

"It is. Beyond that, really. Are you okay?" I was watching the screens, and no one on our side looked okay, but I figured it was better I didn't let Reader know that.

"I'd be better if I wasn't talking to you while trying to get what appears to be an in-control superbeing down. Not that I don't have a lot of options, because we're not dealing with just one. Of course."

They were dealing with twenty, easily, and that was if I was counting correctly, which was hard to do, what with all the explosions.

"Of course. But you can't kill them. We don't want them destroyed or even damaged."

"What?"

"Pay close attention. We're about to be invaded by a huge alien armada that's driving an unreal number of parasites in front of it. Chuckie figured out the controls on the supersoldiers we confiscated at the end of Operation Assassination. We need to do the same with these."

"Wow, is that all?"

"No. We also need to figure out where they came from."

"First a daddy and a mommy parasite fall in love and then—"

"Nice to see you're keeping firm hold of your sense of humor. I'm serious."

"Seriously crazy."

"Which is right in line with Chuckie's orders."

"You've found Reynolds and Jeff?" He sounded relieved.

"No. We've found Chuckie's failsafe. And, apparently, that failsafe is me."

Reader was quiet for a long moment. "Okay. Jeff always listened to you when he was the Head of Field. I'm willing to do the same. If we can."

"Pull every agent away from the International One World Festival. What the bad guys wanted to have happen already has. Split them—send half to Paraguay, half to you in France. I don't care what you have to do, but we need to keep these things alive and get them under our control somehow. And we don't have a lot of time to do it in. So use every international favor we have to make it happen."

"Why did they attack now if we're supposed to capture them?"

This should have been a hard question for me to answer. It wasn't. Clarity crackled through my brain like lighting. Marling had essentially told us what was coming, after all. *Compared to what else is out there, these are your friends.* I'd thought he'd meant the androids were a worse threat than the supersoldiers. Clearly, he'd meant what was on our solar horizon.

"They want us to destroy the only things that have a fighting chance against the invaders."

Reader sighed. "Let's say you're right. Let's say we can capture, contain, and control all the superbeings and supersoldiers. They're not enough to fight an armada."

"We'll find the androids, too."

"How, Kitty? I mean, seriously, how? Your mother and Reynolds have been searching for these things for months or more. They have nothing."

"They have nothing they've told us about. Because they have to be really careful. If they accuse the wrong person without a ton of proof, their careers are destroyed."

He was quiet again. "You have a career you're willing to destroy."

"Got it in one."

"If this goes wrong, Kitty, all the A-Cs will have to go back to Alpha Four."

"James, if this goes wrong, we're all dead or worse. I'll risk that the worst thing that can happen will be an extended visit with the distant relatives."

"Speaking of whom, why aren't they helping us?"

"It's the start of World War Two. We're England. They're the United States."

"It worries me that I understand exactly what's going on based on that explanation."

"I like to think it's because we're so in tune with each other."

"Whatever spin works, girlfriend." He cleared his throat. "This is the real test, isn't it? If Tim and I can handle things. If any of us can, without Jeff or Reynolds."

Reader rarely indulged in self-doubt. And even though I'd had that exact same thought, this wasn't the time for him to take that particular plunge. "Every time is a test, James. Every time one of these freaking fugly monsters, insane politicians, or demented evil geniuses decides to go for their version of the gold is a test. And we pass those tests. Every time."

"We're going to take casualties on this one. I can guarantee it."

I knew he could because I'd just seen that jet go down. And that might be where his self-doubt was coming from. But I didn't want Reader to know we were watching any more than I wanted him to doubt himself. Knowing might affect him negatively in some way. Frankly, having to talk about someone in his command who'd just died might affect him. So I pretended.

"You mean if we haven't already? Yeah, I'm sure we are. I just want to do everything in our power to ensure the casualties happen to their side, not ours."

"We've been lucky. Luck doesn't last."

"Per our enemies and the C.I.A., I exhibit extreme random tendencies."

"What the hell does that mean?"

"It means I'm your Lady Luck."

"You always have been, girlfriend. And you always will be. You still my girl?"

"Always have been and always will be."

"Then everything's still right with my world. We'll make it happen, Kitty. Or die trying."

CHAPTER 76

WE HUNG UP AND I REJOINED THE OTHERS. Jamie's Poof jumped onto my shoulder, rubbed and purred, then disappeared. Hoped it was heading back to Jamie.

Bruno, job done for the moment, went back to his nest in Omega Red's crap and went right back to sleep. Bruno was clearly an A-C animal and fully on board with the A-C idea of napping anywhere and anytime the opportunity presented itself.

Bellie, being an Earth animal, wasn't cooperating in that way. However, she and Oliver had obviously bonded, because she was happily snuggling with him and staying mercifully quiet. I'd been given to understand parrots were one-person birds. Clearly Bellie didn't go in for that sort of nonsense and was of the opinion that she wanted a sugar daddy to nuzzle at all times, regardless of where her cage resided. Worked for me.

The people weren't napping, which was nice. Abigail gave me the thumbs up, so I assumed this meant Tim was clear on his part of our current Plan O' Fun. The hackers were hacking, everyone else was looking stressed and concerned, and Tito was holding a box. I looked in it. It was filled with printouts.

"Are you trying to take over the job of doing the light reading?"

"No. We need to get these in for analysis. And it has to be fast analysis. Due to what's going on, the person who takes these to the Dome needs to be someone Paul, Christopher, and Serene will listen to. Came down to me or Richard. I'm less necessary."

"Hardly. You're our medic and chief butt-kicker."

Tito grinned. "Thanks. But we're not fighting here, Kitty. And I can get back fast if you need me. We need the information, and you need the A-Cs here focused on something other than analysis."

He was right, and I knew better than to argue. "Tell Christopher he's the acting Chief Ambassador right now, because I'm abdicating."

"Not a good time for jokes," Abigail said.

"I'm not joking. Jeff's disappeared, so he's abdicating, too, or whatever the proper term is for an ambassador who's been kidnapped and so can't make any decisions. I'm about to make a call, and when I do, I'm going to get some high-level information. When I get that, I'm going to commit political suicide. Ergo, I'm not the Ambassador any more and am not speaking for American Centaurion in any way."

White nodded. "That makes sense. I'm not convinced anyone will believe it, however. At least, not anyone who matters."

Oliver coughed. "I can make one call and get this story onto the front page of the *World Weekly News*. I realize that's not the same thing as the *Washington Post*, but it's still a legitimate news outlet, in that sense, and if it's followed up by an official announcement from other sources, it will indeed be believed."

"And if you're right, then you don't have to resign in reality," Armstrong added.

"What do you mean?"

He shrugged. "Your mother and Mister Reynolds have been trying to find out how far and deep various connections run. Gaultier, Marling, Yates, Al Dejahl . . . to name only four. These people were connected at the highest levels. Therefore, the P.T.C.U. and the ETD have to be politically careful. You're distancing yourself so you don't have to be careful at all. However, if you can prove their suspicions correct, then you're a hero."

"Or she's dead," Mona said. "Political intrigue is fraught with danger."

"Everything is fraught with danger right now. I'm not doing the math—how long do we have until the alien armada shows up close enough for people to know or them to hit us?"

"We have no idea how long-range their weapons are," Franklin said. "But the estimate is that they'll hit the outskirts of our solar system by late tomorrow."

"Wow, that's going to bring new meaning to the term Blue Monday, isn't it? Okay, do we need to call for a floater gate? It's a long walk back to Colonel Franklin's office."

Hacker International all looked a little shifty suddenly. Franklin noted it, too. "Gentlemen, what are you trying to hide?"

They didn't seem to want to share. "Guys, seriously, now isn't the time to hide anything. Now's the time to come through like heroes. Or, you know, I can just kick you until you talk, which is always nice for working out my stress issues."

Stryker sighed. "Fine, fine. Keep your feet away from my groin and shins. Chuck had a gate installed here. So he could come and go without anyone at Andrews or the C.I.A. knowing about it."

"Classic Chuckie. But how did he do that?"

White cleared his throat. "Under the circumstances, once you moved to the Diplomatic Corps, Charles requested a variety of additional security measures, which Paul approved. I'd assume this gate was one of them."

"Why weren't we told about this, though?"

White shrugged. "Need to know, and we didn't."

"Right," Stryker said. "So, if you can see it and make it work, go for it."

"You can't see it or make it work?"

"You've known him how long and you somehow think Chuck trusted us with that information?" Stryker shook his head, obviously dismayed with my naïve nature.

I decided not to spend the time going for a battle of the witty put-downs. Instead, I did what the A-Cs with us were doing—I looked for the gate. Well, all the A-Cs other than Jennifer, who was clearly engrossed in helping Ravi. She seemed intently engrossed, meaning that she was probably giving in to the Dazzler Weakness—brains. Which spelled potentially lucky times for Ravi.

However, we needed to get the gate found and calibrated. Which wasn't as easy as it sounded. "I don't see it anywhere in the room," Naomi said.

"I looked behind all the pizza boxes and other crap, too," Abigail added.

"Seriously, why aren't we going for the obvious? Dudes, where's the bathroom?"

Henry led us to a door behind a bank of large servers. He opened the door. We all stepped back. "Wow. Does the cleaning lady like never come here?"

Henry gave me a dirty look. "It's fine for our delicate needs."

"I'm refraining from comment. So I don't have to breathe. Jeremy, you're low man on the totem pole. Find the gate."

The Gower girls, White, and I backed away. Jeremy shot me a look that said he'd liked me just fine up until now, then stuck his head into the room. He pulled it out fast. "If it's in there, it's really hidden well."

Henry closed the door. "Sorry. Feel free to clean it to your personal requirements."

"Dude, that would require a self-contained nuke." I looked around. "Where does Chuckie appear from, when he drops in via Gate Express?"

"No idea," Henry said. "He sneaks up on us."

We left the bathroom area. "Yuri, when Chuckie sneaks up on you guys, do you hear him coming from one area more than any other?"

Omega Red seemed to give this consideration. At least, he cocked his head to the right, instead of to the left, which I chose to believe meant he'd stopped thinking about one thing to concentrate on my question.

"I'm not positive. But I believe he comes from the side nearest the bathroom."

We trooped back to the area. A pseudo wall/hallway was created by the servers, separating the bathroom area from the rest of Hacker Central. But Jeremy said the gate wasn't in the bathroom.

My brain chose to remind me that NASA Base had apparently had a server box that had contained a dead body instead of computer equipment. "Open the server boxes."

"No!" Stryker shouted. "Don't do it!"

CHAPTER 77

WE ALL FROZE. "Um, why not, Eddy?"

"You'll damage everything, including what we're working on."

We all relaxed somewhat. "Fine. Thanks for the total freak-out—we hadn't had one of those in, what, a minute, minute and a half? Besides, one of these things is not like the others." I listened at each one. They all hummed as though they had computer stuff going on inside them. I touched them. All felt warm or hot, depending.

I noted something—this room wasn't freezing cold. "Eddy, how are the big servers kept from overheating? This room doesn't feel like a meat locker."

"Individual cooling units directly above and below the servers."

"Jeremy, you're tall. See which server top doesn't seem ice cold."

He checked the top of each server. "All seem cold, all have air conditioning ducts directly over them, and all ducts are blowing cold air.

I sighed to myself. Someone was going to have to check out the floor level. I knew who that someone was going to end up being. Always the way.

I got down on my hands and knees and carefully put a hand under each server. Naturally, it wasn't until I reached the server closest to the wall that it didn't feel cold. "I may have it. Let's open this sucker up."

"Kitty, if you're wrong, you slow us down or worse," Stryker said. In a normal tone this time. How refreshing.

"Eddy, if I'm right, I speed us up a lot." I stood up. There was a panel back here. Hit it with my hand, then jumped back. Hey, the last time I'd done that, a dead body had fallen onto me.

This time, however and thankfully, nothing fell out. The back panel did pop open, though, silently. The door had equipment attached to it, but it was obviously there to make noise and warmth, because the server was empty inside. Well, empty if you were looking with human eyes. "I've found the gate."

White calibrated while Tito and his big box of papers joined us. "What do you want me to tell everyone?" he asked as White stepped out of the server box and indicated it was ready to go.

"The truth. Make sure they're focused on figuring out how to control the superbeings, supersoldiers, and androids. Beyond that, I'm open to suggestions."

He nodded. "We'll manage, Kitty. We had just as much bad going on when I joined up, and we handled it. We'll do it again."

"God, I love your optimism."

Tito grinned. "One of us has to look on the bright side."

"Will you check on Jamie and make sure she's okay? Not missing me or Jeff too much? Not worried? That's she's been fed and changed and—"

"Kitty," Tito interrupted me gently. "She's fine. Your father's there, Amy's there, Alfred and Lucinda are there, right?" I nodded. "Plus the rest of the Embassy staff. She's in good hands. But I promise I'll make a hundred percent sure she's fine."

"Thanks, Tito."

"No problem. She's my patient, remember. That means I have to watch out for her, too." He stepped through the gate. The slow fade was still icky to watch.

"Christopher confirms Tito's there," Naomi said. "Glad our phones still work."

"Oh, they'll knock them out soon enough. They know how dependent we are on telecommunications."

"Well, let's hope they don't do that before we find what you're looking for," Henry said.

"Speaking of which, where do we actually start digging?" Big George asked. "A direction, any direction, would be helpful."

Armstrong cleared his throat. "Gaultier Enterprises would be where I'd recommend. As well as determining the whereabouts of Esteban Cantu and Colonel Hamlin."

"Titan Enterprises, too, along with anything related to Antony Marling." I gave them the spelling. "And the Pentagon. Search anything related to Madeline Cartwright. Oh, and lest we forget, anything related to Ronald Yates."

"Most of those people are dead," Stryker pointed out.

"Yeah. 'Cause all those dead people pissed me off, tried to kill people I love, and also tried to take over the world."

Hacker International turned as one, Ravi included, hell, Omega Red included, and stared at me. "Kitty, are you saying you killed all of them?" Stryker asked carefully.

"I killed Yates. Christopher actually killed Gaultier. Adriana killed Cartwright. And Marling killed himself."

"Oh. So, you've only killed one bad guy?" Henry asked nervously.

"No, I've killed more. Leventhal Reid and Howard Taft, for example. Well, really, Jeff killed Reid." I considered. "I think I'm losing count." Hacker International all looked mildly terrified. "So, um, get to work." They flung themselves back to their tasks at hand.

"Found Esteban Cantu through GPS in his cell phone," Omega Red said shortly. "He's in his home. Same with Colonel Marvin Hamlin. He's in his residence."

"Bet you fifty bucks their phones are home but they aren't."

"We don't have surveillance in their residences," Omega Red shared. "So I have no way of knowing."

"I can't ask for an A-C field team to investigate; they're all deployed."

"Search for alternate signatures," Franklin said. "I'll send people to both locations."

He made the call while I tried not to fret, drum my fingers, or tap my foot. Human speeds really lacked a certain something when time was of the essence.

"Yuri, track Hamlin from Friday. That's the day he disappeared."

"I saw Esteban this morning," Armstrong said.

"Track Cantu from today, then."

"Oh, yes, no problem," Omega Red said under his breath.

"I heard that, and good." A thought occurred. I sent a text to Lorraine. She replied quickly in the affirmative. I went to Omega Red. "Yuri, put the addresses up on screen." He did as requested. I sent them to Lorraine. "Colonel, tell your people to expect some Alpha Centaurion agents to be joining them. They'll probably be at the locations, searching, by the time your teams arrive."

"I thought all Field teams were deployed."

I shrugged. "They are. But in times of war, we let the gals help out."

"Do you mean what I suspect you mean, Missus Martini?"

"You know it, Mister White. Lorraine and Claudia just promoted some of the younger female A-Cs who want to expand past math, science, and medicine into the exciting world of action, danger, and romance. Welcome to the future."

CHAPTER 78

"THEY WON'T HAVE MUCH TRAINING," White said. He sounded worried.

"Ah, that's where you're wrong. Apparently Lorraine and Claudia have been approached by a good number of gals who want to expand their horizons. They've been training them."

"Do James and Tim know about this?"

I coughed. Not if I knew my girls. I'd trained them to do whatever and beg forgiveness later. Hey, it'd been working for us so far. "Oh, I'm sure they'll be great with it. I mean, look at Jennifer here! She's an active imageer, blazing the trail for her sisters in butt kicking. So to speak."

Of course, now we both had to look at her. Jennifer didn't seem ready for action right now. She was comfortably settled on Ravi's desk and appeared to be staying there. However, I'd seen her earlier in the day, so I chose to remain optimistic.

"Ah, yes. I'm completely reassured." White's sarcasm knob was firmly at eleven.

Henry cursed quietly. "Kitty, you're not going to like this," he said, saving me from any more uncomfortable explanations.

"I haven't liked much this weekend, Henry, so what's next on my Anti Hit Parade?"

"I have the news feeds running. Senator Armstrong has been listed as missing by his limo driver. 'Hasn't been seen since he entered the American Centaurion Embassy' is a direct line from this article."

"Doesn't one have to be missing for forty-eight hours before the authorities panic?" Armstrong asked.

"Regular people, yes," Henry said. "Public figures who disappear before public meetings in mysterious ways, however, get press."

"I was at the One World Festival," Armstrong said.

"For too brief a time," Khalid said. "You spent that time assisting us."

"Yes, and I think he was seen," Henry replied. "However, that's not necessarily good news, either. There's another article that's insinuating the senator was kidnapped along with the Bahraini Ambassadress. And another asking if the senator did the kidnapping of the Ambassadress."

"What are the reactions?" Franklin asked.

"Not good. Sending them to the guest terminal." Henry pointed to a space that was relatively clean, if you didn't mind that there were stacks of books and file folders around the terminal and in the guest chair.

Oliver and the Middle Eastern Contingent went to have a look. Well, Oliver and Mona went to look. The Middle Eastern Muscle spent their time moving things so that Mona, at least, could sit down.

"There is more talk of war," Mona said. She sounded on the verge of tears.

"Ugly talk," Oliver added. "The kind that can cause buttons to be pushed down."

"Well, that's not good."

"Your way with the understatement remains intact, I see, Missus Martini."

"Rick, honey, I'm going to have to hurt you."

"Kitty!" Ravi shouted, sparing us from more news updates, fretting, and sarcasm. "I've communicated with the scientists who are reverse engineering the android. We've been able to identify and isolate a homing signal. It was tricky, because the signal was within the self-destruct mechanism, but we've got it."

"Ravi found it," Jennifer added proudly. I refrained from humming U2's "Two Hearts Beat as One" but only because I didn't want to have to explain myself or give White the opening for another Sarcasm Zinger. I wondered if Jennifer was going to share the news of Hacker International with the rest of the Dazzlers or keep them all for herself.

"Ravi, you continue to rock above all other reverse engineers who have come before, exist now, or shall come in the future." Good news, any good news, was such a pleasant shock, I wanted to kiss Ravi. But figured I'd let Jennifer handle that.

"Thanks, Kitty. Always nice to be appreciated. I've sent the information to everyone here, as well as to Dulce. They're tracking as well." He cleared his throat. "When this is over, I'd like to visit. If it's okay."

"I'll show you around," Jennifer said quickly.

"Let's survive to see next week before anyone plans any tours," Franklin said. "Gentlemen, let's get to work. Everyone's depending on you."

As Hacker International focused on their new information, William came over to me. "I've checked in with Walter. He says they're all clear at the Embassy. He's activated the shields, so if we head there, we need to let him know, because the shield can cause an issue with the gate."

"Wait, what? Our Embassy has a shield on it? Seriously?"

William laughed. "It's not standard. It was discovered while you were in Florida. The assumption is that the former Diplomatic Corps installed it as part of their overall plan to destroy us. It's been checked out and tested. Perfectly safe, very effective. Which we should be happy about, because also according to Walter someone's been trying to get in. Moving too fast to see."

"Clarence wants into the tunnels."

"I'll call Walter and tell him you're pretty sure it's Valentino. What do you want him to do?"

"Sit tight and not let him in. I don't know that we can catch him, but the only ones who'll have a shot are Jeff and Christopher."

William nodded and stepped away to make his next call. It occurred to me that if telecommunications went down, not only would we not have anything to work with here in Hacker Central, but I wouldn't be able to call the person I was fairly sure could point us in the right direction.

I followed William's suit, stepped away from the group, and dialed. Got the "all circuits are busy" message. Tried several more times. Same thing. Sent a text. It bounced back. Several times. I felt cut off and more than a little stressed.

Armstrong joined me. "You look upset."

"Senator, I thought they could get calls in and out of the President's bunker."

"Only with special phones." He gave me a rather fatherly look. "Trying to reach your mother?"

I nodded. "She'd know what to do. She undoubtedly knows who's behind this or at least has suspects."

"I'm one, I promise you."

"Yeah, I know." I sighed. "But at this point, better the enemy you know. Not that I'm calling you our enemy. At the moment. I mean, you've been helpful. And all that."

He chuckled and patted my shoulder. "No offense taken. And chin up. Your mother's counting on you to figure things out without her. And I must be honest—if anyone can make sense of what's going on, it's going to be you."

"I suppose."

"I'll do my best to help. You mentioned a name I haven't heard in a while. I believe we should have them looking for connections with Reid as well."

"He's been dead a long time."

"Yes, but as you well know, influence can continue long after someone's death."

"True enough, and considering our visit from the Club Fifty-One contingent, it's a good bet his influence and some cronies are still around."

"Yes, and likely still following his game plan. I knew Reid, and a more anti-alien politician you'll be hard-pressed to find."

"No argument there. He must have funded or been funded by the Club of Crazed Evil Geniuses in some way, too, because Gaultier is the one who created Surcenthumain, but Reid and Taft were the ones who did the testing on Serene and Jeff."

"I agree. And who knows how many others. I'm glad you see my point."

"Did you like him?"

"Reid?" Armstrong shook his head. "Happily I'm a senator and he was a representative, and we were in different parties, so I didn't have to socialize as much as might have been required otherwise."

"You hang with Cantu."

"I'll take anything Esteban wants to do, including what I'm sure he's doing right now, over Leventhal Reid and his ideas of a good time."

I remembered how Reid had wanted to kill me, what he'd wanted to do to me, and how he planned to ensure I'd be conscious all the way through it. I shuddered involuntarily. Armstrong was right—no one had been more sick and twisted than Reid.

I took a deep breath and got myself back to the here and now. "Yo, Eddy! Add in searches for Leventhal Reid, Howard Taft who was not the late president, and Club Fifty-One. Oh, and special attention should be paid to France, particularly Paris, and Paraguay, particularly in the Chaco. In addition to the special attention Big George is supposedly already giving those areas."

"You sure you don't want a five-course meal and some entertainment while you're at it?"

No sooner were the words out of Stryker's mouth than I heard something. It was faint, and sounded far away. "Did anyone else hear that?"

Franklin's phone rang before anyone replied. A quiet beeping noise started from somewhere inside the room. Stryker went to the sound and moved a variety of papers, pizza boxes and other things I chose not to identify.

"I heard it," Buchanan said. "But I can't place what it is."

"I can," Oren said. "It's the sound of an explosion." I looked around. The Middle Eastern Contingent had that "ready for fight or flight" look going.

Franklin hung up. He looked worried and a little sick to his stomach. "It's a good thing you wanted everyone with us."

"Why's that?"

"Headquarters was just blown up. We've lost some airmen for certain. Base is going into full lockdown." So Reader had been proven right within a few minutes—we were already taking casualties.

Everyone was quiet for a few seconds. The shock of an unprovoked attack will do that to you. "I'm so sorry," I said finally.

Franklin shook his head. "We're at war. They knew it. The rest of the population might not yet, but unless we keep on, our enemies win and my men died for nothing."

Had to clear my throat, mostly because it was that or cry, and we didn't have time for crying. "Do they know how the bomb was detonated?"

"No. One moment everything was fine. The next, the building went up. It wasn't an airborne bomb."

"We're secure here," Stryker said.

"For now." White looked pensive.

"What is it, Mister White?"

"Why did anyone blow up Commander Franklin's office? And why now?"

"Because we were there, it's the only logical reason."

"So either they thought we were still there, or they're trying to figure out where we are and blow us up," Buchanan said.

"Or it's where the main gate is for this air base." As I said it I knew I was right. "They don't want us able to get out of here quickly."

"But that doesn't mean that they aren't trying to figure out where we've gone and blow that up, too," White said. "I lean toward both you and Mister Buchanan being correct in this situation."

"Who's 'they'?" Mona asked.

"My bet is that Andrews has some Club Fifty-One Faithful working here. They're really good at covering all the pawn moves, and this kind of destruction is their go-to move. I'd bet the order was to start blowing things up once Mister White and I arrived."

"You're sure this is about you?" Franklin asked.

"I'm certain," Oliver answered for me. "Whoever's behind this has been anticipating what Missus Martini would do. That she would come here was a given, if you recall our earlier discussion."

I heard another sound. This one was closer. I felt a small tremor. Bruno woke up, looked around, and came over to me, squawking quietly.

"We need to get out of here, pronto. Eddy, do you have everything backed up?"

"Yes, but we need this equipment, not to mention the network, to do whatever you want us to do."

"Will, tell Walter we're going to be coming, hopefully through Chuckie's secret gate, and we need to get everything in this room into the Ballroom at the Embassy, and we need to do it fast." William pulled out his phone and started talking. "And tell him we're going to need the top folks who handle the Imageering set up onsite, too."

Harlie, Poofikins, and a number of other Poofs appeared out of nowhere. They were large, in charge, and growling. I was clear on what they were trying to tell us, even without Bruno screaming at the top of his bird lungs. We were out of time.

Abigail grabbed Naomi's hand. "Incoming!"

CHAPTER 79

A PROTECTIVE BUBBLE WENT AROUND ALL OF US, around the entire contents of the room, really. It was similar to the ones I'd seen ACE create when we were in the middle of Operation Drug Addict in Florida. Similar also to the one I'd created with ACE's help during Operation Confusion to dissipate the gaseous form of Surcenthumain. Only much bigger.

The room shook, and the electrical went haywire. The room started to shake as if we were in California during a major quake. Most of us started to lose our balance. Like so many events of my life, it had the potential to be a funny memory in about fifty years.

"Everyone out!" Franklin shouted.

We turned, but the wall with the door sort of collapsed and in a way that indicated it was going to take more than a couple of shoves to get through. We were a long way underground, and I had a feeling someone was going for the idea of burying all of us alive. And there was no time to calibrate—let alone get everyone through —the gate.

Naomi grabbed me, and I felt an electric surge. "Kitty, get us out of here!"

Me? I wasn't a Wonder Twin. Then again, getting out of here sounded fabulous. I considered all of our options. Went with the sane idea for once. "American Centaurion Embassy, second floor, ballroom."

I'd done this time warp before, during Operation Invasion, when ACE had sent us to Alpha Four and back. But no one else with me had.

The bubble surrounding us shifted, taking all its contents along.

It felt like I always imagined a time warp would. First the airbase, then the parts of D.C. between Andrews and our Embassy flashed by as we went past or through them, depending.

I saw a lot of freaked out looking expressions. Even Omega Red looked freaked, and I knew he couldn't see us all fly through everything like the fastest form of hyperspeed available. Even White looked freaked, and that had to be some kind of red-letter moment.

Thankfully, since we weren't changing solar systems, the trip was brief. There we were, safe and sound in the ballroom. "Everyone okay?" I asked as I checked Bruno and the Poofs, who were back to small.

Everyone proclaimed themselves to be in once piece, even Ravi, who was a little freaked seeing as he hadn't been sure if his head was going to explode or not. Senator Armstrong had his arm around Mona, who clearly was wondering why she'd gotten out of bed this morning, but otherwise, our folks looked a damned sight better than we would have if the Gower girls weren't amazing. And if Chuckie hadn't spent a lot of time training them.

The Poofs bounced up and down, mewled at me, and disappeared. Their work here was, apparently, done for the time being, and they were back on the hunt for other evil to thwart. At least, that was my take on it.

"Girls, that was, I must say, amazing. And timely. Did we get the entire room?"

"I think so," Stryker said, sounding shaky. "But we need to get everything hooked back up."

"Really? Because everything still looks . . . active." It did. The screens were still showing their images, the computers and such had stopped going haywire and appeared to be running, even the big servers.

"Hurry," Naomi said through gritted teeth. "It's harder to keep this going than it looks."

"Com on! Walter! Need some help here!"

"On it, Chief." No sooner said than a large number of A-Cs arrived and started plugging things in to what appeared to be portable generators. More came in with what looked like telecommunications apparatus.

"Not that I mind, but how did so many agents become available?"

"Sent over from Imageering Main," William shared. "They're always the last imageers pulled into Field situations."

"And because you didn't use the gate, Chief, they were able to come through without delay," Walter added. "Embassy shield is back at full power."

"Okey-dokey, good job, and keep the com line open."

"Will do, Chief."

Everyone did what they could to speed things up, but being A-Cs, they were done quickly even without the additional hands. Hacker International confirmed all their stuff was working. But Naomi and Abigail still looked taxed. "What hasn't been reconnected?"

"The gate," Abigail replied.

"Wow, you brought the gate, too?"

"It was in the room. We left the bathroom, though."

"Wise choice. So, um, what do we do about the gate?"

William zipped over to the server box containing the gate. "Hang on, I think I can fix it so that it'll function like a stable floater." A couple of other agents went to help him. "Okay, let go."

Naomi and Abigail relaxed, took deep breaths, and let them out slowly. "I don't want to have to do that again," Naomi said.

"Was it a big power drain?"

She shook her head. "Not as bad as it could have been. But controlling all the electrical and information and so on isn't easy."

Abigail nodded. "I just wasn't sure we'd be able to react in time."

"You girls did great, and now isn't the time to start doubting your abilities." We had had enough of that already. "Do you need to go into isolation or anything?"

Naomi shook her head. "We need to be quiet and meditate."

"That'll be easy."

The Gower girls both laughed, then they moved a few feet away, sat down, and appeared to become one with the mystic forces. Or they went to sleep. Being personally quite poor with meditation, I couldn't tell. Decided there were more pressing things that needed my attention. "Eddy, talk to me. Are we up and running as if we never stopped?"

"Close to, yeah."

"Super. Walt, ensure that whatever electronic information we're getting is being housed here and sent to Home Base, NASA Base, and any other Base it makes sense to go to for backup and analysis."

"On it, Chief."

"Excellent. Will, is that gate really functioning?" If we could keep the gate here, then we saved valuable seconds if we had to evacuate again and the Gower girls weren't ready.

"Yes, I think so, though no personnel have tried it yet."

"How did they know where you were?" Franklin asked. "That bunker was secured, and yet they took it down as if it were a cardboard box."

"Tell me the President's bunker is more secure than that one was."

"I hope so." Franklin didn't sound convinced.

"The electronic trail," Big George said. "That's how they found you. Who else would be looking at what you've had us investigating?"

"Yeah, I agree. You gave us the printouts so whoever's been keeping nasty files on us and away from Chuckie wouldn't know who had that intelligence. However, it must have triggered a destruction mechanism or sent a destruction order."

"That sounds like Esteban's work," Armstrong said. "And to reassure everyone, the President's bunker is far more secure than the one we just escaped."

"Good." My mother was there. I cared about the President and everyone else who would be down there, but not like I cared about Mom. Whom I even more desperately wanted to talk to. Mom wasn't here. However, it was time to do what she'd taught me and keep things moving. "Can we get eyes on Andrews and the One World Festival?"

"We don't have the spare screens," Stryker said.

"We will have in a moment, Chief," Walter shared. "Last contingent from Imageering Main on their way, with extra equipment of all kinds."

"Good. Colonel, can we alert our Bases that we have both an attack by unknown parties on Andrews and an alien invasion heading our way?" The last of our assigned agents arrived, equipment in tow. They bustled about, getting more screens, phones, computer terminals and such set up.

Franklin nodded. "We're in a state of emergency, and as of right now, I'm the highest-ranking officer on site, so, yes, please warn all Centaurion divisions, bases, and personnel that we're under attack."

"Advising Gladys now, Chief. She'll get information out and personnel prepped."

"Thanks, Walt. Henry, let's get eyes on Andrews and the One World Festival *if* it isn't too much trouble, and, yes, I'll keep on nagging until we have the visuals. Speaking of nagging, Eddy, I still want all the information I asked you for right before our enemies tried to blow us to kingdom come."

"Your wish is my command."

"I wish we could find Jeff and Chuckie alive, well, and un-harmed. Make it so."

No sooner were the words out of my mouth than a weird beep-ing filled the room.

CHAPTER 80

"TELL ME THE EMBASSY ISN'T being bombed. And I'm not kidding about that."

"We are not under attack, Chief," Walter shared. "And I'm not kidding about that, either."

The biggest screen in the room—which heretofore had had the schematic of the world with all the dead zones and tunnels on it—flashed to much more active life.

"We have action in the D.C. area tunnels," Big George shouted.

"We have action in areas other than the tunnels," Omega Red added as more beeping started. "France and Paraguay have gone hot."

"Ah, Kitty?" Henry said nervously. "What did you do?"

"I didn't do anything." Well, I'd made a wish. "I wish the alien armada would go away without harming us or the Alpha Centaurion system. Make it so."

"Kitty, are you high?" Stryker asked.

"No. Just in case I've somehow gotten super wishing powers, though, I figured I'd toss another one out there to the Powers That Be. Yuri, what do you mean about hot in terms of France and Paraguay? We've seen and are seeing the action onscreen, and it's been hot there for a while now."

"Not what I mean. It's a long explanation that I'm not going to try to give you because Chuck isn't here to translate it for you. Suffice to say, we've got some electronic signals that aren't normal."

"They match the ones Ravi isolated," Henry shared.

"Hone in and confirm locations, numbers, access points, and potential hostiles," Franklin said.

Before I could ask Big George what was going on in the tunnels, I heard a step behind me. I spun around to see Christopher standing there, Patented Glare #3 going strong.

"What are you doing here?"

"And how did you get in?" William asked. "The basement gate is secured because of the Embassy's shield."

Christopher shared Patented Glare #4 with William. "I came in via the floater gate you have in this room. And, Kitty, I'm doing what I spent my life training for. You're not the only one who can 'resign.' "

"But we need you managing things at the Dome."

He snorted. "The last time you were there? Sure. Now? Now I have five women running things."

"Claudia and Lorraine are taking over?"

"Oh, yes, believe me, but they're actually not the ones running the show." He shook his head. "Commander Dwyer reminded everyone that with James and Tim off dealing with the superbeings and supersoldiers, she, as the Head of Imageering, was in charge."

"Serene countermanded you? Really? How did she say this?" I normally thought of Serene as sweetness and innocence on the hoof.

"She didn't exactly say it." Christopher looked slightly embarrassed. "She snarled it. Over the intercom system."

"She's very pregnant."

"And she's apparently been watching you, because she pulled rank faster than I can run."

I could see White. He looked quietly pleased. "Okay, but how did the Security team handle it?"

"You mean after they wet themselves? Trust me, when she's angry, Serene's really able to channel when she was crazy and trying to kill you and anyone around you."

"That's my girl. But still, why are you here? You weren't supposed to resign. We need someone to be the face of American Centaurion if everything goes to hell."

Christopher snorted again and switched to Patented Glare #1. "The moment Tito shared what was going on, Doreen said that if anyone was going to actually pretend to be the Ambassador in charge, it was going to be the one person with actual experience. She said to tell you that she has no issue returning to her regular position within the Embassy once things are normal, but until then, she said she's taken over the diplomatic responsibilities."

"What did Paul say about this?"

"You mean our Pontifex? Our Pontifex was politely told that, while he is indeed a member of Alpha Team, it's more of a figurehead position, and as the religious ruler of our people and the vessel for ACE, he'd be sitting in his chair, under guard. He's allowed to speak, I think, but only when spoken to. ACE, by the way, can butt in whenever, not that I think that's going to happen. Before I was told to leave, Paul was allowed to share that ACE still seems distracted and distant."

"Works for me." Well, the part about ACE didn't, but hopefully we'd solve ACE's problems, too. "So, Serene, Doreen, Claudia, and Lorraine is four. Who's the fifth gal in the A-C Girl Power Club?"

"My wife. And I can't thank you enough for that."

"How is Amy being one of the ones in charge my fault?"

"Oh, I don't know. 'Kitty's not the only one who can handle an emergency or keep things going. Get out of here and do something useful and let those of us who understand crisis management handle the civilians.' So, basically, thanks to you, my own wife kicked me out of the Dome."

I managed to keep a straight face, but it took effort. "But they let Tito stay?"

"They like me better," Tito said, as he rejoined us. "Glad you brought the gate along. I'll ask how later."

"Abigail and Naomi are hella awesome is how."

"What about Captain Morgan?" Franklin asked. "Is he returning as well?"

"No." Tito was also having trouble keeping a straight face. "We have a lot of single girls over there, for a variety of reasons. It was requested that he remain to help protect them and to ensure we had U.S. Military presence and advice."

"Wow, awesome spin." Nice to know Morgan met Dazzler requirements.

"Captain Morgan was deemed particularly necessary because all the single women were recruited into active duty," Tito added with a rather wicked grin. "Supposedly our Head of Recruitment authorized it."

"And I want to know when, where, how, and why you did that." Christopher sounded pissed off and a little impressed.

"I'm sure I did authorize it, but it's all a blur. Been so very, very busy and all that. But back to our missing captain. Are you saying the ladies liked Captain Morgan more than you, Tito?"

He laughed. "Nope. But he's fresh meat."

"Excuse me?" Franklin asked, sounding shocked and a little worried.

"A-C women prefer brains and brain capacity over anything else, Colonel. So, be happy, you have a smart guy as your adjunct."

"It's called being sapiosexual," Tito added. "And it's a definite perk that comes with working for Centaurion. Unlike Christopher, I was given the choice of staying or going. Serene's close but not due yet, and there are plenty of doctors there, including Melanie and Emily, who are heading up whatever the other gals aren't, assisted by Magdalena," he said to White.

"And yet you chose to come back to help us?"

"I went to the bathroom before I came back, just in case. But everyone having moved back to the Embassy was the deciding factor."

"You are the smart one, I've always said so. But not to worry—the Gower girls left Hacker International's bathroom to be destroyed with the rest of the bunker."

"Confirming their intelligence."

"Too true. How's Jamie?"

"Fine," Tito said with a grin as Christopher snorted.

"Why does Christopher find that question funny?"

"Because Serene told me that as far as helpers went, Jamie was always more useful than I am. Jamie's sitting with her Uncle Paul, along with Aunt Lucinda and Uncle Alfred and your father, and she's having the time of her life."

"Sorry Serene thinks Jamie's more useful than you, Christopher."

"I had to demand to be given a good-bye kiss. From Jamie *and* Amy."

"Awww. She doesn't seem to miss her mommy, and I'm not acting all down about it. Besides, I'm sure the girls are all just focused on doing their jobs and averting international and interstellar crises of epic proportions."

"They're crazed with power, you mean. I'm familiar with how it looks—I've seen it with you for over two years now."

"Choosing to ignore your snippy attitude because things are going on. Right before you arrived, Big George said there was action in the tunnels."

"Tunnels? Big George? What *is* going on?" Christopher sounded one syllable away from a full on snark fest.

"I thought you were briefed."

"No. The *Commanders* and *Chiefs* were briefed. I was allowed to resign pending the end of the world."

"Kitty," Big George said urgently. "You need to look at this."

CHAPTER 81

"TITO, RICHARD, MALCOLM—I need to focus. Someone catch Christopher up on what's going on."

"I'll do it," White said. "I can talk the fastest."

"I'll assist," William added with a grin. "I can talk fast, too."

"True enough. Just do it in a far corner and at low levels." As they did as requested, I did my best to ignore the sounds—A-Cs could talk at hyperspeed and hear at that level as well. But it was so fast that it had a negative effect on most humans, me in particular. Enhancement hadn't made that any easier, either.

Instead, I focused on the screen as most of those standing clustered around to watch as well. "All I see is tunnel, Big George."

"I've got heat readings. I'm following them. They were extremely faint before, but are slowly getting stronger, so whatever's giving off the heat is getting closer to our sensors."

"We don't have sensors throughout the tunnels?"

"No. NASA's been generous, but we're talking thousands of miles of tunnels, limited personnel, and somewhat limited budget. Chuck's been extremely careful about who goes down there, let alone who knows about this in the first place. We have cameras and security sensors all along what we call the Embassy Tunnel. We have security sensors along the tunnels we've finished mapping, but cameras are only placed intermittently, mostly near the dead zones."

I saw a long, dark hallway. The camera was moving. "How is the camera moving?"

"It's on a tread."

"Wow."

"It's hardly amazing, Kitty. We've had things like this since the moon landing, if not before. It's how we patrol the sections that don't have stationary cameras set up."

"You aren't going to tell me the moon landing was faked are you?"

"No, that's Omega Red's thing. I know it was real."

"Okey-dokey. You can share your pet conspiracy theory with me later."

"You'll want me to. I've proven that the world governments create boy bands in order to subliminally control the citizenry."

"Yeah, I'll wait until we've saved the world to get into that one."

"Fine. You like rock anyway."

I chose to refrain from mentioning that I also had a nostalgic fondness for *NSYNC and the Backstreet Boys. I didn't listen to them all that often, though, so I was probably safe from the musical mind control.

Studied the picture on screen as the camera rolled along. Big George had said this was part of the D.C. tunnels, meaning it was connected to "our" tunnel and the Embassy.

Based on the use of a roving camera, knew it wasn't near the Secret Lab, where they'd been creating Gaultier's Zombie Army of Hot Guys. Even without the roving camera clue, we'd blown that up, and though A-C fail-safes meant the lab had exploded in on itself, there had still been rubble. And I saw no rubble.

However, dark halls with murky-to-no lighting didn't offer a lot of landmarks to compare against, and I'd only been down in our part of the tunnel system once.

Decided to stop keeping my questions to myself. "Big George, where is this, in the schematic of the underground tunnels?"

He tapped something onto his keyboard and another screen tossed up the D.C. area underground map. "It's heading for the last dead zone, the one we're not done mapping, but it's not there yet. The sensors react and interfere with our mapping equipment, so we have very few sensors in this area."

Because Big George had put up the map for this one underground area only, I could actually make out some of the words. "From the map, that dead zone looks to be near Langley."

"It is."

"But it's also near Arlington, in that sense, and D.C.," Stryker said. "It's under the Washington Golf and Country Club."

"Seriously?" Armstrong sounded concerned. "The President's a member there. I'm a member there."

"Everyone who's anyone is a member there or good friends with a member there," Franklin said. "It's a perfect place to have a secret underground tunnel and room, too, because even if you're not a member, if you're someone's invited guest, you're 'in' once you're there, and no one's going to bother you."

"If it's really a room." There were many other possibilities, which I chose not to share aloud. Why say "hidden bomb" right now? What good would it do if we couldn't access the dead zones to verify?

"I think Amy's father was a member there," Christopher said quietly to me, as he, White, and William joined us.

"I'm sure he was. And that means LaRue probably still is." I figured Ronald Yates, Antony Marling, and heck, even Madeline Cartwright had been members there. Or been pals with one. It was a safe bet every enemy we had was no more than two degrees of separation from a full-fledged member.

"No wonder your mother and Mister Reynolds have been careful," Armstrong said. "The members of this country club are among the most powerful in the nation."

"You should know, Senator. Are Mimi and Abby done meditating?"

"Yes," Naomi said. "What do you need?"

"You two and Christopher—see if you can get a reading on Jeff or Chuckie." Just because Big George had found some heat signatures, it didn't mean they were emanating from the bodies we were looking for.

Christopher muttered something about every woman he knew bossing him around, but otherwise I could tell the three of them were concentrating.

Tried to be quiet while they were focused. Failed. "How deep are these tunnels?"

"Deep," Big George said.

"There are tunnels under Washington," Stryker added. "These are deeper. You did know that there were tunnels under the city, didn't you?"

"Yes, Eddy. Just like Disneyland, there's a whole lot more underground that the regular folks don't know about."

"Just checking," he grumbled. "Geez, bite a guy's head off."

"Get back to work, Eddy."

"I've got something," Naomi said. She and Abigail were already holding hands, but Naomi grabbed Christopher's hand, too. "Need your help."

"Two people," Christopher said slowly. "The interference is extreme. I can't tell if they're human or A-C, let alone if they're Jeff and Reynolds. I can just get that there's something living in there and they . . . seem personlike."

"Same here," Abigail confirmed. Naomi nodded.

Something was bothering me. Something important. "I have a question."

"Yes?" Big George asked.

"Why is it that three of the most powerful A-Cs on the planet are having more trouble reading what's in that tunnel than a roving camera and some heat sensors?"

CHAPTER 82

"WHAT DO YOU MEAN?" Abigail asked.

"I mean that you three should be able to see everything about these tunnels, let alone who's in them. Christopher can see people in the Alpha Centauri system, for God's sake. Yet, whatever these tunnels are reinforced with, it's harder for an empath, imageer, or hybrid to see through them. Video feeds are doing better than the three of you, and that should be impossible."

"They knew what they were doing, I guess," Christopher said. "Though I don't know how anyone would be able to predict the powers Naomi and Abigail have."

"Let alone the ones you, Jeff, and Serene got from the Surcenthumain boost." Which bothered me even more. "The other locations where there are dead zones, what are they under or near? I mean, one's close to our Embassy. So where are the others?"

"In this area that we're focused on, the Pentagon, Langley, Camp David, and Norfolk, all of which we've mapped," Henry answered. "The Gaultier America research facility in McLean is mapped, but there's more going on there. The main Gaultier America research facility in upstate New York is also mapped, by the way, and linked to this tunnel system."

"For all we know, all the tunnels are linked," Big George said. "As I told you earlier, we are nowhere close to done with this project."

"Fabulous. But all of these are under our control now?"

"As far as we know, yes," Henry said.

"All of them are mapped, and have sensors installed," Big

George corrected. "And none of those other sensors are showing signs of activity."

"So, the only one that's still essentially an unknown is this one under the Country Club of the Political Stars, right?"

"Right." Henry sighed. "As Big George said, there are plenty that we haven't confirmed. We now know what the tunnels and dead zones look like to our scanning equipment, but there's a lot more than we have resources to deal with immediately."

The lack of resources comments were interesting. Centaurion Division had the resources to help search. We had the resources to make the search go infinitely faster, too. But, to my knowledge, Chuckie hadn't asked for help. I wanted to know why, but in order to find out, I also had to get Jeff and Chuckie back alive. But no pressure.

"Where are the tunnel access points? I mean, I know they're accessible via our Embassy, but to my knowledge, Chuckie hasn't been sending teams down through our basement to look at this stuff."

"No," Big George said with a chuckle. "Far from it. Your Embassy is off limits, remember? No, there are access points near the dead zones."

"Easy to find access points?"

"Some yes, some no."

"Fabulous. So, are there any actual guards on the access points?"

"Personnel, no. Sensors only."

"Including by the country club?"

"Yes. Its access point is actually fairly easy to get to."

"How so?"

"It's in some dense, older foliage that's part of the golf course."

"Big trees and bushes and such? Secluded area that's sort of in plain sight but no one really looks at because they're focused on the main attraction?"

"Yes."

A brand new question was begged. "Walt, is someone, presumably Clarence Valentino, still trying to get into our Embassy?"

"Yes, Chief."

"So why is Clarence spending his time trying to get in here, if he wants to get into the tunnels, instead of trotting over to the country club?"

"No idea," Christopher said. "Maybe he wants into the Embassy for a different reason."

"Why?" Buchanan asked. He'd been so quiet I'd almost forgotten he was there. Tried to remember if I'd seen him in the last few minutes. Decided there were more important things going on than my figuring out if he was really Dr. Strange in disguise. "What could he want in the Embassy?"

"He can't need a gate," Christopher said. "He can go to any airport and calibrate one for wherever he needs to go."

"But can he use them to get into the tunnels or the dead zones?"

"Probably not," Christopher said. "But we can't tell without being able to access these dead zones."

"Maybe it's the only access point Clarence knows about," Naomi suggested.

"Maybe. You know, what's 'our' secret lab actually under? It's not all that close to the Embassy."

Big George cleared his throat. "Your dead zone is under the Lincoln Memorial. Its entrance is, like the country club's, within some dense foliage along the side of the Memorial."

"I have Bad Guy Bingo!"

"Then I have Bad Guy Bingo, too, because Clarence wanted Sis and me to follow him into the trees by the Memorial," Abigail said. "I think that means he knew exactly where the entrance was."

"What does that prove, though?" Christopher asked.

"That Clarence cannot be trying to get into the Embassy in order to access the tunnels. Because he could do it from the Lincoln Memorial and be anywhere on Earth, it looks like. Do your sensors show anything in the tunnels from earlier today or this week?"

"I've got the reports, let me check," Henry said. "Interesting. Heat signature triggered the sensors in the tunnel near the Memorial, but it was so quick the program assumed a small foreign body."

"You mean like a little Japanese girl or something?"

Received a slew of "duh" looks from Hacker International and a lot of "really?" looks from everyone else.

"No," Stryker said as he rolled his eyes. "He means like insects."

Henry nodded. "The sensors are very delicately tuned, so they pick up everything. The heat registered so quickly it appears to be nonhuman in nature."

"Oh, it's nonhuman. I'm betting that Clarence was moving so fast he fooled the sensors."

White nodded. "It makes sense, and having seen him running this afternoon, it's very believable."

"So he's been in the tunnels. Henry, check for more 'oh, it's nothing' readings from the sensors. We think Clarence has been back for about a week. Eddy."

"Yes? You want me to add something onto what I'm already doing, don't you?"

"You're still sharp as a knife. Yeah. I need help with the conspiracy theories, and since Chuckie's not here, you're my next go-to guy."

"I'm so honored." His tone didn't say "honored," of course. But I chose to ignore that.

"You have a good understanding of what's going on, so suck it up. First off, we have a massive, deep underground, tunnel system and a whole lot of big, cubelike dead zones, right?"

"Right."

"So, what are the bad guys using these underground tunnels and supersecret rooms or whatever they really are for?"

"As near as we can tell, not a damn thing."

"So why are these tunnels and dead zones in place? The one secret lab we destroyed, okay, I get why that was there. But why this intricate tunnel system, which clearly extends beyond the D.C. area? From what I can see, it doesn't look like a vehicle could fit in there, so really amazing drug running can't be the answer."

"It's so nice that you just assume I know what you're talking about."

"You saying you don't?"

"No. Just commenting on your faith in me." Stryker was quiet for a few moments. "Obviously there's more going on. But you're wrong about the vehicle thing. I mean, a motorcycle would have no problem in these. Something larger could make it, too."

"But not a tank."

"No." Stryker cleared his throat. "But you could probably use these tunnels to transport illegal weapons."

"But why?" Christopher asked. "These had to be put in place with the help of our former Diplomatic Corps. We were fooled by them for decades. Why go to all this trouble and then not use them for anything?"

"I have a better question—do we think the tunnels are either manmade or A-C made?"

CHAPTER 83

"WHAT ARE YOU QUESTIONING?" Franklin asked. "Who put this system in place, when, or why?"

"Colonel, all of the above. My other question, though, is how in the world could anyone on Earth put in something this intricate, this far underground, that's also cloaked from everything we can throw at it, either human or A-C? I could buy the tunnel and secret lab when that's all it seemed to be. Now? What's on the screen is too intricate even for the most devious and dedicated of A-Cs, let alone humans."

It was silent except for the beeping. Nice to know I'd stumped the room.

Franklin cleared his throat. I sensed a trend starting. "Ah, do you have a theory?"

"Oh, sadly, I think I do. Can we see those pictures of the space armada on one of the screens again, please and thank you?" The pictures appeared. "You know, these spaceships look like what literally every human on Earth who's reported a UFO describes as what they've seen."

"We can't get any reading on them from the probes," Franklin said. "But we can see them and photograph them. So they're not hidden."

"No, they're not hidden from our eyes or our cameras, apparently. For whatever reason, they don't cloak like that." I considered why. "Possibly because the last times they were here in force, we were so primitive it didn't matter if they allowed themselves to be seen. Possibly because they don't think we can hurt them even if we see them."

"Then explain that secret lab you, my father, and Reynolds found and destroyed."

"My guess? It was a coinkydink. The bad guys get them so much more frequently than the good guys do, after all. I'd bet they wanted their secret lab and discovered the tunnel and room by happy accident. They could have been drawn there, too. There are a lot of possibilities.

"You think these aliens have been here before, just like the Ancients, don't you?" Christopher asked.

"Yeah, I do." My feminine intuition shared that it thought so, too. It also thought we were screwed. Had to stop listening to the negative intuitive parts. "If they arrived before the A-Cs were sent here, Earth wouldn't know about them and neither would any of you."

"Yates was here far longer than the rest of us," White said quietly.

"Yeah, I know. And I'm betting he knew whoever's coming to visit." Chances were they'd liked him, too, because they'd have had more in common with him. "Maybe they even brought the right parasite here, to join with him." They were driving enough parasites in front of them, effectively, that this seemed extremely likely. Figured. A guy like Yates wouldn't connect with the Mephistopheles parasite by accident. Not in the world I got to live in.

Stryker cleared his throat. Apparently the trend was really catching on. "Ah, Kitty? Didn't you say you killed Yates?"

"Yep. So, I'll offer three guesses for who this group is going to be the most pissed off at, and the first two don't count."

"But all of the secret rooms are under or near important places in the U.S.," Buchanan pointed out. "How is that possible?"

"Maybe they give off some kind of power. Maybe they've got some kind of attractor in them. Heck, maybe they emit some form of mind control. I doubt that the locations are random, either way. But based on what these ships look like, I'd say they've been dropping by frequently. Give the right person the suggestion for where to put the Pentagon, and presto, the Pentagon is on top of your dead zone. Oh, let's call them what they are—hidden strongholds with God knows what inside."

"There are green circles around other places of importance outside of the United States, too," Mona said.

"Many," Khalid chimed in. "I count at least fifty in our part of the world alone."

"Including in Israel," Jakob added.

"At least as many in Europe, even more in Asia," Oren shared.

"What does it all mean?" Jeremy asked.

"We don't know. Yet." We needed to figure it out, before the invaders arrived to explain it to us.

"So all the people who say they've been abducted by aliens are telling the truth?" Franklin asked.

I looked at Stryker. He contrived to look innocent. "Oh, I'd say many, but certainly not all." Stryker opened his mouth. "Eddy, think carefully before you let your ego do the talking." He slammed his mouth shut. "Knew you were more intelligent than you seem."

"Does this mean the invasion has been in place for some time?" Armstrong asked. "As opposed to being something your enemies started on their own?"

"Captains in place!" Bellie squawked. "Paraguay and Paris! Paraguay and Paris!"

Oliver and the Middle Eastern Contingent were all trying to shush the bird. "I'm sorry," Mona said. "She was doing so well."

"The bird knows something," Omega Red said.

"Yes, Yuri, we know. Problem is, she only knows some things, not everything. And I don't think we've asked her the right questions."

"Gil felt the bird had identified Esteban Cantu as one of those captains," Franklin said.

"Gil?" Christopher asked.

"Captain Morgan. I thought you met him."

"I did. We weren't on a first name basis before I was tossed out of the Dome. So, Cantu being involved isn't a surprise. Bellie said he was a good man."

"Or she was identifying Goodman as another captain," Buchanan added.

"Or Hammy, who everyone says is a good man."

"Hammy?" Christopher asked.

"Colonel Hamlin, as in Colonel Franklin's mysteriously vanished predecessor. That's his nickname. At any rate, Bellie knows something. Good luck to anyone figuring out what it is."

"We'll work on it," Oliver said.

"You don't want in on the alien invasion theories, MJO?"

"When your thinking diverges from mine, I'll chime in."

"Nice to get the *World Weekly News* stamp of approval." I was about to toss off another witticism, when something caught my eye. It was a little something, and if I wasn't enhanced, I'd never have seen it at all. "Wait a minute." I stared at the space ships. "Is there any way to make the picture bigger? Just zoom in on one of the ships, doesn't matter which one."

The image got larger. "Say when," Henry said.

It took several magnifications. "When. Okay, everyone, look at the top of the space ship. It's a rounded dome, right?" The room chorused agreement. "Okay, inside that dome, does it look like there's a more sparkly cube?"

"Can't tell," Big George said. "The picture's too degraded."

Christopher went to the screen and touched it. He held his hand there a good minute. He turned back, and his face was pale. "I recognize something in that area of the ship. It's faint, but familiar enough."

"You used one when you were little, right?"

He stared at me. "My mother told you?" he asked finally. I felt White stiffen, just a bit.

"In a way." When I'd first met the Gang from A-C, Jeff had implanted something into me, which turned out to be a message from his late aunt. I'd only had an essence of a tiny bit of Terry within me, and ACE had removed that when we'd found him, but it had been enough.

I'd seen Terry give ten-year-old Jeff a glowing cube, telling him it was just for him and Christopher to use. It was part of the memory she'd programmed Jeff to implant, so my seeing the cube was intentional on Terry's part.

Since then I'd always wondered how it had worked, how she'd created it, because I'd never seen anything like it before or since. We had no idea, because the cube had been taken by a person or persons unknown sometime after the boys had used it. Jeff and I had hoped it was his parents who had found it, but they insisted they hadn't.

I now had a good idea of who had. "Clarence found the Power Cube, took it, and that's what they used to find our invading friends."

"Most likely." Christopher's face had drained of color. "If they've used it, then they know everything Jeff and I can do."

CHAPTER 84

"MAYBE THEY DO, BUT MAYBE THEY DON'T."
Shockingly, my fabulous words of wisdom and comfort
didn't seem to make Christopher feel any better.

White went to his son, put his arm around Christopher's shoulders, and brought him away from the screen. "Let's sit down for a moment, son."

While White and Christopher took time to calm down and forestall freaking out, I considered the latest fun facts.

Terry hadn't been stupid, and she'd been very aware of what was going on. Based on the cube, she might have known more than any other A-C who wasn't close to Yates. Plus, A-Cs were big on the failsafes. I put my money on her installing something to protect her only son and nephew. Whether that had been broken or not was probably the issue. And the baddies had had over twenty years to try.

Less, though, because LaRue was the real brains of this particular operation, especially now that Yates was a deader. The trophy wife, who'd only been around for about ten years or so. Still might have been enough time.

I found myself wishing Madeline Cartwright were still alive. She'd been the brains behind the whole Titan Makes Scary Weapons stuff, and more besides, but she'd understood me and I'd understood her. We'd liked each other in that sense, once all the masks were off, even though we were enemies. I knew she'd known about this.

So, had to think like she had. But not aloud. For once. First time for everything. But Cartwright had done all her work in secret. So, to think like she did, I couldn't share.

Normally not getting to think aloud would allow my mind to wander off topic. But I was honestly too mad and afraid to allow it. I couldn't afford to wander until Jeff and Chuckie were back, and we had some handle on how to protect our world.

What would Cartwright have done with the knowledge that there were hidden rooms all over the place? If they were rooms at all? I felt certain she'd have come to the same conclusion I had—that they'd been put into place long ago and well before the A-Cs had ever arrived.

Like the rest of the Bad Guys League, Cartwright had wanted to live forever, and she wanted to be the one in charge. She wasn't into the fame portion, but she was all about the power stuff. So, what do you do, when you know someone out there is more powerful than you and also not as nice as the people you're used to dealing with?

My brain kicked, and I jerked. "Marling and Cartwright made the supersoldiers and androids to fight the invaders. It's not their only purpose, obviously, but that's their double duty. Which means they have something in them that we can set off to make them react and fight for us, not against us."

"Then let's hope James and Tim are successful," Christopher said. "Because I don't think we can fit the entire population of the planet into the Dome."

"The Dome . . ."

"What?" White asked.

"Big George, can we zoom over to New Mexico and take a look at one of the red circles?"

"Sure." The picture on the big screen changed. "You want Area Fifty-One?"

It was circled in red, but that wasn't my main focus. Yet. "No, the one over here." I went to his terminal and pointed it out. "That's the Crash Site Dome, where the Ancients crash-landed in the nineteen-fifties."

"It's off limits."

"Note the red circle. Yeah, no kidding. The Dome is an incredible power source, but it's so well hidden, and so well protected, that it's always been left alone, by our enemies on Earth and from much farther away. What I want to know is this—is there a dead zone under the Dome, or secret tunnels leading to it?"

"We haven't had time to really map the Southwest," Big George admitted. "There's been so much to do locally, and much of that state is off limits anyway."

"Then let's bet on the side of yes." ACE had been far too specific about the Dome, far too willing to let me shove as many people in there as possible. The Dome was key to whatever was going on; that's why it was ACE's entire protection focus.

"Why?" Christopher asked. He looked and sounded normal. Good. "The Dome goes down several levels. If our builders had discovered an almost impregnable secret room, I think they would have told us."

"Not if they were Yates loyalists, and, trust me, you have a lot more of them than you realize. There were even more when you were first exiled here. It would explain a lot, including how the Dome is the most hidden of all your Bases, why it's never been attacked, and why it has so much power."

"It's the half-life from the Ancients' ship."

I had to remind myself that A-Cs were really raised not to question their elders. If the older folks said something, it was taken at face value unless and until pointedly proven to be incorrect.

"We've been told it's the half-life from the Ancients' power supply. And I'm sure that's true, in its way." I was sure because 99.9% of A-Cs couldn't lie believably to anyone, and the best lies were based in truth. They got around the deficiency by leaving things out, versus making things up. "What they left out, I'm almost a hundred percent certain, was that they found some other power source when they were building the Dome."

"If so, I was never informed," White said.

"I'm sure you weren't, because I'm sure whoever found whatever's under the Dome was a Yates loyalist."

"Let's say that's true. Why would the Ancients' ship crash right over a dead zone?" Christopher countered.

"Oh, sadly for all of us, I have an easy answer for that. Because it was brought down by something and landed pretty much on top of its killer, so to speak."

CHAPTER 85

"A LRIGHT," BUCHANAN SAID SLOWLY. "Let's say you're right."

Christopher sighed. "She's usually right."

I went to him and put my hand on his forehead. "You okay?" Christopher rolled his eyes while Buchanan chuckled.

"Your file indicates a high degree of accuracy," Big George said.

"I'll bet it doesn't say it that nicely. But, Malcolm, where were you going with this?"

"What do we do about it? Race to the Dome? Get everyone out of the Dome? Shove them into these tunnels? Try to breach one of the dead zones? Evacuate half the world? And I think some focus has to be given to what Valentino wants in the Embassy."

"Those are all good questions. I think we leave everyone in the Dome for right now. As for Clarence . . . no guess for why he's trying to get into the Embassy. I'll toss 'he's trying to find something he or the others hid in the Embassy' into the collective hat. It's someone else's turn now."

Ravi cleared his throat, confirming the trend was now an epidemic. I realized he'd been quiet for quite a while. Checked. Nope, he and Jennifer weren't making out.

"Yes, Ravi? What have you been up to while the rest of us have been fretting?"

"Well, it occurred to me that we have these dead spots all over the globe. Chuck's had us focus mainly on the D.C. ones and some of the Eastern Seaboard, but he's also had us take a cursory glance at France and Paraguay."

"Do tell."

"There's a full tunnel network in the Paris area. A less sophisticated system is in Paraguay, in the Chaco region. We've been paying attention to these anyway, but our monitoring went hot earlier, remember?"

"Yeah, it was like fifteen minutes ago. I'm not that forgetful."

"Closer to twenty minutes, maybe a half hour," Stryker muttered.

Ravi chose to ignore my sarcasm while I ignored Stryker. I chalked both up to personal growth. "So, based on the information I have on the androids, they don't need a special sized room. They could be stored anywhere, including in the tunnel system, just waiting to activate."

"Are they in the tunnels somewhere?" Franklin asked hopefully.

"No. However, I then considered the supersoldiers. Chuck told us a very little bit about them, but I'm clear they were close to twelve feet tall, meaning no dead zone we've mapped so far could hold them. They're also too big to go through the tunnels. At least, the tunnels in the U.S."

"You're saying the tunnels and dead zones in France and Paraguay are bigger?"

Ravi shot me a hurt look. "Way to steal a man's big moment, Kitty."

"Just part of my charm."

"So you've always said. Anyway, yes. The android signatures were erratic, in part, I believe, because they're so well done that they appear almost a hundred percent human. But we also have a signal for the supersoldiers to work with, because Chuck brought one back here for me to play with."

"What the hell?" Stryker said. "I didn't know about that."

Ravi shrugged and looked smug. "You thought he was joking, so he knew you wouldn't take it seriously. Besides, you can't reverse engineer." Jennifer looked as if she'd made her future life choice and was already picking out curtains and china patterns. I checked—Jeremy looked as though he wished they were both back at the Mall. Brothers were like that, at least so far as I'd been told.

"Can too," Stryker muttered.

"So, what's the bottom line, Ravi?"

"The supersoldiers aren't trying to pass as human, so their signals are far more basic. With the information gleaned from the android we were able to identify commonalities between the android and supersoldier signals and isolate them from the general electronic chatter that runs twenty-four-seven."

"We?"

"I'm working remotely with the team in Dulce. Which is why we've moved so quickly. Anyway, we've identified where the signals came on-radar, if you will, cross-referenced against known formations and attacks, particularly the one at the President's Ball, which was the clearest data we have. Most of this data is from Centaurion Division, which Dulce shared with me, and I've cross-referenced. Then I cross-mapped it with dead zone parameters of enough presumed size to be able to house them, focused on Paris and the Chaco, and radiated out from there."

"And?" Franklin sounded impatient. I couldn't blame him. I didn't care how Ravi and his A-C team did it, if his answer was going to help.

"I've sent the coordinates to Commanders Reader and Crawford. Teams are converging."

"Um, the last I heard, Commanders Reader and Crawford were trying to bring down superbeings and supersoldiers alive while also trying not to die."

"Oh." Ravi looked surprised. "Sorry. I sent the kill switch information to them while you were all discussing everything else. Supersoldiers are down and under control."

We all turned and looked at the screen that had been running our Paris feed. Sure enough, there were no more explosions, and the supersoldiers were in a nice formation. I could see the Eiffel tower in the far distance. Happily, it appeared to be standing and in one piece. I put this into the win column, because said column was pretty empty.

"That covers France, right?"

"Yes."

"Awesome. So, what's going on in Paraguay? Are Tim and his team dead or still fighting? The kill switch can't work on a superbeing."

Ravi shrugged. "It can when they're not real."

CHAPTER 86

I LET THAT ONE SIT ON THE AIR for a bit while I considered how to phrase the next thing I was going to say. Went with the classics. "What the hell?"

Ravi sighed again. "They look like superbeings, but they aren't. They're supersoldiers designed to look like superbeings."

"How in the world is that possible?"

"The same way the supersoldiers are made, only these are covered with a clear metal, which is why they appear to be superbeings. The point is, though, that they have a kill switch, just as the others do."

"Wow, the Evil Genius Club really likes to give you options in your personal choice of destruction method, don't they?"

"How long have you had this information?" Christopher asked, voice tight.

"I've had the remnants of the supersoldier for about a week," Ravi said. "Because what happened at the President's Ball wasn't hidden from those in power, Chuck couldn't bring it to me until the release was cleared by his higher-ups. I had to work on it in secret because Chuck didn't want the other guys to know."

"Bastard," Stryker muttered.

"Why does Ravi get all the fun jobs?" Henry whined.

"Who authorized that, do you know?" Armstrong asked, before the rest of the guys could whine and complain.

"I can check if it's important."

"It is."

"What're you thinking, Senator?"

"It'll depend on who gave Reynolds the release."

Ravi typed away. I noted he was using both hands. "Ravi, your head hasn't exploded."

"No. I was able to reverse the tracker, with help from the good people at the Science Center. It won't make Chuck's head explode, don't panic."

"Who said I was panicking?"

"I know you. Anyway, while doing this I was also able to remove the kill switch. I've tried to track Chuck, but it's like everything else, the signal's not clear enough to be sure where he is. On the other hand, your team in Paraguay is, as we speak, taking control of the supersoldiers and pseudosuperbeings, just as the team in Paris is."

"How did you figure this out?" Christopher asked. "You didn't have one of the 'fake' superbeings to work with."

"Their signal signatures are similar to the one Chuck brought me. There are minor variations per supersoldier, of course, but frankly, the differences are more pronounced per 'batch' than per supersoldier."

"I was told . . . by someone who would know, that the supersoldiers Chuckie has under his control are different from all the others."

"Yes, their signals are indeed different. Stronger. I can't speak for anything else about them other than the signal they send. It's different, but not that different, if you will."

"Awesome. So, this is good news. Right?"

"Right."

"How many are there, can you tell?"

"Yes. Based on the signatures I can identify, we have at least a thousand."

That sat on the air for a longer bit. "Wow. That's, um, a lot."

"Only if they can fight the invaders," Franklin said. "Otherwise, ten thousand honestly wouldn't be that many."

I'd seen these things in action, Franklin hadn't. "Trust me, that's a lot. Good lord, do they have some factory or something?"

"Want my hypothesis?" Ravi asked.

"Sure."

"I believe the dead zones function as sections of a factory."

Henry snorted. "Too far apart to be useful."

"Oh, I don't know," Omega Red said. "It's quite possible. They do it with cars all the time."

"It's unwieldy," Big George shared, backing the Dr. Wu Team.

"How does this get Jeff and Reynolds back?" Christopher asked before Hacker International could go into a full-fledged, completely off-tangent discussion that would turn into a shouting match followed by a group sulk, none of which we had time to indulge, even though it tended to be worth the price of admission.

They were all quiet for a moment while Christopher treated everyone to Patented Glare #4. "It doesn't," Ravi said finally. "Sorry." He cleared his throat, ensuring the epidemic would continue. "Senator, just found it—Clifford Goodman from Homeland Security authorized the release."

"That's good, right? Cliff's a friend of Chuckie's."

Armstrong nodded slowly. "I think so."

"Interesting," Stryker said. "I've been looking at the C.I.A. files Big George found on all of you. Not sure what your teams are going to come up with, but this section seems key for what's going on. 'Team works well together. Separately they are much less effective. Separation of Katt-Martini from the rest of the team causes faster degeneration of effectiveness.'"

"Who wrote that report?" Buchanan asked.

Stryker shook his head. "It's been added to, by a variety of operatives, all of whom are using code names. It'll take time to decipher and use resources we have focused elsewhere."

"Really?"

"Really. You've used up all our servers and focus, Kitty, including the ones your folks added. If you want me to put resources here, you have to choose what other vital search or program you want stopped."

"Who added that information doesn't matter," Christopher said. "It proves why they spent so much effort getting Kitty away from the rest of us."

"I think they're selling your team short," Franklin said.

"Depends on who put that information in." I looked at Armstrong. "Senator, you and I discussed Leventhal Reid only a little while ago. I'm sure you were aware of what went down during Operation Drug Addict."

"Yes. Honestly, if my briefings have been even remotely accurate, this assessment is correct."

"Only if it presumes our personnel remain stagnant, and that's not the case. I point to what the gals are doing in the Dome as Exhibit A."

"Kitty, more activity in the tunnels," Big George said, as the picture on the big screen flashed from the map of New Mexico to the murky tunnel interior.

Sure enough, there was activity. Of a sort.

CHAPTER 87

"I SEE WHAT COULD POSSIBLY BE humanlike shapes," I said finally. "Christopher, can you get anything?"

"Not really," he admitted. "I can't confirm we're looking at humans or A-Cs."

"Mimi, Abby, anything?"

"No," Naomi said. "Like with Christopher, I can't really feel them or see their minds."

"Me either," Abigail added. "Could be people, could be androids, could be something else."

"Moving camera closer," Big George said. It didn't help much. The shapes were still indistinct.

"Do we have extra lighting or something down there?"

No sooner were those words out of my mouth than there was a flash of something that could have been an A-C moving at the fast hyperspeed, could have been a gun firing, or could have been something else. The screen went dark.

"Either they can hear us, read our minds, or they spotted the camera," Franklin said. "Regardless, this likely moves them into enemy camp."

"If they're hostiles, then they might know where Jeff and Chuckie are. That means we need to capture them, sooner as opposed to later. Will, can you get me and Richard into the tunnels via our new floater gate, or should we use the Jolly Green Giant's tunnel downstairs?"

"The elevator will be safer, Chief," Walter answered for his brother. "I can coordinate the shield to let you through."

"I'd prefer military personnel to go," Franklin said.

"Well, Colonel, under the current circumstances, that would mean you. Or Hacker International, here. And I think you need to stay here, and I know without asking that Hacker International has no intention of leaving their assigned posts. Besides, Mister White and I kick butt on a regular basis."

"True enough. You do have precedent on your side. Of course, in my experience, you sometimes need the full might of the U.S. military to help you."

"Everyone's a critic. Let's focus on the positive side, shall we?" Bruno warbled.

"No, Bruno, my bird. You're staying here to ensure that someone's in charge of our animal kingdom."

Bruno wasn't happy, but, with a bird grumble, he acquiesced.

"I'm going, too," Christopher stated with authority.

"No, you're not," I said with more authority, as in, I channeled Mom. "Right now, you're King Alexander's closest relative on Earth. You're not going anywhere. We need you alive, well, and able to figure out how the hell to let Alexander and Councilor Leonidas know that we need their help."

"She's right," Colonel Franklin said. "And while I don't want to have to pull rank, since you seem touchy about that, I have to insist you stay here."

Christopher's mouth opened, to argue no doubt, but White put his hand up. "Son, they're right. Stay here. If we need you, you'll know."

"How?" Christopher shot Patented Glare #1 at us. "None of us can read into those tunnels."

Omega Red cleared his throat. "You could go old school."

"Come again?"

He held out his hand. There were two Bluetooth earpieces sitting on his palm. "I realize you're all used to using your special powers and holding your phones to your ears, but, as *The Matrix* has shown us, earpieces work really well, too."

"Yuri, welcome to the Land of Sarcasm. I'm not even gonna ask how you 'saw' *The Matrix*."

"There's a specialized program we created—"

"Yuri! I pointedly said I wasn't going to ask. Are these tuned to our frequency, whatever that frequency may be?"

"They're tuned to the system," Henry said as White and I put the earpieces on.

"Can't stop the signal. Okay, so we'll keep you updated and vice versa, right?"

"Yes," Big George confirmed. "We'll be monitoring you."

"Kitty, I mention this as a favor and as someone who's known you a long time," Stryker said. "Please remember that we'll be able to hear everything, even things you mutter under your breath."

"You don't know me," I muttered under my breath.

"Yes, I do," Stryker said.

"I could have been there and back in this time," Christopher snapped. He had a point.

"Fine, fine, we're going. Ready, Mister White?"

"Willing and eager as well, Missus Martini." White took my hand, and we headed down to the basement.

Since discovering the hidden elevator and all the other fun things the former Diplomatic Corps had installed way back when, we'd removed all the basement clutter they'd had strewn around to disguise said elevator and such. We'd also uncloaked the switch that turned the elevator on. This only helped the humans, but said humans appreciated it.

I appreciated that we could quickly hit the button and head down the three stories to the start of the Tunnels of Murky Doom without tripping over boxes. "Walt, we're in the elevator."

"Go ahead, Chief, you're cleared. Advise when leaving and I'll close that shield back up."

"Is the entire Embassy unshielded?" I asked as White hit the down button.

"No, Chief. I put this section under its own shielding once you were all back. Even if someone were to breach the tunnel and make it into the elevator, they couldn't come into the Embassy."

"Excellent, Walt, you rock above all others." The elevator wasn't the fastest in the world, but that gave me time to test out our equipment. "So, how many people besides Walter can hear me?"

"Everyone," Stryker said in my ear. "We have the two of you on speaker."

"Nice. Who's going to talk us through the tunnels?" The sounds of arguing came through clearly. While we waited, I rummaged around in my purse and pulled out my Glock. "I'm ready. Whenever, you know, someone's going to agree to tell us which ways to turn and all that."

"I will," Christopher said finally. "Since none of the humans are going to actually be able to see the two of you on camera."

"You won't see us, either. The cameras can't catch hyperspeed."

"No kidding. I can judge where you'll be when."

I looked at White. "You think he'll really be able to?"

"I can hear you," Christopher snarled.

"Oh, I'm sure Christopher is more than up to the task," White said with a chuckle, as the elevator stopped. I kicked the Gaultier Enterprises symbol, the door opened. "Leaving the elevator now, son, and we'll be going at the slower speeds to avoid overshooting turns and targets. Walter, please lock up behind us." White took my free hand, and we zipped off.

"And I'd like to miss booby traps."

"We've cleared the tunnels," Stryker said.

"I know Chuckie, and all of you, and I'm betting that they're not cleared so much as suspended for a moment or two." There was some grumbling from the room, but no one denied the charge. "As I thought. Mister White, keep the eyeballs peeled."

"I always do, Missus Martini. Especially when teamed with you."

"Careful, Rick honey, or I'll have to hurt you."

Suppressed a shudder as we ran past the former secret lab, which I now thought of as the Burial Ground of the Hot Zombies. Tried to spot where around here would lead up to the Lincoln Memorial, but either we were moving too fast or I didn't look in the right places, because I saw nothing but murk and really well-made walls.

True to his own hype, Christopher told us each turn right about when we'd need it. Since White was on the fifty-miles-plus plan, I let him again do the major hyperspeed work.

Did my best to register where we were and what our surroundings looked like, but the cameras hadn't sold the tunnels short—even with enhanced A-C vision, it was hard to make much out. But because we passed a couple of the dead-zone rooms on the way, I was able to spot similarities. The tunnel walls were smoother around the dead zones. And there was a kind of gentle tug as we went past, as if the areas wanted us to slow down and check them out. But I hadn't experienced that tug when we were near the destroyed secret lab room.

"Slow down," Christopher said after a variety of twists and turns that seemed close together but I knew were actually miles apart. "You should be coming up on the area where the camera went off-line."

White slowed us to a walk. The tunnel turned. We put our backs to the near wall and inched toward the curve.

"You hear anything?" I asked as softly as possible.

"No," White said.

"We're picking up the same general being readings," Christopher shared. "Now we can make out four instead of two. Even though I know the new bodies are the two of you, I can't tell based on my talents, and neither can Naomi and Abigail."

Figured I'd save stating the obvious—that we needed to figure out what these tunnels were made or lined with as fast as possible—for another time.

Instead, I pondered our situation. A-Cs had advanced hearing as well as all the other goodies. Maybe my hearing wasn't yet up to *Bionic Woman* standards, but White was well past the *Six Million Dollar Man*. Therefore, if he couldn't hear anything, when we were sure there were two other things around the corner, it meant they'd heard us and were doing the same as we were—trying not to make noise while sneaking up on the enemy.

White had likely figured the same, as he put his hand on my arm and tried to move me behind him. I shook my head and waved my Glock. He didn't seem impressed.

"I can shoot who or whatever," I whispered in his ear.

"Or they can shoot you," he whispered back. "I'd prefer no bloodshed on our side if at all possible."

Heaved a sigh I ensured I kept silent. Considered other options and checked my purse. Harlie, Poofikins, and Fluffy were all there, looking expectant. "Poofies," I said softly, "can you let Kitty know if whatever or whoever is around this corner is going to be dangerous for Kitty and Richard to meet?"

The Poofs looked at me, then at each other, then back at me. They mewled softly. I had no idea what they meant and found myself wishing I'd brought Bruno along for translation services if nothing else.

"Kitty doesn't understand."

Three Poofy sighs greeted this. I got the distinct impression they were all disappointed in me and thinking I was none too swift. Or else they didn't understand me, which, while it seemed unlikely, was always possible. They didn't budge, however.

"Maybe go big and toothy? So whatever it is can't hurt my Poofies?"

Three Poof heads cocked to the side then snorted at me in a way that was both derisive and incredibly adorable. Clearly, however, this wasn't an option they were thrilled with.

Feeling like a catcher with three really stubborn rookie pitchers in front of me, I tried again. "Can you sneak over and see who's there, and report back to Kitty? Or something, anything?"

Poofikins jumped onto my shoulder. Harlie and Fluffy bounded around the corner. Now, with my most vague directive, was when they were choosing to listen?

"No, wait." I flung myself around the curve, dragging White, who was still trying to hold me back, along with me. I needed to be ready to back the Poofs if at all necessary.

Of course, once I rounded the curve, I realized the Poofs were right—I was an idiot.

CHAPTER 88

"WHOA THERE, WONDER WOMAN.** Still against the rules to shoot your boss."

"Kitty, Chuck's signal is finally stabilizing," Ravi said urgently in our ears. "I can see where they are." He coughed. "Ah, they're pretty much where we figure you are."

True enough, because we were staring at Jeff and Chuckie, who each now had a Poof on their shoulders giving them happy Poofy love rubs.

"Fantastic. Thanks for that eleventh-hour confirmation, Ravi. For the record, this isn't your finest moment, though your earlier moments make up for it." Examined Jeff and Chuckie. They seemed ambulatory and I didn't see signs of loss of limbs or even bleeding. "You know, if you two are actually okay, I think I'm going to kill you."

I put my Glock carefully back into my purse, removed the Bluetooth and dropped it in, then moved Poofikins back in as well. Took my purse off and handed it to White. Then I ran at top speed for Jeff.

He caught me, picked me up, and hugged me tightly. "We're okay, baby, I promise." His hug felt normal, but I could tell he was holding something in his hand.

"Define 'okay,' " Chuckie said. "I feel like crap." Looked over at him. Yeah, Chuckie didn't look as though he'd had the best day ever. He was also holding something, and in such a way that neither I nor White could see what it was.

"What happened and where the *hell* have you two been?" Okay, it wasn't actually what I'd been planning to say, during all the time I'd been worried about them. But it was so appropriate, nonetheless.

"Long story," Jeff said.

"I'd like some of it."

"I would as well, Jeffrey. I'm particularly interested in what you and Charles are both hiding from us. Currently, we have no proof the two of you are actually yourselves, if you catch my drift, Missus Martini."

Jeff's hold on me tightened. "We're not androids."

"Proof would be awesome."

Jeff shifted me a little and kissed me. Like always, it was great and I had to control myself from grinding against him. However, that could potentially be duplicated. And if it could, I wanted the patent, because a machine that could kiss like Jeff would be the path to instant wealth.

Once our kiss was over, I let my worry continue. Jeff, however, just put me down. I sidled over to White. "We may want to be ready to run like hell," I said quietly.

Jeff heaved a sigh. "Baby, it's really me. I can't feel you right now. I can't feel anyone."

"Which is part of why we look this bad," Chuckie said dryly. "Because someone went for the 'throw a temper tantrum and see if that works' method."

"I was distraught," Jeff said as he shot a sideways look of annoyance at Chuckie. "You weren't exactly Mister Calm, either, for a while there."

The Poofs all jumped down in front of me and White. They were mewling and jumping up and down. "Kitty's got nothing, Poofies, sorry."

White jerked. "The tunnels are affecting your talents. Meaning they're affecting Jeffrey as well."

"What do you mean?"

"You can't understand the Poofs right now. We already knew the tunnels were affecting our people. I should have considered that before we left."

"Okay, makes sense. So, Jeff, Chuckie, prove you're who we want you to be and show us what you're hiding from us. Now. Or Richard and I do a runner." Neither Jeff nor Chuckie looked up to catching me and White. If they could, it might also prove they were androids. I currently hated where my mind was going.

"Camera's down," Chuckie said with a shrug.

"Yeah, thanks for that. We were trying to find you guys or whoever was down here. That equipment's not cheap."

Chuckie shot me his "really?" look. "I'm aware of what they cost, Kitty. I'm also aware that we've got enemies everywhere." His eyes narrowed. "In fact, how do we know the two of you aren't androids? Martini can't feel anyone in here."

"Look, we're in this weird Mexican Standoff. Someone needs to prove who's who to the others."

The Poofs started jumping up and down again, mewling loudly. They bounded between the four of us, purring and rubbing. Then they stood in front of me, and all three of them stared at me with, what I was positive, were "duh" expressions on their faces.

The light dawned, albeit really slowly. "The Poofs say we're all who we think we are, the real people." The Poofs jumped up and down again, then Harlie went back to Jeff, Fluffy went back to Chuckie, and Poofikins jumped onto my shoulder, grumbling quietly. "Fine, fine, Kitty's being an idiot again. *Excuse me*. It's been a long weekend."

"Since we've confirmed we're all who we say we are, when are you boys going to share what it is you're hiding from us?" White asked.

"We should probably wait until we're back somewhere secure," Jeff said.

"How far away are we from wherever you're basing, Kitty?" Chuckie asked.

"Far."

"Miles," White corrected. "And we're going back to the Embassy. Speed is of the essence. There are things you two don't know about that require our attention."

"I can't handle any more hyperspeed right now," Chuckie said. "I had enough of that today—I honestly don't think my body can take it."

"That's the main reason we've been moving so slowly," Jeff said.

I looked at his expression. "No, it's not. I mean, I'm not doubting Chuckie, but you two are doing more than staggering homeward."

"True enough," Chuckie said. "We had to move slowly, so we were examining the tunnels as we went. We can do more of that later. However, I can't move fast. If I have to deal with more hyperspeed reactions today, I'm going to be bedridden."

"We can't afford to have either one of you out. But we have to get back."

Jeff sighed. "Fine, fine." He fiddled with whatever he was holding. I stepped closer and took a good look. It was a shiny cube, and it looked familiar. "Where, exactly, are we headed, baby?"

"The Embassy ballroom. It's loaded with people and equipment, though."

"Shouldn't be a problem. Richard, hold onto Kitty and Chuck, will you?"

My jaw dropped. This was the first time I'd ever heard Jeff call Chuckie anything other than Reynolds. White took our hands as requested, Jeff finished his fiddling, grabbed my free hand, and we moved.

This felt nothing like a gate transfer or hyperspeed. There was no nausea, no feeling of movement, really. But we could see where we were going, in a sense, but we were moving by everything so fast it was something of a blur. The movement and feeling was very similar to how ACE had shifted us all to Alpha Four and back again at the end of Operation Invasion.

We stopped quickly enough, right in the middle of the ballroom. It dawned on me that I'd forgotten to tell Jeff that the Embassy was shielded, but apparently that hadn't been an issue, because we were all okay.

"Jeff! Jeff! Jeff!" Bellie sounded overjoyed. But she stayed with Oliver. I wasn't sure if he had a death grip on her legs or what, but I was thankful for the small favor.

Jeff winced. "Whoa. All of you are really stressed and upset."

"Why wouldn't we be?" Christopher snapped.

"Why are you all mad at us?" Jeff asked.

"You do realize we've thought you were kidnapped all this time," White said calmly. "Therefore, while Missus Martini and I have had a few moments to come to grips with the fact that the two of you are back with us, most of the rest of the room is relieved to see the two of you alive and reasonably well, while at the same time being remarkably perturbed that you have waited so very long to reassure us of your health and well-being."

"What Richard said. Only not nearly as nicely."

Naomi stared at Chuckie. "We thought you might be dead," she said finally.

"Clarence said he had you," Abigail added. "He almost convinced Sis to go with him to save you."

"I'm sorry." Chuckie looked as though he had no idea of what to say in this situation. Come to think of it, he probably didn't.

"You didn't call," Naomi added. She walked over to him. "In fact, you didn't text, send a mental message, or send an emotional message, either. Nothing. I thought you were *dead*."

"I didn't mean to worry you." Chuckie looked and sounded worried.

"Clarence actually sort of had us—" Jeff said.

Before he could finish, Naomi burst into tears. Chuckie pulled her into his arms, held her, and did the soothing murmur thing. He also did the nuzzling of the head thing, as well as the stroking of the back in an intimate way thing. I heard a couple of terms of endearment in there, too.

This didn't shock me all that much. I'd had a strong suspicion for quite a while, after all, and if White calling him Charles the moment we were with Naomi hadn't been the clear clue, her actions when Chuckie was in danger certainly left no room for confusion. And some of the Poof Population Explosion was also explained. But not all. Wondered if the Poofs somehow knew what was coming and had been staffing up in preparation. Decided I could find out another time.

I looked at Jeff. In contrast to what I would have guessed even this morning, he didn't look shocked at all. He also didn't look angry. He looked incredibly pleased. Clearly their time alone together had been great for bonding.

Jeff looked at me, and the pleased look left his face to be replaced by a guilty and apologetic look. He ran his hand through his hair. Now that we were in the light, I could see that he'd definitely taken some kind of beating. Because A-Cs healed fast, he didn't look as bad as he'd probably looked a couple hours prior, but Jeff was definitely going to need adrenaline. He probably needed isolation, but I doubted we had time for that.

"I'm not going to turn on the waterworks. Because I've been too busy to focus on the fretting, so I'm not nearly as upset as Mimi is, and because I'm just under the emotional level where I'm so angry that I'm going to cry. But if you don't tell us all exactly what the hell is going on, quickly, succinctly, and immediately, I'm going to show you that Naomi has nothing on me in terms of histrionics."

Jeff looked at Chuckie, who nodded.

"I told you he wasn't in love with me any more," I said quietly.

"Yeah, yeah. You know, he's a great guy. I have no idea why I didn't realize it before."

Christopher coughed. We'd moved from throat clearing to coughing as the new noises epidemic. "No idea at all, Jeff. Wouldn't be your typical jealousy thing, would it?"

"Or the Alpha Male fighting thing."

Jeff shrugged. "Things of the past."

Christopher and I both coughed. It was the new epidemic for sure. "I'll start the betting pool," Christopher said to me.

"This is touching," Franklin said. "But since we have an alien armada about to invade and likely conquer us, I believe we'd all appreciate knowing what you two gentlemen have been up to."

"What do you mean, we have an alien armada on the way?" Jeff asked, Commander voice back on full.

"I'm pulling rank," Franklin said. "As Commander of Andrews Air Force Base, or whatever's left of it, I want your intel first. We'll catch you up after that."

"What do you mean, whatever's left of it?" Chuckie asked.

"Long story. I'm with Colonel Franklin—you show us yours and then we'll show you ours. And make it snappy. We don't know how much time we actually have before they show up."

Jeff nodded and looked around. "Who are all—"

"Later. They've all done the spit shake and pinky swear, or will do as soon as we have time. Your intel now. Introductions after you get some adrenaline. Now, Jeff. I mean it. We're all seriously tired, pissed, and stressed."

"Fine. You told me to find Reynolds, which I did."

"Just as Clarence showed up out of nowhere," Chuckie added, still holding onto Naomi.

"Clarence tried to grab Reynolds, I was able to get him first. I saw that Clarence had . . . something of mine." I could tell he didn't want me sharing what I'd seen him use to get us back here with anyone else.

"The glowing cube Terry gave you when you were ten."

Jeff gaped at me. "Why are you discussing that here when—?"

"Seriously, Jeff, hurry the hell up and stop being coy. Figure everyone in this room knows or should know all about what's going on. You two are way behind on the Bad Guy Scheme du Jour."

"Fine. I saw the cube, realized he must have been the one who took it from my parents' home. Then Clarence took off. We were both fine, and Reynolds agreed Clarence was the highest security risk at the Festival. So we followed him."

"For miles," Chuckie said. "At hyperspeed."

"Right. So, we caught him at some golf course. While Reynolds was on his hands and knees throwing up, Clarence and I got into a fight."

"He's taken Surcenthumain. A lot of it, from what I could see."

"Yeah, baby, he has. I was able to get the cube away from him, but only because he knocked me down and I grabbed it as I was falling. Once I had it, I grabbed Reynolds, only Clarence attacked us again. He hits hard, and I hadn't been winning the fight in the first place. I wanted to get the hell away and get the two of us to safety."

"And?"

Jeff shrugged. "And all of a sudden, we weren't on a golf course anymore."

CHAPTER 89

"WE WERE IN A ROOM," Chuckie said. "The movement that took us there was similar to when we were all taken to Alpha Four, only much faster."

"Just like Jeff used to get us back here."

He nodded. "So, once inside, we were safe from Clarence."

"And anything else," Jeff said. "We couldn't get out."

Chuckie looked around the room. "You activated the protocols?"

"Yes, we're all caught up, Director Fury. And everyone here knows about the tunnel system and the rooms."

"Great. Based on what I already knew, I realized we had to be in a dead zone, and based on where we'd been when the cube activated, I figured we were inside the dead zone still being mapped. We couldn't receive or send any electronic signals, and Martini had no empathic abilities at all."

"I couldn't read Reynolds, and he was right next to me."

"Wow, we've officially found A-C kryptonite. Wonderful."

"Our watches stopped working, too," Chuckie said. "So we didn't have a clear idea of the passage of time."

Naomi sniffled and looked up at him. "Great excuse. I don't think I buy it any more than Kitty will."

Chuckie smiled at her, and it was a smile I remembered from long ago. I savored the warm, fuzzy moment. I wasn't sure how many more we were going to get. "Sorry," he said again. "But we didn't realize anyone was looking for us."

"Seriously? With Clarence running amok? With me point blank telling Jeff to get you because you were the assassination target of the day?"

Jeff sighed. "Baby, there was more going on. We weren't alone in the room." He reached into his jacket pocket and pulled out the glowing cube. "It turned out that this wasn't the one Christopher and I had when we were little."

Chuckie released one arm from around Naomi and reached into his pocket. "The only thing the room contained was this." He pulled out another glowing cube. "Per Martini, this one isn't the one he had as a child, either."

"So, did you try the wishing we were somewhere else thing?"

"Yeah, after the 'throw himself against every part of the walls' attempt that lasted far longer than was good for anyone's health, your husband did," Chuckie said. He looked like he was trying not to laugh. "For what I'm guessing was an hour. With no success."

"Yeah, yeah. It was more like fifteen minutes, if that. Reynolds finally convinced me to sit down and tell him what I knew about our cube and how it worked."

"From what I can tell, your mother," Chuckie said to Christopher, "was able to alter the cube you two used to be trained on your DNA signature. Maybe tuned to your talents. But set up just for the two of you. The ones Clarence had and we found are more . . . general."

"How would my mother have ever found a cube like this?" Christopher asked. "They aren't manmade and they aren't something from our home world. Are they?" he asked White.

"I'd never heard of these until today, son."

Chuckie's wasn't the only human mind that could move fast when needed. Mine liked to comply now and again as well. "Richard, I'm sorry, I know you don't know this, but now's apparently the time. I know Terry went to see Yates right after the Mephistopheles superbeing showed up. She was going to ask for his help. Instead, he infected her in some way. Whether it was with a parasite or something else, I'm not sure, but that's what killed her."

White clenched his jaw but otherwise didn't betray emotion. Christopher put his arm around his father; Abigail took and squeezed White's hand. "I'm fine, children," he said quietly. "Confirmation of long suspected truth is something of a relief."

"I know it was a long time ago, but do you know where Yates was the week before Terry got sick?"

"It still feels like yesterday most of the time, so yes, I do remember. He was in Washington, D.C. Rumors put him at his club."

"Which we can safely assume was the same country club the dead zone is under. So, maybe he had the cube, maybe Terry followed him, something, but somewhere along the way, she found it. Figured out how to program it and brought it back with her. So she could pass on what Jeff and Christopher would need in order to survive without her."

"But she never told me where she got it," Jeff said. "Why not?"

"The same reason she didn't tell you many other things. You were ten years old, and she was already giving you more responsibility than any child should have to bear."

"So, how did you two get out?" Stryker asked. "The room's impregnable."

"With our tools, yes," Chuckie said. "But not if you use the cubes properly."

"Only works if you're with the smartest guy in not just the room you're in, but any room in the world," Jeff said. Proudly. Wow. This was a red-letter day in a lot of ways.

"Thanks. It's based on mental telepathy, which would sound like so much New Age junk if we didn't have A-Cs doing similar every day of their lives. It requires more than wishing to make it work, however."

"So how did Jeff manage it?"

They both chuckled. "Lucky accident, as near as we can tell," Chuckie said. "He was pressing the right points of the cube at the right time, and was completely focused on his goal, which was a clear and simple goal."

"How do you mean?" Buchanan asked.

"Martini wanted to get the two of us away from Clarence and to safety. That's a clear goal. 'I want to be rich' isn't as clear a goal, for example, because it's not saying how you're going to get rich, it's not saying what you consider rich to be, and so on."

"Makes sense." Who was I to argue? I could talk to animals now. I had no That's So Crazy leg to stand on.

"If you look at the cube, it's set up almost exactly like a Rubik's Cube," Chuckie continued. He held up his cube. It glowed, but I could see that each side was faintly different in color from the others. "It moves similarly, so each square, row, and side means something. I'm nowhere close to determining how it works all the way around, but after a variety of experiments, we determined the right formation for traveling through the dead zone. We tested and ended up outside the walls."

"We each went back in, separately," Jeff said. "So the one in the tunnel could go for help if the one in the room couldn't get back out. But the pattern is consistent. And the goal was simple—I want to be on the other side of this wall, in the room."

"Or I want to be outside this room, in the tunnel. I was glad to be right on that one," Chuckie said as he fiddled with his cube.

"We were looking to see what we could pick up from the tunnels when you found us," Jeff added.

"Why were you two just sauntering along?" Christopher asked. "You were moving slowly by any standards, let alone ours.

"Because Reynolds threw up for ten minutes straight while I spent time on the losing end of a fight with Clarence, and then we both got to enjoy Clarence hitting us for a while, and then we were locked in a room with no water or food, and we've both used a lot of energy, and, speaking for both of us, we feel like crap. I have no hyperspeed left, and as Reynolds confirmed earlier, he can't take hyperspeed right now anyway. We had no choice but to 'saunter.' "

I looked at both their expressions. "You need adrenaline, don't you?" I asked Jeff.

"No, I'm sure I'm fine."

Tito sighed. "I'm sure you're not, and we have a world of hurt heading for us, so let's get you taken care of."

While Jeff whined and complained and Tito, Christopher, and White overruled him, I put on my Recap Girl cape yet again and brought Jeff and Chuckie up to speed on what had gone on in their absence, which included introductions of those here and elsewhere they hadn't officially met and all the other niceties.

I might have mentioned how distressed we all were with their being kidnapped and all that more than once, but who could blame me? Not Naomi, if her chiming in was any indication.

Chuckie was overjoyed to discover Franklin was truly now the man in charge at Andrews and concerned about Hamlin's disappearance, which he hadn't been briefed on.

Ravi interrupted to demand information from Chuckie about how he controlled the nine supersoldiers in his charge. Once the information was relayed, and Chuckie confirmed that he, Reader, and Tim—and only he, Reader, and Tim—had access to where these nine supersoldiers were housed, I went back to theories and recaps. I'd gotten so good at this over the past couple of days that I didn't miss a thing. White, Buchanan,

Oliver, and the Middle Eastern Contingent even applauded when I was done.

The nice thing about Tito being here and Jeff not being at death's door was that the adrenaline could go in via the vein in his arm rather than stabbed into his hearts. It was the most pleasant adrenaline injection of his I'd ever experienced.

Ravi chimed in again as all this finished up and Jeff was rolling his sleeve down. "We have confirmation of control of all supersoldiers, from teams in Paris and Paraguay. I've also apprised Commanders Reader and Crawford of our status."

My phone beeped. I had a text. "James says that he and Tim are so thrilled that the two of you are alive and well, they plan to celebrate by kicking alien invader butt." Another beep. "Tim says that he appreciates that we took forever to let them know you two were okay."

"Enough with the guilt," Jeff said. "Does my mother know I was missing?"

"Yes, indeed. And I'm sure she'll make you feel even guiltier than I possibly can." Another beep. "James says that, under the circumstances, now that Chuckie's back, he'd like to suggest that we get Alpha Four's help, pronto."

Chuckie shook his head. "I don't know why they wouldn't be helping you already, even with me gone."

"I explained that. World War Two. And such."

"Yes, I know," he said patiently. "But you're at least as trusted by them as I am, Kitty." He gave a mirthless chuckle. "Besides, what we really need is an ozone shield."

"Why?" Jeff asked.

"It stopped the parasites when Alpha Four had theirs up." My mind raced. "Oh. Wow. Um, I have a really clear and focused goal, Chuckie."

"On it."

"Do you think these things can do that?" Jeff asked, looking at the cube in his hand.

"Worth a shot. So, while Chuckie plays with our Outer Space Rubik's Cube, where is the one Terry programmed? I'd figured Clarence stole it way back when."

"Makes sense, but if he is the one who took it, he hid it somewhere," Jeff said.

"The Embassy," William said, before I could. "That's why he's trying to get in here. He lost his cube and knows where a spare is stored."

"That must be how they were able to enter the dead zone they used for the secret lab—they had the cube and figured out how to work it."

"We think each dead zone houses a cube," Chuckie said. "I was hoping to test and see if we could get into one of the others with one of the two we have."

"So does that mean our world is littered with these cubes?" Oren asked.

"Too little data to make an accurate hypothesis," Henry said.

"Oh, but I'm here, and I'm great with making a really good guess. Yes, assume there are Power Cubes in every dead zone. And if we could find the one Clarence hid in here, we'd have three." An idea formed. "Poofies, can you find the missing cube that mean old Clarence stole and hid?"

The three Poofs with us appeared from wherever they'd been. Harlie did a mewl-growl thing, and a few more Poofs appeared out of nowhere. I decided not to question. The Poofs bounced up and down, then disappeared.

"Great, the Poofs are on the hunt." One problem down. I thought faster. "So, based on our earlier assumptions, I'm going to make another leap."

"Why not?" Omega Red said. "It's all speculation right now."

"Oh, it won't be speculation for long, Yuri. We know the Ancients came by more than once. I think it's a safe bet that whatever the aliens are that are headed toward us, they dropped by, too. The Ancients hung around and interacted. But maybe these other aliens didn't. They could have been like ACE—they came to watch and observe, maybe take some tests, but they're supposed to be leaving us alone. They put their cubes and tunnels into the earth a long time ago, and they're using building materials we can't access or probe with A-C talents or Earth-based technology, so that probably means metals from another world."

"Why are so many important things on top of these cube rooms, then?" Buchanan asked. "It can't be random chance."

"No, I agree with you. I go back to the idea that they're working as attractors of some kind. Maybe they probe and give subliminal suggestions. I felt a kind of tug when Richard and I went by the dead zones we passed on the way to find Jeff and Chuckie."

"I did as well," White confirmed.

"So I think they've been influencing us in some ways, either the cubes, the space invaders, or both."

"I can agree," Chuckie said, still fiddling with his cube. "Because while we both wanted to get out of the room, there was a strong draw to stay in it."

"I think if I'd been in there by myself, I might not have gotten out," Jeff said. "And not only because Reynolds figured out part of the cube when I couldn't. Once I calmed down it was very . . . soothing to be there."

"So maybe that's why you were both so calm when we found you—the room chilled you out."

"Maybe." Chuckie shrugged. "We don't have enough data to even make an educated guess at this time."

"Okay, fine," Christopher said. "So why did you mention the Ancients, Kitty?"

"Because of the Dome. I think that Ancients' ship was shot down by the cube that probably resides under the Dome. And I think that happened because these guys and the Ancients didn't get along."

"Enough to shoot another vessel out of the air?" Jeremy asked.

"Look, I realize that we humans like to think that sentient life on other planets will have found a way to get along with everyone and would only come visit when they want to share how to make world peace a reality. But we have examples in the Alpha Centauri system that say it's a nice idea but not something that happens in reality. Utopia's a great vision. But it's a hard thing to actually create or maintain."

"Let's say you're right," Henry said. "Why build the way they have? The tunnels and rooms are so small. We discussed this earlier—you can't get a car, let alone a tank, in there."

"Maybe the aliens aren't as big as we are."

"There was plenty of room for me and Reynolds in the tunnels," Jeff said. "The room was pretty big, too. About the size of our old apartments in the Science Center."

I missed the Lair. Wondered if we'd ever see it again, then decided it was currently the least of my worries.

"The denizens of the Alpha Centauri planets are roughly our size," White said.

"Maybe we grow them taller out here in the Boondocks of the Milky Way. Maybe I'm wrong. We're going to find out, I'm sure."

The computers started beeping like crazy. "You're right about the world of hurt, Tito," Big George said. "And Kitty, you're right, we're going to find out about the invaders, and soon. Chuck, we need you to hurry."

"Why?"

"Because everyone's wrong about the armada arriving Monday. It's here, right now."

"In our part of the galaxy?" Christopher asked.

"No," Stryker answered, voice shaking. "In our solar system."

CHAPTER 90

THE IMAGE ON THE SCREEN was indeed the armada. "Is that Jupiter?"

"Yes," Big George said.

"Military worldwide is going to DEFCON One," Henry said.

"Wow. I think we're really beyond that. I put us at DEFCON Total Freak-Out, but what do I know?"

"I don't have enough time to figure this out," Chuckie said quietly. "If I did, I might be able to put an ozone shield up. But I don't think that's an option now."

"Where are the missiles aimed?" Franklin asked.

"Some external," Stryker said. "Some internal."

Everyone was very quiet. I could hear R.E.M. singing in my mind—this could very well be the end of the world as we knew it. The heck with that. I dug my iPod out of my purse.

"What are you doing?" Jeff asked softly.

"The instructions Chuckie left for us were to activate the Avenger Initiative. That initiative said 'go with the crazy.' We're all scared. I'd personally rather be having sex with you than facing space invaders so powerful that we can't even comprehend how they're traveling as fast as they are. However, duty, apparently, calls."

"But Reynolds is here now," Jeff pointed out.

"I have no idea of what to do," Chuckie said. "I honestly wasn't prepared for our enemies to come back so soon, let alone with this kind of backup."

Wanted to hear tunes but needed to make calls. Decided I could

do both until telecommunications went down. God alone knew if
that was all that would be taken out. No, couldn't go there, even
though I was terrified. Everyone was terrified, even the men used to
dealing with the biggest, fugliest monsters around.

This situation was threatening everyone and everything I cared
about. And that flipped me from frightened to what had been working for me since Day One with Centaurion, and even more so since
Jamie had been born—I was really, really angry.

Put my earbuds in, spun the dial without looking, hit the button
for play at random. Made sure the volume was such that I could still
everyone in the room. Didn't care what was playing, as long as it
was music. Interestingly enough, hard rock didn't come on. Adam
Ant singing "Viva le Rock" came on.

Sent a group text out. Happily, telecommunications was still
working. "Where do we think they're going to come?"

"Alien arrivals seem to happen in the Southwest the most,"
Stryker shared.

"Why do you think they're going to bother to land?" Jennifer
asked.

"Because they've put some time into this planet."

"What if these aren't the same beings who built the tunnels and
made the cubes?" Jeremy asked.

"They are. And if they're not, no one travels this far out of
their way to blow things up from afar." I looked at the picture as
"Apollo 9" came on. I'd hit my Adam Ant playlist. No worries,
it was helping. "William and Jennifer tried reading the aliens
inside the ships, but they were too far away. They're not far
away now."

Christopher and Jeff went to the screen. Christopher put his
hand on the ships, and Jeff put his on top of Christopher's. "Not
human," Christopher said. "Not mammalian at all. It's a mind that
seems vaguely familiar, but not like a mind I've read before."

Jeff pulled his hand away. "Bellie, come to Jeff." She squawked
happily and flew to him. While she nuzzled him, Jeff put his hand
onto her head. "Their minds are like Bellie's."

"Great, they'll love you and want to kill me. Well, we knew that
last part already."

"Not what I mean. They're more . . . sentient than Bellie is, but
they feel much more like she does."

"So, they're birds?"

"Birdlike. Like the Canus Majorians are doglike or the Feliniads are catlike." He went back, still holding Bellie, and put his hand over Christopher's again. "They're . . . worried?"

"Worried about what?"

Jeff shook his head. "I can't tell. But they don't feel angry or bloodthirsty or anything like that."

"Desperate but not serious?" Hey, it was playing, and again seemed helpful. I'd never have guessed that Adam Ant was going to be my go-to guy for a major space invasion, but I never argued with serendipity. And Jeff's kisses did drive me delirious, even if I didn't have time for them at this moment.

He managed a chuckle. "I suppose. Some are more excited, some are frightened. They're running the same gamut of emotions as we do or the different races from Alpha Centauri do. They're closer to the Reptilians than to us or any of the rest of the Alpha Centauri species, but they feel familiar enough. At least, I think so."

"Christopher, find the ship that has LaRue and Ronaldo in it." He nodded and started touching each ship. William and Jennifer went to assist, as did Jeremy. Didn't know if he and Jennifer routinely did the Go Team move or were just fast learners, but they were doing it now.

"Kings of the Wild Frontier" came on now. Maybe it was the asymmetrical drumbeats, but Adam Ant's music was really firing my brain up. The lyrics of this song were incredibly helpful, at least to me in this situation.

"Chuckie, give Naomi your cube. Mimi, Abby, you're up."

"What are we doing?"

"Moving galaxies, probably. But right now I'd like you to figure out how the cube works and get an ozone shield, or some kind of parasite shield up around the Earth, pronto."

They gaped at me. "How—" Naomi started.

"This is what Chuckie's been training you for," I snapped. "I realize the situation sucks, but we don't get to be heroic when things are quiet. Not that they ever are, mind you, but still. You two are the most powerful adult A-Cs we have. You can do more than Serene, Jeff, and Christopher, and that's without the Surcenthumain boost. Stop acting like you can abdicate responsibility now that the menfolk are home and unharmed. It doesn't work like that."

The Gower girls looked at each other, then back at me. "You're right," Naomi said.

"Yes, but we have no idea what an ozone shield would be like," Abigail added.

"I do," Chuckie replied.

"Time for the Wonder Twins to go to triplets."

"We need Jeff, too," Naomi said. "He understands the cube, possibly better than Chuck does."

"I doubt it, but it's worth a shot," Jeff said. He handed Bellie back to Oliver, then took Abigail's free hand. I left them to it.

Buchanan had been quiet, and I needed some input. "Malcolm, where do you think they're going to choose as their main arrival location? Or are you thinking they're just going to blow us to smithereens?"

"I'm with you, Missus Chief. They're going to land and see what's going on. As for where, it's going to depend on whether they want a show of force, to create panic and terror, or to create a diplomatic illusion."

"MJO?"

"New York is always popular for this kind of thing."

"Hacker International, Stryker's already voted for the Southwest. Any other ideas?"

"Major cities are always popular," Henry said.

"Tokyo," Ravi said immediately.

"Moscow," Yuri countered. "Going for an area with a lot of nukes."

"Middle East, maybe?" Big George suggested. "They're trying to start a war there, after all."

Turned to the Middle Eastern Contingent. "What do you guys think?"

To their credit, the four of them didn't waste time asking me why I was asking for their opinions. Instead, four brows furrowed in thought.

"May I ask a question?" Mona asked.

"Sure."

"Why would so much have gone on here, in Washington, D.C., if this was not the landing site?" The others nodded their agreement. So did Buchanan, Tito, and White.

"Wow, we need to swear you into the Kickbutt Gang fast."

I sent another group text out as the song changed again. Happily, the teams in Paraguay and Paris were in supersonic jets, and the supersoldiers were capable of supersonic flight as well. A day ago this would have been horrible news. Today it made me want to dig Antony Marling up from his grave and hug him.

"I know what we're going to do." Everyone looked at me expectantly, even the four doing the Wonder Twins Squared. "We're going to do exactly what you told us to, Chuckie. The Avengers are going to assemble. And then, as my man Adam Ant suggests, we're going to demand that our invaders stand and deliver."

CHAPTER 91

"**WHAT SHOULD I TELL THE TOP BRASS?**" Franklin asked.

"Tell them Centaurion is going to give it their best shot, and we'd appreciate it if the rest of the world didn't fire until we said to. We'd also appreciate it if the worldwide Mexican Standoff could be defused. Senator, MJO, you're going to have to assist our good colonel with that."

"Why bring the reporter along?" Armstrong asked.

"Because certain people know that he's the best investigative journalist in the world and they'll listen to him."

"What about our lovely Miss Bellie?" Oliver asked.

"Much as I'd love to send her with you, I think that would be pushing it for the Top Brass. She'll stay with Jeff." I looked over. Jeff was still busy. Heaved a sigh. "With me." Bellie and I eyed each other. "With Bruno." Oliver nodded and put Bellie gently next to Bruno. Bruno didn't react, but Bellie stayed put, so that was good enough for me.

"What are the rest of you going to be doing?" Franklin asked.

"Choosing our spot. I think it's already been selected, which is nice. Oh, and you have a few more on your team, Colonel. Mister White, you, Tito, William, and Malcolm are going to wherever the Colonel's going, along with our Middle Eastern Contingent."

White looked surprised. "Why so, Missus Martini?"

"I say this all the time, and no one listens. You're actually the best diplomat we have, and we need a diplomat to smooth things over more than I need my partner with me right now. You're also an A-C and can get our people out fast if things turn ugly. Same with

William, and he's our best imageer after Christopher and Serene, so he can read things you may need read. Tito kicks butt better than anyone else around, Malcolm's Mister Skills, and we need to prove that Mona's alive and well and willingly with Mossad. Show up en masse, make the statement, dress for success, sort of thing."

William looked at Christopher, who nodded. There was a lot of that going around.

Buchanan looked ready to argue. "Malcolm, this is you protecting me. Someone Colonel Franklin goes to see isn't going to be on our side. Someone there wants this invasion to succeed. More than one, probably. Do whatever you need to, but accept that you're the one most likely to spot them, whoever they are."

"You sounded just like your mother," he said with a small smile.

"Thanks. I imagine you'll be seeing her soon. Tell her . . ." I was going to have him tell her I loved her, but Mom knew that, and besides, that sounded like good-bye, and I didn't want any of us focusing on the end. "Tell her I want my security clearance back."

"Shall we?" Franklin asked as the others chuckled.

"If you know where we're going, we can go via the nearest gate," White said.

Franklin nodded and shook my hand. Armstrong did as well. "Missus Martini, I'll see you on the other side."

"Hopefully with the negatives from my wild nights of passion in your hand."

He laughed. "One never knows."

The others going with Franklin all hugged me, even Buchanan. "Be careful," he said in a low voice. "Clarence is still at large, and Cantu and the other captain won't be where I'm going. And they'll all be gunning for you."

With that the Colonel's team headed for the Server Box Floater Gate. That thing was getting a lot of work today. Made a mental note to have someone service it when this was all over.

"Now what?" Stryker asked.

"Found it!" Christopher's hand was on a ship at the rear of the armada. "They're here. They're the only Earthlings on the ship. All the rest are, like Jeff said, birdlike. This ship is at the back, but I think it's the command ship."

I paused Adam Ant in the middle of "Whip in My Valise" and pulled out my earbuds. "Isn't that opposite the way our birds work?"

Jennifer touched the ship. "This one was at the head before. The beings in it feel familiar."

"They're kind of flying in a triangle shape, aren't they?"

"Yes, not that I know if this will mean anything for us," Christopher said.

"We'll find out shortly. Migratory birds shift around the bird in the lead all the time, maybe it's the same for them. Now that we have confirmation, see if you can help Jeff and the others make the cube work right."

Christopher trotted over to enlarge and enhance Team Wonder.

Amazingly enough, Bruno was still snoozing, though Bellie looked alert. I went to the avians. "Bruno, my bird, it's almost show time. Bigger birds are coming. You and your flock are awesome, but I'm not sure you're up to taking on an entire avian armada."

He pulled his head out of his wing and warbled nicely at me.

"Wow. No idea of what you're saying. Hope this isn't me losing our connection at the worst time possible."

Bruno stretched his neck out and rubbed against my cheek.

"Aww, thanks. Okay, I'll stop stressing. Bellie, my girl, what's the good word?"

Bellie looked right at me. "Evolution."

"Time to move it, gang! We need to get prepped and get to the Mall."

"We're not done," Jeff said.

"We're not close to done," Abigail added.

"Then screw it. Time is of the essence." Bruno hopped down and stared at me. "Okay, we have a little time. Bruno says we can use the cube."

"I don't want us using it too much," Chuckie said. "I'm worried about what it's doing to our minds and bodies."

"Seems to have done Jeff a world of good."

"Hilarious. We need weapons before we run off anywhere."

"I'll get them ready," Christopher said. "What do you want, Kitty, a rocket launcher?"

"Just extra clips for my Glock."

"You're optimistic."

"Oh, you'll have the rocket launcher, I'm not worried."

Bruno warbled at me, then disappeared. "Where's your bird going?" Jeff asked.

"He's getting his own reinforcements. He'll meet us at the Mall."

"You're sure that's where they're coming?"

"Is the International One World Festival there? Has it already been the scene of at least one 'kidnapping,' if not more? Does that not mean there are more reporters than you can shake a stick at around or nearby? Is it not our nation's capital? And, to Mona's point, isn't this right where Clarence, Cantu, and whoever the other captain Bellie's talking about are?"

"She's right," Chuckie said. "Let's get prepped for this. As much as we can."

"Bruno said we probably have a couple minutes. Which is good, because I want to change my clothes." The ones I was in had already seen a lot of action.

"I'll go with you," Jeff said. "Because, I need to change, too."

"I'll stick with looking beat up and disheveled," Chuckie said.

"It looks good on you," Naomi said with a laugh.

"Liar." Chuckie grinned at her and gave her a one-armed hug.

"Don't you need to wait for Christopher to get back with weapons?" Abigail asked.

"James and Tim are bringing our real weapons. Chuckie, you need to get the nine you have control of out of storage and activated. I want them with us."

"I want Mimi and Abby with me. But I'm not convinced any of this will be enough," Chuckie said quietly. "That's a huge armada."

"And there are thousands of parasites in front of it," Christopher added as he returned with the first ton of weapons, which he dumped on the floor at our feet.

While the menfolk divvied up the guns and explosives, I trotted over to Ravi. Time to try the next thing that might not work. "I know we have control of the supersoldiers. But have you found the androids yet?"

"Not really. There are a huge number of them, but their signals aren't as clear as the supersoldiers' are."

"Can you communicate with them?"

"I suppose we could send a signal to them, but so far they haven't responded to anything we've tried, so I'm not convinced we're getting through."

"Send one word to them, see if it changes anything. Evolution."

Ravi typed away. I held my breath. Taking cues from a parrot seemed crazy—but that was our Initiative. And the way Bellie had reacted made me think I'd given her a code phrase to react to. Or else she liked to say "evolution" a lot and just hadn't around me this weekend.

Ravi drew in his breath sharply. "It worked. The signals are all more clear. They're listening to me now."

"Great. Christopher, can you help Ravi get the androids over to the Mall?"

"I'll do my best. You want me to stay if we can only control them from here?"

"Yes," Jeff said firmly. "You have combat experience, these guys don't."

"I have the androids' attention, but nothing I'm telling them appears to be working," Ravi muttered as he typed furiously. "Dulce's having the same lack of success."

"Kitty, we still can't find Colonel Hamlin," Stryker said. "He's completely off grid. But we've identified an older cell phone of Cantu's that's active and in use. He's in D.C., near the Lincoln Memorial."

"Can I call 'em or can I call 'em?"

"You can call them," Jeff said. "Let's all get going."

"Meet here or at the Mall?" Chuckie asked.

"Mall. Get your soldiers in place. Coordinate with James and Tim, and don't forget Serene."

"Or she'll take your head off," Christopher said.

"Take Bellie." Jeff handed the parrot off to his cousin.

"Why?"

"We'll go faster without her right now."

"No argument from me. She might share more code words with you, too. I asked her what the good word was."

"Evolution," Bellie squawked.

Ravi looked at Bellie. "Protocol." Nothing. "Initiative." Nada. He looked disappointed.

"If those were her trigger words, I think she'd have already tossed them out." I thought about it, what I'd said that had triggered her in the first place, and then her reaction word. "Survival of the fittest."

"Protocol two-two-six-three-seven-one-two. Protocol eight-seven-one-four-five. Protocol six-six-six-one-four-nine-two."

Ravi typed. "That's it! They're obeying!"

"My work here is done. Someone give this parrot some major bird treats. If you need more, try words or phrases related to evolution."

Hacker International all looked at me. To a dude, they looked impressed. "Kitty, I have to say, that was amazing." Stryker sounded as shocked as he looked. "I didn't know you had it in you."

"Eddy? I'll be really offended later. Right now we have a world to save."

Jeff grinned. "And you're just the girl to save it."

CHAPTER 92

JEFF PULLED A BUNCH OF BIRD TREATS out of his pocket and handed them to Christopher, who fed Bellie while she looked smug. Decided she had the right. Jeff took my hand, and we left the ballroom.

He headed us for the elevator. "We're not taking the stairs?"

"No." The doors opened, we got in. He hit the button for our floor.

"Is everything okay?"

Jeff hit the Stop Elevator button. "No." He turned to me. "This isn't an invasion from the Home World, where we have some allies helping us and we know what we're up against. This could be the end of Earth, and no matter what I tell you, I know you'll be right there on the front lines with me. And . . ." He reached out and stroked my face. "If we're going to die, I want to make love to my wife one last time."

"I have no argument. Well, I do, because we need to get into place at the Mall and all that, and I think it's against the rules in the Heroes' Handbook to stop for nookie when the end of the world looms." But Jeff's eyes were smoldering, he had the "jungle cat about to eat me" look on his face, and, frankly, I wanted to make love to my husband once more before we died, too.

"Screw the Heroes' Handbook."

"I'd rather you screwed me."

Jeff laughed. "Good. We'll use hyperspeed," he said with a sexy half-smile. "Normally I'm against any kind of a quickie, but trust me, baby, you'll like it." I always liked it, especially in an elevator, so there was no worry about this on my part.

"I know you just got some adrenaline, but are you sure you're okay enough to go for the gusto?"

His jungle cat smile widened. "Let me prove it to you."

We didn't undress fully, though Jeff got my purse, shoes, pants, and panties off in a split second. I got his shirt opened just as fast and ran my hands over his awesome pecs. He had me up against the side of the elevator, my shirt shoved up, bra opened, his pants undone, and himself inside me in another second or so.

He kissed me deeply, and as his tongue twined with and controlled mine, I wrapped my legs around his waist, stopped worrying about what we should be doing, and focused on what we wanted to do. And moaned, because Jeff was the world's greatest kisser.

Jeff had made love to me before using hyperspeed, right before the last interstellar invasion had arrived, but I hadn't been enhanced at the time. It had been intense when I was fully human. Now that I wasn't, it was even better.

In this position, he was deep inside me, especially when he slid one arm under my thigh. I had my hands on either side of his face, because I wanted to kiss him and never stop kissing him.

My breasts rubbed against the hair on his chest and, as always, it made my hips buck against him even harder. We were going fast, but because I could do it, too, it didn't seem faster than normal now.

My hands slid into his hair as Jeff ended our kiss and moved his mouth to my neck. He ran his teeth over the spot that made me incoherent while I started my cat in heat yowling, and my hips went nuts.

I clutched at his back as he bit me gently. As had happened before, my climax seemed to come out of nowhere. It hit—strong, hard, and incredible—and I stopped yowling because the feeling was so intense I couldn't make noise.

Jeff changed the speed of his thrusts, just a little, but it was enough, and another orgasm built up. He ran his tongue up my neck. "Again," he whispered in my ear, a moment before my next orgasm crashed over me.

He changed his rhythm again, building me up a little more slowly this time. We weren't being fancy, we weren't trying anything new, but we didn't have to. Every time with Jeff was great, and even though we didn't have time to review our entire sexual repertoire, it was still wonderful.

My thighs tightened around his sides and I used my lower legs to push against his butt, or as I liked to think of it, gave his amazing thrusters an assist.

His mouth moved to the other side of my neck, and I yowled again. He nibbled up this side of my neck as we both sped up. I was gasping and panting and so very, very ready to go over the edge. "Again, baby."

Sure enough, my third orgasm hit. This time, he joined me and roared against my neck as I hit high C, each throb from him causing spikes in my climax.

Finally our bodies slowed and stilled, and I could tell we weren't moving at hyperspeed any more. Jeff kissed me again as he slid out of me and put me gently on the floor.

He hit the Stop Elevator button again, and we dressed as the elevator continued up. Jeff used hyperspeed, so it took him about a second to finish. I didn't feel confident enough to use hyperspeed to dress, seeing as I didn't want to risk ripping my jeans. However, Jeff helped me, so I was dressed before we reached our floor.

He pulled me into his arms, and I leaned my head against his chest.

"I love you, baby," he said softly.

"I love you, too." I looked up at him. "And I forgive you for being alive and well instead of kidnapped and not letting me know for hours."

Jeff grinned. "Good to know." He kissed my forehead. "Now, let's go save the world."

"Oh, good. Routine."

CHAPTER 93

WE ZIPPED OUT OF THE ELEVATOR and into our rooms. I
changed out of my cool Aerosmith shirt into one of my more
badass Aerosmith shirts. I worked best with Steven, Joe, and the
rest of my boys on my chest. Decided the rest of my ensemble
could remain, though I left my Lifehouse jacket in the room—it had
been through enough today.

Jeff changed into a new suit. Looked just like the suit he took
off, only this one wasn't dirty. We each had our clothing ritual, and
his was no better or worse than mine.

Made sure his adrenaline harpoon and my Glock were in my
purse. "Huh."

"What?"

"I have no Poofs." Checked the Poof Condos. No Poofs there,
either.

"You sent them off to search for the missing cube."

"I just sort of thought they'd be back by now. Or, you know, that
other Poofs would be along for the ride." I was Poofless? This
didn't seem like the right time for the Poofs to not be around. Then
again, they worked in mysterious, Poofy ways, and every other time
they'd done a runner, it had always been for the greater good.

"Maybe they're all at the Dome. Protecting Jamie. Which is
what they should be doing."

"No. I mean, some are there, but I sent most of them to find and
help you and Chuckie. You and Chuckie are found."

"No help from the Poofs on that one."

"Yeah. You know, Fluffy was with the group I sent out, as a matter of fact."

"Huh. You know, the Poof was with Reynolds when we got attacked. But I don't think it went into the room with us."

"But you're not sure?" Jeff shook his head. "It doesn't seem possible if Fluffy was with Chuckie. That would mean the Poofs could get in and out of the impregnable rooms, and, if so, why wouldn't they have brought you with them?"

"No idea. Let's table that concern for when we don't have alien birds attacking us. Gate or hyperspeed?"

"Bruno said to use the cube."

"I'm not taking orders from a bird, and besides, I think Chuck may be right."

"The shock of you using his first name is still almost enough to make me faint."

"Noted. Besides, I'm not confident I can land us somewhere I'm not familiar with, especially when there are a lot of people around."

"It's up to you, then. We can use our handy dandy floater gate or take in the sights."

"I'm tired. Let's take the gate."

We headed to the ballroom and checked on Hacker International first. "Glad you two didn't stop to have sex," Christopher said. He didn't appear to be saying this sarcastically, so apparently hyperspeed sexy time had been a brilliant choice. "They're here." He pointed to one of the screens.

The armada was hanging out by the moon. They wouldn't be visible to the human eye, but anyone looking through a telescope would have no problem seeing them.

"You should still stay here," Jeff told Christopher, though he didn't sound as though he really meant it.

"No," Christopher said firmly. "The hackers know what to do. The Barones are here, and they can interface. And I know you'll need me there."

"You sure you want us to stay here?" Jennifer asked. I could tell she wanted to stay. Jeremy looked torn. But who knew what was going to hit over here? Hacker International would need as many A-Cs as possible if they needed to clear out fast.

"Yes, at least for now. Stick around, do what you can here. Walter, you still listening?"

"Yes, Chief."

"Excellent. Please advise everyone who might not know that the invaders have arrived. No idea what the parasite situation is, but we need to figure it's going to be bad. Keep some Security and other available A-Cs here with the Barones and Hacker International. Help them as you're able. Lock up behind us."

"Roger that, Chief."

"Christopher, you want to spin the floater gate dial?"

He shook his head. "I think, under the circumstances, we're better off going on foot. I want to get an idea of what's going on before we're immediately involved in it."

"Nothing's on screen yet," Ravi shared. "There are no signs of human panic."

"Oh, give it a few minutes. Or less." I put my purse over my neck, Jeff and Christopher each grabbed one of my hands, and the three of us took off.

Christopher might have been Cyclops in Chuckie's mind, but as far as I was concerned, he was the Flash all the way. He controlled the hyperspeeding; we were at the Mall in what seemed like a second flat.

Which was great, because that meant we got to enjoy the invaders' big reveal moment and, therefore, more of the total chaos it created. I'd been right—the armada had made its presence known in much less than a few minutes.

If Michael Bay and Steven Spielberg got together to make an alien invasion movie that didn't involve shapeshifting robots, they couldn't come up with anything better than the scene in front of us.

The sky, which had been clear only a few seconds prior, filled with flying saucers. I couldn't tell if they were spread out around the planet or not, but there were a large number of them massed overhead.

The certainty that these aliens, whoever they were, had been here before and dropped by regularly for routine checkups settled firmly into my stomach. We were looking at classic, stereotypical flying saucers.

Interestingly enough, the parasites weren't landing and splatting onto people. They appeared to be in a giant bubble. The sun was low in the sky, and that was probably the only reason the bubble was obvious—the sun's rays were hitting it in a way that showed its outline. The bubble was similar to the one I'd created with ACE's help in order to safely dispose of the gaseous Surcenthumain during Operation Confusion. Only about a zillion times bigger.

There had easily been tens of thousands of people at the One World Festival, and they were all panicked. People were screaming and running and generally acting like it was the end of the world. Because it sure looked like it.

"The invaders don't have to do anything," Christopher shouted as we jumped onto the wall of the Reflecting Pool to avoid getting trampled. "Everyone's going to kill themselves just to get away."

"We have to do something." Not that I had any idea of what.

"Stop it!" Jeff bellowed. "Calm down!"

No one bellowed like my man. He was easily heard above the others. And the people around us sort of stumbled to a halt.

If we'd had time, Jeff probably could have gotten the calm to spread. But we didn't have time.

CHAPTER 94

ONE OF THE FLYING SAUCERS FIRED what looked like a laser beam toward the Washington Monument. But the beam didn't hit the monument. It hit a supersoldier.

Our army was here.

Amazingly enough, the supersoldier didn't disintegrate. It took its licking and kept on ticking. Nice to know Titan Security had created the Timex Line of supersoldiers. Especially since they were fighting on our side.

Whether this shocked the space invaders or not I couldn't tell, but the ships fired again. And more supersoldiers lifted up and took the hits. The sky was already too filled, and the ground was too chaotic for me to be able to determine if any of the lasers had hit anything other than a supersoldier.

However, giant metal monsters fighting on our side or not, the people here didn't know and didn't care. The screams increased, as did the panic.

"People are being trampled!" I almost jumped off and tried to help, but Jeff grabbed me.

"Our goal isn't one person, it's the world."

He was right. Dug my phone out and tried to make a call. As far as I could tell, I connected with Tim, but I couldn't hear anything. "We need help with crowd control!" I shouted into the phone. Then I hung up and contemplated my options. It wasn't a great idea to casually stand around texting while the world blew up around me. Hopefully that one call to Tim made an impact, because that was it for telecommunications.

The invaders hadn't needed to knock those out after all. The human herd was panicking, and that was all it took. Jeff and Christopher both had their phones out and seemed to be having the same kind of one-sided, mostly useless conversations I'd had. Dropped my phone back into my purse as they hung up and put their phones away.

A group of people slammed into us. I got separated from Jeff and slammed into Christopher. We both went into the water, but he managed to keep us steady and, more importantly, upright. Jeff shoved through, grabbed my hand, and pulled us out of the water. "Run!" We took off.

We were moving so fast that we were actually running on top of the water. Didn't have time to marvel—we were too busy dodging people who were scrambling to get out of the way of either the lasers or the supersoldiers. Or each other. The Reflecting Pool was only a minor roadblock—plenty were willing to get wet if it meant they could get out of the way faster.

Jumped off the end and raced to the World War II Memorial. People were running all over it, but this Memorial had two small, raised stone gazebolike structures on either side of it. A-Cs could jump well, and these weren't that high, so we leaped up onto one of them, which got us out of the way of the crowd.

"How long before someone launches a nuke?" I asked.

"Soon, I'm sure." Jeff leaned on me.

"You okay?"

"I'm blocking. The terror's too much. I'd already be out if not for the adrenaline." He took a deep breath and let it out slowly. "Okay, I'm good. I can't feel anything much, baby, so don't get lost."

"I wasn't the one who was missing for half the afternoon."

The crowd was running in all directions. More lasers shot down on us. The supersoldiers blocked most of them. But not all.

A blast went through the Reflecting Pool. Which would have been okay—it was repairable. The people in the pool, however, weren't. There were a lot of them, all blown to bits.

I was thankful Jeff couldn't feel anyone's reactions, though I'm sure my screaming was probably enough. I knew I was at the dog-only register. Not that it mattered. No dog was going to pick my screams of horror out from the rest of the crowd.

The water that was left in the Reflecting Pool was red, and so was much of the stone. Body parts were strewn all over, in the pool and around it.

Another laser hit the street that separated the World War II memorial from the Washington Monument. The streets within the Mall had all been blocked off for the Festival, so no cars were there. However, once again, there were plenty of people running on the street because it seemed to provide a safer path.

Many dodged the strike itself, but not all. The blast not only sent bodies flying but also threw up chunks of tar and pavement into the air—and they came down indiscriminately. Booths, stages, old people, young people—destruction rained down.

Another downside of having to use supersoldiers in this kind of situation was that they were a lot bigger than any human, and they clearly weren't programmed to watch where they were stepping. They seemed focused on protecting the monuments, which was great, but innocent people were getting trampled under their feet.

A thought managed to crawl into my horrified mind. "If we can get people into those tunnels, they'll be safer than anywhere out here."

"How?" Christopher asked. "There's only three of us."

I spotted something. A lot of somethings. Lots of guys in black suits, moving really fast. The Field teams were here.

CHAPTER 95

"OVER HERE!" JEFF BELLOWED.

More than a few teams heard him, and we had a lot of A-Cs in front of us in moments.

"Grab as many people as you can and head for the Lincoln Memorial," I shouted. "We're going to have you take them underground. Pass it on!"

The agents nodded and took off. Well, some did. Some grabbed people nearby.

"Link hands!" I shouted as we jumped down and ran past.

Jeff bellowed that order as the three of us continued to the Lincoln Memorial.

We couldn't run at hyperspeed. Well, we tried, but slammed into a group of people who'd reversed direction at the last moment because of a laser blast in front of them.

I lost my hold on both Jeff and Christopher and went flying. Landed on some bodies. "I'm so sorry," I said as I scrambled to my feet. "Are you—"

I was going to ask if they were okay. But they were all dead. I could tell because none of the bodies were whole, and no one was breathing.

Backed away and got slammed into someone else, spun around, shoved, and generally manhandled. If my purse hadn't been over my neck, I'd have lost it, and not because anyone was trying to steal it.

A supersoldier was barreling toward where I was. I grabbed the people nearest me and ran in the opposite direction. Spotted some black Armani suits in the crowd and tried to head for them.

"No!" a man I had hold of screamed. He yanked away. As I tried to grab for him, he moved out of my reach and right under a super-soldier's foot. He was crushed in front of me.

I turned away to head back toward the Field agents I'd spotted but saw now why the man had pulled away. They'd been shot by a direct laser hit, probably what the supersoldier had been trying to block. The other person I held yanked out of my hand and ran off. I couldn't move.

The air was filled with dust and smoke now. Not so much that I couldn't see, but enough to make your eyes water and throat dry. Fear has a smell, and this much fear smelled the way a kick in the gut felt. We were animals, after all, and animals pick up the panic from other animals. I wanted to run away screaming, just like every-one else.

Thought I heard someone calling my name and turned around. There was a little girl standing on the grass, alone, crying. Somehow, no one had run her over yet. However, it was just a mat-ter of time.

I ran toward her, dodging people, and got to her just before a clutch of people ran her down. Managed to get us to another clear patch.

Against all odds, a woman ran to us. "Oh, thank you!" she said as she took the little girl from me.

"Let's get out of here. Head for the Lincoln Memorial."

She nodded and we took off. I was doing better with someone specific to actually protect. I couldn't be afraid, I had to take care of them. I had the woman by her arm so I wouldn't lose her.

Dodged and weaved us around people, like salmon swimming upstream against a thousand grizzly bears. Felt the ground shaking, moved to hyperspeed, and got us out of the way of another super-soldier. It just missed us as it took a laser blast. And then another. And then more. These blasts were more rapid fire, like machine guns versus cannonballs.

"Wow, that was close."

I backed us away, keeping them behind me, as the supersoldier took another hit and went onto its, for want of a better word, knees. It fell over onto its face and more people.

Heard more than felt something. A little sound that I shouldn't have been able to hear at all. A sigh, almost.

Looked at the mother and daughter with me. I still had hold of the woman's arm. But half of her was gone. And so was half of her daughter. They'd been sliced through by laser fire. I'd put them behind me to protect them, but that act had killed them.

Horror, despair, and rage vied for supremacy. Horror and despair really had the most going for them. But as I forced my fingers to let go of the woman's arm and watched what was left of their bodies fall to the ground, rage won.

These invaders didn't even have the decency to come fight us one on one. I might have no love for the beings from Alpha Centauri who had sided with King Adolphus and come here to destroy me and my friends, but they'd had the balls to face us on a reasonably fair field of battle.

But these invaders had come and started shooting at us, at innocent people. There was a word for what they were. In one way or another, I'd been fighting against what they were since the first minutes I'd joined up with Centaurion Division.

They were terrorists. And they had to be stopped. Because everyone who died today deserved for their survivors to live free. And I was going to make sure that happened.

Or die trying.

CHAPTER 96

SOMEONE GRABBED ME, AND I JUMPED. "Come on, baby," Jeff said. "Let's get this stopped before more innocent people get . . . hurt."

"How'd you find me?"

"I read your mind. Kitty, just remember . . . this isn't your fault. You didn't bring these beings down on us. They brought themselves. Now let's go stop them. Permanently."

I nodded. I wasn't sure I believed him, but I was sure that we needed to stop the madness. We headed for the Lincoln Memorial again.

I'd planned to head for the area Clarence had been when he'd tried to lure the Gower girls to the dark side. But Christopher was at the base of the steps leading up to the Memorial, and we joined him there.

It didn't take long to figure out why Christopher had stopped here. Clarence was here on the steps of the Memorial—and he wasn't alone. He had Jamie in his arms and a gun at her head. "Come any closer and I kill her," Clarence shouted.

We stopped. "How did he get her?" Jeff asked. "I thought she was safe."

"No idea." My throat was tight. I wanted to run and grab her out of his arms, but I knew that would just mean he shot my baby in front of me. "I shouldn't have left her alone at the Dome."

"She wasn't alone," Christopher said, voice filled with dread. He didn't have to voice his thoughts—if Clarence had Jamie, what had happened to everyone else at the Dome? What had happened to ACE?

Agents were bringing people, and they headed for us. Jeff and Christopher both put their hands up, and everyone stopped. Just in time.

Light beamed down out of the sky, coming from the flying saucer closest to us. Just like in the movies. I could see bodies coming down inside the light. Several of them.

The light disappeared, and there were five beings with Clarence. We knew two of them—Ronaldo Al Dejahl and LaRue Demorte Gaultier.

Al Dejahl didn't have an image overlay on, so he looked like himself—tall, midtwenties, handsome, well built, dark hair and eyes. Since I wasn't fighting for my life at the moment, I could spot the resemblance to White easily, and Serene as well.

The woman with him I also knew, but not in the same way. She was a tall, thin, bleached blonde about my age, maybe a little older, but not much. The Trophy Wife, aka LaRue Demorte Gaultier. I'd met her a few times, both before Amy's mother had died—when she'd been Herbert Gaultier's assistant—and after, when she'd become his second wife. I'd never liked her then, which was nice, because I certainly loathed her now.

They were both dressed in what I could only think of as an intergalactic robe and muumuu combination. The fabric sort of hung off their shoulders like drapes, which hid their body shapes. The robes had loose sleeves that went down to their wrists. I got the impression that if they'd held their arms straight out to their sides, they'd look like half of a white balloon each.

Of course, they were in them because the beings they were with were wearing the same outfits. And, on five-foot-tall bird people, they looked okay, sort of like extra long and luxurious feathers. But on humans and human-looking aliens it was pretentious, funny, and basically unflattering.

"We do not come in peace," Al Dejahl said, voice booming. I was sure everyone around us could hear him. Possibly everyone on the Mall could hear him. That's right, he had troubadour talent, along with imageering. And mind control. Couldn't forget about the mind control, because he was undoubtedly going to start using it shortly.

"No kidding," I muttered under my breath.

LaRue looked at the three of us. "You." She pointed to me. "You will come to us. The others will stay away."

Jeff growled. I could tell he was ready to attack. "No," I said quietly. "I'll go. You figure out what the hell's going on and how to stop it. And coordinate our forces, because we seem to be lacking things like air support, Chuckie, the Gower girls, and androids."

I squeezed his hand, and Christopher's, then let go and trotted up the stairs. This was really reminiscent of my short trip to Alpha Four, only I'd had a lot more and better backup then, and I hadn't been sick to my stomach from horror.

Stopped a few steps away from them so that I'd have an easy time jumping back and falling down the stairs should one of them lunge for me. "Give me back my daughter." Jamie appeared to be calm and asleep. I hoped it was sleep and not drugs, but I put nothing past these people.

The bird-people had heads that looked something like a humanoid version of an eagle, with an extra-large lower jaw. Unlike most birds, their eyes were more centered. I cocked my head. From another angle, they looked like something else vaguely familiar. Couldn't place what, but I had a feeling I needed to.

Their bodies were completely hidden by their Space Togas, so I had no guess there, but I did spot six large talons sticking out from under each muumuu. The talons were painted with designs I didn't have time to focus on.

Feathers stuck out of their Space Toga sleeves. Didn't know if this meant they only had wings, had feathers for fingers like an avian version of *Edward Scissorhands*, or something else. The way things were going, I put my money on "something else."

LaRue smirked. "I don't think so. If you'd just let us have her before, none of this would be happening now."

"Right, you'd have enacted whatever horrible world domination plan you had and enslaved us all already. Instead you headed out of town to find new friends." I looked at their companions. "So, just who are the Bird People of Outer Space?"

"They are the Z'porrah," Al Dejahl replied. "An ancient race."

The three birds looked at me. I looked back. "Can you understand me?"

They nodded.

"Good. Then understand that you've invaded and attacked a world that hasn't done anything to you or yours. You've slaughtered innocent people—not warriors but people, civilians. Children, the elderly, the infirm. None of these people deserved to die, and certainly not in this way and with no warning. That's an act of war no matter what part of the galaxy you're from. And around here, it's also considered an act of terrorism."

They stared at me, the way birds will.

"And I'm kind of interested in how, in addition to every other heinous crime you've committed and are committing, the kidnapping and threatening of an innocent baby, or chick, is considered okay where you people come from."

More bird stares. Contemplated doing a staredown with them. Decided even if I won, I was still likely to lose. Supersoldiers taking the laser blasts or no, we weren't in a good position.

No sooner thought than a supersoldier took a major hit and plummeted to the ground, barely missing the building and people. The wreckage only missed the people because the A-Cs had managed to shove everyone away.

I looked back to LaRue. I had to get it together and keep it together, and that meant I needed to, shock of shocks, run my mouth.

"Great dresses you and Ronnie are wearing. They really say 'I'm a wise elder god wannabe.' And, wow, LaRue, let me just applaud you for managing to find a way to dye your hair all the way out in the far reaches of space. Lesser women would have let their hair go back to its natural color, but not you. Way to focus on the priorities, babe."

She smirked. "You still have a mouth on you, I see. It won't do you any good, but it's nice to see you sticking with what worked for you when you were a kid."

"You mean when we were kids, though you *are* older than me. By a good few years." Her eyes narrowed. Good. "I have to give it to you though—Ronnie here is a much more age-appropriate choice than your very late and not-at-all lamented sugar daddy, even if Ronnie is, what, a decade younger than you. He's a lot better than his father was, too. And let me point out that I'm emphasizing the word 'was.' "

"My father was a brilliant man whom you murdered in cold blood," Al Dejahl said. The bird people nodded. Okay, this was part of the party line, apparently.

"Yeah, is that the story you're telling? He was the Devil incarnate. We called him an insane megalomaniac who tried to destroy every living person on this world, and killing him was in self- and world-defense. Nice to see you still desperately trying to fill his fugly hooves, though, because if you take a look around, we have the very definitions of murdering innocents in cold blood littered all over the Mall."

Al Dejahl shrugged. "In any offensive, pawns are there to be sacrificed."

"You really are your father's son, aren't you? Of course, I'm kind of shocked you're mobile and all. The last time we met, Jeff put quite the beat-down on you. Our Pontifex is the only reason you're alive."

"Weak people don't last long," Al Dejahl sneered. "We'll take care of my dear half-brother later."

Surely they knew Gower had taken over as Pontifex. Of course, it had happened when Al Dejahl was unconscious, Clarence was imprisoned, and LaRue was scrambling to save the remnants of their operation. So either their intel wasn't two-way and they didn't know, or they wanted to get a rise out of me. Either option meant I needed to give them nothing they could work with. Fortunately, years spent with Chuckie had honed my ability to keep a poker face, and my mother had ensured that, despite the evidence, I knew when to shut the hell up.

"So, you headed off for galactic parts unknown, found a planet that would let you land, said 'help, help, we're freedom fighters, please come help us save our people from an oppressive regime,' and then kept on going, until you found a planet that would both let you land and was interested in helping you brave saviors to free your world. That about right?"

"What a smart little girl you are," LaRue sneered. "If only you were going to live longer, there might be hope for you yet. But humans die so much more easily than A-Cs do, and I assure you, you'll be dying shortly."

"But don't worry," Al Dejahl chimed in. "We'll be happy to raise your daughter for you. It'll ensure she becomes a useful member of our new society."

Thanked them silently for the extra boost of rage. But did they not know I was enhanced? Chuckie had done a good job of keeping it quiet, and every bad guy who'd seen me use the new skills was dead, so maybe not.

"Really? That's the plan? Stealing other people's innocent children and making the world over into some goose-stepping, conformist culture? As if that'll really work."

"It works well when you have the right backup," LaRue said. Probably true. After all, their new friends were big birds. Goose-stepping might seem right and natural to them. And many cultures seemed to place order and conformity higher up on the scale than creativity and freedom.

Al Dejahl nodded. "None of your husband's people will be welcome here. I don't mean him, of course. You'll both be dead. But his people will be exiled again. Only we'll be visiting the 'home

world' after this. And they won't be welcome there, either, or anywhere in that system."

"How *Mein Kampf* of you. They're your people, too. Technically,
at least."

He shrugged. "People are sheep, regardless of what they look
like. They crave order. Chaos has descended, and they'll do anything to make it stop. We'll only be doing what they want."

What *was* it with the League of Evil Bad Guys? Just once,
couldn't one of them be shooting for anarchy as the final goal?
What about peace, love, harmony, and Billy Zane in a role where
he didn't have to chew scenery? Heck, even a simple money grab.
But no, to a crazed lunatic they went for the total domination idea.
Always the way.

"A-Cs don't crave order?" Which ones did he know? The ones I
knew liked order just fine. In fact, until I'd shown up, as near as I
could tell, they'd had all of two rebels, Terry and Jeff. Not really a
large percentage of the available population.

"They tend to be . . . far too creative for our plans."

"You mean smart."

"You say tomato."

"Actually, I say whatever, but I get your general drift. So you're
just going to kill all the A-Cs here? At least they're like you, in that
sense. Not even going for the ever-popular enslavement plan? You
don't want your own A-C army?"

Al Dejahl's eyes narrowed, and he leaned toward me. "I don't
need any of them," he hissed. "I have many things that are so much
better. And much more effectively controlled."

Had to figure out if they were the King and Queen of the Big
Bluff or if they really had no idea that we'd taken control of the
supersoldiers and, hopefully, the androids. Did they think the supersoldiers were taking hits on Marling's order? Then again, maybe
they weren't talking about those and were referring to the Z'porrah.

Decided not to push it. Keeping the bad guys monologing was
my specialty, and hopefully it'd give us time for reinforcements of
some kind to arrive. "Really? You know, Jamie's an A-C, too."

"She's a hybrid. More powerful. More useful, too." Al Dejahl
grinned at me. "Your husband should have killed me when he had
the chance."

"Yeah. You're part of the group that mistakes kindness and char-
ity for weakness." I looked at the three Z'porrah in front of me. "So,
Big Birds, you're good with this? Our people showed mercy to this
man and didn't kill him. He and his pals exiled themselves as

opposed to facing fair trial. And they've lied to you about who they are in our world, they're threatening an infant as well as thousands of innocent people—and you're still willing to stand with them?"

The Z'porrah stared at me. "You are rude," one said.

"Um, sorry, but you invaded our world and attacked. No introductions, no declarations of war, no polite requests for surrender. Just wham, bam, look at my parasites, ma'am. Where I come from, we call that being *extremely* rude."

"None stand with you," the second Z'porrah said.

I looked behind me. Yep, all the people were there. And more. Turned back. "I see a heck of a lot of people standing there."

The third Z'porrah shook its head. "Your own flock is not what we mean."

"You mean that because we don't have other alien races other than human and A-C here that this means we're okay to be destroyed?"

The Z'porrah all rolled their eyes. In unison. As the unison thing went, eye rolling in unison was the most icky and unsettling of any I'd experienced so far. "None stand with you. You have destroyed life on this planet. We see no reason not to destroy you."

"Ohhhh, you're doing this for ecology! Got it. You're ecoterrorists and we're your next target. Gotcha. Of course, you destroying us makes you no better than we are, but I doubt that matters to birdbrains."

"You insult us," the first Z'porrah said.

"No. You're ugly and your mother hen dresses you funny is an insult. Calling you what you are isn't an insult. By the way? We're sick and tired of you coming by, probing and freaking out our people. Why you have that intricate tunnel system is a little confusing, though, because you aren't blinking in the sunlight, so you don't live underground."

The second Z'porrah's eyes narrowed. "You have found the network?"

I thought about it, what the subterranean tunnels and dead zones had looked like. Could it be their version of a computer network? Wished Chuckie was here, or anyone from Hacker International, because they'd have known right off.

Decided to go for it. "Yes."

The three birds screeched in unison. They sounded like Bruno and the rest of the Peregrines, only at least a hundred times louder.

"Destroy them!" the third Z'porrah screamed. "The apes must not have network!"

Whoops.

CHAPTER 97

I WASN'T SURE WHAT THE Z'PORRAH were expecting when they gave their destruction order. But I had to bet that what happened wasn't it.

Jamie woke up, screaming and clawing. She also turned into a Peregrine. Lola, to be exact. Lola clawed and bit at Clarence, who also started screaming and hitting at her.

Big mistake. The rest of the Peregrine flock appeared, and they were pissed. They attacked Clarence and the others, clawing at their Space Togas and everything underneath. The scene in front of me turned into a lot of claws, beaks, and feathers.

At the same time, I heard screams from behind me. Risked a look. People were pointing and running in the opposite direction. Looked where they were pointing, which was at the downed supersoldier. The soldier part was destroyed. The super part wasn't.

A superbeing staggered out of its shell. It might have been hurt, but it wasn't dead by a long shot. Claws, talons, other scary projections jutted from what I charitably chose to think of as its body. As near as I could tell, its head was in what on a human would be its stomach. It screamed, and really gave the Z'porrah a run for their screeching money.

The superbeing did what superbeings did—it destroyed.

Had to assume it was seriously pissed from being trapped and controlled inside the supersoldier shell—after all, ACE had told me that whatever was inside the supersoldiers was sentient. It swiped viciously at the people near it, most of whom were Field agents. Not that only our people took hits. The ground was now officially red with blood.

Supersoldiers ran toward us, trampling people who were, yet again, running away in panic. The superbeing was definitely of the tooth, claws, slice and dice variety, and it was slashing through the crowd.

But not everyone was running away from it. Some people ran toward it. And, shockingly, they weren't wearing black Armani suits.

They looked like regular people, but as they swarmed over the superbeing, I realized they were androids, because no human or A-C could take the damage the superbeing was handing out and still hang on and fight back.

This was great in one way, but we were now in between the proverbial rock and hard place. If a supersoldier was downed by one of the Z'porrah ships, it was going to open up and release its special surprise inside, which would then start destroying all the things it had been protecting previously.

When we had battles like this in the middle of the desert, nothing really got messed up other than the cacti and poor desert animals. Here, though, there was so much to destroy—it already looked like World War III, and the attack hadn't been going on for more than thirty minutes, if that.

Checked on the Peregrines. They were definitely holding their own. The Z'porrah's Space Togas were in shreds, and LaRue and Al Dejahl didn't look any better. But I could see what the Z'porrah looked like without their clothes on. And, to me, they no longer looked like birds. But I did realize what their heads had reminded me of.

They looked like miniature Tyrannosaurus Rexes. With wings.

So much seemed explained, but I had no one to share my new insights with. Not a problem, I had plenty of other things to do. Like not let my head hit the pavement when Al Dejahl broke through my Peregrine line and tackled me.

Tucked my head against him as we rolled down the stairs. Managed to flip him an extra time so that he landed on the bottom when we hit the pavement.

"What is it with you and beating up girls?" I slammed my fist into his face. He seemed shocked. So I hit him again. And again. Really, really hard. "You are not a nice guy." Punctuated each word with a punch.

Sadly, he recovered and flipped us again. Tucked my head again so it didn't hit, which was good. But he was on top of me, which was bad. He grabbed my throat so I couldn't move my head, reared back, fist ready to slam into me.

Just like the last time he'd been attacking me, Al Dejahl wasn't paying attention to one important piece of information. Jeff was around.

I heard the roar before I saw his fist hit, so I grabbed the fingers around my throat and pulled them apart. I was fairly sure I felt bones break. Then Jeff's fist landed and Al Dejahl flew off me.

"You okay, baby?"

"Yes, because of you. Go get him, I'll get LaRue." Jeff took off; I scrambled to my feet and took a look around.

Clarence was down. I wasn't sure if he was dead, but he wasn't moving. The three Z'porrah were still fighting my Peregrines. LaRue wasn't there with them, though. Scanned the crowd. Spotted her, running for the side of the Lincoln Memorial. The hell with that—I wasn't letting her get into the tunnels.

Amazingly enough, there weren't a lot of people where LaRue was heading. I didn't really know why. I'd have thought the trees would have looked like inviting hiding places to someone, but apparently not. Fine, it would make it easier for me, and our side needed any break it could get.

Took off at hyperspeed. I was one with the rage at this point, power flowing through me, not having to think about running fast, dodging nimbly, hitting hard, seeing far. I caught LaRue within two seconds.

Slammed her into the ground, hit her face into the dirt a couple of times, flipped her over, and landed on her stomach with both knees.

"Ooof!" She didn't make any other noise, possibly because I'd knocked all the wind out of her.

Pulled out my phone and selected the voice recorder. "Tell me who your contacts on Earth are." She didn't speak. I slapped her. "Tell me who your contacts on Earth are." She glared at me. I leaned closer. "Tell me or I'll kill you, right now. I've killed plenty of evil people by now, more than I think you know about. Killing you won't make up for even one of the innocents who died here today. But it'll be a good start. So talk . . . or die."

I heard a gun cock and felt something hard at the back of my head. "I don't think LaRue needs to cooperate with a traitor, Missus Martini."

"Speaking of traitors, Cantu, I was wondering when you'd show up." I slid my thumb on my phone from voice recorder to main menu. Hit the speed dial button and hoped he was in a position to answer. "So, were you the captain in Paraguay or Paris?"

"Paraguay, of course. South America is my turf, so to speak. Stand up slowly with your hands up."

Held my phone so that he couldn't see the face. "So, Esteban Cantu of the Central Intelligence Agency, how long have you been conspiring with extraterrestrials known as the Z'porrah and known traitors and terrorists Clarence Valentino, LaRue Demorte Gaultier, Ronaldo Al Dejahl, and possibly the remnants and new beginnings of Club Fifty-One to overthrow Earth and take over?"

Cantu laughed. "I'm here to broker our surrender to a more powerful force. For the good of the country and the world, of course."

"Of course. But you didn't answer my very specific question. I just want to be sure that I'm hating you for the right reasons."

"And not because you hope that you'll be able to catch me in a confession? I'm disappointed in you."

"As much as you're disappointed in Senator Armstrong?"

"Some people don't like to get their hands dirty."

"Unlike you."

"I do what needs to be done. Carefully."

My back was still to Cantu, so I couldn't tell how close the gun was to my head. Hyperspeed did nothing for you if the bullet hit, and at this range, he wasn't likely to miss.

Had a good view of LaRue, though. Between our little scuffle and what the Peregrines had done, she wasn't looking too good. "Kill her, Esteban," she said as she struggled to her feet. "And let's get this moving." She was in front of me but just too far away for me to grab.

"I agree. Good-bye, Missus Martini. Unlike all the rest of the people you've faced, I have no ego attached to gloating about having bested you. Power and survival are the best revenge."

I dropped to the ground as the gunshot rang out.

CHAPTER 98

HIT THE GROUND, ROLLED, flipped to my feet, and landed in a fighting crouch. Did this all at hyperspeed, which was why I was still amazingly alive to channel Bruce Lee.

But Cantu wasn't paying attention to me anymore. He was looking at LaRue, and his expression was shocked.

I looked at LaRue, too. She had a bullet in her brain. I could tell because there was a hole in her forehead, her eyes were wide with surprise, and she was falling backward in what seemed like slow motion.

Apparently we were all surprised. I recovered from the shock the quickest. Well, LaRue wasn't going to recover from anything anymore. But I tackled Cantu as LaRue's body hit the ground.

Didn't go for anything fancy, just broke the wrist that was holding his gun. He screamed. I shoved his gun away out of his reach but where I could still see it. Then I backhanded him.

"Who else is involved in this?" He didn't answer. "Tell me or I'll break the other wrist. And that's just for starters."

"You . . . won't," he said between gritted teeth. "You don't . . . work like that."

A man's shoe stepped onto Cantu's broken wrist. The shoe had a foot in it, too, which was nice. I wasn't taking anything for granted right now.

"She doesn't," Chuckie said icily, gun trained on Cantu. "But as you well know, *we* do."

Cantu managed to bark a laugh. "There won't be any 'we' left, Reynolds, don't you get it? They're here, and they're going to destroy us. Surrender would at least mean we got to survive. But you and your self-righteous do-gooder ideals—you're the one who's going to doom Earth. Not me. Never me."

"Cantu, enough with your blah, blah, blah. Dude, seriously, what kept you?"

Chuckie helped me to my feet, and I took a look around. He wasn't alone. My mother was here, along with Kevin and Buchanan and several guys who looked as if they were familiar with Guantanamo and extracting information. Everyone other than Chuckie and Buchanan was wearing their P.T.C.U. caps and vests.

"We couldn't use a gate," Chuckie said. "Floaters aren't stable, and we're not sure how long the gate system is going to last so it's reserved for Field agents only right now."

"Dammit. We could use a few floaters to get the people out of here. There's a lot of dead and probably even more injured."

"Can't help them until we can be sure medical teams can get in without being destroyed themselves. Right now we have everything focused on the invaders."

The muscle guys picked up Cantu and handcuffed him, despite his broken wrist. I chose not to care. Cantu glared at me. "This isn't over."

"No, but it's over for you." The muscle moved him away from the rest of us. Not too far, but to where he couldn't hear us.

"Good work, kitten."

"Thanks, Mom." I hugged her and got her breath-stopping bear hug in return. "Air . . . Mom . . . need air . . ."

She laughed and let me go. "I was just worried about you. Nice work on the phone. It's not enough, but it's a good start."

"Yeah, great. But Cantu here makes a good point—we need to get the Z'porrah under control or gone before someone launches a nuke. Oh, but, Chuckie, you and Hacker International need to know that the Z'porrah are an ancient race, they've been here before, a lot, and the underground tunnels and such are their version of a computer network."

"Really? Interesting."

"Yeah, I thought you'd enjoy that. They also look like mini T-Rexes with wings. Don't even ask. And by mini, I mean shorter than me. But I think that they and the Ancients had rival breeding programs or species advancement programs in place. My bet is that the Z'porrah are why we had dinosaurs, and they're still bitter that the dinos died out."

"Maybe the Ancients got rid of them to make way for the mammals," Buchanan suggested.

"Could be. At any rate, that's what's in those spaceships. And the three who beamed down don't like me much. At all. They said I was rude, can you believe it?"

Mom, Chuckie, Kevin, and Buchanan all gave me looks that said they could easily believe it. Always the way.

Forged on. "Lola did an awesome fake out. Clarence thought he had Jamie when he had a really pissed off Peregrine instead."

Chuckie and Mom exchanged a worried glance. "The Dome was evacuated," Chuckie said slowly. "The Z'porrah have half their fleet firing directly on it."

"Crap." Well, that explained why we were having problems with the gates. "They're trying to blow the planet. If the tunnels really are a computer network kind of setup, then the Dome is where the heart of everything is."

"You're sure?" Chuckie asked.

"Pretty darned." ACE was guarding the Dome, not Washington D.C. I was positive.

"The U.S., Russia, and Israel already launched nuclear weapons at the Z'porrah ships," Kevin said. "The nukes were destroyed in the air."

"The Z'porrah fired on the Dome after those attacks," Buchanan said. "They may not consider that they're attacking us; in their minds they may think we started it."

"Possibly, but I'm not willing to give them the benefit of the doubt right now." I could still see the faces of the dead, wounded, and terrified. "What's it like elsewhere?"

"As far as we know, they're only attacking here and at the Dome," Kevin said. "No retaliation was sent toward Russia or Israel, despite their having launched nukes, and the Z'porrah aren't firing at the part of our country where the nukes launched from, either."

"Was there fallout?" If there was, we were really seeing the start of World War III.

"No," Mom said. "Something engulfed the fallout, all of it. And then the nuclear codes went dead. No one can fire anything world-destroying, nuclear or otherwise."

"Did Naomi and Abigail do that?"

Chuckie shook his head. "They're using the two Power Cubes we have to create shielding over this area. The Cubes are boosting their powers, and they already know how to create shields. It's why the buildings aren't completely destroyed. Yet."

So ACE was still protecting us. I was certain he was the one who'd engulfed the fallout and then killed our ability to fire more bombs. "Why are the girls protecting the buildings? I mean, I get it, priceless, rare things, can't be replaced and all that. But the people . . . they can't be replaced either."

"It's easier for them to cover the buildings because it gives them a shape to follow and also means they're not protecting superbeings. They're taking fewer direct hits this way, too. And they're covering every building attached to the Mall, which means all the contents of those buildings, which includes people."

"I didn't see anyone running inside anything."

"Reader gave the order for the Field teams to get all the civilians into the museums and memorials, other than Lincoln, so in addition to architecture, they've got countless people inside by now. It's tricky to let people in and out of the shields, though, so I don't know how much longer Mimi and Abby will be able to hold out."

"The girls are tougher than you think. Where did everyone in the Dome go?"

"Into the tunnels," Chuckie said. "The hackers were able to find the entrance for them. Easily."

ACE again, I was sure. "Have we talked to anyone in the tunnels?"

"No, Mimi and Abby can't spare the focus, White, Reader, and Crawford are busy, and Serene's presumably in those tunnels. It's a long way from New Mexico to D.C., and there are no gates in the tunnels."

"Only Power Cubes. If you can find them." I looked in my purse. No Poofs still. "You think the Poofs are with Jamie and the others in the tunnels?" I asked hopefully.

"Haven't seen a Poof," Mom said.

"I haven't seen Fluffy since you sent the Poofs off to try to find the cube that used to belong to White and your husband."

My husband. Last I'd seen him, he was fighting Al Dejahl. "I need to find Jeff."

"We need to stop this invasion," Mom corrected. "We were hoping you had some ideas."

"I don't know, how do you stop a flock of birds or a bunch of dinosaurs? Kill the leader?"

"Maybe, but we don't know who the leader is or are," Chuckie said. "The three who came to the planet might be, but they might just be diplomats."

"Duck hunting," Buchanan said.

"Not sure a decoy will work, Malcolm."

He shook his head. "Lure them out, one by one, and finish them off that way."

"It could work, but it's slow," Chuckie said.

"Take out the quarterback," Kevin said. "Or get the ball away from them."

"Football?" Mom said. "Right now? Really?"

"That could work, too," Buchanan said.

"Super Agent Man, any ideas?"

"Take the king."

"So, you're suggesting duck hunting, football, and chess?" Mom said. "No wonder you all work well with Kitty."

"Thanks so much, Mom."

She shook her head. "I say shoot to kill and let God sort 'em out."

"I like where your head's at. But, there's only one way to find out which one of these great plans is going to work. Find the tunnel entrance that's around here, and get anyone you can down into it." I gave Mom a quick kiss and took off for the front of the Memorial.

To find more chaos than I remembered. And I remembered quite a bit.

CHAPTER 99

THERE WERE SUPERSOLDIERS EVERYWHERE, most of them leaping into the path of laser beams. Some of them looked like they could take flight, but they weren't doing so.

I assumed they weren't flying because we finally had jets in the air, firing on the Z'porrah ships. There were a good number of them, but I recognized the flying signatures of several of our aircraft—my flyboys were in the air.

There were fewer people out and about, as Chuckie had said. In fact, I was fairly sure the only mobile people I was seeing were actually androids, because every one of them was fighting in some way. Did my best not to look at the nonmobile people and also tried to ignore the screams. They were farther away, but still, not all the innocents were safe. But I had enough rage, and I couldn't let despair back until this was all over.

Now that I knew the Gower girls were creating shields, I could just make them out—a slight shimmering around every building.

Which was good, because several of the supersoldiers were down, and every one of them had let a superbeing loose.

The supersoldiers that weren't taking the Z'porrah laser hits were fighting the superbeings. It was sort of a fair fight, but as I watched, a superbeing sliced through a supersoldier. And released a new friend. At the rate this was going, we were going to have more superbeings than supersoldiers fast.

Speaking of which, the Z'porrah had brought a whole slew of parasites with them. Somehow, they were still held in their protective bubble, but shots were being fired at and around them. Our aircraft weren't firing at the parasites—the Z'porrah ships were. It dawned on me that ACE had to be who was keeping that protective covering around the parasites, and the Z'porrah were trying to release them.

ACE might be powerful, but he wasn't limitless. Like the Gower girls, ACE had to be close to tapped out.

The Z'porrah ships started to take an interest in our jets. Our jets were nimble, small, and well piloted, so they were hard to hit. But the flying saucers could shoot from what seemed like any part of their saucer rim, so they could make up for a lack of precision by just flinging a lot of shots all over the place.

Tried to keep track of the jets I was sure were flown by my guys. It was a lot like watching a shell game, and I lost them here and there.

Falling debris forced me to run away from the Lincoln Memorial. I backed into some trees. I was good with hiding for a moment and figuring out where Jeff was, along with my next move. Running around being a target seemed stupid and futile.

I was in trees but had a pretty unobstructed view of the air. Five jets converged on one Z'porrah ship. As they zipped around it in death-defying ways, all their firepower focused at the dome on top, I knew without asking that these were my guys.

One of them hit the magic spot, and the Z'porrah ship started to crack. The jets took off as the flying saucer exploded.

"Yeah! Take that!" I jumped up and down. One small victory was still better than none.

Flying saucer debris rained down, and I hugged the trees. Another downside of this fight was that the debris wasn't just hitting the Mall. I had no idea how much of it was falling on D.C. and the surrounding area, but I had to figure quite a lot.

My flyboys were at it again, targeting another Z'porrah ship. This time, they knew where the weakness was, and they hit it much faster. Another flying saucer broke apart into a lot of smaller chunks.

Wanted to call someone and tell them the rest of the jets needed to do this same technique. If we could get enough up there, we'd have the Z'porrah on the run. And I might have tried to reach Reader or Tim as the flyboys went after their next target.

But before I could decide if a call or text right now would be the height of bad timing or just what the doctor ordered, several Z'porrah ships released a barrage of firepower.

Three of the jets sheared off, spinning and flipping themselves in the air. They were safe, and I didn't think they'd taken a hit. I looked for the other two.

They weren't doing as well. The Z'porrah had blocked them, and they were having to maneuver between flying saucers, laser fire, and each other. They were doing a great job, but all it was going to take was one good hit and they were toast.

My guys were the best pilots out there, though. I didn't need to worry or hold my breath. But I was doing both.

Another Z'porrah ship came down from above just as the two jets were making a break for the sky. The Z'porrah's shots hit. One jet was on fire, and one had a wing sheared off.

Even hit, the pilots were the best of the best. They managed to maneuver away from the laser shots. But they were both crashing.

I judged their trajectories and was pretty sure they were trying to hit the tidal basin the Jefferson Memorial overlooked. It was filled with water, and would have far less water traffic than the Potomac.

But they were coming down fast, and even if they managed to hit the water, their chances of survival weren't good.

I ran for the tidal basin. It wasn't too far away from where I was, and I had the smoke trail from the jets to follow. Heard the crashes before I reached the water; they'd hit close together.

Jeff could swim almost as fast as he could run. And we'd run on top of the water today, we'd gone so fast. So I didn't slow down when I reached the tidal basin, I sped up.

Both jets were in the water and on fire. How I didn't bother to question. The way our luck ran, one or both were going to explode. With my guys in there. My feet barely touched the water I was moving so fast.

Had to come to a screeching halt because I'd reached the downed jets. One canopy was off, and there was no pilot inside. The other was still on.

Ripped it off as if it were tissue paper, to see Chip Walker inside. He was bleeding from a variety of areas, including his head.

I couldn't unlock the restraints. So I pulled them out. Grabbed Walker as carefully as I could. I was back at the high level of rage where everything worked just the way I wanted it to. Walker was light as a feather, and I took off toward the Jefferson Memorial. Put him down gently and scanned for my other pilot.

I didn't see anyone in the water. But that didn't mean he wasn't in there. Took my purse off and left it with Walker, just in case. Then I ran on the water again, around the edge and then crisscrossing so that I could see every part. No one.

Ran back to the jets and searched around them. Took a deep breath and dove under. I was moving so fast that I was able to swim around the wreckage without issue. Which was good. Because I found him, pinned under a jet.

I wouldn't have thought it possible, but I shoved the jet off, grabbed my guy, and hauled him to the surface. It was Matt Hughes, and he looked worse than Walker. Put him into the carry position and ran like hell for where I'd left Walker.

Laid Hughes next to him as the jets exploded. I didn't even turn around. Hughes needed mouth-to-mouth, but I had to slow down to do it or I'd kill him. If he wasn't already dead.

"Excuse me," a man said softly.

I looked up. An older couple was nearby. "You need to get to safety."

The man looked around. "My dear, safety is an illusion." He had an accent, but I was too distraught to figure out where that meant they were from. "But you look as though you need help."

"Can you do CPR?"

"Yes." The man spoke to his wife in their native tongue. She nodded, knelt down next to Hughes, and started the pressing and blowing process.

The man knelt down next to Walker. "He is unconscious. I don't believe CPR will help."

More people crept out of the Memorial. Somehow, nothing was really hitting over here, though I didn't expect that to last.

"Help me get them inside," the man with Walker said to them.

My purse was still next to Walker, and I put it back over my neck while I dug my phone out and called the one person I knew would be able to handle this situation.

"Kitty, where are you?" Tito asked. He was shouting, and I could tell he was somewhere close by.

"Hughes and Walker are down, and they both look worse than bad. We're at the Jefferson Memorial. Some good Samaritans are trying to help us. I need you here, right now."

"Gates aren't working."

"Then tell me where you are."

"In front of the Washington Monument."

"Stay there." I looked at the man as I dropped my phone into my purse. "Please get them inside. I'll be right back."

I took off running. Ran on top of the water again. It was the straightest line to where Tito was.

There were fewer people out now. I hated myself for it, but I didn't run around the dead bodies. I hurdled them, but I didn't avoid them.

I was going so fast I sailed under supersoldier feet and past superbeings that moved as if they were standing still. It took only seconds to reach Tito.

Grabbed him and ran back the same way. I'd worry about him throwing up once we were there. Ran across the water, managed to stop before we ran past the Jefferson Memorial.

"Wow," Tito said.

"You're not throwing up."

"Nope. I've been experimenting with an antinausea serum in my off time. I took it before you sent us off with Colonel Franklin, when it looked like we might see action. Seems to be working."

"Extremely glad your Super-Dramamine is a success because Hughes and Walker don't look like they're working." I'd been so fast that the people were basically where they'd been when I'd left, with the woman still doing CPR on Hughes and her husband checking Walker for all the places he was bleeding.

They'd seen me arrive, so this group didn't look as shocked as you'd expect. Either that or what with a space armada attacking, maybe someone appearing and disappearing in the blink of an eye seemed perfectly normal.

"He's a doctor," I told them, pointing to Tito. "Please do what he says."

Tito knelt down between the two pilots and did a fast check. "Please continue CPR," he said to the woman. Her husband translated. She nodded and kept on.

The man stood up and dug a handkerchief out of his jacket. "Here."

"Why are you giving me this?"

He smiled and gently wiped my face. "Because you are crying."

I was? Put my fingers to my cheeks. I was. Wanted to say I was crying because I was so angry. But I knew I wasn't. I was crying because Hughes wasn't breathing and Walker wasn't moving. "Thank you." I sniffled and did my best to keep it together. Had to focus on the rage. Hughes and Walker expected me to avenge them. If I broke down, then I wasn't going to be good for anything.

Tito made a call. He was requesting emergency support, and he sounded grim.

"How are they?" I asked when he hung up.

He stood up and took my hand. "Kitty, last time we were in this situation, I lied to you. You want lies or the truth this time?"

My throat felt tight. "That bad, huh?" My face was wet. Should have kept the handkerchief.

"Not looking good for either one of them, no."

"I'll take the lies. Because you're a better doctor than you give yourself credit for." Heard an explosion behind me. Turned to see a fireball going up into the sky. I was fairly sure it was near the Lincoln Memorial. "Tito, I—"

"Have to go. I know. Be careful, Kitty. I'll do my best here."

I hugged him. "I know you will. And I'll do my best there. Please make sure all these people get to some kind of safety. They're the only ones who stopped to help anyone else."

"No," the man who'd wiped my tears said. "We hid. You stopped. We came out to help you, but only because you were here to be helped." He gently wiped my tears away again. "Never forget that you stopped." He nodded his head toward the spaceships. "Now go stop them."

"Yes, sir, that's exactly my plan."

I turned and ran across the water again, heading for the fireball.

CHAPTER 100

THE SOUND OF EMERGENCY VEHICLES managed to float over on the breeze as I reached the Lincoln Memorial. I hoped some of them were heading to help Tito, but couldn't think about that now.

The fireball was already high enough up that I couldn't be sure where it had originated, though there were a couple of smoking supersoldiers on the far side from where I was, so I had a good guess.

Saw no activity at the top of the Lincoln Memorial steps, but there was a congregation of superbeings and supersoldiers near the bottom of the steps, so I ran over there. Not because I was crazy, but because I had to figure that if Jeff and Christopher were anywhere, they were there.

Sure enough, and they weren't the only ones. The Peregrines were with them, as were some Field agents, along with the three Z'porrah. They were all fighting—each other and the superbeings—while dodging the supersoldiers. Everyone was moving fast, but the Z'porrah didn't seem to have the same speed as anyone I'd ever met from the Alpha Centauri system. One small favor.

A group of androids ran into the fray, and I joined them. "What are you doing here?" Christopher shouted as he ran past me. "Get to safety!"

"There is no safety right now! And I'm trying help you guys."

Of course, I needed a weapon. A Glock wasn't going to do squat against anything I was looking at here. Had a nostalgic moment for our last intergalactic battle. I'd had a cool Amazon Battle Staff then. Now, I had, well, me. I'd been great with the really fast running, but otherwise, I wasn't feeling the Living Weapon jazz. Started to consider Christopher's wisdom. But I hadn't found Jeff yet.

Ran through the fight, jumping out of the way here, dodging a supersoldier foot there, sliding past a superbeing attack, to end up at the home plate of where Jeff was, fighting Al Dejahl and all three of the Z'porrah.

One of the Z'porrah had its back to me, and I jumped on he, she, or it, wrapped an arm around its neck, and started hitting.

"Get off me, you damned naked ape!"

"Not gonna happen, Flying Dino Dude. And only my friends get to call me a Naked Ape." Wrapped my legs around the thing's waist—sort of the inverse of doing this with Jeff. My mind shared that it hated where I'd taken it and wanted a chlorine rinse.

The Z'porrah spun and thrashed, and I held on and pounded its beak. Its wings were very ineffectual—had the distinct impression they were décor at this point, not useful appendages.

Tried to do the twist and break the neck thing, but its neck was really thick, and while it didn't have the Alpha Centauri hyperspeed or superstrength, it certainly wasn't a ninety-pound weakling, either.

The Z'porrah put it's little T-Rex arms out and made some weird, high-pitched sounds. They were almost musical, but not quite. Then it rolled its eyes back so it could look right at me. "Your world will be over now."

We waited a couple of seconds. Nothing seemed different. "That thing you do with your eyes is pretty freaky, but it doesn't seem to be working."

The Z'porrah looked shocked and confused. I tried to twist its neck again. Sadly, no luck, and my attempt seemed to remind it that we were fighting. It went back to thrashing around, and I went back to hanging on and hitting it.

We spun around like this for a little bit, which gave me a weird view of the action and also the chance to hit Al Dejahl on the back of his head with my purse as my bucking Z'porrah and I went by him.

I lasted more than eight seconds before the Z'porrah managed to flip me off its back, so I had a future career as a bull rider, should we have a future.

Flipped in the air so that I'd be able to roll as I landed. Did and rolled into Jeff.

As I did, one of the Field agents got hit and staggered back, right into the Z'porrah I'd been fighting. It opened its jaws and bit. The agent screamed as the Z'porrah ripped his arm off. And ate it. The agent tried to get away, but the Z'porrah literally bit his head off, crunched it up, and swallowed. I wasn't positive, but the Z'porrah looked a little bit bigger after this.

"Get out of here, baby," Jeff said as he pulled me to my feet.

"No." I found my Glock, made sure the safety was off, and walked over to the Z'porrah. It opened its beak, presumably to bite my head off. I aimed and did the rapid-fire technique Mom had taught me. Unloaded all fifteen rounds into the thing's head.

Its head exploded. It didn't bring the agent back, or Hughes and Walker, but it was incredibly satisfying.

My satisfaction didn't last long. Jeff grabbed me just before a supersoldier stomped where I'd been. The rest of the Z'porrah was squished flat, so that was one for the win column.

However, the superbeings and supersoldiers were boiling around us, and we had to leap out of the way of a variety of feet, or at least things that hit the ground. Decided it was time to be a good wife and obey my husband's orders, just this once.

However, before I could get out of the action, there was a loud sound from above. Suddenly, all of us were in shade. And it was spreading.

Looked up to see what was causing our growing shadow. A Z'porrah ship had been hit enough that it was breaking up, but it wasn't breaking apart. Instead, it was crashing. Right onto us.

The crush of supersoldiers, superbeings, remaining Carnivorous Flying Dinos, and androids left us no escape openings. More supersoldiers were tearing toward us, firing whatever projectiles they had at the falling ship.

Felt someone hit up against my back and looked over my shoulder to see Christopher back-to-back with me. Jeff was at my side. And I knew we were all going to die, right here and right now.

I took Jeff's hand. Time for last words. Or something. As I watched the Z'porrah ship head toward us, I felt compelled to say something. "I really wish we had a protective shield around us right now, and, barring that, I wish we'd gotten to say good-bye to Jamie."

And as soon as the words were out of my mouth, there she was.

CHAPTER 101

MY BABY WAS RIGHT THERE, on the ground at my feet. She was standing and had her hands up in the air, as if she wanted me to pick her up.

I let go of Jeff, dropped to the ground, grabbed Jamie, and pulled her to me, while I did the wrap and cover every mother's ever done to put herself between her child and something horrible.

While I did this, my mind shared that it had a few questions. Was this really Jamie or another Peregrine? If it was Jamie, how did she get here? And how in the world was she standing up on her own?

Jeff stepped in front of us, Christopher blocked us from the rear. I cringed. And Jamie pulled away from me a little, so that she could look up at the sky. And she kept her hands up.

After a second or two, I realized that we were all still alive and unsmooshed. Looked up to see the flying saucer just hanging in the air above us. Everything and everyone around us was still fighting, but they were avoiding us, as if our little area was repelling them. Other than the Peregrines, who, to a bird, gathered around us, cooing.

Thought about all the times Jamie had done something she'd heard me say and chose my words carefully.

"It would be nice if the big, round, metal space ship were to be put down, very carefully, so that it didn't hurt anyone or anything on the ground."

Sure enough, the flying saucer sailed slowly and landed, bottom side down, balanced on the reflecting pool.

"What a good girl you are." I hugged her. "Mommy loves you so much. And look at my big girl, standing up all by herself!" And so early, too. She'd be walking sooner than average, but then she wasn't an average baby. I snuggled her, and she giggled at me.

"Ah, Kitty? Could we maybe be sure we're going to survive this before you go into full on Mommy Mode?"

"Uncle Christopher's just a little jumpy, Jamie-Kat. Let's make him feel better. Why don't you, Mommy, Daddy, Uncle Christopher, and all our wonderful Peregrine birdies all get away from where we are right now and go where it's a little safer?"

The Power Cube had moved us faster and more smoothly than a gate ever had. We moved the same way now. One moment, we were in the middle of Fighting Fugly Stew, the next we were on the top of the Lincoln Memorial steps.

I stood up, holding Jamie in my arms. She reached for Jeff, who took her and cuddled her. "My Jamie-Kat is such a good girl," he said as he gave her lots of Daddy Kisses, and she giggled happily.

"How is she doing all this?" Christopher asked me quietly. He sounded a little freaked out.

"No idea. Just glad she can."

Supersoldiers surrounded the downed Z'porrah ship, but no one came out of it. Which was probably good, seeing as there were still superbeings loose, and the rest of the supersoldiers, assisted by the androids, were fighting them and/or taking the hits the Z'porrah were still sending toward us.

"We're going to need to bring in artillery to get rid of the superbeings," Jeff said. "Before they destroy all the supersoldiers and we have even more superbeings."

"We could call Stryker's team and tell them to have the supersoldiers stand down," Christopher said. "But I'm not sure that we want them stopping, because some of the supersoldiers are destroying the superbeings."

"I think we need to stop the Z'porrah ships from blowing us all up first."

The Lincoln Memorial was set up so that you could, from the top, see everything across the Mall. So we had a good view of what happened next.

More spaceships appeared.

It was another armada. Only these ships weren't flying saucers. Some looked like big cat's paws, some like big dog heads, some like giant lizards with wings. These were accompanied by three ships that screamed "I'm an Imperial Battle Cruiser from *Star Wars*" only with extra bells and whistles.

Our friends were here, and Earth wasn't standing alone any more.

The Z'porrah ships were a little slow to react to the new arrivals, which gave our allies a chance to blast some of them out of the air without trying too hard.

However, that didn't last long. All the Z'porrah ships stopped firing at targets on the ground and focused on those in the air. The Feliniad, Canus Majorian, and Reptilian ships fired back.

The sun was beginning to set, but you couldn't tell because there was so much light in the sky. The Z'porrah ships could fire from various points around their saucer. The Feliniad, Canus Majorian, and Reptilian ships couldn't, but apparently they made up for this inability with stronger firepower. Both sides seemed equally matched in terms of flying agility, other than the Alpha Four Battle Cruisers, which were just as unwieldy as you'd expect a huge battle cruiser to be.

The Z'porrah obviously realized this too, as they started focusing much of their attack on the cruisers.

Jets appeared again and reengaged with the battle. They'd learned from my flyboys and were focusing their firepower on the tops of the Z'porrah ships. Some of the Feliniad and Canus Majorian ships caught on and followed our fighters, firing where they were.

A handful of the Z'porrah ships decided to start firing at the ground again. Or, rather, at the supersoldiers. Couldn't guess whether they'd realized that once a supersoldier was destroyed, a weapon that worked against us was released, or if they just wanted to get rid of our backup, but they were sending a lot of firepower at our sort of living weapons.

Over a dozen supersoldiers went down, and over a dozen superbeings came out. They started the usual superbeing attacks, flailing at anything near them. Other than two. Two of them noticed us. And headed for us.

"Time to run?" Christopher asked.

Three jets disengaged from the big battle and flew low. Their shots were carefully placed, focused solely on the superbeings. "Wait." I recognized the flying signatures again. "It's the rest of the flyboys."

"What do you mean, the rest?" Jeff asked.

"Hughes and Walker are . . . down. It . . . doesn't look good. But Tito's with them."

Jeff took my hand. "They'll pull through, baby. But I think Christopher's right, we need to get out of here." He had a point—one of the superbeings was at the stairs.

No sooner said than one of the flyboys drilled the superbeing. It exploded. Body parts just missed us. "Awesome! Of course, now we have the lovely smell of fried fugly to add to the rest of the day's fun sights and sounds."

"We also still have a superbeing after us," Christopher shared. "And more being created every minute."

This was true, but the flyboys were the best, and they were undoubtedly upset about Hughes and Walker. My guys didn't let their friends get shot down and not retaliate to the fullest measure.

Of course, better safe than sorry. I was about to agree that running away from the next superbeing heading up the stairs was the right choice when something big exploded in the sky.

Looked up to see a Reptilian ship breaking apart, just like the three Z'porrah ships it had collided with. All of which were directly overhead. Over our heads.

CHAPTER 102

I CRINGED AGAINST JEFF as he pulled me and Jamie both closer in to him, and the debris plummeted out of the sky. But it never reached us.

The debris floated in the air, a good way above the tops of the buildings. "Is, ah, Jamie doing that?" Christopher asked.

Tore my eyes away from the sky and looked at my daughter. She didn't seem to be concentrating. "Not sure, but I don't think so."

Noticed something. The sounds of battle were far, far less. Took a better look at the sky. No one was firing any more.

Well, no one up high was. There were still fighter jets flying around, but they were focusing on the superbeings.

"What's going on?" Jeff asked.

"No idea. We need to get our guys out of the sky. Once all the superbeings are down." Tried not to think about the Reptilians on board their downed ship. What if Jareen and Neeraj, my Reptilian Soul Sister and her hubby, had been on board?

"Already handling," Chuckie said.

"Where did you come from this time?"

"The ground. I walked up the steps while you all were focused on the sky."

"Well, can you blame us? Um, what happened?"

"The Reptilian Sacrifice is what it's called."

I steeled myself. "How many of them died?"

"None."

"Excuse me? Their ship rammed three others and broke apart."

"Right, but we're talking about beings that routinely create spatiotemporal warps as part of their marriage rituals. The Reptilians get into position, sacrifice their ship while taking out several others, then warp over to other enemy ships. It's amazingly effective, especially on beings they don't routinely tangle with."

"Well, who expects the other guy to sacrifice his entire spaceship?"

"No one." Chuckie grinned. "Most races aren't willing to lose a ship, but the Reptilians make new ships quickly and easily, so it's a very worthwhile tactic."

"So, the fight's over?" Jeff didn't sound like he believed it. Couldn't blame him.

"Pretty much. The Reptilians have control of all the rest of the Z'porrah ships."

"That's great, but I'm still worried about what we're going to do with the supersoldiers," Christopher said. "I'm not the only one who's noticed that the minute they're broken we get an extra-resilient superbeing, right?"

"No, you're not the only one," Chuckie said. He had something in his ear.

"Did you just join *The Matrix,* or are you on a weird headset?" It certainly wasn't a Bluetooth from Hacker International.

He grinned. "Weird headset. I'm talking to the Alpha Four command ship. They're aware of all of our various problems. Just handling them in order of need."

One of the Alpha Four battle cruisers hovered over the debris, and another hovered over the parasites. Both drew their targets inside the ships' bellies.

"Wow, I hope they have some sort of antiparasite lining inside there."

"We do."

Turned to see Alexander standing there. Correction—King Alexander. He looked much less like the unsure kid we'd befriended and much more like a ruler.

Chuckie bowed his head. "Your Highness."

"Good to see you . . . Your Highness." I followed suit and did the head bow. Jeff and Christopher did as well.

Alexander smiled at me. "Our apologies for being late."

"Yeah, we know, you had to be sure all the crap with Ronaldo and LaRue wasn't just a really elaborate ruse on Earth's part to bring the Z'porrah to conquer your system."

"True enough."

"Took you long enough to figure it out and get here," Jeff said. Then he handed Jamie to me, grabbed Alexander and hugged him, and it was back to informal. Christopher and Alexander also hugged, Chuckie shook his hand, and Jamie and I got a joint hug. Then Alexander took Jamie from me and did all the goo-goo stuff people do with babies.

"Thanks for the Peregrines, they rock. We were a little slow on the warning messages, though."

Alexander shrugged as he patted Bruno's head. "It happens."

"By the way, why did Christopher and I wake up before the Peregrines arrived?"

Alexander looked surprised. "Because of your talents. And because Christopher is the Primary, and therefore the overall protection of the principality rests with him."

Christopher and I exchanged an "oh really?" glance. "Great, good to know. Just checking and all that."

Jeff took Jamie back as the last superbeing on the ground was destroyed. "What are you going to do with the Z'porrah ships?"

"We've destroyed at least half of the fleet they sent," Alexander said. "We could destroy them all. But we'll show them mercy, and they'll be clear that we've so done. We will also ensure they understand that should they try this again, we *will* destroy them all."

Chuckie was having a quiet conversation with no one, so I assumed he was talking to the Command Ship again. "Yes, thank you." He turned back to us. "The Z'porrah have officially surrendered. The ones in the air are being sent back to their solar system. Their command ship is the one on Earth, and we will be taking the crew as political prisoners."

"Is their ruler here?"

"Hardly," Alexander said. "Their ruler is back on their home world."

"Where most rulers tend to hang out. Why are you here?"

"Because my family and principality were being threatened, and we needed to show the Z'porrah we are not cowardly. My mother and Councilor Leonidas, as well as the rest of the Planetary Council, are still on Alpha Four. And this way, I got to get out of the palace and do something exciting."

"Oh. So Jareen isn't here? Or Queen Renata, Felicia, or Wahoa?" Now that I knew we'd see tomorrow, it would have been nice to see the rest of my friends, too.

Alexander grinned. "The others wanted to come with me. However, Jareen is expecting, and warp space travel is not recommended for pregnant women of any race. The rest needed to remain to ensure our solar system was protected in case we were not successful in protecting Earth. Everyone sends their good wishes to you and suggests you visit our solar system for once."

The Feliniad and Canus Majorian ships encircled the Z'porrah ships and herded them toward the remaining Reptilian ships. The sky between the Reptilian ships had a weird, wavering sheen to it. "Have they created a spatiotemporal warp net thing?"

"Yes," Chuckie replied. "It's got a more official name, but I know better than to waste breath telling you what it is. It'll send the Z'porrah back to their part of the galaxy."

"Where we all hope they'll stay." The first Z'porrah ship went into the net thing and did a fast fade. Not much better than a slow fade, really, at least per my stomach.

"You're right," Chuckie said. "They visit here a lot. We're going to put a stop to that. Somehow."

Alexander coughed discreetly. "Handled."

"How?"

He shrugged. "In addition to the fact that we're explaining to the Z'porran leadership that Earth solar is considered as off limits as Alpha Centauri solar, we gave your . . . special friend . . . some much needed new instructions."

"By 'special friend' I hope you mean ACE."

"I do."

"What instructions?"

"Permissions might be a better choice of words. We removed several overriding initiatives within the PPB Net programming."

"As in, you removed the guilt?"

"Hopefully. I'm sure ACE will need some adjustment time." Alexander looked me in the eyes. "He may choose to leave."

"And if he does, I'll birth him, just like I said I would when we fought your late brother for your throne."

Alexander nodded. "Good. I feel more than a little . . . responsibility toward him."

"Good." Alpha Four finally had a leader who cared about more than himself. While that wasn't the only requirement for good, effective leadership, it was a requirement I personally found vital.

"If ACE does leave you, we will provide some kind of assistance to ensure the Z'porrah aren't able to casually use Earth as their playground."

"Thanks. And wise. Because they were planning to head over to you guys the moment they had us subjugated."

"We were impressed with your world's restraint," Alexander

said. "Once the first wave of nuclear missiles didn't work, the fact that you sent no more toward the Z'porrah was quite intelligent."

We all smiled and nodded. If Alexander wanted to think humans had been smarter than we normally were, why disabuse him of that notion? ACE wouldn't mind us taking the credit on this one, I was sure.

"How's the Dome?"

"Safe," Chuckie said. "Our allies arrived before it was damaged. Our people are back inside, everyone's accounted for."

Heard a soft mewling behind us. Turned to see some Poofs. "Harlie, Poofikins! Where have all my Poofies been? Kitty's been so worried."

The Poof that was Jamie's bounded to her. "Mous-Mous!" Jamie squealed.

We all stared. "Did she just say her first word?" Jeff asked.

"I think so."

"And instead of Daddy or Mommy, she said Mous-Mous?"

"Yes. I think . . . I think that's her Poof's name. Mous-Mous?" The Poof in Jamie's arms looked at me and purred. "Mous-Mous it is."

Jamie seemed to be saying moose-moose, but I knew she wasn't spelling it that way in her mind. Which was a bizarre thing to be thinking. The Poof looked at me, and I realized that it knew how its name was spelled, which was why I knew how its name was spelled. I sensed another new career option—pet psychic.

Mous-Mous hopped out of Jamie's arms and over to my feet. It went large and toothy. It was a younger Poof, so it didn't go Jeff-sized, but it was easily as big as one of the Z'porrah. Mous-Mous opened its mouth and hacked.

"You're kidding me," Christopher said. "It's throwing up on us?"

It was indeed throwing up, but what Mous-Mous tossed up wasn't regurgitated food. It was a glowing Power Cube.

"Hey, that's the one we had growing up," Jeff said.

"Mous-Mous, did you find the cube at home?"

Mous-Mous mewled and looked pleased with itself.

"Oh, really? That was Part Two of your mission after you came by to remind me to get the supersoldiers active? Well done." I looked at the other Poofs. They all looked exceedingly pleased with themselves. "Did you each take a Power Cube?" Many purrs. "And you could because as long as one Poof had a Power Cube, all Poofies have access to use the Power Cube and so can go in and out of the dead-zone rooms?" More purrs. "And are the Power Cubes safe inside my Poofies, and vice versa?" Many purrs again.

Thought about my one-on-one fight with the Z'porrah. "Did my Poofies take the Power Cubes so the nasty Carnivorous Flying Dinos wouldn't be able to sing their funny song and blow us up?" More purrs, some jumping up and down. Got the impression the Poofs were pleased with how I was once again impressively insightful and rightfully proud of themselves.

Mous-Mous swallowed the Power Cube and went back to small and fluffy.

"Damn," Chuckie said under his breath.

"Will the Poofies give the Power Cubes to Kitty, or Jeff, or Chuckie, or some of the others, if we need them?"

There was some mewling about this. The Peregrines got involved.

"What are they saying?" Christopher asked finally.

"Oh, the Poofs and Peregrines both want to be sure the Power Cubes don't get used against us or abused by anyone. They're working out who should have access when, their own Avenger Initiative sort of thing. I think our Power Cube access is going to be on a need-to-have basis, not a want-to have, but they're still working it out."

"I'm so pleased you have found a way to have the Poofs and Peregrines work together," Alexander said. "It's a rare talent, but we had faith in you."

"Per Stryker, without the Power Cubes in place, we're now able to 'see' and map all the dead zones and tunnel system," Chuckie said. "So, good initiative from the Poofs."

"My Poofies and Peregrines know how to get the job done."

"Only my girl." Jeff put his arm around me. "You know there's no way Imageering was able to hide all of this."

"Or that the Field teams can alter memories enough," Christopher added.

"We're outed." Jeff sighed. "Alexander, any chance we can all move back to Alpha Four?"

"Absolutely, if you wish it. We are prepared to evacuate our people, if it's requested or necessary. And any humans who are in danger as well."

"You're the best, Alex. But I don't know . . . maybe we won't have to."

"Love your optimism, baby. Why do you think we won't be run off the Earth?"

I looked around. "Because the A-Cs being here is the only reason our allies came to help. Without the A-Cs, Earth would already be conquered."

"Think that's going to be a viewpoint the average person will buy?" Jeff asked.

"Depends on how it's spun," Chuckie replied. "I honestly have no guess. Could be the best thing to happen to the A-Cs, could be talked up as one huge Hollywood marketing ploy, could mean we're all running for our lives."

"Guess we're going to find out."

"Can't wait," Christopher said, sounding as though he actually could wait.

"We have friends in high places. And low ones. And far, far away ones. We'll be okay."

As I said this, the last Z'porrah ship was shoved through the Reptilians warp net. Three Feliniad ships swooped down and carefully and accurately hovered over each superbeing. There wasn't as much air blowback as a bunch of helicopters, but I could still feel the air moving.

However, being blown around a little bit was well worth the outcome, because when they finished, the superbeings were no more, sucked up into the Feliniad ships. And as soon as the superbeings were gone, the supersoldiers and androids all went still.

"Who flipped their switches?"

"Ravi," Chuckie said. "King Alexander, I'd like to formally request that you demand that the supersoldiers and androids be given into the custody of Alpha Four and removed from Earth."

"Why?" I asked before Alexander could reply. "They held off the Z'porrah until the cavalry arrived."

"Because if we can control them, so can someone else," Jeff replied. "They aren't benign. They were all programmed to destroy. We were lucky this time. I don't want to bet that we'll be lucky again."

"We will make that demand," Alexander said. "And then we will have them all destroyed. Charles, I assume you would like to bear witness to their destruction?"

"Yes, thank you. We need to catalog who the androids were impersonating before they're disposed of, but otherwise, the sooner we can remove these creatures the better."

"If one megalomaniac can think these things up, another one can as well."

"Which is why I don't want to leave any parts around for the next wave of evil geniuses to find," Chuckie said. "Reader and Crawford know where the bases in Paris and Paraguay are. We'll be razing those in the next few days."

"No argument, I'm with you. Why risk a *Terminator* scenario? Especially since we just had *War of the Worlds*. And then some."

Chuckie sighed. "True enough. Ravi doesn't think we found all of the androids, by the way, just the ones in the U.S."

Before anyone could reply, ask questions, or fret about our android situation, the hatch of the Z'porrah ship opened, and a beam of light came from it.

CHAPTER 103

WE ALL BRACED FOR ANOTHER ATTACK, but there was none. Apparently the beam of light thing was how the Z'porrah got in and out of their ships every time, even if they were only traveling about three feet.

The six of us zipped down the stairs and over to the flying saucer. We were joined by a lot of Field agents. Reader and Tim were there as well. "Military's on the way," Reader said as we joined him.

"Why aren't they here already?"

"Same reason we're not looking forward to a nuclear winter—nothing would work."

I leaned against Jeff. ACE, are you there?

Yes, Kitty, ACE is here. And Alexander is wrong. ACE does not wish to leave.

I'm glad. Thank you for keeping us from destroying ourselves while trying to destroy the Z'porrah.

ACE does not like the Z'porrah.

Because they're evil, or because what they do is evil?

The Z'porrah are not evil. But the Z'porrah are wrong.

About what? Silence. Do I need to know?

Kitty does not need to know right now. The machines will work again now. ACE cannot always interfere.

We understand. Thank you again for saving us.

ACE only did some. Others helped ACE.

Who? ACE was quiet, but he didn't feel distressed. Time to guess. The Poofs?

To some extent. Control of the Power Cubes is important. The Poofs did well.

There had to be more. Thought about it. Jamie and the rest of the hybrid babies?

Yes. ACE will not leave. ACE has many new penguins to care for, and these need ACE. ACE is happy to be needed.

And loved, ACE. Never forget that.

ACE does not.

ACE? How did Jamie get to us in time?

Jamie knew Kitty and Jeff and Christopher needed Jamie. There was a bit of evasiveness in his tone.

Why did she come when she did? No reply. Thought about it. Did she come because I specifically mentioned her?

In a way.

Thought about it some more. Were you keeping her in the Dome and safe?

ACE . . . did not want Jamie to go into danger until Jamie had to.

So, did you let her go or did she get away from you?

There was another long pause. Even ACE can lose concentration. He sounded embarrassed.

It happens, even to the most watchful of parents, ACE. And she really did save the day.

ACE is happy Jamie did well and that Kitty and Jeff and Christopher and all the others are still alive. ACE wishes ACE could have saved everyone. But ACE could not.

He sounded so sad, regretful, and tired I wanted to hug and hold him, but that wasn't really something I could do, unless I found Gower and hugged him, and that wasn't quite the same thing.

No, but ACE appreciates Kitty's caring for ACE.

Were you hurt?

ACE would like . . . time to rest.

Are you able to rest? Is it over?

Yes. For now.

Well, that's all we can hope for, isn't it?

Yes. Kitty is wise. Kitty thinks right. ACE is always thankful for Kitty.

And I'm always thankful for you, ACE.

Felt ACE hug my mind, and then he was gone.

Reader was barking orders, telling each Field team to take control of one Z'porrah. Wasn't sure how many Z'porrah there were, but hopefully we had enough A-Cs to handle it.

"Ambassadors Martini," Armstrong's voice boomed behind us. "There you are. Safe and sound, I see."

Armstrong wasn't alone. White was with him, which was nice, but a number of other people who looked vaguely familiar were with him, too—meaning they were probably politicians I'd met but hadn't really interacted with—which wasn't. Fabulous. On the plus side, Oliver was with him as well, looking as though all his dreams had come true at the exact moment he didn't have a camera on him.

"Senator," Jeff said a trifle suspiciously. "Good to see you."

"Better to see you," Armstrong said. "Excellent work on the experimental aircraft. American Centaurion truly does amazing work. Doesn't it, Mister Reynolds?"

Chuckie stared at Armstrong for a good long few moments. I had a feeling that Chuckie's answer was going to determine how hard the Powers That Be pressed for Centaurion to become the War Division. "These weren't American Centaurion design," he said finally. "These ships weren't created in this solar system."

"If you say so." Armstrong's smile didn't falter. He and Chuckie were having a stare down. Good luck to Armstrong. I'd beaten him, and he was now trying to take on one of the only two people I couldn't outstare.

"I do." Chuckie sounded calm.

Jeff looked at his uncle. White nodded. "I do as well," Jeff said.

Armstrong shrugged. "We can discuss it with the President." Got the impression Chuckie had won but wasn't sure what he'd won, exactly.

"I think that would be wise," Chuckie agreed. "The heads of the C.I.A. and the P.T.C.U. should be involved as well."

"Already safely back in the Oval Office. Homeland Security is there as well, along with a number of world leaders, most of whom were already in town for the Festival. They're just waiting for you and the Ambassadors here to join them." Armstrong's smile went back to Cheerful Politician. "Some of your pets have been spotted. I believe several of our finer companies would like to breed them."

"Not just no, but hell no," Jeff said pleasantly.

"Or create plush toys based on them," Armstrong said smoothly, without missing a beat.

"Maybe, but only if American Centaurion holds the patents as well as majority share in stock and profits," Chuckie said just as smoothly.

I caught Oliver's eye, and he came over. "MJO, what do you recommend?" I asked quietly.

"About Poof toys?"

"Don't be coy."

"Oh, but it's such fun. Mister Reynolds will need support. I'd suggest your husband go with him, while you take your baby home to her Embassy physician, to ensure she's safe and well."

"Gotcha." Wondered if my Embassy physician was home, at a hospital, or taking two of my friends to the morgue. Decided I had to focus on the here and now, not the worry in the pit of my stomach.

"We will accompany Our friend and kinsman," Alexander said, and he was definitely using the Royal We. "We would like to meet your President and other world leaders." It wasn't a request or a suggestion—it was an order.

"Yes, Your Highness," Armstrong said smoothly. "We appreciate your help with this matter."

"We only came to help because some of Our people reside here," Alexander said, speaking clearly and projecting his voice. "If they were not considered welcomed members of your society, We would not have chosen to lend Our support."

Oliver chuckled. "Then again, perhaps Mister Reynolds has all the support he'll need with your King along."

Armstrong smiled as the people with him nodded their heads a little too emphatically. "Well put, Your Highness. I couldn't have said it better myself."

Military vehicles arrived, and the Field agents began loading the captured Z'porrah onto the trucks. Several Field teams entered their ship, returning quickly to declare it devoid of any more Little Big Birds.

"They're off limits for experiments." I hated them, but still. If we let them experiment on the Z'porrah, it was only a matter of time before the same was done on the A-Cs.

Alexander nodded. "Should We discover that these prisoners of war are being mistreated in any way We deem inappropriate—and We deem medical experiments to absolutely be inappropriate—We will take steps to ensure their safety."

The politicians with Armstrong looked worried. Armstrong didn't. He looked pleased. I'd spent most of this weekend with him, and I still wasn't sure if we'd just given an enemy the keys to the city, or if we now had an even more powerful ally. Figured I'd better bet a little on both.

Alexander nodded to Reader, who made a call. One of the Alpha Four Battle Cruisers moved into position over us. "Step away from the saucer," Reader shouted. "Everyone."

We did as we were told. A beam came down from the Alpha

Four ship and hit the Z'porrah saucer. The saucer lifted and was pulled up into the belly of the cruiser. Much faster than they did it in the movies. Maybe it was easier when you weren't using models.

All the Alpha Centauri ships disappeared. "You're staying?" I asked Alexander.

"Only for a short time. Our ships have moved off, past Earth satellites, so that the rest of this can be handled more . . . diplomatically."

"Works for me. As long as they're close by if we need them."

"They are. And they're all monitoring."

Several black limos arrived, and Secret Service stepped out of them. The politicians were ushered inside.

"MJO, what's your destination?"

"I've been told I can't attend the summit meeting, so I'm going to drop off my stories." He shook his head. "This could be the first time in the history of journalism that the kidnapping of an ambassadress and world war being averted is going to be on the back page, because we have such a better lead story."

"Try not to explode from the awesome of it all."

He grinned. "I'll do my best."

A gray limo pulled up, and Buchanan and Jeremy got out of it. "We'll take our own car," Jeff said. "Oliver, if you need a ride, we'll drop you."

"The lift is very much appreciated, Ambassador."

"And if we forget to drop you and take you with us by accident, please be sure to take good notes and let me know immediately if someone's handing us a line of crap."

Oliver beamed. "Absolutely, Ambassador Martini."

Jeff kissed me and Jamie. "Get home safely."

"I'll do my best. I'm not the one who got lost, I have to say yet again."

Jeff grinned. "I'll let you punish me for it later."

"Can't wait." Truly. We still hadn't had nearly enough sex to make up for being apart for a month, let alone to celebrate the world not ending again.

Jeff, White, Alexander, Oliver, and Chuckie got into our limo. Buchanan and Jeremy got back in. Decided to table how and why Jeremy had left his post at the Embassy for later. Presumably because he'd been requested. I assumed Jennifer was still back at the Embassy, attached to Ravi's hip. I had no problem with this.

All the limos but one pulled away. The last one was still waiting for Armstrong.

He came over to me instead. "Ambassador Katt-Martini, it appears all's well that ends well."

"For right now, I guess. What's the word on who was blackmailing us?"

"Your mother was finally able to authorize a search of all of Esteban's holdings. A variety of pictures were found, each of them with a portion of the finished product visible, so to speak. Ample proof of his attempts to blackmail us."

"Conveniently found or really found?"

"You'll have to ask your mother about that. She can tell you now—your security clearance has been reinstated. At a higher level than before, too."

"Thanks, I think."

"Oh, don't worry. I'll have ways for you to thank me later. Just as you'll have them for me."

"We're officially in bed together, even if the dirty pictures were faked, is that what you're saying?"

Armstrong laughed. "Better the devil you know, Ambassador, rather than the devils you don't."

"Dude, for the first time, you and I totally agree."

CHAPTER 104

WE WERE FINALLY ALL BACK in the Embassy, which was pretty much stuffed to the gills with people.

Pierre had, of course, managed to create a fab "It's Not Really the End of the World and We Feel More Than Fine" party in about five minutes, and everyone was having a good time. "Don't Get Mad, Get Even" by Aerosmith played in the background, followed by "Crazy Days" from Adam Gregory. I approved of the musical choices.

No one was positive about what the fallout was going to be from the Z'porrah attack, but until they showed up with torches and pitchforks at our doors, we'd decided to count this as one for the win column and not worry about it.

Len and Kyle were with Adriana and Olga, all of whom were being entertained by Hacker International, with an assist from the Barones. Jennifer was sitting on Ravi's lap. Jeremy was chatting up Adriana, and he suddenly seemed much less against the idea of humans and A-Cs matching up.

My parents were with Jeff's parents. They looked like they were plotting something. Knowing the four of them, probably when to start suggesting we have another baby. Embassy folks were with their significant others, and everyone was mingling. Pierre knew how to throw a good party.

I was with Lorraine and Claudia. We'd caught each other up on what had happened at our various locations and were now just enjoying passing our babies back and forth among ourselves.

"Speech, speech!" Michael Gower shouted.

Chuckie had his arm around Naomi, and it was clear he was the one Michael was shouting at. Chuckie looked a little embarrassed but a lot happy. "Not a long speech. We just wanted to announce that, given that the world hasn't ended, and with her parents', sister's, and brothers' approval—especially brothers'—Naomi and I are officially engaged."

"Not that I have a ring yet," Naomi shouted.

"Hey, I was busy helping avert intergalactic war," Chuckie countered with a laugh.

"As Supreme Pontifex, I think my sister needs a giant rock, Chuck," Gower said with a grin. He was sitting next to White and looked tired. Because, as he'd told me, he'd had to provide some power for ACE, just as the hybrid children had. However, the drain on Gower had been much more than the drain on the kids. Gower wasn't sure why, though we both suspected it was because the kids were more powerful.

There were lots of cheers and congratulations, which was nice. Someone, probably Kyle, put on "Chuck E's In Love" by Rickie Lee Jones.

"You know what I don't get?"

"What?" Claudia asked.

"Why did it take so long for an A-C girl to claim Chuckie? I mean, he's the smartest guy around."

"Oh, yeah, he is," Lorraine said. "But, well . . . we don't go for guys if they're in a committed relationship."

"When was Chuckie in a serious relationship?" He'd certainly never told me about one.

The girls exchanged glances. Claudia laughed. "Wow, on this one, you're as dense as Jeff and Christopher usually are."

"Huh?"

Lorraine sighed. "He was committed to *you*, Kitty. For years. After your wedding, there was a window of about a week when he was available. And then, well, a big 'off limits' signal got beamed to the rest of us. We know when to back off."

"Off limits? Oh! Naomi staked her claim."

"Strongly," Claudia said. "Can't blame her, really. I mean, a guy like Chuck wasn't going to remain on the market long."

"Relatively speaking." Chuckie probably felt he'd been on the market a lot longer than the Dazzlers did. But as Armstrong had plagiarized from the Bard, all was well that ended well.

Tito and Nurse Carter came in with Hughes and Walker, both in wheelchairs. Hughes had a broken leg, Walker had a cracked skull, but for the most part, Jeff had been right—they were going to pull through.

I gave Jamie to Lorraine, trotted over, and gave both of them big hugs. "I thought I'd never see you guys again."

"You almost didn't," Tito said. "It was a close thing for both of them."

"Don't hug them too hard," Nurse Carter added. "They both have internal injuries. Because we have A-C medical advances, they can be up and out of bed, even though they shouldn't be," she added sternly, which earned fake guilty looks from both flyboys. "You two get a half an hour here, and then it's back into the infirmary."

"You need to get rest, too, Kitty, just like Jeff, Christopher, Paul, Naomi, and Abigail do," Tito said. "And by rest I mean all of you are headed for isolation tonight." I opened my mouth, but he put his hand up. "Everyone's on an adrenaline high still, I know. Just don't plan on staying up much longer than my two main patients here."

Tito and Nurse Carter tactfully took their leave. Tito joined Christopher and Amy and the rest of the flyboys, who were near the food, while Nurse Carter went and joined White, who pulled her onto his lap. Christopher noted this, and I saw him smile, then turn back and give Amy a kiss.

Turned my attention back to Hughes and Walker. "Glad you two were able to get out of bed, let alone join the party."

Hughes smiled. "We're only here because I hear tell someone ran on water to save us. And because Tito's the best doctor on any planet."

Walker nodded, then winced. "I gotta remember my head's not on tight right now." He took my hand and Hughes took the other. "Thanks, Kitty."

"I may not be the Head of Airborne anymore, but you'll always be my guys."

"And you'll always be our commander," Walker said.

"Even if we don't officially report to you any more," Hughes added.

Before we could get too mushy, we were interrupted by parrot squawks. "Mister! Mister! Mister!" Bellie was flying around the room, clearly searching for Oliver.

Jeff caught her near Claudia's head, and I went back to claim my baby and let the extra Dazzler nurses Tito employed fuss over Hughes and Walker.

"She sure wants to find our favorite reporter," Jeff said, sounding a little hurt.

"He was here a second ago."

"I went to use the facilities," Oliver said as he rejoined us.

Bellie squawked happily and flew to Oliver's shoulder, giving him a nuzzle. Jeff looked shocked.

"Bellie, you really are a cheap slut, aren't you?" I was fine with this of course, and I had a feeling Bellie was smart enough to know that, ultimately, between me and her, I was going to win in the fight for Jeff's love and affection.

She looked at me. "Jeff has Kitty. Bellie has Mister."

"I like where your birdbrain's at, Bellie. MJO, you okay with another pet?"

"Actually, yes. I haven't had any in the last few years because I'm gone so often, but Miss Bellie is so bright and well trained, I can take her with me. And, as events have shown, I know Button can take care of itself anywhere. May I assume if I have to go to dangerous parts of the world that I may leave Miss Bellie in your good care?"

"Absolutely," Jeff said quickly.

"Aww, your avian mistress has chosen a different sugar daddy. You'll just have to make do with me."

Jeff grinned as he put his arm around me, and the music switched to "Hold Me" by Jamie Grace. "I'll take that deal."

My parents commandeered Jamie under the legitimate excuse of not having seen her for a month. The rest of Alpha, Airborne, and our extended Embassy team floated over one by one, each one sharing what they'd done during the weekend, how close a shave they'd had with death, what they'd been worried about. No one was topping Hughes and Walker on the close shaves, but that was okay by me.

Jeff looked around the room. "You know, this was the big test—how would we handle things when it looked like the world was going to end. I think everyone did a great job. And the right people are where they need to be."

"Girlfriend was right," Reader said, flashing me the cover-boy grin. "When it came down to it, what we had that our enemies didn't was us. As long as we're together, nothing can break us."

"Together forever, right, James?"

Everyone agreed we were a team 'til the bitter end, as "Last Days on Earth" by Tears for Fears came onto our sound system.

"Right," Jeff whispered in my ear. "You're mine until the worlds ends, and then for the rest of eternity." He kissed me, and, as always, everything else faded into the background.

So we were outed to the world. So what? Maybe they'd chase us off Earth. Maybe they'd try to turn to us for every emergency. Or maybe they'd accept that we were just like everybody else—people who loved each other and would fight to protect our world from all the bad things out there trying to destroy it.

Ultimately, it didn't matter. I was with Jeff, and we had Jamie, and that meant we had everything we'd ever need.

Bad guys of the galaxy beware. And all that.

Coming in May 2013:
the seventh novel in the *Alien* series
from Gini Koch

ALIEN IN THE HOUSE

Read on for a sneak preview

"WHY ARE YOU BOTH HERE SO EARLY?" Reader asked. He sounded mildly annoyed. This seemed to be the Standard Reaction Mode for whoever was the Head of Field for Centaurion Division when dealing with Chuckie.

"Not that it isn't great to see you both," I added. Hey, I was the co-Head Diplomat and I tried to practice my diplomatic skills whenever it was convenient and easy. "Unless you're bringing news of doom and gloom, and then come back later, okay?" I also didn't like to overdo the practicing.

Chuckie grinned. "No, for once, not coming by to share how the world's going to end tomorrow."

Good. I wouldn't have to tell Walter to spin "Paint it Black" by the Rolling Stones. Though I had Stones songs on the playlist for tonight's festivities because the British Counsel was supposed to be in attendance and I wanted to play more nicely than I had before and pretend I thought the Stones were sort of in the same league as Aerosmith, even though Aerosmith was the greatest and the Stones were merely good.

Cliff nodded. "Under the circumstances, the Department wanted to ensure that you and we feel your Embassy is secure. I decided to come by with Chuck, as opposed to sending a team here."

"Thanks, we appreciate that," Jeff said. "So what do you need to see?"

"Any common areas the guests will be in," Cliff replied. "This is really just a formality, not a white glove test."

"Excuse me?" Jeff sounded confused, which wasn't a surprise.

"Earth saying. Your mother would understand it." This I knew for a fact. Happily, the A-C Operations team, who I called the Elves because I never, ever saw them perform their wondrous and magical duties, handled the cleaning of every A-C facility, including the Embassy. If the cleaning was left up to me, we'd be decorating in the finest of Washington, D.C. dust. I didn't hate housekeeping, but we weren't exactly best buds forever, either.

Jeff grunted. "So, where do we start?"

"Basement," Cliff said. "Let's do this quickly so you can all get back to prepping for the party tonight."

"You all go on ahead," Chuckie said. "I need to talk to Kitty for a minute."

Jeff gave us both a searching look, shrugged, kissed my cheek, and he and the other men trotted off. This was the result of massive personal growth on Jeff's part, much of which had happened because he'd finally caught on that Chuckie was no longer in love with me and was, in fact, in love with Naomi Gower, who was one of Jeff's cousins.

I waited until the others were out of earshot. "Okay, what's going on?"

"I need to run some things by you, and I don't want an audience for it."

"Is this about the two dead Representatives and the one really sick one?"

"No." He gave me the "you so crazy" look. I got that look a lot. "Why would those incidents, however tragic, be related to tonight's party or any of us in any way?"

"Dude, I figured it was safer to ask. You know how they teach you how to spell 'assume,' right?"

Chuckie shook his head and laughed, then led me down the hall into Jeff's office, closing the door behind us. He sat at the edge of Jeff's desk. "I need you to talk to ACE."

ACE was a collective superconsciousness I'd managed to channel into Paul Gower what seemed like aeons ago but was, in reality, only about two years prior. Gower was not only one of Chuckie's future brothers-in-law, but he was also the current Supreme Pontifex for the A-Cs, or, as I liked to think of it, their Pope With Benefits.

"Why don't you ask Paul whatever it is you need to ask ACE?"

"I have. He says that ACE doesn't want to talk to me."

"Huh." ACE had never had any issue with Chuckie in the past. "What do Naomi and Abigail think?" The Gower girls were the most powerful of the talented A-Cs, to the point where no one, not even Chuckie and the girls themselves, knew the full extent of their powers.

At least, they had been. Until the interstellar invasion.

Naomi and Abigail had used their powers to protect all the various D.C. monuments at the National Mall—and all the people inside them. They'd managed to preserve our nation's capital and history as well as many thousands of innocent people, but it had come at a cost. They'd had to use so much power for such an extended period of time, it had burned them both out. No one was sure if the burnout was temporary or permanent. The girls seemed to be handling this well, but I didn't sleep with them, in that sense.

Chuckie shook his head. "They haven't talked to ACE since . . . right after the invasion attempt."

"Operation Destruction was pretty hard on everyone."

"Yes, it was. We test Mimi and Abby all the time. They still have no more powers than a non-talented A-C."

"I know you'll get mad at me for the suggestion, but have you considered giving them a Surcenthumain boost?" Surcenthumain had been created by a whole host of our enemies, and it was the reason Jeff, his cousin, Christopher White, and Christopher's "lost aunt" Serene all had beyond expanded powers. It was also the reason I wasn't fully human anymore, Jamie having done the mother and child feedback that turned me into a semi-alien.

Chuckie sighed. "All moral and ethical issues aside, Mimi and Abby aren't handling being 'normal' as well as they think they are, so I've thought about it. But I don't want to risk it without some sort of confirmation that it would actually work."

"What does Tito think?"

"Doctor Hernandez isn't convinced that we have enough data to safely guess, and none of us like the idea of using Mimi and Abby, let alone anyone else, as test subjects."

Chuckie was giving me a look that said I was asking stupid questions. I decided to take the logic leap. "So that's why you want to talk to ACE."

"Finally. Yes."

"Does Paul·know why you want to talk to ACE?"

"Yes."

"Huh. Well, okay, let me give it a shot." I'd been the one who'd figured out what was going on with ACE when we'd first "met," and therefore ACE had a soft spot for me. As Reader put it, ACE cared most about me and Gower.

Because I never wanted ACE to feel that I took him for granted,

I only contacted when it was important. Nothing had been Earth-shattering, either literally or figuratively, for these past months, so I'd left ACE alone.

I sat in one of the chairs in Jeff's office, closed my eyes, and thought in my mind. ACE, are you there?

I waited. ACE?

I waited a bit longer, while doing my best to hold down the panic. Maybe leaving ACE alone hadn't been a wise plan.

ACE? ACE, are you there, are you okay?

Waited a few more long, silent moments. Opened my eyes, cleared my throat, and shared the scary news. "He didn't answer. And I . . . I couldn't feel him."

Chuckie nodded. "That's what I was afraid of."

"Do you think ACE has left us? Or . . . died?" I didn't know if ACE could die in the ways a human would understand, but I did know he could be injured, and we'd dissipated a similar superconsciousness, so ACE wasn't invulnerable.

"I don't know. I do know, based on the intel we got from Richard White, that if Gower were killed while ACE was joined with him then the PPB-Net that represents ACE will collapse in on itself and destroy the Earth. I'd have to guess if ACE were to . . . die that it would negatively affect Gower, perhaps even kill him. Gower's alive and well and we're all still here, so I don't know that ACE is dead, at least as we'd be able to comprehend it."

White was Christopher's father and the former Pontifex, who now also resided at the Embassy and was my partner whenever we got to kick evil butt, which happened with a lot less frequency these days. "Have you asked Richard about this?"

"No. The people who are most likely to get a reply from ACE are you and Gower, Mimi, Abby, and Serene. Serene's tried to reach ACE, as have Mimi and Abby. None of them could get a response. Mimi and Abby put it down to their talent loss. Serene thinks it's because she's not as close to ACE as the others."

"But you don't think that at all."

"Of course not. ACE has never shown himself to be unwilling to talk to any of them. And he was talking to you well before you gained any kind of A-C talents."

"Yeah, he's always there for his favorite penguins."

"I'm worried that our benevolent observer has left us, and if that's the case, Earth is back to being very alone, lonely, and vulnerable."

"Why so? Alpha Four are our friends, and so are the rest of the planets in that system."

"Yes," Chuckie said patiently, "they are. And how do we contact our friends when we need them?"

"We ask ACE to connect us. Crap." I felt sick to my stomach. I hadn't worried about ACE much. I'd checked on him after we'd all survived the Dino-Bird alien invasion attempt, of course. "The last I spoke with ACE was when we were doing cleanup after Operation Destruction. He told me he was tired and needed to rest, just like the rest of us did."

"There's a possibility that ACE left us in case he was going to die, so he wouldn't destroy the Earth."

"There's also a possibility that he's so hurt that he can't talk to us. I have no vote for which one of those ideas is worse, by the way, but thanks so much for choosing to have this conversation with me right before I have to entertain a bunch of politicians."

He shook his head. "We've become reliant on ACE. If he's not there for us any more, we need to be prepared for it."

"Why are you discussing this with me and not Jeff or James or anyone else?"

"Because Gower isn't willing to admit that ACE isn't chatting with him on a regular basis. As far as I can tell, he hasn't told Reader." Reader was not only the Head of Field, he was Gower's husband. "And if he hasn't told Reader, then he hasn't told anyone."

"Yeah, I can agree there." Chuckie was the smartest person in any and all rooms, so it didn't shock me that he'd figured out what was going on. "So, you think Paul knows, or suspects something's wrong with ACE and is hiding it to avoid mass panic?"

"Yes, nice of your brain to join the party."

"Blah, blah, blah. Does anyone else suspect?"

"No, I don't think so, mostly because no one else really understands how we work with ACE, and most don't know that he exists, in that sense."

"What about Naomi, Abigail, and Serene?"

"I told them I didn't want to bother the Pontifex with my request. When they couldn't reach ACE, I said I'd talk to Gower about it. Mimi and Abby can no longer tell if I'm lying, and Serene can only do it if she's touching a picture of me, and I gave her no reason to race out to grab a camera."

"Not dissing the skills, Secret Agent Man, just checking. Have you talked to Cliff about it?"

"Absolutely not, and you shouldn't, either. I don't even want you talking to your husband about this. This is the highest security issue we have right now, and it affects the entire world."

"Well, I can do my best to take this news to my grave, but where have you missed the fact that, since his special Surcenthumain boost, Jeff can pretty much read my mind when he wants to?"

The door opened and Jeff came in, closed and locked the door behind him. "And I also pick up when she's stressed, simply by being the strongest empath on the planet. Though, I get why you don't want this spread around," he said to Chuckie.

"Can you feel ACE?" Chuckie asked him.

Jeff shook his head. "No. I've never even thought to try before, so I wouldn't know what ACE would feel like emotionally, even if I could access him."

"Can you get Gower to tell me the truth about what he knows?" Chuckie asked.

"Possibly, but not tonight. The party has to take precedence unless you're going to tell us to declare a state of emergency."

"No, I agree." Chuckie rubbed the back of his neck. "The last thing I want is anyone actually knowing that we have no idea where ACE is...."

Gini Koch lives in Hell's Orientation Area (aka Phoenix, Arizona), works her butt off (sadly, not literally) by day, and writes by night with the rest of the beautiful people. She lives with her awesome husband, three dogs (aka The Canine Death Squad), and two cats (aka The Killer Kitties). She has one very wonderful and spoiled daughter, who will still tell you she's not as spoiled as the pets (and she'd be right).

When she's not writing, Gini spends her time cracking wise, staring at pictures of good looking leading men for "inspiration," teaching her pets to "bring it," and driving her husband insane asking, "Have I told you about this story idea yet?" She listens to every kind of music 24/7 (from Lifehouse to Pitbull and everything in between, particularly Aerosmith) and is a proud comics geek-girl willing to discuss at any time why Wolverine is the best superhero ever (even if Deadpool does get all the best lines). You can reach her via her website (www.ginikoch.com), email (gini@ginikoch .com), Twitter (@GiniKoch), Facebook (facebook.com/Gini.Koch), or Facebook Fan Page (Hairspray and Rock 'n' Roll).

Gini Koch
The Alien *Novels*

"Amusing and interesting...a hilarious romp in the vein of 'Men in Black' or 'Ghostbusters'."—*VOYA*

TOUCHED BY AN ALIEN
978-0-7564-0600-4

ALIEN TANGO
978-0-7564-0632-5

ALIEN IN THE FAMILY
978-0-7564-0668-4

ALIEN PROLIFERATION
978-0-7564-0697-4

ALIEN DIPLOMACY
978-0-7564-0716-2

ALIEN vs. ALIEN
978-0-7564-0770-4

ALIEN IN THE HOUSE
978-0-7564-0757-5
(Available May 2013)

To Order Call: 1-800-788-6262
www.dawbooks.com

DAW 160

Diana Rowland

"Rowland's delightful novel jumps genre lines with a little something for everyone—mystery, horror, humor, and even a smattering of romance. Not to be missed—all that's required is a high tolerance for gray matter. For true zombiephiles, of course, that's a no brainer."

—*Library Journal*

"An intriguing mystery and a hilarious mix of the horrific and mundane aspects of zombie life open a promising new series...Humor and gore are balanced by surprisingly touching moments as Angel tries to turn her (un)life around."

—*Publishers Weekly*

My Life as a White Trash Zombie
978-0-7564-0675-2

Even White Trash Zombies Get the Blues
978-0-7564-0750-6

To Order Call: 1-800-788-6262
www.dawbooks.com

DAW 201

Tanya Huff
The *Confederation* Novels

"As a heroine, Kerr shines. She is cut from the same mold as Ellen Ripley of the Aliens films. Like her heroine, Huff delivers the goods." —*SF Weekly*

A CONFEDERATION OF VALOR
Omnibus Edition
(*Valor's Choice, The Better Part of Valor*)
978-0-7564-0399-7

THE HEART OF VALOR
978-0-7564-0481-9

VALOR'S TRIAL
978-0-7564-0557-1

THE TRUTH OF VALOR
978-0-7564-0684-4

To Order Call: 1-800-788-6262
www.dawbooks.com

DAW 73

RM Meluch

The Tour of the Merrimack

"An action-packed space opera. For readers who like romps through outer space, lots of battles with gooey horrific insects, and character sexploitation, *The Myriad* delivers..."   —*SciFi.com*

"Like *The Myriad*, this one is grand space opera. You will enjoy it."   —*Analog*

"This is grand old-fashioned space opera, so toss your disbelief out the nearest airlock and dive in."
                    —*Publishers Weekly* (Starred Review)

THE MYRIAD   0-7564-0320-1

WOLF STAR   0-7564-0383-6

THE SAGITTARIUS COMMAND
                    978-0-7564-0490-1

STRENGTH AND HONOR
                    978-0-7564-0578-6

THE NINTH CIRCLE
                    978-0-7564-0764-3

To Order Call: 1-800-788-6262

www.dawbooks.com

Celia Jerome

The Willow Tate *Novels*

"Readers will love the first Willow Tate book. Willow is funny, brave and open to possibilities most people would not have even considered as she meets her perfect foil in Thaddeus Grant, a British agent assigned to look over the strange occurrences following Willow like a shadow. Together they make a wonderful pair and readers will love their unconventional courtship." —*RT Book Review*

TROLLS IN THE HAMPTONS
978-0-7564-0630-1

NIGHT MARES IN THE HAMPTONS
978-0-7564-0663-9

FIRE WORKS IN THE HAMPTONS
978-0-7564-0688-2

LIFE GUARDS IN THE HAMPTONS
978-0-7564-0725-4

SAND WITCHES IN THE HAMPTONS
978-0-7564-0767-4

To Order Call: 1-800-788-6262
www.dawbooks.com